Night Maw

Gerald W. Locke

Night Maw

Published by Locke Publishing

ISBN: 979-8-89170-576-0

Cover and interior design: Gerald Locke
Printed in the United States of America

Discover more books by Gerald Locke:
GeraldLocke.com
Follow for updates and new releases:
TikTok: @geraldlockeauthor
Facebook: Gerald Locke – Author

Contents

Night Maw
The Legend of Shadows

by

Gerald Locke

"The dark isn't empty. It's patient."

Night Maw
Copyright © 2026 by Gerald Locke

Published by Bookllo Publishing

ISBN: 979-8-89170-576-0

Cover and interior design: Gerald Locke
Printed in the United States of America

Discover more books by Gerald Locke:

GeraldLocke.com

Follow for updates and new releases:

TikTok: @geraldlockeauthor

Facebook: Gerald Locke – Author

Table of Contents

"The corners have always been watching.
Humanity just learned to stop looking back."

— **Gerald Locke**, *Night Maw*

The Legend of Night Maw

As told through centuries of whispers

They say that long before people trusted the night, long before lamps pushed back the dark, something waited in the thin place between the last ember of light and the first breath of shadow. People didn't dare give it a real name. They whispered around it, walked around it, and prayed it would never follow them home.

Some called it the Corner Watcher. Others the Dark-Bent Man. But most, when pressed, used only a trembling word passed from generation to generation:

the Night Maw.

The old ones claimed the Night Maw was ancient before the first fire was stolen, before language shaped fear, before shadows had owners. It didn't belong to the living, and it didn't belong to the dead. It lived in the **between**—where the dark pools, thickens, and remembers.

They said it forms itself in the places you refuse to look: the farthest corner of your bedroom, the slice of darkness beneath your bed, the narrow void between two failing streetlights. And it waits for one thing.

Not sleep.

Not movement.

Awareness.

Children were warned never to lie awake in fear, because the Night Maw hunts only those who *wake up afraid.* If your shadow twitches, if the room chills enough to sting your teeth, if the silence changes weight—don't blink, don't breathe, don't stay conscious. Let sleep claim you.

Because the Night Maw loves open, frightened eyes.

They say it finds you through **the smallest betrayals** of being alive.

The lonely breath you didn't mean to let out.

The heartbeat that stutters or skips.

The shadow that lags behind your body by half a second.

When all three align, the Maw begins to crawl toward you—slow at first, dragging its long, joint-loose limbs across the floor. And as it moves, every other shadow in the room leans toward it, bowing like servants greeting an ancient king.

Those who lived the longest described seeing it only in fragments: something too tall to be human, too thin to stand, arms long enough to reach the ground, head bent as though broken long ago. Its skin doesn't reflect light—*it erases it.* If you stare too long, it blurs, twitches, or appears closer than it should. By the time your mind admits what you're looking at, it's already near.

One rule survives in every culture that feared it:

Never turn toward the breathing.

Because if you hear it—wet, thick, hungry breathing just behind you—and you turn, the Maw opens its mouth. They say its jaw unhinges ear to ear, revealing two rows of teeth like polished needles. And they say you don't die instantly.

You simply lose the ability to scream.

There's a story the elders loved to repeat: a boy who mocked the legend, bragging that shadows were harmless. One night he sat alone in the dark to prove his courage. When the silence thickened, he smirked. When the air turned freezing, he stayed put. When his shadow bent backward along the wall, he still didn't move.

But when he heard the wet, rattling breath behind him—deep, slow, dragging through a throat too long and too narrow—he turned.

They found him at sunrise, sitting upright in the corner, eyes wide and glassy, mouth stretched too far as if pulled from within. His shadow lay beside him like a collapsed puppet, twisted into a shape nothing human could cast.

Some say the Night Maw chooses its prey: the forgotten, the lonely, the ones who cry in silence, the ones who stare into corners too long. They say the dark itself keeps a record of every person who looks into it—and the Maw remembers every person who looks back.

And so the warnings persist:

Never linger awake in a dark room.

Never look at the farthest corner.

Never follow a shadow that moves wrong.

Never listen to breathing that doesn't belong to you.

And above all—

never, ever turn around when the air goes cold.

Because if you do…

if you acknowledge it…

if your fear wakes you fully…

then the Night Maw knows you are aware.

And once it knows—

it comes.

Every retelling in every country, every century ends the same way:

Do not wake in fear when the shadows thicken.

If you are conscious when it arrives,

you will not see the morning.

Prologue I — 1347, Iberian Hill Village

The winter settled early over the hill village, a quiet, bone-deep cold that felt older than the mountains themselves. Frost clung to the thatch roofs long before the first snow, glittering like a thin crust of glass beneath the moonlight. The villagers moved quietly through the narrow paths between their stone huts, shoulders hunched against the wind, every step sounding louder than it should in the stillness. Even the livestock seemed subdued, bleating only once or twice before falling into a nervous quiet.

No one said it aloud, but everyone felt it—that something in the winter had changed. The nights no longer felt merely cold; they felt **aware**.

The first child went missing on a moonless night when the lamps burned low. His mother woke to a cold so sharp it stung her gums when she breathed. She thought at first the hearth fire had died, but when she lifted her head from her blanket, the embers still glowed faintly. The air around her son's cot, however, felt wrong—heavy in a way cold alone couldn't explain.

She reached into the darkness and touched only straw.

By morning, the village searched the terraces and the frozen paths, calling his name until their throats cracked. They found nothing—not a trail, not a cry for help, not a single mark in the frost. Only the child's little blanket lay crumpled on the floor beside the cot, stiff with cold as if it had been left outside for hours.

After that, people began watching their corners more carefully.

A week later, a young boy swore he saw his shadow bend backward along the wall, lifting as if tugged by something behind him. His father slapped him for speaking nonsense, but that night the man refused to blow out the lamp.

By the time midwinter arrived, mothers whispered warnings as they tucked their children into bed. **Do not lie awake. Do not look into the far corner. Close your eyes before fear wakes you too fully.** None of the families agreed on the name, but all agreed on the habit: cover the lamps, keep the rooms dim but not dark, leave no corner unlit.

Still, the cold deepened.

Still, the nights grew stranger.

A shepherd returning late one evening claimed he felt breathing behind him—wet, thick, as though passing through a throat that had forgotten how to work. He ran the whole way down the hill, bursting into the communal hut drenched in sweat even as his clothes crackled stiff with frost. He tried to laugh it off, but the villagers noticed the tremor in his hands and the whiteness in his beard where ice had clung to it.

Then came the tenth night. The one the elders would not speak of afterward.

Lamplight flickered along the walls of one of the huts, the flame shivering though there was no draft. The mother inside stirred at a sound she didn't recognize—slow, dragging, like something heavy being pulled across packed earth. She sat up, breath held tight in her chest, and listened.

The sound came again.

Not from outside.

From the corner of the room.

She whispered her son's name. No answer. The cold in that corner had a presence to it, a weight that made her eyes water. The lamplight thinned, stretching away from the corner as though pushed by an unseen pressure. Something tall shifted inside the dark—so tall the rafters seemed to bend to make room for it. She couldn't make out its shape, but she saw movement, impossible movement: a twitch to the side, too fast and too abrupt to be human, as if the darkness itself had lurched forward.

Her scream never left her throat. A pressure closed around it—cold, silent, absolute.

At dawn, the villagers found the boy sitting upright beside his cot, his eyes open and unfocused, frost clinging to his lashes. His mouth hung wider than it should, as if stretched from within. He looked as though he had tried to scream but had forgotten how.

Others were found the same that morning. Ten, in total. Some vanished entirely. Others left behind with their bodies twisted at strange angles, or their shadows stretched across the floor in shapes that made no sense.

A traveling monk who passed through days later recorded what the villagers could not voice. In the margin of a small leather-bound journal, he sketched a figure too tall and too bent to be human. Its limbs hung long enough to drag across the ground. Its head angled sharply downward, as though broken. The monk pressed his quill so hard in places that the parchment tore.

Under the drawing he wrote only:

Ten, and then it slept.

Prologue II — Awakening Hunger

The cold hit him before he understood anything was wrong.

One moment the street was mild and empty; the next, a thin ache pressed into his lungs, as if the air had been sucked dry around him. He exhaled, and the breath left his mouth as a pale ribbon that drifted too slowly to vanish.

He stopped and looked up.

The streetlight above him flickered—once, sharp as a camera flash—then blew with a hard metallic pop. Darkness didn't spill across the sidewalk. It dropped. A clean-edged pocket of black settled where the light had been, a wedge carved out of the block with borders too sharp to be natural.

He took one step back.

The silence around him thickened. No wind. No passing cars. Even his own breathing sounded muffled, trapped against the inside of his skull.

Something shifted in the dark pocket.

Not a figure. Not a person.

A vertical smear of deeper black, straightening from a low crouch. Its proportions were wrong—limbs too long, angles too sharp, as if it had remembered a human shape imperfectly. The head hung forward at a broken tilt.

His throat tightened. "Hey—hey, who's there?"

His voice landed flat, swallowed before it crossed the street.

The silhouette unfolded further, joints bending the wrong direction, shoulders stretching upward until it stood nearly twice his height. It didn't walk. It didn't sway. It simply *straightened* in the dead light, its edges too crooked to belong to anything living.

He stumbled backward, palm skidding across cold metal as he caught the nearest parked car. His pulse hammered against his ribs hard enough to hurt.

The silhouette in the pocket didn't move.

He blinked—

—and something breathed behind his left ear.

He whipped around.

The street behind him was empty...

but the dark pocket was still in front of him.

He blinked again, breath catching high in his chest.

The crooked silhouette was gone.

Every part of it.

But the sensation of height behind him—of something tall and bent leaning over his shoulders—didn't fade.

He opened his mouth to scream.

Only a rasp came out.

The rasp in his throat stalled mid-breath.

A shape brushed the back of his jaw—not a hand, not a touch. A pressure. A presence. A wrong closeness. His knees tried to lock, but his body wouldn't obey the command to run.

Thin warmth rose off his skin.

Then something opened behind him.

Teeth.

Not a jaw—just teeth, suspended in a slice of darkness that hadn't been there a blink before. The outer row looked almost human, except each tooth bent inward, hooked as if they'd grown toward the throat they were meant to enter. Behind them, a second row of impossibly long needles trembled in a faint, hungry rhythm.

They didn't come toward him.

They were *already inside* him.

A cold spike punched through the soft tissue beneath his voice box—ice-hard, razor-precise. His mouth snapped open soundlessly as the inner needles slid through the cartilage from behind, piercing it in perfect alignment. There was no external break. No blood. Just the sudden collapse of his own airway around a set of teeth that shouldn't exist.

He convulsed, hands clawing at unbroken skin.

The next breath he tried to drag in froze halfway down, crystallizing as it formed. Frost spidered along the inner wall of his throat. The cartilage folded inward, compressing under pressure that he couldn't locate, couldn't track, couldn't understand.

Inside his neck, the inner teeth flexed.

A long, wet pull followed—like a siphon drawing heat instead of air. His vision jerked sideways as the muscles along his spine seized.

His shadow on the pavement twisted sharply, bending around something that wasn't visible, its angles pulled toward a point behind him where no object stood. One leg of the shadow elongated; the torso warped, as if light had found a new shape to obey.

He tried to scream again.

The sound died in the crushed column of his throat.

Cold raced outward from the wound that didn't exist, blooming deep in his chest cavity. His heartbeat staggered, tripped, then fluttered weakly as the warmth inside him drained too fast to comprehend.

His knees buckled.

He hit the pavement hard on his side. The teeth shifted with him—anchored inside the collapsed cartilage—needle points dragging shallow grooves along the inner airway as they took the last of his heat in short, greedy pulses.

His vision tunneled.

Then the pressure vanished.

His body sagged fully against the asphalt, throat steaming faintly in the open air.

The dark pocket where the teeth had been—where something impossibly tall had stood—flattened back into ordinary shadow. No silhouette. No depth. No sign of anything at all.

Just empty night.

The radio on Maya's hip chirped once—short, clipped, too calm for the hour.

"Medic Twelve, respond for a person down. Caller was a passing motorist and did not remain. Brookside and Alder. PD responding."

Maya closed her locker, the echo too loud in the half-lit bay. Her pulse hadn't settled since the last call, and the muscles between her ribs still felt tight, like her body was bracing for something she couldn't name.

She keyed the mic.

"Medic Twelve en route."

Ruiz already had the ambulance rolling, tires crunching over uneven pavement as they swung out of the station. No siren—protocol didn't allow it without confirmation—but the lights flashed blue across storefront glass as they accelerated through the empty blocks.

Maya sat on the bench seat, elbows braced on her knees, hands clasped too tightly. She didn't want another call like the last one. She didn't want any call. The inside of her skull buzzed, the kind of tired that made her vision grainy around the edges.

Ruiz glanced at her in the rearview mirror.

"You holding up?"

"Fine."

She wasn't.

He didn't push.

The MDT beeped as they turned onto Alder. Ruiz slowed.

Maya's chest tightened.

Halfway down the block, a streetlight flickered weakly over a shape on the asphalt. A blown lamp next to it left a dead patch of darkness that looked too sharp-edged for a normal outage.

Ruiz hadn't even stopped the rig before Maya was out the door.

She jogged to the body, dropping to her knees beside a man sprawled on his back, limbs loose, eyes half-lidded. His skin looked pale in the lamplight—paler than it should at this hour.

"Sir, can you hear me?"

Nothing.

She pressed two fingers to his carotid.

Nothing there, either.

Her breath caught as her glove touched his neck.

Cold.

Not cool.

Not cooling.

Cold.

The kind that belonged on bodies hours dead, not minutes. The skin gave slightly beneath her fingers, pliable instead of stiff, which made the temperature feel even more wrong.

"Ruiz," she said quietly, "you feel this?"

He crouched beside her, reached out, and jerked his hand back. "Jesus. How long has he been down?"

"No idea," Maya murmured. "Caller didn't stay."

She grabbed her shears and cut the collar of the man's shirt, tilting his head gently to visualize the airway.

Her stomach clenched.

The larynx had collapsed inward—clean, symmetrical, impossible. No bruising. No abrasions. No external signs of pressure. The tracheal rings looked as if something had crushed them from the inside out.

She'd seen strangulations, blunt-force, motor vehicle trauma, even bizarre industrial accidents. None looked like this.

None.

"This isn't right," she whispered.

Ruiz hovered behind her, the hair on his arms standing up. "You want compressions?"

"No. Don't… don't touch him."

She leaned closer.

A thin trail of steam still rose from the man's throat—fading, fragile.

Bodies didn't do that unless heat was still escaping.

But everything about him felt empty.

Drained.

She swallowed hard, her throat suddenly dry.

All she could hear was her own breathing, too loud in the quiet.

The street felt wrong again—silent in a way that had nothing to do with time of night. No wind. No distant engines. Just a pressure in the air, like the block hadn't fully settled after something passed through it.

Maya lifted her head slightly.

"PD's two minutes out," Ruiz said behind her.

She nodded, eyes fixed on the collapsed airway.

The last time she'd felt this unsettled was the night her brother died.

But this…

this was different.

Worse, somehow.

And she didn't know why.

A cruiser rolled onto the block, headlights cutting a narrow path between the parked cars. The engine quieted, then clicked as it cooled. Detective Graves stepped out before it fully settled, tugging his jacket straight with a tired, precise motion.

He saw Maya kneeling beside the body and crossed the pavement toward her, boots crunching on scattered glass from the blown streetlamp.

"Maya," he said, voice low. "Talk to me."

"Male," she said, forcing steadiness into her tone. "No pulse. No external trauma. Airway collapse—internal. And he's cold."

Graves crouched, the movement slow with age or long hours or both. He touched the man's cheek with two gloved fingers and froze, his brow tightening almost imperceptibly.

"That's… not normal," he muttered.

"No," Maya said. "It isn't."

He tilted the man's head gently and examined the throat the way he'd done a hundred times in other cases. His frown deepened. "This looks punched in."

He paused. "But from the wrong direction."

"Exactly."

Graves shifted his weight, bones cracking softly with the motion. His eyes scanned the neck again—no bruising, no abrasions, no discoloration. Nothing to explain how the cartilage had folded inward so cleanly.

"Any obstruction?" he asked.

"None."

"No sign of choking?"

"No petechiae. No swelling. No pressure marks."

Graves exhaled slowly through his nose. The faint rise of steam from the man's throat caught in the lamplight, thin as breath but wrong in every way.

"Time on scene?" he asked.

"Seconds before we got here," Maya said. "Motorist didn't stay."

Graves nodded once. He stayed crouched a moment longer, staring at the collapsed airway like it might rearrange itself into something rational if he gave it enough time.

It didn't.

Behind them, Ruiz stood silent, hands locked behind his back, unwilling to step closer.

The blown streetlamp above them buzzed faintly, a dying pulse of electricity. The dark patch beneath it—just ordinary shadow now—stretched across the pavement with nothing unusual in its shape. Nothing to suggest anything had ever stood there.

But the stillness on the block felt tightened somehow, like a muscle that hadn't unclenched.

Graves rose slowly, knees popping.

"You feel that?" he asked.

Maya didn't trust her voice, so she nodded once.

Graves didn't elaborate. Didn't speculate. Didn't guess. He just looked down at the body again, jaw set with the kind of quiet he only used when something refused to make sense.

"Whatever happened here," he said, "is outside anything I've dealt with."

Maya swallowed, throat tight.

He stepped back, giving her space.

The silence on the street pressed in again. No cars. No wind. No movement. Just the man on the pavement and the faint, lingering curl of steam rising from his neck as the last trace of warmth left him.

Maya finally pulled off her gloves with slow, uneasy fingers. Calls didn't usually stay with her.

This one already had.

Chapter 1 — First Watch

Maya locked her apartment door behind her and stood there, hand still on the deadbolt, pulse tapping hard against her palm. The hallway outside had been silent, but too silent. The kind of silence that left her nerves stretched thin even after she stepped inside.

She kicked off her boots and moved through the dark without turning on a light. Light felt wrong tonight. Too sharp. Too revealing.

Her body was bone-tired, but her mind was running hot—flashes of the collapsed airway hitting her in short, vicious bursts. The cartilage folding inward. The cold beneath her glove. The faint curl of steam lifting off dead skin.

She rubbed her hands over her face. It didn't help.

She hadn't slept in… what, thirty-six hours? Forty? It had been getting harder to track. Insomnia had carved itself into her bones since her brother died—something fractured in her, something sleep was supposed to fix but never did.

She tried anyway.

Maya stripped down, stepped into the shower, and let the water hit her shoulders. The warmth should've eased her tension. Instead, her muscles stayed tight, coiled, waiting for a sound that didn't come.

She kept replaying the scene.

The man's throat giving under her fingers.

The wrong cold.

The way the street had felt like it was... holding its breath.

She shut off the water abruptly and stepped out, towel wrapped around her with a tightness that bordered on defensive. Her reflection in the bathroom mirror looked washed-out, pupils slightly blown, the faint tremor in her hand starting again despite the heat.

She ignored it.

She walked to the bedroom, dropped onto the mattress, and pulled the blankets up without bothering to dry her hair. The sheets were cold against her skin. She curled onto her side, eyes closed tight.

Sleep didn't come.

Her mind kept dragging her back to the alley, to the body, to the exact moment she'd tilted the man's head and seen the impossible shape of his throat.

Maya pressed the heel of her hand to her chest, trying to slow her breathing. The memory of her brother's last night surfaced—sharp, fast, a flash that cut through her like glass—but she forced it back down before it could take shape. She didn't want to see that. Not tonight.

Not ever.

The apartment creaked softly as the building settled. She flinched anyway.

Her phone buzzed on the nightstand.

Unknown part of her hoped it was dispatch again—an easy transport, a lift assist, anything to pull her away from her own thoughts. But when she reached over and checked the screen, her stomach tightened.

Clara.

She stared at the name for a long moment, thumb hovering over the answer icon. The room felt colder suddenly, though she told herself that was just the shower moisture evaporating.

Finally, she swiped to accept the call and brought the phone to her ear.

"Maya?" Clara's voice was soft. Careful. Too careful.

"Yeah," Maya said. Her voice sounded flat, scraped thin.

"You home?"

"Yeah."

"Are you okay?"

Maya swallowed. Her throat felt bruised, though she knew it wasn't. "Long night."

A beat of silence. Clara always knew what silence meant.

"I saw the alert come through," Clara said quietly. "That call out on Brookside… it looked bad."

Maya didn't answer.

"You want to talk about it?"

"No."

Another pause. Longer this time.

"Maya… I'm not trying to push. I just—"

"I said no." The words came out sharper than she meant, enough that guilt flickered through her chest before she could stop it.

Clara exhaled softly, the hurt muted but unmistakable. "Okay. Just… please sleep tonight. You sound exhausted."

"Yeah. I will."

It was a lie and they both knew it.

"Goodnight, Maya."

"Night."

She hung up before Clara could say anything else.

The room felt heavier afterward, the silence pressing in around her again. Maya put the phone screen-down on the nightstand and lay back, staring at the ceiling.

Her heart wouldn't settle. Her thoughts wouldn't slow. Every time she blinked, she saw the man's throat collapse inward all over again.

She pulled the blankets up to her chin, but it didn't help.

Sleep didn't come.

It didn't even try.

Morning hit like a punishment.

Maya hadn't slept—she knew that before she opened her eyes. Her body felt hollowed out, her muscles tight from clenching through the night. The gray light leaking through the blinds didn't soften anything; it only made the apartment look smaller, corners darker, edges sharper.

Clara's call lingered faintly in her head, not because of what was said but because of everything Maya wouldn't let herself say back. She pushed the thought away and dragged herself upright. Her reflection in the hallway mirror looked worse than last night—eyes rimmed red, dark circles smearing down toward her cheekbones, her expression a dull, exhausted mask she barely recognized anymore.

She got dressed on autopilot.

Uniform. Boots. Hair pulled back with a tie that felt too tight. She checked her pockets, keys, radio, trauma shears—muscle memory carrying her through motions her thoughts weren't awake enough to follow.

Outside, the air bit at her skin—not cold, not really, but sharp from lack of sleep. She drove in silence, gripping the steering wheel tighter than she should, replaying the night in painful flashes she couldn't control.

By the time she walked into the station, she could feel the exhaustion beneath her ribs like a bruise. The chatter hit her immediately—officers clustered around the coffee machine, voices pitched too casually for the subject they were discussing.

"Dude, I swear my neck froze when I walked past him," Holt was saying. "Like someone opened a freezer right next to me."

"Yeah, sure," another officer laughed. "Maybe the guy died in an ice bath."

Holt scowled. "I'm telling you, there was a draft."

"There was no draft," someone else chimed in. "You freak out at spiders. Maybe it was your imagination."

"Then why was the guy's throat—?"

Maya stepped into the break room doorway. The officers quieted just enough to signal they'd noticed her but not enough to stop talking.

"…crushed from the inside," one of them muttered, lowering his voice too late.

Holt looked over at her. "You were first on scene, right?"

Maya nodded once. She didn't want to be part of the conversation, but Holt's gaze lingered on her face like he was looking for confirmation—or absolution.

"Did you feel it?" he asked. "The cold?"

The room went quiet. Waiting.

Maya's jaw tightened. "I don't know what I felt," she said flatly. "I was working."

It was the truth. And also a lie. She'd felt something, but naming it would make it real. And nothing about that scene deserved a name.

Graves had already pulled her aside that morning for a brief follow-up. It hadn't clarified anything; if anything, it sharpened the unease that had been gnawing at her since the night before.

The officers exchanged looks. A few shrugged it off. One laughed under his breath. Holt went back to his coffee, unsettled in a way he didn't try to hide.

Maya walked past them without another word and headed for her locker. She grabbed the incident file from the printout stack—she hadn't planned on it, but her hand moved before she could stop it.

She stood alone in the hallway reading it.

Then reading it again.

Internal airway collapse.

No external trauma.

Core temperature inconsistent with time of death.

No signs of asphyxiation.

No intoxicants detected.

No struggle.

No explanation.

She flicked her thumb against the edge of the paper, the repetition grounding her in a way sleep hadn't.

Dispatch logs sat clipped behind the report. She flipped to them.

Call routed directly to her unit.

Time-stamped.

Verified.

Clean.

She wasn't imagining any part of last night. Her exhaustion might be gnawing at her, but the facts were in black and white. Someone—or something—had destroyed that man's airway from the inside.

She felt her pulse spike.

Her hands tightened on the file.

She tried to breathe evenly, but each inhale came in too shallow, like she could feel the collapsed airway from last night pressing into her thoughts.

"This isn't helping," she muttered to herself.

But she didn't put the papers down.

Her shift began. Calls came in. Small things. Routine things. She handled them on muscle memory, the way she always did when her head wasn't cooperating.

But every quiet moment between calls pulled her back to the report, back to the angles of that broken throat, back to the cold beneath her glove that she still felt if she thought too hard about it.

She told herself it was just fatigue making her fixate.

Then, walking down the hallway near the supply closet, she felt a ripple crawl up the back of her neck.

Not a sound.

Not a draft.

Just... awareness.

Like someone was standing close behind her.

She stopped and turned.

No one.

Her heartbeat kicked harder in her chest. She swallowed, trying to shake off the feeling. It didn't shake easily.

She walked on, jaw clenched, exhaustion dragging at her feet.

By mid-afternoon, the station felt too bright.

The fluorescents buzzed overhead, a thin, sharp sound that bored into Maya's skull with every passing hour. She tried drinking water. Tried stretching. Tried focusing on the ambulance inventory. Nothing cut through the exhaustion dragging at her nerves.

Every time she closed her eyes—even for a single blink—the collapsed airway flashed behind her eyelids.

She hated that.

She hated even more that she kept rereading the report tucked into her back pocket.

Ruiz found her at the rig, leaning against the side panel with her arms crossed too tight. "You okay?" he asked quietly.

"I'm fine," she said.

He didn't buy it, but Ruiz knew her well enough not to push.

"We've got five before the next check." He hesitated. "You want coffee?"

"No."

He nodded and headed inside, leaving her with the hum of the engine block and the faint sting of cold air slipping through the open garage bay.

She pulled the report out again.

The same lines.

The same impossibilities.

The same wrongness.

Her eyes snagged on the temperature reading for the victim's skin. The differential was off. Way off. Something about it tugged at a memory from her training—the specialized modules paramedics took when they wanted to deal with rare emergency presentations.

The case studies no one talked about.

The ones written without real explanations.

She flipped through the back of the folder and pulled one of the older sheets she'd tucked in years ago—an archived printout she barely remembered saving.

Unclassified airway collapse – internal.
Cold differential inconsistent with environmental exposure.
No external trauma.
No documented cause.

Her fingers pressed into the paper hard enough to crinkle the edge.

This wasn't new.

Not exactly.

Another unit got toned out for a routine CHF call, the radio chatter echoing across the bay. Familiar voices. Normal rhythms. The world moving on like nothing had happened.

Maya's heartbeat didn't match it.

She pushed off the rig and went back inside, needing a distraction, any distraction. Holt and two other officers were still at the coffee machine, the humor in their voices dulling but not gone.

"Look, I'm just saying," Holt muttered, "that cold air didn't feel right. It wasn't weather. It was like—"

"Like the guy had an AC shoved down his throat?" one officer joked.

"Shut up. I know what I felt."

Maya kept walking, but Holt's words caught in her chest like a hook.

She didn't want to agree with him.
She didn't want to feel validated.
She didn't want anyone else to have experienced that wrongness.

Because that made it real.

Her thoughts started spiraling, so she forced herself into the supply closet, breathing slow. She braced her hands on the counter, grounding herself in the feel of solid surface and metal fixtures.

A paramedic's anchor.

She closed her eyes.

One breath.

Two.

When she opened them, the reflection in the small supply-room mirror jumped a fraction behind her movement—as if her body turned before her shadow caught up.

Her pulse surged brutally.

She whipped around.

The hallway behind her was empty.

She blinked hard, jaw tightening. "You're exhausted," she whispered to herself. "You're overtired. It's nothing."

But her skin prickled, a crawling sensation under the surface like her nerves were firing warnings they couldn't articulate.

The supply-room door creaked softly as she pushed it open. Normal building sounds, she told herself. Normal day. Normal fatigue.

But she didn't fully believe it.

As she walked back down the hall, she noticed the overhead lights buzzing in an uneven rhythm—barely off-beat, barely perceptible, but just enough to tighten something deep inside her chest.

It felt like the building was holding its breath.

Her shift finally wound down. Ruiz gave her a long, assessing look as she signed the end-of-shift paperwork.

"You need sleep," he said plainly.

"I know."

"You actually gonna get some?"

She didn't answer.

That was answer enough.

The apartment felt different when Maya stepped inside.

Not colder. Not darker.

Just… tighter.

As if the air didn't want to move around her.

Moxie trotted toward her from the living room, tail up, chirping a greeting—but halfway across the rug the cat stopped dead, pupils dilating to black coins.

Maya frowned. "Hey, what's wrong?"

Moxie didn't look at her.

She stared past Maya's shoulder, toward the corner of the apartment near the bookshelf. The fur along her spine lifted in a rigid line, mouth sliding open in a silent hiss.

Maya closed the door slowly and turned to look.

Nothing there.

Just the same corner. Same bookshelf. Same shadow pooling behind it from the single lamp she'd left on before her shift.

"Mox," she murmured, "it's fine."

It wasn't.

Moxie backed away, ears flat, gaze fixed. When Maya tried to scoop her up, the cat twisted and bolted down the hall, disappearing under the bed.

Maya rubbed a hand down her face. "Jesus, I need sleep."

She set her bag down and crossed the living room to the kitchen counter. Her legs felt heavy, her head fogged, her vision grainy with the kind of exhaustion that bordered on nausea.

She grabbed a glass from the cabinet.

As she reached for the sink, a faint prickle crawled up the back of her neck, the same one she'd felt earlier in the station hallway. A warning too soft to classify as fear, but too sharp to ignore.

She paused her movement.

The glass in her hand stayed steady.

Her shadow on the floor did not.

It hesitated—a fraction of a second—before following her arm's motion. A delayed echo, the silhouette catching up to her body like it was running a half-second behind reality.

She froze.

Her breath hitched, then shortened.

Slowly, she moved her hand again.

Forward.

Back.

Her real arm obeyed immediately.

Her shadow stuttered.

Then followed.

A cold pulse went through her—not supernatural cold, not environmental cold, just the sick, inner freeze of adrenaline dumping hard into an already-exhausted system.

"Fuck," she whispered under her breath.

She stepped backward.

Her shadow didn't.

Not at first.

It lingered in the original posture—an outline that wasn't quite hers—and then slurred into place like light had miscalculated its job.

Maya's heartbeat thudded hard enough to make her throat tighten.

"It's sleep deprivation," she told herself. "It's just sleep deprivation."

She didn't quite believe it.

Behind her, from the hallway, she heard the faint scrape of Moxie shifting under the bed. A soft growl followed—low, guttural, animal, aimed at the same corner the cat had been staring at when Maya came in.

Maya turned slowly.

The corner looked unchanged.

Shadows exactly where they should be.

Except—

as she stepped forward, the tallest shadow on the wall didn't shift in sync with her body. It slid a heartbeat late, dragging slightly behind the movement like it was attached by something elastic.

Not wrong enough to scream.

Not clear enough to name.

But unmistakably off.

Her fingers curled around the edge of the countertop, grip tightening.

She shut off the lamp.

Darkness washed the room clean. The shadows vanished into one uniform shape. The apartment felt still again. Normal again. Almost.

Almost.

Maya breathed out slowly, jaw clenched until it ached.

She stood there in the dark for a long time before finally moving toward the bedroom, each step careful, measured, as if the floor might shift under her if she stepped wrong.

The corner stayed quiet.

Moxie hid under the bed.

The apartment held its breath.

And Maya couldn't shake the feeling that something had noticed her noticing.

Chapter 2 — A Broken Throat

Detective Graves hadn't gone home.

The overhead lights in his office buzzed with a faint, irregular pulse—just enough to irritate him, not enough to justify changing the bulb. He sat hunched over his desk, elbows planted on either side of the keyboard, the bodycam footage from Brookside paused at the moment he'd reached the victim.

He hit play again.

The video flickered once before stabilizing. The timestamp rolled forward. His recorded voice came through tinny and detached: *"Maya, talk to me."*

He watched the frame carefully—not for Maya, not for the victim, but for the dark behind them. That pocket beneath the blown streetlamp. Too clean-edged. Too still.

He scrubbed back two seconds and watched it again.

Then again.

Then frame-by-frame.

One frame caught him.

The victim's torso had a strange lean, not quite aligned with the previous frame. His shadow—barely visible on the pavement—bent at an angle that didn't match the light source. And in the darkness behind him, something shifted. Not movement. Not shape. Just a momentary deepening, like the black had flexed inward.

Graves' breath lodged in his throat for a heartbeat.

He blinked hard, leaning closer, squinting at the pixels.

Artifacting.

It had to be artifacting.

Night shots always rendered weird angles. Compression errors. Shitty hardware.

He forced himself to keep moving.

He clicked to the next frame.

Everything looked normal.

The one after that.

Normal.

He went back—

—there it was again.

That wrong angle in the shadow.

That half-inch lean that shouldn't exist between frames.

His stomach tightened with a feeling he didn't have a name for. Something between irritation and unease.

Graves straightened, jaw flexing. "No," he muttered. "Not doing this."

He opened the bodycam menu, hovered over the anomalous still frame, and selected **Delete Frame**.

A confirmation prompt appeared.

He deleted it without hesitation.

Not because he wasn't unsettled—

but because he refused to give that feeling shape.

Ghost stories, conspiracy theories, shadow bullshit—that wasn't his world. His world was evidence. Mechanisms. Motive. Opportunity. Bodies that made sense.

He hit play again.

Without the strange frame, the footage flowed cleanly. The victim. Maya kneeling beside him. Ruiz hovering nearby. A blown streetlamp. A normal, tragic scene that deserved a normal, tragic explanation.

Graves exhaled and muted the playback. His reflection in the darkened office window looked older than he felt—lines deeper, eyes heavier. He rubbed his jaw, trying to ground himself in the familiar scratch of stubble.

"What you felt wasn't real," he told himself. "Stick to procedure."

He closed the video file and pushed back from the desk, breath steadying. There were still steps he needed to take—steps that didn't involve staring at pixels until they turned into ghosts.

He grabbed his coat from the back of the chair.

He wasn't done with this case.

Not even close.

The hallway outside Graves' office felt colder than it should have—not drafty, just emptied-out, like the building hadn't fully woken for the day. His boots echoed too loudly as he crossed the tiled floor, coat slung over one arm, body cam thumbnail still burned into the back of his eyes.

He pushed through the double doors into the forensic wing.

Autopsy Suite 2's lights were already on.

Dr. Imani Ward didn't look up when Graves entered; he was adjusting the overhead lamp, gloved hands steady, face set in its usual expression of focused neutrality.

"Morning," Ward said, tone clipped but not unfriendly.

"Morning," Graves replied, stepping up beside him.

The Brookside victim lay on the table, chest plate retracted, skin drained of anything resembling life. Under the harsh lights, he almost looked sculpted—unnatural in his stillness, the throat already showing that subtle inward bow Maya had described.

Ward gestured with a nod. "I was about to begin the airway exam. You're here just in time."

Graves said nothing, jaw tightening as he pulled on a pair of gloves.

Ward started with the external survey, his voice clinical, detached. "No external signs of strangulation. No bruising. No petechiae. No swelling. No abrasions. Nothing to suggest pressure was applied from the outside."

Graves folded his arms. "We already knew that from the scene."

"Knowing isn't confirming," Ward replied.

He repositioned the light and made a precise incision along the anterior neck. The tissue parted cleanly. Graves forced himself to watch—he'd done this a thousand times, but something about *this* felt wrong before Ward even touched the cartilage.

"Here's the part that's bothering me," Ward said quietly.

He inserted two fingers beneath the laryngeal structure and lifted.

The cartilage collapsed inward like it had been hollowed.

Graves felt a slow pulse of dread crawl up from the base of his spine.

Ward continued, "Blunt force trauma causes outward fractures or crushes from an external source. Here—" He angled the light. "The damage originates inside. From pressure pushing outward against the rings, forcing them inward."

"I've only seen this once — in those 14th-century plague diagrams Vander presented last year."

Graves leaned closer, eyes narrowing at the subtle tunnels along the inner airway wall—tiny punctures like the start of drilled paths, but too organic. Too numerous.

Ward picked up a thin probe. "Watch."

He slid it into one of the punctures.

It traveled far deeper than it should have.

No resistance. No tear.

Just a clean glide through a space that should not exist.

Graves' stomach tightened.

Ward withdrew the probe. "There are multiple of these. Uniform size. No external entry. Whatever caused them originated internally."

"Could he have swallowed something corrosive?" Graves asked.

"No burns. No chemical residue. And corrosion doesn't create per-fect punctures." Ward shook his head. "This wasn't chemical. And it wasn't mechanical."

Graves stared down at the mangled airway. A memory flickered uninvited—something he'd seen years ago, in a case file older detectives dismissed as 'misfiled folklore.' A throat collapsed inward, puncture-like structures described as "tunneling." But that case had been chalked up to decomposition artifacts and poor preservation.

He shut the thought down immediately.

Ward set the probe aside. "Temperature's another problem."

Graves didn't look up. "How low?"

"Lower than it should be for his documented time of death—and lower than it should be without prolonged exposure to cold environments."

"It wasn't that cold outside."

"No." Ward's tone darkened. "It wasn't."

Graves dragged a hand across his mouth. "You think this was staged? Moved?"

Ward gave him a look that said *don't insult me.* "No relocation indicators. No fluids out of place. No lividity inconsistencies. This man died where he was found."

Graves' jaw flexed.

Ward's voice softened. "Detective… this doesn't match any category. Not strangulation. Not choking. Not trauma. Not environmental. It's something else."

Graves shut that down instantly. "Then label it inconclusive until we have more."

Ward hesitated. "I can do that. But you know this isn't going to stay inconclusive for long."

"I'll worry about that when we get there," Graves said.

He peeled off his gloves and tossed them into the bin with more force than necessary.

Ward watched him—curious, uneasy, thoughtful.

Graves avoided the look entirely.

He pushed the door open and stepped back into the hall, the stale air of the forensic wing pressing tight against his chest. The fluorescent lights hummed overhead, the pitch just off enough to make his teeth ache.

He didn't admit it aloud, but he could feel it:

Something about this case was already digging into him.

And he hated that.

Graves didn't go back to his desk.

Didn't return calls.

Didn't check messages.

He walked straight out of the forensic wing and into the brittle morning light, the cold air hitting his lungs like he'd stepped into a different case entirely. He kept moving until he reached his car.

If the autopsy results were going to make any sense, he needed the first set of hands that touched the victim. Someone who felt things before the clinical layer got applied. Someone who didn't filter their perceptions through procedure.

He needed Maya Raine.

He keyed the engine, turned out of the precinct lot, and headed for the Sycamore EMS station—a squat brick building tucked behind the medical center, half-warehouse, half-habitat for people who ran into chaos without blinking.

He pulled into the lot as an ambulance bay door rolled open. Morning shift was gearing up: medics swapping clipboards, checking rigs, uncoiling hoses, the rhythm of people who'd been up longer than anyone realized.

Inside the front lobby, he flashed his badge.

"Detective Graves," he said. "I need EMT Maya Raine for a follow-up."

The receptionist hit a button on the landline, voice calm and practiced.

"Raine, PD is here to see you. Bring your ID."

A pause. Then footsteps down the interior hallway.

Maya Raine appeared—buttoned uniform, hair pulled back, expression neutral but watchful. The fatigue in her posture was obvious, but so was her composure. A night of no sleep could do that. Trauma could do that too.

Graves gestured to a small conference room off the lobby.

"Can we talk in here?"

She nodded once. "Sure."

They stepped inside. The room was small: training diagrams on one wall, a stack of trauma kits on another, a single table with mismatched chairs. Graves shut the door behind them.

He didn't sit right away.

"Maya," he said, "walk me through it again. Not the report. Not the phrasing you think sounds official. I want the moment."

She sat, folding her hands in her lap. "All right."

He lowered into the opposite chair.

"You were first on scene," he began.

"Yes."

"And your impressions haven't changed since last night?"

"No."

Her voice held no defensiveness, just fact.

Graves opened his notebook. "You said the victim's temperature was abnormal."

"He was cold," she said. "Deep cold. Like refrigeration." She paused. "But without the stiffness you'd expect."

"That's subjective."

"It's also accurate."

He watched her. She didn't back down, didn't revise, didn't soften.

"And the throat?" he asked.

Her jaw tensed slightly. "Compromised. Internally. The airway felt… collapsed from the inside. Not crushed by an external strike."

"There were no external injuries."

"I know."

"That's highly unlikely."

"I know."

The simplicity of her tone grated at him—not because she was dismissive, but because she wasn't rattled. She wasn't guessing. She wasn't even speculating. She was just telling him what happened, and he hated that there was no ambiguity to grab onto.

His pen hovered over the page. "You mentioned something else yesterday. On scene. The shadow."

Maya's gaze flicked away for half a second—just enough to confirm she remembered it clearly.

"I saw something move where nothing should've moved," she said. "I wrote that it might've been the light glitching off a cruiser's headlights."

"But you don't believe that."

"No," she admitted quietly.

He leaned in. "Explain."

She took a breath. "The victim was on the ground. Holt was coming around the far side of the street. There shouldn't have been anything between us. But when the ambulance headlights swept over, something—something tall—cut the light for a fraction of a second." She hesitated. "And then it wasn't there."

"You're exhausted."

"Yes," she said. "But I wasn't hallucinating."

Her honesty was disarming.

Her clarity, worse.

He tapped his pen against the notebook. "Anything else stand out?"

"You already know the answer," she said. "You wouldn't be here otherwise."

He looked up.

She met his stare evenly. "Something about that scene was wrong, Detective. I can't tell you what. But it was wrong. The cold, the airway collapse, the way Holt reacted, the… whatever I saw in the light. None of it fits."

Graves closed the notebook.

For a long moment, neither of them spoke.

Outside, an ambulance backup alarm beeped steadily. Inside, the fluorescent in the corner hummed—not flickering, not failing, just humming in a pitch that irritated the back of Graves' teeth.

He stood.

"Thank you for your time," he said.

Maya didn't rise.

She didn't press him.

She didn't try to make him believe anything.

Which made her easier to believe.

Graves put a hand on the door handle.

"Detective," she said.

He turned.

"You saw something too," she said quietly. "You wouldn't have deleted footage otherwise."

He froze—but only for a second.

"No," he said. "I saw a corrupted frame."

Maya gave the faintest shake of her head. Not defiant—just unconvinced.

"You can lie to the department," she said softly. "You don't need to lie to yourself."

He opened the door before he could answer.

But as he stepped into the bay, the morning sunlight hit a metal gurney in just the wrong way, casting a long, clean shadow across the concrete.

He walked past it.

It stayed still.

He kept going.

And two steps later—just two—he had the uncanny, hair-raising sense that the shadow had moved a fraction behind him.

He did not look back.

He refused to look back.

Graves didn't remember half the drive home.

He remembered the station door shutting behind him, the air outside hitting warmer than it should've been, his fingers tightening around the steering wheel until the leather creaked. He remembered traffic lights blurring past and the muted drone of a morning radio show he didn't recall turning on.

Beyond that, his brain filed everything into static.

By the time he reached his townhouse, the sun was dipping low enough to lay long bands of orange across the siding. He killed the engine and sat there for a moment, staring at his own front door like it belonged to someone else.

He wasn't jumpy.

He wasn't rattled.

He told himself that twice.

Then he stepped out.

The neighborhood was quiet—driveways filling as people returned home from work, kids' bikes abandoned near curbs, the distant thump of a basketball somewhere down the block. Normal. Entirely normal.

He walked to his door, keyed in the lock, and stepped inside.

The air was still.

Not cold. Not warm. Just still.

He shut the door behind him and tossed his keys onto the counter. The metal clatter echoed a shade too loudly in the small space. He ignored it, loosened his tie, and shrugged out of his jacket, draping it over the back of his dining chair.

He didn't turn on the main light—just the one over the stove, a low amber rectangle that barely illuminated the kitchen. Habit more than mood.

He reached for a glass from the cabinet, rubbing the bridge of his nose with the heel of his hand. His skull felt tight. Not aching, not throbbing—tight, like something inside was chewing on the edges of his thoughts.

When he lowered his hand, he saw movement.

Just a flicker.

At the edge of the refrigerator door.

Graves froze.

The fridge was stainless steel, clean enough to reflect light in a dull, warped way. The amber glow from the stove light cast his shadow across it—long, soft, distorted by the angle.

He moved to the right, just slightly.

His shadow moved with him.

A beat late.

Not even a full second—maybe a quarter, maybe less.

A slip.

A misfire.

He didn't breathe.

He moved again, this time deliberately shifting his weight.

His shadow followed.

Late again.

The hair on his arms rose.

The refrigerator hummed quietly, steady as ever. The house didn't creak. The furnace didn't kick on. Nothing else in the room moved.

Just him.

And the shadow that lagged behind like it was waiting for permission.

Graves tore his gaze away, reaching for the glass with stiff fingers. He set it under the tap and let the water run until it was cold enough to mask the tremor in his hand.

He shut off the faucet.

He forced himself to look back.

The shadow looked perfectly normal again.

He swallowed, throat clicking dryly, and took a drink. The water felt thick going down, like he was swallowing gravity.

He pulled his phone from his pocket and checked the time.

Not late.

Not even dusk.

Too early for hallucinations.

Too early for fatigue-induced distortions.

He set the phone down and braced both hands on the counter, head lowered.

"Get it together," he muttered.

But the words didn't feel like they belonged to him.

He straightened, carried the glass to the living room, and sat heavily on the couch. He didn't turn on the TV. Didn't check the mail. Didn't move for long enough that his legs began to feel numb.

His mind kept circling back to the body.

To the collapsing airway.

To the cold that wasn't environmental.

To the throat damage Ward couldn't explain.

To Maya Raine and the unflinching certainty in her voice.

To the flickered shadow in his own kitchen.

He scrubbed a hand over his face.

The refrigerator hummed again—steady, monotone, familiar.

He looked up.

The shadow cast across the far wall stretched long and thin, exactly where it should be.

Exactly how it should be.

But his pulse didn't slow.

Because he didn't trust it anymore.

He leaned back against the couch cushions and let his eyes close, just for a moment, the weight of the day pressing down on him like a hand on his chest.

He told himself he'd open them in a second.

He told himself he was fine.

He told himself nothing was wrong.

And somewhere behind those assurances, where the truth always lived, something cold and thin threaded itself through his thoughts—

Not ice.

Not temperature.

Just wrongness.

The kind that didn't need a name to hollow you out.

Chapter 3 – The Corner Moves

Lila Mercer woke to the sound of breathing.

Not her own.

Not her mother's.

Something wetter. Thick. Rattling. Like someone trying to inhale through a throat full of cold syrup.

The darkness in her room felt wrong before she was fully awake. The air was too heavy, too cold—not freezing, not icy, just... wrong. A cold that didn't live on the skin, but inside the room itself, like the walls were holding their breath.

She curled tighter under her blanket, heart thudding so loud she could feel it in her teeth.

The breathing came again.

Right there.

Near the foot of her bed.

Close enough she could almost feel the air shift when it exhaled.

Lila's hand moved on its own, sliding up to her face, covering her mouth so she wouldn't make a sound. Her eyes strained in the dark, adjusting, searching.

Her room didn't change.

But the corner did.

The far corner—between her dresser and the cracked poster of dancing unicorns—looked deeper. It was subtle at first, like the shadows had sunk backward, pulling the corner with them. The straight lines of the walls didn't meet at the right angle anymore; the space looked stretched, pulled open by some invisible force.

A breath hitched in her throat.

The corner wasn't supposed to look like that.

Corners didn't have extra room.

She rubbed her eyes and blinked hard.

It stayed wrong.

The angle dipped. The darkness pulled downward, as if that corner of the room had quietly exhaled and hollowed itself out. Her nightlight—the soft pink one shaped like a rabbit—sat on her dresser, but its glow stopped a few inches short of where the shadow began. Like it knew better than to touch it.

Then something in the corner shifted.

Not a shape.

Not a body.

Just the shadow itself bending—longer, thinner, like someone had pressed a finger into the darkness and dragged it down the wall.

Lila's breath caught in her chest.

The wet, rattling inhale came again.

Closer this time.

She clamped her eyes shut and whispered the thing her abuela always said when Lila was scared at night:

"Duérmete o el Cucuy te llevará."

Sleep, or the Cucuy will take you.

She didn't know whether saying it was supposed to help or if she was calling something even closer. But she whispered it again—so quietly even she could barely hear it.

The breathing stopped.

Her heart thudded once, twice—hard enough to make her ribs hurt.

Then the breathing started again.

Closer.

Right next to her bed.

Like it had bent down to listen.

Lila swallowed a scream, trembling so hard her teeth almost clicked.

She forced herself to open her eyes.

The corner was deeper now—much deeper. Not like a shadow. Not like a trick. It looked like the wall had caved away, like there was more room back there than there should be. Like the corner led somewhere else entirely.

Something moved in that too-deep space. A faint, inward pull she felt rather than saw—like the dark was leaning closer.

Lila's throat tightened.

"Mom…" she whispered, so thin the word barely existed.

The breathing stopped again.

Silence stretched—heavy, awful, waiting.

Then she felt it:

A warm, moist exhale against her toes.

That broke her.

Lila screamed—a small, scraped, animal sound that tore out of her before she could breathe again.

Footsteps rushed down the hall.

A door handle turned.

Light exploded into the room.

The breathing vanished.

The corner snapped back to normal—flat, shallow, harmless.

Her mother burst inside, voice sharp and scared—

"Lila? ¡Mija, what happened?"

The overhead light washed the room in a flat, yellow glow.

The corner stood there, perfectly ordinary again—two walls, a right angle, the faint reflection of the nightlight on the dresser.

But Lila couldn't stop staring at it, shaking so hard her blanket slipped from her shoulders. The look in her eyes told her mother everything:

Whatever had been in that room wasn't gone.

It was just hiding.

Her mother crossed the room in three strides, pulling Lila into her arms before the girl could speak. Lila clung to her with both fists, shaking so hard that her mother felt it through her own ribs.

"Shh, shh, mija, estás bien—tell me what happened," she murmured, brushing Lila's hair back, scanning her face for any sign of injury.

Lila pointed toward the far corner with a trembling hand.

"There," she whispered. "It was breathing."

Her mother followed the direction of her finger.

There was nothing there.

Just the wall, the dresser, the familiar wallpaper seam she kept meaning to fix.

"It was just a nightmare," her mother said gently. "You scared yourself awake."

"No," Lila insisted, pulling back enough to look at her. Fresh tears clung to her lashes. "It was there. It was standing there. The corner—" She swallowed hard. "The corner got bigger."

Her mother blinked. "Bigger? What do you mean bigger?"

Lila tried to explain, words stumbling over each other. "It... stretched. Like the room got... wrong. And it was breathing like it was sick."

Her mother tightened her hold, kissing the side of her head. "Sweetheart, you're tired. You fell asleep with the nightlight on, and shadows play tricks—"

"It wasn't a shadow," Lila whispered urgently. "It was in the room with me."

Her mother wanted to dismiss it. Wanted to call it imagination, or a dream, or something childish and harmless. But as she shifted slightly on the bed, she felt it too—

The temperature.

She glanced toward the vent. Warm air flowed steadily through it, humming softly, but the room itself felt cold enough to bite at her arms. A wrong cold. Not winter cold, not broken-heater cold—just out of place.

"Why is it freezing in here?" she muttered, rubbing her forearm.

Lila's breath hitched. "I told you."

"Maybe the thermostat—" Her mother stood, crossing to check the digital display on the wall. Normal numbers. Normal settings. No reason the room should feel like a refrigerator.

When she turned back toward the bed, Lila had shifted closer to the doorway, the hall light casting her shadow long across the carpet.

Her mother froze.

For a heartbeat—just one—Lila's shadow didn't line up.

The girl's shoulders moved a second before the shadow caught up. The head tilted a fraction too slow. Then everything snapped into alignment, seamless and ordinary again.

Her mother's stomach tightened.

She forced herself to blink, to breathe. "It's... it's nothing. Just the hallway bulb flickering."

"It wasn't flickering," Lila whispered behind her.

Her mother didn't argue.

Instead she sat beside her again, wrapping one arm around Lila's back and pulling her close.

"You're safe," she said quietly. "I'm right here."

Lila pushed her face into her mother's shoulder. "Don't turn the light off. Please don't."

"I won't," her mother promised.

She smoothed Lila's hair again, though her own hands were trembling now. The cold was deeper near the corner, she noticed—subtle, but present, like the air itself carried a memory of someone exhaling there.

She stood only long enough to twist the bedroom light into a softer glow, then returned to the bed.

Lila's grip was iron.

"I'll stay," her mother said. "Until you fall asleep."

Lila shook her head violently. "I can't sleep. If I sleep, it comes."

Her mother swallowed hard.

She didn't understand what Lila meant.

But she believed that Lila believed it.

She tightened her arm around her daughter.

"It can't hurt you," she whispered. "Nothing can hurt you while I'm here."

Lila didn't answer.

She just kept staring at the corner.

As if she expected it to move again.

Her mother kept her arm around Lila until her breathing finally steadied, though she never stopped staring at the far corner. Every time her mother shifted, even slightly, Lila's grip tightened again, as if movement alone might invite the dark back in.

"Do you want water?" her mother asked softly.

Lila shook her head. Hard.

Her mother exhaled, brushing a thumb over Lila's cheek, wiping away a tear that had dried cold. "Okay. I'm not going anywhere."

She meant it.

But she still needed a moment to check the window—just a second to convince herself the draft wasn't coming from outside, to tether the evening back to something recognizable.

"I'm right here," she said, easing Lila gently back toward her pillows. "I'm not leaving. I just need to close the window—two steps, that's it."

Lila released her only because she could still see her hands.

Her mother crossed the room. The window was shut, locked, sealed. No draft. No gap. No reason the room should feel twenty degrees colder than the hallway.

The cold was strongest near the corner.

She felt it before she reached it—a subtle tightening in her chest, as if she were stepping into a place the house didn't own anymore.

She shut the window anyway, because doing anything at all made her feel less helpless. When she turned back, Lila was sitting upright again, eyes wide, fixed on her.

"I'm here," her mother repeated.

She started toward the bed.

Then she stopped.

Not because she heard anything.

Not because she saw anything.

Because the corner behind her seemed… deeper again.

Just a breath of difference.

Just enough to unsettle her vision.

Just enough to make her step falter.

The angle of the ceiling dipped a fraction lower into the dark, like gravity was pulling downward on that exact spot. Her mother blinked rapidly, trying to force the geometry back into shape.

The corner remained still.

But the stillness felt wrong—too heavy, too expectant.

Her heart tripped against her ribs.

"Lila," she said quietly, "don't look at the corner."

Lila's voice trembled. "I can't not look."

Her mother crossed the room quickly, sat beside her, and pulled her close again. She tucked Lila's head under her chin and held her there, shielding her view.

"It's nothing," she said.

She didn't believe that.

Not after feeling the cold.

Not after seeing the shadow hesitate.

Not after watching the room bend where it shouldn't.

"It's nothing," she insisted anyway.

Lila's breath stuttered. "It'll come back."

"No," her mother whispered. "No, it won't."

She reached over and flipped the hall light on again—brighter this time, enough to spill a wide yellow band across the threshold of the room. Lila watched it like it was a lifeline.

Her mother stood for only a second—just to get the extra blanket from the chair—but even that moment made Lila's fingers clench the sheets so tightly they strained.

"I'm right here," her mother said again, returning instantly.

She wrapped the blanket around both of them and held Lila against her chest. The girl's pulse hammered through the fabric.

The corner stayed still.

But the room felt wrong in a way she couldn't name—like something was waiting just out of sight, one breath behind the world they recognized.

Lila whispered, "Don't let it take me."

"It's not taking anybody," her mother said, tightening her arms.

Lila buried her face in her shoulder.

Her mother stared at the corner.

The darkness there didn't move.

Didn't shift.

Didn't breathe.

Her mother held her until the shaking eased, though Lila never fully relaxed.

Every few seconds her eyes darted back toward the corner, as if expecting something to peel away from it.

The heater hummed.

The room stayed cold.

Her mother tried not to look, but she couldn't help it.

The corner sat there—ordinary, still, harmless.

It looked harmless.

She pulled the blanket tighter around them both and breathed in slowly through her nose, steadying herself.

"Close your eyes," she whispered into Lila's hair. "I'm right here."

Lila didn't close them.

Not all the way.

Her mother didn't press her.

She just kept her arms around her daughter, staring at a corner that refused to feel like a corner anymore, waiting for the room to feel like her house again.

It didn't.

Not for the rest of the night.

Chapter 4 — Half-Eaten

Holt tasted iron in the back of his throat before he even saw the body.

The call had come in as a possible medical emergency—runner down, unresponsive—but the moment he stepped off the gravel and into the tree line, he knew this wasn't medical. The woods were too quiet. Too still. Even the insects had gone silent, as if something had wrung the sound out of the air.

Dusk leaked through the branches in sick, thin streaks. The temperature dipped without warning—cold enough that Holt rubbed his arms through his uniform sleeves, breath fogging faintly even though it was nowhere near cold enough for that.

Then he saw the man on the ground.

Face-down. One arm tucked under him, the other flung outward like he'd tried to catch himself and failed. Sweat still slicked the back of his neck. He hadn't been dead long.

But Holt's stomach turned when he saw the ribs.

They were wrong.

The jogger's shirt had ridden up during the fall—or whatever it was—and the whole ribcage looked... lifted. As if something beneath the sternum had tried to force its way out. The ribs bent upward, not snapped. No tearing. No lacerations. Skin intact.

Just a cage pushed open from the inside.

"Jesus Christ…" Holt crouched, swallowing hard as bile crept up his throat. He'd seen stabbings, crash victims, a guy who took a sharpened broom handle through the abdomen—nothing made him feel like this. Nothing ever felt this… hollow.

He reached out and touched the runner's side. The skin was cold. Not environmental cold—absence-of-warmth cold. The kind of cold you feel walking into a morgue at three a.m.

Holt jerked his hand back.

A faint dragging noise came from somewhere deeper in the woods.

He froze.

Not footsteps.

Not an animal.

Something heavy grazing bark—slow, deliberate, almost curious.

He turned toward the sound, pulse hammering in his ears.

Between the trees, something slipped out of sight.

He didn't see a shape.

Didn't see a creature.

Didn't see a person.

All he saw was movement—massive, wrong, angles bending where they shouldn't. Long something—limb? branch? shadow?—scraped along a tree trunk with a noise that raised every hair on Holt's body.

The scrape was eight feet up the bark.

No human reached that high without a ladder.

No deer.

No bear.

Nothing he knew.

His breath came hard and uneven. His chest tightened.

"Hello?" he called, voice too thin. "Police—identify yourself!"

The woods didn't answer.

Another whisper of bark-shred carried through the trees, farther now, as if whatever made it was choosing where to go next.

Holt's legs shook.

He'd never admit it later, but he shook.

His flashlight beam jittered across tree trunks, catching nothing. No silhouette. No eyes. No outline. Just long, vertical shadows that looked too stiff to be branches.

Holt backed up toward the body.

"Dispatch," he said into the radio, trying to steady his voice. "Start EMS and Detective Graves. This scene is… it's not right. I need them now."

Another crack of bark. This time closer.

Holt spun, nearly losing his footing, the beam snapping to the right just in time to catch—

Nothing.

Nothing but trees.

Nothing but the trail running back toward daylight.

Nothing but the kind of shadows that made the brain lie.

But he'd seen something.

Something tall.

Something that moved like bone without flesh.

Something whose shape he couldn't get his mind to hold onto.

He swallowed hard enough it hurt.

"…a shadow with bones," he muttered under his breath.

He didn't know why he said it. It didn't make sense. The words just spilled out, scraped raw from whatever fear was clawing at his spine.

He crouched again by the jogger, forcing himself to focus on the body—on the thing he could touch. The ribs bowed up like someone had hooked fingers around them and pulled until they flexed. No tearing. No tool marks. No bruising. Just a quiet, impossible distortion.

"What the hell did this to you…" Holt whispered.

The woods groaned softly in response—branches shifting in wind that wasn't there.

Holt didn't look back toward the trees.

He kept his eyes on the body.

Because looking anywhere else felt like an invitation.

Maya felt the wrongness before she saw the body.

The air shifted the second she stepped off the trail—pressure dropping, temperature dipping, that same hollow pull she'd felt on Brookside. Her breath left her in a thin plume as she followed Holt's shouted "Over here!"

She ducked under a low branch, boots sinking into soft earth, Ruiz right behind her with the trauma pack slung over his shoulder.

Holt stood ten feet from the corpse, gun still drawn, not pointed at anything—just held there like a lifeline. His face was gray; sweat carved cold tracks down his temples.

Maya dropped to her knees beside the jogger without waiting for Holt to explain. Training overrode dread.

"Male, late twenties to mid-thirties," she muttered, gloved hands working with a practiced speed. "Rigidity—none. Skin temperature—Jesus." She stiffened.

Ruiz knelt beside her. "What?"

She didn't answer. She pressed the thermometer to the jogger's neck. The small device beeped immediately—far too quickly.

A cold-band reading. Same problem as Brookside.

She lifted the corner of the man's shirt.

The ribs were bowed outward.

Not cracked.

Not crushed.

Bent.

Ruiz let out a low, involuntary curse. "What the hell…?"

Maya leaned in, jaw clenched. The angles were wrong—even for trauma. The sternum was still intact, but each rib curved up and out as if something had forced them apart from inside the thoracic cavity, then stopped before breaking through.

She pressed gently along the rib margins. The cartilage underneath felt hollow—absent, like something had scooped through and left the structure softened.

Her stomach tightened.

Brookside hadn't been a fluke.

She shifted her penlight into her left hand and checked the abdominal skin. No tearing. No puncture wounds. No bruising. But the underlying organs—liver, stomach, soft structures—were displaced slightly inward. As if pulled toward a vacuum that no longer existed.

Ruiz whispered, "Is this some kind of animal attack?"

"No," Maya said flatly.

"Then what the fu—"

"Holt," she said, eyes still on the body. "What did you see?"

He didn't answer.

She looked up.

The man was barely breathing, chest rising shallowly in panic rather than effort. His eyes were wide, staring at something behind her that wasn't there.

"Holt," Maya said again.

He snapped his gaze toward her. "It wasn't—" His breath hitched. "It wasn't a guy. Or an animal. I don't know what the fuck it was."

"Describe it anyway."

Holt wiped his mouth with the back of his shaking hand. "It moved like... like bone. But wrong. Tall. Slipped between trees like it didn't need space to do it." His voice cracked. "A shadow with bones. That's what it looked like."

Ruiz exhaled sharply. "What does that even mean?"

"It means," Maya said quietly, "he saw something his brain isn't built to categorize."

Holt flinched at that. "I'm not crazy."

"I didn't say you were."

She looked back at the body, running her fingers lightly along the ribcage. The flex was unnatural—pliable in a way she'd never felt on a fresh body. No bruising. No evidence of external force. But internal collapse, internal suction, and the cold.

Always the cold.

She checked the lungs: faint crackle, but no visible trauma. Abdominal cavity: displaced, but intact. Heart: still present, still full, no external rupture.

If this was a feed, something had stopped it. Interrupted it mid-extraction.

She motioned to Ruiz. "Give me the thermometer again."

He handed it over. She placed it against the jogger's sternum.

Another cold-band reading. Lower than ambient by a solid ten degrees.

Her skin prickled.

"Same cold-zoning as Brookside," she murmured.

Ruiz stiffened. "Seriously?"

She nodded. "Exact same pattern."

Holt swallowed hard. "What the hell does that mean?"

"It means whatever did this," Maya said, "wasn't finished."

Holt's face drained of color. He glanced toward the trees again.

"Hey," Maya said sharply. "Look at me. Stay focused."

He tried. He really did. But his gaze kept dragging toward that dense stretch of trees like a magnet.

Maya rose from her crouch, sweeping her flashlight up the nearest trunk.

Her breath caught.

Scratches—fresh, raw, bark peeled clean—ran nearly nine feet up the trunk.

Ruiz saw it too. "No fucking way."

Holt whispered, "I told you."

Maya stepped closer. The marks weren't claws, weren't knives, weren't tools. They were long, parallel drags—like something had braced weight against the tree and slid downward.

She lifted her flashlight higher, checking the angle.

Only one word fit, and she hated that it did:

Height.

Not human height.

Not animal height.

Something else.

She forced her breath steady, backing away from the tree.

Holt stood rigid, like he expected something to peel out of the woods and finish what it started.

"Ruiz," Maya said quietly, "call Graves again and confirm ETA. Tell him this one's not... normal."

Ruiz keyed the mic with a trembling hand.

Holt stared at the dark between the trunks.

And Maya felt it—that same hollow wrongness she'd felt at Brookside.

A pocket of air that didn't match the environment.

Something absent rather than present.

She didn't look into the woods.

She didn't need to.

Whatever had been here had left its mark.

And whatever interrupted it was worse.

Graves arrived pissed off.

The moment he stepped under the crime-scene tape, he was already muttering under his breath—about the hour, about the location, about idiots running in the woods at dusk. Anything to keep his mind off the way the shadows between the trees made his skin crawl.

Holt stood a few yards away, arms wrapped tight across his chest like he was holding himself together. Maya crouched beside the body again, her penlight tracing the warped ribs.

Graves ignored the officer first, heading straight for her.

"Tell me this isn't what it looks like," he said.

Maya didn't look up. "Depends what you think it looks like."

He clenched his jaw. "A goddamn animal attack."

"No," she said quietly.

"Then a fall, a crush injury, maybe a—"

"Detective." She finally looked at him. "His ribs bent outward without breaking the skin. You can see the curvature. There's no bruising, no contusion, no external force. Nothing hit him."

Graves stared at the body. For a moment the world tilted—not visually, not literally, just in the stomach-lurching way reality sometimes slips when it's asked to hold something it can't support.

He forced himself to swallow it.

"So he collapsed on something," he said. "A branch, a rock—"

"No." Maya touched the rib line with gloved fingers. "This is internal pressure. Something pulled his thoracic cavity open from the inside."

Holt made a strangled noise behind them.

Graves rounded on him. "What did you see?"

Holt's jaw worked uselessly before words came. "Something was out there." He pointed shakily toward the tree line. "Tall. Wrong. I heard it scrape the bark. Eight feet up. At least."

Graves folded his arms. "You're jumpy. Dark woods, dead body—that'll mess with anyone's head."

"It wasn't in my head," Holt said, voice cracking.

"You saw movement," Graves said. "Everything makes movement out here—wind, branches, deer—"

"There was no wind," Holt shot back, louder than he meant to. His hands trembled.

Maya rose to her feet, stepping between them. "Detective, the bark scrapes are real."

Graves turned on her. Too fast. Too defensive. "Plenty of things climb."

"Not at that angle," she said. "And the suction pattern in the abdomen matches Brookside."

He blinked. "Brookside? No. Brookside was—"

"Brookside was this," she said, her voice low. "But in the throat instead of the torso."

Ruiz added quietly, "We got another cold-band reading."

Graves shot Maya a look that was half accusation, half something more fragile.

"You're telling me the same abnormality happened twice in two days."

"Yes."

"You're telling me the ribs bent from the inside."

"Yes."

"You're telling me an animal, or a person, or—hell, anything we know about—did this without leaving a single external mark."

"Yes."

He stared at her for a long, silent moment.

She stared back, steady.

He felt the same pressure he felt at Brookside—a hollow, sinking weight behind his ribs, as if his own heartbeat had faltered for half a beat.

But he refused to give that feeling oxygen.

Graves turned away, exhaling sharply. "Fine. We're calling this an interrupted assault. Maybe two perpetrators. Maybe some psycho with a hydraulic—"

"Hydraulics don't do this," Maya snapped.

He hated how much that shook him.

"Enough," he said. "I'm not arguing biology in the woods."

"It's not biology," Holt whispered. "It's something else."

Graves spun on him. "What you saw was panic-induced pareidolia. You got spooked. It happens."

Holt's face flushed with anger and fear. "It wasn't pareidolia, sir. It moved like—like it didn't care how bodies work."

Graves stalked toward him. "And what does that even mean?"

Holt flinched. "I don't know. But it wasn't human."

Silence fell thick over the clearing.

The woods behind them stood tall and dark and impossibly still.

Maya broke it softly. "Detective, the suction pattern... the cold-band... the internal force... this wasn't an everyday call."

Graves dragged a hand down his face, stopping just long enough to pinch the bridge of his nose. His breath hissed between his teeth.

He bent down beside the body, examining the ribs up close, forcing logic into a shape it could not hold.

"This is… an anomaly," he said finally. "An odd one. But nothing supernatural. Nothing impossible."

The word *impossible* hung in the air like bait.

Maya didn't take it.

Holt didn't either. He just stared at the trees behind them like something was still watching.

Graves stood, dusting off his hands even though nothing clung to them.

"Bag him," he told Ruiz. "Get him to the ME. We're done here."

But as he turned to leave, a breeze that didn't come from the weather stirred the leaves overhead—just enough to shift the shadows, just enough to make all three freeze.

Holt's breath hitched.

Maya's shoulders tensed.

Graves refused to turn around.

He kept walking.

And the woods stayed silent behind him.

The body was loaded by the time Graves made it back to the trailhead. Ruiz and the techs had zipped the bag and lifted the stretcher onto the gurney, wheels clattering over roots and uneven ground as they maneuvered toward the path.

Holt followed a few paces behind them, still pale, still shaking, eyes fixed anywhere but the treeline. He looked like someone trying very hard not to revisit whatever he'd seen.

Maya walked in silence at his side, her jaw locked, gloves still on her hands even though the exam was over. She kept staring at the ridge of the runner's ribs through the body bag—like the shape itself was trying to rearrange something in her memory.

Graves stopped near the parked cruisers, pinching the bridge of his nose hard enough to leave marks. "Alright," he said, exhaling sharply. "We're not doing this out here."

Maya glanced over. "Doing what?"

"Speculating. Jumping at shadows. Turning a freak accident into a horror show." He dropped his hand. "I need statements. Real ones.

Not whatever that"—he jerked his chin toward the woods—"did to your heads."

Holt stiffened. "Detective—"

"Not here." Graves' voice was rougher than he meant. "Not with the body still warm."

Maya didn't argue. She peeled off her gloves and tossed them into the biohazard bag Ruiz held out, but she didn't look away from Graves.

"You need me to write it up?" she asked quietly.

"No," he said. "I need you at the precinct."
He turned to Ruiz. "Your partner's coming with me."

Ruiz nodded without hesitation. "Go. I'll secure the rig."

Maya hesitated only a second. Long enough for the wrongness in the woods to press faintly against her ribs again. Long enough for the cold-band memory to crawl up her spine.

Then she stepped away from Ruiz and walked toward Graves.

Holt swallowed, lifting a hand like he needed to say something—wanted to say something—but he couldn't shape the words. He looked back over his shoulder at the trees instead, pupils blown wide, breath fast.

Graves caught the expression and forced the edge from his voice. "Holt. You'll come in after her. We'll get your statement too."

Holt gave a short nod. "End of shift for me. I'll file it first thing tomorrow," but he didn't take his eyes off the dark between the trunks.

Maya paused beside him. "Drink some water," she said quietly. "You're hyperventilating."

He blinked at her like he'd forgotten the concept.

She squeezed his shoulder—brief, grounding—then followed Graves to his cruiser.

The trail felt smaller as they walked. Like the woods had inched closer while no one was looking. The air was dense, heavy enough to make each breath feel measured.

When Graves opened the passenger door, Maya didn't get in immediately. She stood there, scanning the perimeter one last time, as if expecting something to peel itself out of the trees—but there was nothing.

Just stillness.

Too much of it.

She finally slid into the seat. Graves shut the door harder than necessary, circled the car, and got behind the wheel.

As he started the engine, Maya spoke without looking at him.

"You think Holt hallucinated."

"I think," Graves said, shifting into drive, "that two bizarre scenes in two days is already too damn much, and I'm not letting panic dictate the narrative."

Maya didn't argue.

The cruiser rolled forward, tires crunching over gravel. The woods receded in the mirrors—dark, silent, uninviting.

Halfway down the access road, Maya turned her head slightly toward the passenger window, staring out at the treeline one last time.

A thin layer of fog hovered low to the ground, clinging to the underbrush like it didn't want to leave.

Graves exhaled through his teeth. "Let's get this over with."

They drove toward the city lights—toward paperwork, statements, and the illusion of normalcy—leaving the trail behind like a wound that hadn't closed.

Chapter 5 — Old Warnings

Maya followed Graves into the precinct lobby, the fluorescent lights too bright after the woods. The air smelled like stale coffee and disinfectant—normal things that felt wrong in her lungs. She still had the jogger's ribs in her head, bowed up like something had tried to push its way out.

Graves looked just as wrecked. He didn't hide it well anymore—his jaw clenched too tight, the muscle twitch in his cheek starting again. They walked in silence toward the front desk.

They weren't alone.

A man stood at the counter, arms full of rolled papers, old folders, and something that looked like photocopied carvings sticking out of a binder. He tapped one foot rapidly against the tile, pacing little half-circles like he'd been waiting for hours.

He turned as they approached.

"Detective Graves?" His voice carried a clipped academic precision, as if every syllable had been sharpened.

Graves blinked. "Do I know you?"

"Ellis Vander," the man said. "Doctor Vander, technically. Ward called me."

Maya's stomach tightened.

Graves exhaled hard. "Oh, Christ. Of course he did." He rubbed his forehead. "Look, whatever Ward thinks he saw—"

"He didn't see anything," Vander cut in. "He examined something. Something he's only encountered once before."

Maya froze.

Ward's voice from last night echoed back:

I've only seen this once — in those 14th-century plague diagrams Vander presented last year.

Graves' patience evaporated. "Doctor, this is an active investigation. And you were not invited."

"Incorrect," Vander said. "Ward consulted me. I'm here to offer context."

"Context?" Graves scoffed. "From medieval woodcuts?"

"Yes," Vander said simply.

He stepped closer and slid a sheet out from the top of his stack—a photocopy of an old Iberian carving. The edges were worn, the image grainy, but the details were unmistakable:

A bent figure, elongated arms dragging near the floor. Beside it—a child with a torso collapsed inward like the chest had caved from the inside.

Maya's breath caught.

Graves started to turn away, but Vander spoke again, quieter now. "Ward told me about the throat."

Graves stopped.

"The inward collapse pattern," Vander continued. "Symmetrical. Clean. No external trauma. The cartilage hollowed before it folded."

Maya's skin prickled.

"That is not blunt force," Vander said. "That is not strangulation. That is not any known mechanical injury. And it is not the first time it has appeared in this city."

Graves turned slowly. "What does that mean?"

"It means," Vander said, "your Brookside victim's injuries match documented anomalies from plague-era Europe, early Iberian folklore, and a series of unexplained deaths in 1911 and 1978."

Maya's pulse kicked hard against her ribs.

Graves looked furious. "You're suggesting our victim was killed by a story."

"No," Vander corrected. "I'm suggesting your victim was killed the same way as others were."

He unrolled another sheet—a medieval woodcut. A man lying on the ground, chest collapsed inward. A tall shape beside him with arms long enough to touch the man's ribs without bending.

"It's crude," Vander said, "but the anatomical ratio is consistent. Arm length. Posture. And—"

He tapped the victim's neck in the woodcut.

"—the same puncture-track pattern Ward noted inside the airway."

Maya felt cold.

Graves did too. She could see it in the way his jaw flexed, the way his breath hitched for a fraction of a second.

But he pushed back. Hard.

"This is pareidolia," he snapped. "People in the 1300s didn't understand disease—of course they imagined monsters."

"I'm not talking about monsters," Vander said. "I'm talking about patterns."

He dropped another photocopy onto the counter.

Another collapsed chest.

Another inward torque of the ribs.

Another elongated shadow sketched beside the victim.

Maya didn't want to touch it. She already saw the jogger's body superimposed over it.

Vander watched her—not in a predatory way, but with academic interest sharpened by something like dread.

"You were first on scene at Brookside," he said.

Not a question.

Maya nodded slowly.

"Did you feel the temperature drop?"

Her throat tightened. "Yes."

"Did the throat collapse appear symmetrical?"

"Yes."

"And did the body retain surface warmth longer than the internal organs?"

Maya's heart thudded. "How would you—"

"Because it always starts that way," Vander said.

Graves stepped between them. "Enough."

Vander didn't flinch. "You can ignore me if you want. Most do. But Ward didn't call me because he's superstitious. He called me because he recognized a specific pattern from historical medical anomalies no one ever explained."

Graves opened his mouth to retort—

But Vander wasn't finished.

"Detective," he said softly, "what you found at Brookside was not unique. And it was not isolated."

He straightened a little, the weight behind his eyes suddenly deeper.

"And if the pattern has resurfaced," he said, "it has never resurfaced alone."

Maya felt the floor tilt beneath her.

Graves didn't move. He didn't breathe.

He just stared at Vander like he'd suddenly become the most dangerous man in the room.

Graves snatched the nearest photocopy off the counter and slapped it back into Vander's chest.

"These are drawings," he said. "Paranoid monks and grieving parents trying to explain death before microscopes existed."

"And yet," Vander replied calmly, "their descriptions align with injuries your coroner cannot classify."

Graves bristled. "Coincidence."

"Coincidence does not replicate anatomical ratios across centuries."

Vander opened another folder—this one thinner, filled with photocopied carvings and translated footnotes.

"You want to call these superstition," he said, "but the descriptions are too consistent across cultures to ignore."

Graves rolled his eyes. "Here we go."

Vander ignored him. He pointed to a margin note beneath an Iberian carving.

"El Coco," he said. "Cucuy stories. The earliest versions don't describe a man-shaped boogeyman. They describe a long-limbed figure that bends over sleeping children, leaving their ribs collapsed inward by morning."

He flipped the page.

"Shadow People accounts from the 17th and 18th centuries mention the same posture—tall, bent forward, arms too long, heads angled unnaturally. Witnesses always note a cold sensation first."

He turned to one final sheet—an ossuary etching from Eastern Europe.

"And the proto-Reaper figures weren't skeletal. Not originally. They were shadow shapes with disproportionate limbs, depicted beside victims with inward-crushed torsos. After centuries of reinterpretation, the scythe and skeleton replaced the original descriptions."

Maya felt her pulse slow and pound at the same time.

Vander looked directly at her.

"These aren't different stories," he said. "They are the same account, retold across generations, each culture naming it something different while describing the same anatomy."

Graves shook his head hard. "Folklore evolves. People project fear onto whatever kills them."

"And what killed them," Vander said, "left the same marks you saw last night."

Maya's throat tightened.

Graves went still.

For a moment, the fluorescent lights seemed too loud, humming against all the things none of them wanted to say aloud.

Maya swallowed hard. Vander's tone wasn't dramatic. It was quiet, almost clinical, which only made it worse.

He unrolled another sheet—this one cleaner, printed from a high-resolution restoration. The figure beside the victim wasn't detailed, just a dark, elongated silhouette etched with a woodcarver's uneven hand. But the victim's body—

Maya stared.

The ribs were bowed outward like the jogger's.

The sternum was intact.

The abdomen slightly concave.

No skin breaks.

No external trauma.

Her stomach dropped.

Vander tracked her reaction and lowered the page between them so only she could see. "You recognize it."

It wasn't a question.

She didn't answer.

Graves snatched the sheet out of Vander's hands and slapped it face-down on the counter. "We're not indulging this."

"You already are," Vander said. "By refusing to look closely."

Graves' voice sharpened. "What do you want? Credit? A book deal? To turn this into some folklore lecture for your grad students?"

Vander's eyes hardened—something cold and old settling behind them.

"I want you to survive," he said quietly.

The words hit the room like a pressure drop.

Graves scoffed, but the sound was brittle. "Save the theatrics."

Vander stepped closer, lowering his voice. "Ward told me what he saw. The internal puncture paths. The collapse pattern. The cold halo around the airway. These are not random. They are not modern. They are not new."

He slid a thin binder onto the counter and opened it to a photograph—grainy, time-worn.

A victim from 1911.

Ribs bowed inward this time—an incomplete feed.

Neck bent at the exact same angle Maya had seen in Brookside.

Beneath the photograph, handwritten in faded ink:

"Shadow lingered after death."

Maya's breath hitched.

Vander flipped to another page—an autopsy sketch from 1978, margins filled with frantic notes.

Collapsed trachea.

Internal frost pockets.

Cartilage inversion.

Cold-zone differential.

All the things she'd already seen.

All the things she didn't want to admit matched.

Graves stared at the sketch a beat too long.

Then he snapped his fingers at it, dismissive. "Still folklore. Misdiagnosis. Poor documentation."

"If it were just one era," Vander said, "I would agree. But this—" He tapped the binder. "—is eight hundred years of identical anatomical anomalies. Across continents. Across cultures. Across languages."

He looked directly at Maya.

"No matter when it appears," he said, "people describe the same thing."

Maya's throat tightened. She felt her shadow shift at her feet—no lag, no distortion—but she still flinched.

Graves caught the movement.

"Maya," he said, "don't encourage this."

Vander didn't take his eyes off her. "Did you notice anything strange on your scene tonight?"

Her jaw locked.

Her pulse thudded.

"Yes," she said softly.

Graves pivoted toward her. "Raine—"

Vander nodded, almost sadly. "The cold-band. The rib torque. The displacement of the soft organs. All consistent."

"With what?" Graves snapped.

Vander finally looked at him.

"With a feeding pattern that predates your badge," he said. "And mine."

Graves clenched his fists. "We are not doing this. Not on my case."

Vander didn't try to argue. He just gathered his papers, stacking them with an unsettling calm.

"You don't have to believe me," he said. "You will."

He slid one last page across the counter toward them—a monk's journal excerpt, translated in neat handwriting.

Maya read the first translated line before she could stop herself:

"When its hunger begins, the air turns sharp. The shadows warp. The ribs bow. And we cannot bury our dead fast enough."

Her vision tunneled for a moment.

Graves shoved the binder back toward Vander. "I'm not taking medieval horror stories as evidence."

Vander didn't flinch. "Then look at the scene again."

"Oh, I'll look," Graves said sharply, grabbing his jacket. "And you're coming with me—to the perimeter. You stay behind the tape, you don't touch a damn thing, and when your drawings don't line up, you're done. Understood?"

Vander nodded once. "Understood."

Graves rubbed his eyes and pointed at Maya. "Raine, you're done. I'm having a deputy take you home. You look like you're about to fall over."

Maya stiffened. "I'm fine."

"No," Graves said. "You're not. You've seen enough for one night. Go home. Sleep."

He jerked a thumb toward the hallway. "Deputy Keller's on escort."

Maya didn't argue this time.

She didn't trust her voice.

Graves didn't talk during the drive back to the trail. The cruiser's engine hummed under the weight of the silence, headlights cutting narrow tunnels through the trees as dusk collapsed into the deep blue of early night.

Vander sat in the passenger seat, hands folded neatly on the notebook in his lap. He didn't fidget. He didn't look nervous. He looked like a man on his way to verify something he'd already accepted.

Graves hated him more by the minute.

They reached the access road. Patrol units were gone; only a single cruiser remained, lights off, guarding the mouth of the trail. The deputy on watch stepped aside when he saw Graves' badge.

"You two heading in?"

"Just to the tape," Graves said. "Civilian consultant stays behind it. No exceptions."

The deputy nodded. "Scene's cold. No techs left inside."

Good. Graves wanted this done fast.

They walked in. The branches overhead had gone black against the last scrap of sky, and the temperature dipped the deeper they moved — subtle, but enough for Graves to feel air tightening against his ribs.

Vander noticed. Graves saw the way his gaze sharpened, the way he lifted his chin as if testing the air.

"This is residual," Vander murmured.

"Don't," Graves snapped. "You get five minutes. Behind the tape."

They reached the perimeter. The yellow tape fluttered once in a breeze that didn't exist. The indentation in the ground where the jogger had collapsed was still visible — a shallow depression, the outline of where the body bag had been zipped shut.

Vander stopped just short of the tape.

He didn't step over it.

He didn't ask to.

He only looked.

And the way he looked made Graves' skin crawl — not mystical, not entranced, but clinical, like he was aligning a photograph with a memory he'd studied too many times.

Vander pointed with the end of his pen — cautious not to cross the boundary.

"Here," he said. "This is where the collapse initiated."

Graves folded his arms. "You don't know that."

"I do," Vander said quietly. "The soil depresses differently when pressure originates internally rather than from external impact."

Graves felt irritation spike through his chest. "You're not an ME."

"No," Vander agreed. "But the 1911 orchard deaths showed the same shallow depressions. And the 1638 plague sketches show victims arranged similarly — ribs raised, sternum intact, abdominal cavity slightly concave. It's consistent."

Graves clenched his jaw. "This isn't centuries-old Spain. This is a park in our jurisdiction."

"And yet," Vander replied, "the physiology of collapse hasn't changed."

He lifted his gaze to the nearest tree.

The bark-scrape marks were faint in the dim light, but still visible: long, vertical, parallel runs nearly nine feet up.

Vander's breath caught.

Not dramatically — but in recognition.

Graves saw it. And it pissed him off.

"No," Graves said, stepping closer. "Don't you dare tell me that tree looks like one of your woodcuts."

"It doesn't," Vander said. "It looks like the 1911 orchard trunk. Almost exactly, in fact."

He angled his head, noting the drag pattern. "Same directional descent. Same depth variance. Same spacing."

Graves wanted to argue, but the words jammed somewhere behind his teeth. He stared at the marks, at the too-even lines, at the height. His mind tried to fit the pattern into categories he understood — climbers, tools, animals — but everything came up wrong.

Vander knelt in the dirt just beyond the tape, pen hovering over unseen shapes.

"This is where it stood," he said softly. "Here."

"Something stood there," Graves corrected. "Human, animal — we don't know."

"Human height doesn't reach nine feet," Vander murmured, almost apologetically.

"Ladders do," Graves snapped.

"Then show me the ladder marks."

Graves ground his teeth. He couldn't. There were none.

Vander looked back toward the clearing, voice low. "It always starts like this. Pressure from within. Cold pockets in the air. Collapsed structures without external damage."

"'Always,'" Graves repeated, bitterness deep. "As if you've been here before."

"Not here," Vander said. "But I've been close. Close enough."

He stood slowly.

The woods around them were quiet — too quiet. No insects. No wind. No night sounds. Just the pressure of a space that felt like it was holding its breath.

Vander stared into the treeline for a long moment, eyes tracking the dark between the trunks, not with wonder, but with a quiet, exhausted dread.

"Cycles repeat," he said. "Not often. Not predictably. But when the first signs appear... they don't stop."

"This isn't a cycle," Graves growled. "This is two deaths that have nothing in common."

Vander looked at him — not smug, not triumphant, but deeply sad.

"You don't believe that," he said.

Graves' jaw twitched.

Vander turned away from the clearing.

"We should go," he said softly. "Whatever was here... it left. But not long ago."

That line hit something low in Graves' gut, something he refused to name.

He stepped back from the tape, voice tight. "We're going. You're giving your statement when we get back."

Vander nodded and followed him out.

The woods remained silent behind them.

Too silent.

The kind of silence that wasn't emptiness —
but vacancy.

By the time they reached the cruiser, the sky had drained into a dull, metallic blue—the last band of dusk slipping behind the treetops. Not night. Just that uneasy hour where everything looked sharper and flatter than it should, like the world hadn't decided what to do with its own shadows.

Graves unlocked the car and jerked his head. "Get in."

Vander obeyed without a word. He placed his notebook carefully on his lap, palms resting lightly over it as if the weight grounded him.

Graves slid behind the wheel and gripped it hard before starting the engine. He didn't look at Vander. Didn't look at the trees either. Just stared straight ahead, jaw tight, breath shallow.

"You don't mention anything you said out there," Graves said finally. "Not until we're in a room with a recorder. Not in the hallway. Not to another officer. Not to anyone."

Vander nodded once. "Understood."

"I'm serious."

"So am I."

The answer unsettled Graves in a way he couldn't articulate. He started the engine just to break the silence. Headlights poured over the trailhead, catching the tape and the darkening branches in stark, washed-out glare.

They pulled away.

For a few seconds, neither spoke. The tires crunched gravel in long, steady rolls, the trees thinning as they approached the paved road. The world outside the windshield still held the tail-end of daylight—thin, bruised light that didn't warm anything.

Halfway down the access lane, Vander spoke without looking away from the window.

"Two cases within a day..." He exhaled quietly. "That's faster than I expected."

Graves snapped, "Stop. Right there. No more of that cycle bullshit."

Vander's reflection in the passenger window looked almost translucent.

He didn't argue.

Graves wasn't sure if that made it better or worse.

When they reached the main road, the cruiser rolled under a streetlamp flickering to life—the kind of lazy, sputtering ignition that made the pavement glow and fade, glow and fade. The sensation crawled over Graves' skin.

"Listen carefully," Graves said, voice low. "When we get back, you give a normal statement. Facts. Nothing about woodcuts or cucuy monsters or patterns across centuries."

"I can keep my language strictly clinical," Vander said.

"Good," Graves muttered. "Keep it that way."

They drove the rest of the way in silence, the light outside thinning further, but never quite collapsing into night. It was that threshold hour—the kind where even familiar streets felt stretched at the edges.

Graves pulled into the precinct lot, parking hard. The building's exterior lights flickered on overhead, bleaching the concrete in a dead yellow hue.

He cut the engine.

Vander sat still, hands on the notebook, eyes nowhere Graves wanted them to be—somewhere deeper, quieter, more resigned.

"You pull any shit in there," Graves said, "and I'll have three uniforms toss you out. I don't care who Ward is."

Vander nodded. "Detective, my goal isn't to frighten you."

Graves laughed under his breath—short, humorless.

"Trust me," he said. "You're not even close."

He opened the door and stepped out.

He didn't notice the way his shadow lagged—half a heartbeat behind—before it snapped back into alignment beneath him.

But Vander noticed.

His face went pale.

He said nothing.

He just followed Graves into the precinct, dusk clinging to the windows like it wasn't ready to let go.

Chapter 6 — Followed Home

Holt locked his front door and felt the click run up his spine like a warning.

The house was supposed to feel familiar. Safe. A place he could shrug out of the jogger scene and the memory of those scraped trees. Instead, the air inside pressed at him—still, heavy, like the walls had been holding their breath while he was gone.

He dropped his keys in the dish by the entryway and froze.

Breathing.

Not his.

A wet, faintly rattling inhale somewhere deeper in the hall.

He stood motionless, every muscle drawn tight. His own heartbeat filled his ears, loud and unsteady, masking the sound for a moment. Then it came again—low, damp, a drag of air through something too narrow.

He reached for the hallway light and flicked it on.

The breathing stopped.

Nothing moved.

The hall was empty.

"Jesus...," he muttered, rubbing a hand over his face. He hadn't slept right in two days. The jogger, the silhouette he thought he saw in the woods—it was wrecking his nerves. He knew that. Knew he should shower, lie down, get a few hours before start-of-watch tomorrow.

But the quiet… it felt *held*, like the air was waiting for something.

His phone buzzed.

A text from Graves: *Statement at start-of-watch. Don't be late.*

Holt typed back with stiff fingers: *Yeah. First thing. End of shift for me.*

He hovered over send, exhaled, and tapped it.

The breathing didn't return, but something shifted in the hallway—so small he almost missed it. A pressure change. A faint drop in temperature over the bare skin of his forearms. Not cold exactly… just *less warm.*

The kitchen light flickered when he walked under it.

Not the usual kind of flicker—no hum, no bulb about to die. Just a quick pulse, as if something had passed between him and the ceiling.

He blinked up at the fixture, jaw clenching.

"No," he whispered to himself. "No, no. You're tired. That's all."

He turned toward the bathroom. The door stood half-open, dark inside except for a thin slice of hallway light carving across the tile.

Something shifted again.

Not movement.

Not footsteps.

More like… *space adjusting,* the room settling in a way it shouldn't.

His pulse kicked hard.

He took one step backward, then another, until his shoulder hit the wall.

"Okay…," he breathed, forcing air into his lungs. "House noises. Nothing. Just… nothing."

But the house didn't feel empty.

It felt *aware* of him.

He moved back into the living room, forcing himself not to look over his shoulder. The lamp on the side table cast a soft circle of light across the carpet—warm, steady, comforting.

Until he caught a flicker of something at the edge of his vision.

His own shadow.

It lagged behind him by half a second before snapping back into place.

Holt stopped breathing.

He tested it—moved his arm slowly.

Shadow followed.

Then caught up too fast, like a frame skipping forward.

His throat tightened. Sweat prickled at the base of his neck.

"Just… stress," he whispered. "Just stress."

But the words didn't settle anything.

He stood still for a long moment, waiting for the room to act normal again. Waiting to feel normal again. The silence dragged, thick and wrong.

And then—

The breathing came back.

Closer this time.

Coming from the very end of the hall.

Holt's skin crawled.

He didn't move. He didn't speak. He didn't even swallow.

He only listened.

And the breathing—slow, wet, patient—filled the dark like something waiting for him to answer.

Holt forced himself toward the hallway again, one slow step at a time, until he could lean just far enough to hit the bathroom light without taking his eyes off the dark. The switch clicked under his thumb.

White light filled the doorway.

The breathing stopped instantly.

He shouldn't have been relieved. Relief meant he believed it. Meant he expected a cause.

He scanned the bathroom—shower curtain, tile, mirror—and shut the door again. Turned the lock. He didn't need to. He just needed to feel like he had control over something.

The house felt wrong behind him, a silence that pressed against his back as he walked into the living room. His chest tightened with every step.

He flicked on the overhead light.

Too bright. Too sterile. He reached for the lamp instead.

Warm light spread across the room, settling on the couch and the worn hardwood floor. He let himself breathe, just once, slow and steady.

Then something moved.

A flicker of shadow — delayed.

Holt froze, heartbeat spiking.

The far wall held his shadow, but something about it was wrong. It was angled differently than his body. A fraction off. Only noticeable because he wasn't moving.

He lifted his hand.

The shadow lifted a beat later.

Holt's breath stuttered out of him.

"No," he whispered, stepping back.

He moved again, just enough to test it.

The shadow hesitated — then snapped into perfect alignment as if trying not to be caught.

His stomach dropped.

He grabbed his phone and dialed the precinct's non-emergency number, pulse hammering against the side of his throat.

"Dispatch," a bored voice answered.

"This is Officer Holt," he said, trying to control the tremor in his voice. "Badge 4125. I— I just need it noted that I'm... not feeling right tonight. Might be a stress reaction from the jogger scene. I'm staying in. Just log it."

A pause.

"You need a wellness check?"

"No," he said too quickly. "No. I'm fine. Just... log it."

"Logged."

The call ended.

He lowered the phone, staring at the dark spot under the coffee table.

It shifted.

Not big—barely anything—but the darkness there seemed to thicken for just a second, like someone pressing gently into the underside of a mattress.

Holt's breath hitched.

He stepped back until he hit the wall again.

"Stop," he whispered to the empty room. "Just... stop."

The shadows didn't move.

But the air felt like it was watching him.

He kept his eyes fixed on that sliver of dark beneath the table, the one place the lamp didn't quite reach. It didn't flicker. It didn't distort.

It just waited.

He swallowed hard.

The house felt tight around him—every wall too close, every corner too deep. His skin prickled with cold he couldn't shake.

His flashlight lay on the counter.

He forced himself toward it, each step deliberate.

The moment he reached for it—

Something at the end of the hall bent the shadows in a direction the light didn't allow.

He stopped dead.

The dark didn't move.

But it wasn't still either.

Like the moment right before someone steps into view.

His hands shook. The flashlight felt slick in his grip.

He stood there, listening, barely breathing.

And then—

A faint creak of floorboards deeper inside the house.

Not under his feet.

Not where anyone should be.

He was not alone.

He wasn't sure he had ever been alone since he left the woods.

Holt edged backward toward the living room, flashlight trembling in his grip. The house felt too quiet, as if every wall were listening. He kept the beam low, sweeping the baseboards, the hallway, the doorframes.

Nothing.

He exhaled—just barely—then stepped past the doorway into the hall.

A shape slid across the bathroom threshold.

He froze.

At first he thought it was his own shadow again, lagging or bending. But the angle was wrong. The outline was wrong. It stretched too tall, too thin, reaching nearly to the top of the doorframe before folding backward, as if the silhouette had too many joints—or none at all.

The lamp in the living room was still on. His shadow shouldn't even be cast this far.

His chest seized.

"Who's there?" His voice came out cracked, too quiet.

The silhouette didn't answer.

It didn't move.

But the darkness around it deepened—just a fraction—like the outline was condensing into something denser than the shadows it stood in.

Holt's pulse hammered painfully in his neck.

He raised the flashlight.

The beam shook.

The silhouette didn't scatter or distort the way shadows should under direct light.

It didn't react at all.

He stepped back so fast his heel hit the wall. Air scraped in and out of his lungs in short, jagged pulls.

"No," he whispered. "No. No."

The silhouette leaned.

Not forward.

Just *angled*, slowly, impossibly, as if its upper half bent from somewhere above its chest and its lower half stayed perfectly still.

Holt's throat locked.

His hand flew to his holster. He yanked the gun free and leveled it at the figure.

"Get out! I'm armed! I said—"

A wet inhale—behind him.

Directly behind him.

Holt spun, gun raised—

Nothing.

His breath convulsed in his chest. Sweat slid down his spine, cold and sharp.

He turned back toward the bathroom.

The silhouette was gone.

A single, thin line of shadow slipped along the wall, retreating toward the kitchen as if being absorbed into the deeper dark beneath the cupboards.

Holt's vision narrowed.

"Stop it stop it stop it—"

A floorboard creaked behind him.

He whipped around and fired.

The gunshot detonated through the house, ripping a concussive crack through the hallway. Drywall dust drifted in a pale cloud from the fresh crater in the wall. Holt stumbled backward, ears ringing so hard the world went muffled and distant.

For a moment, all he could hear was his own breathing—ragged, panicked, animal.

Then the silence returned.

Not normal silence.

The heavy kind.

The listening kind.

He kept the gun raised, hands trembling so violently the barrel twitched.

Somewhere outside, a door slammed. Another voice called something unclear in the distance—someone reacting to the noise, to the sudden violence echoing off the surrounding houses.

Of course they heard.

A gunshot inside a residential block at this hour? No one would mistake that for anything else.

His pulse hammered harder.

He stayed exactly where he was, muscles locked, staring down the dark seam between the hall and living room.

Two minutes.

Maybe three.

Then he heard it—faint through the walls—the first whoop of approaching sirens. Not urgent. Not full-code. Just the controlled response used for *shots fired / unknown trouble.*

Holt's stomach twisted.

He didn't move. Didn't lower the gun. Didn't blink.

A police radio crackled outside.

Footsteps climbed his porch.

A hard knock rattled the door.

"Officer Holt!" a voice shouted. **"Department! Step into view and announce yourself!"**

His knees nearly buckled with equal parts relief and dread.

But before he could answer, before he holstered the weapon, before he forced his legs toward the entry—

Something deeper in the house shifted again.

A faint drag.

A repositioning.

As if something tall was quietly drawing itself deeper into the dark.

Holt swallowed, throat tight enough to ache.

The door rattled again.

"Holt! Open up!"

He tore his eyes away from the shadowed hallway, breath shaking, and started toward the front door.

Behind him, the house settled into silence.

The kind that waits.

The moment Holt opened the door, the porch lights from the patrol cruiser washed over him, bleaching him out in harsh LED glare.

Two uniformed officers stood with hands near their holsters. Graves was behind them, jacket half-zipped, tie loose, jaw tight enough to crack. He must've been in his car when the call came out.

Holt lowered his gun and set it on the entry table, hands shaking too hard to hide.

Graves stepped forward, voice low, controlled, pissed. "Tell me why the hell there's a round in your wall."

Holt swallowed, throat trembling. "I— I saw someone. In the hall."

"Someone," Graves repeated flatly. "Describe them."

Holt opened his mouth.

His voice wouldn't come out.

Not *can't.*

Wouldn't.

Because whatever he'd seen didn't fit into anything that could be described without sounding insane.

"Tall," he forced out. "Wrong. It— it moved like—"

He shut his mouth before the rest escaped.

Graves studied him for a long, steady beat. Holt could see the calculation behind his eyes — running Holt's words through everything he knew about the man: good cop, good instincts, solid performance, no history of breakdowns.

And what he'd seen at the jogger scene.

"Did you hear anything?" Graves asked, tone shifting — not kinder, but more cautious.

Holt nodded. "Breathing."

The officers behind them exchanged a quick glance. Graves didn't look away from Holt.

"You discharged your weapon at a shadow in your own damn house."

"It wasn't—" Holt's voice cracked. "It wasn't a shadow."

Graves inhaled sharply through his nose. "You're getting written up for this. That's not optional. But you're also going off-duty for the night. You're not clearing another call until you get some sleep."

Holt's pulse hammered. "I'm not— I'm not imagining this."

"Then give me something real," Graves said. "A suspect description. A forced entry. A footprint. A broken lock. Anything."

Holt had nothing.

Just the memory of something tall and bent leaning out of the dark.

Graves' jaw tightened. "We'll finish your statement tomorrow."

He stepped back onto the porch and signaled to the uniforms. "Clear the house."

Holt stayed in the doorway as the officers swept room by room. He flinched at every creak, every open door, every shift of their flashlights.

It took seven minutes.

Seven minutes of Holt's heart beating too loud and the house feeling too still.

"Nothing, Detective," one of the officers said. "No signs of entry."

Of course there weren't.

Graves let out a slow exhale. "Alright. Holt — get some rest. You're done for the night."

Graves stepped closer, lowering his voice so the uniforms wouldn't hear. "Listen carefully. Your weapon's secured. And until a supervisor clears you, you're off-duty. Mandatory wellness eval tomorrow morning. Keller will put it on the schedule."

Holt blinked at him, the words landing slower than they should.

"This isn't optional," Graves added. "You discharged a firearm inside your own home with no verified threat. Policy won't let you back on duty until you're evaluated."

Holt nodded, but it felt automatic.

The officers left. The cruiser pulled away. Graves lingered just long enough to search Holt's face again, some mix of annoyance and concern threading behind his eyes.

"You see anything else tonight," Graves said quietly, "you call me. Not dispatch. Me."

Holt swallowed. "It wasn't nothing."

Graves hesitated — the closest he'd come to admitting doubt.

Then he turned and walked away.

Holt locked the door.

The deadbolt clicked too loudly.

He stood there in the quiet entry, breath shallow, skin prickling with cold that wasn't from the night.

He didn't want to stay awake.

He didn't want to sleep either.

He chose the one option that felt survivable — light.

He grabbed every lamp he owned. Dragged them into the bedroom. Desk lamps, floor lamp, bedside lights — all clustered around the bed in a messy halo of bulbs and cords. The room glowed like the inside of an interrogation booth.

He sat on the edge of the mattress, hands clasped between his knees, gun holstered but within reach.

Light filled every angle.

Every corner.

Every—

Something overhead shifted.

Slow.

Deliberate.

A shadow crawled across the ceiling, sliding against the light instead of retreating from it — thin, long, bending in ways his eyes couldn't follow.

Not cast by anything in the room.

Not shaped like anything alive.

Holt's breath left him in a thin, shaking sound.

The light didn't stop it.

Nothing stopped it.

It moved anyway.

It moved because it wanted to.

And Holt finally understood:

Whatever was in his house wasn't confused.

It wasn't displaced.

It wasn't lost.

It was hunting.

And it liked him scared.

Chapter 7 — Forensic Oddities

The county forensic wing felt colder than the rest of the building—not temperature cold, just the kind that settled under the skin. Graves pushed through the double doors with a stiffness that hadn't left him since the woods. The hum of the overhead fluorescents vibrated at a pitch that made his teeth grit. Stainless steel surfaces. Bleach. Old anxiety ground into tile grout.

A half-assembled briefing waited for him.

A projector cast a pale square onto the wall. Evidence boards lined the front of the room—case numbers stenciled neatly at the top:

CASE 24-117A — Alder Street DOA

CASE 24-119C — Woodline DOA

Photos and temperature logs were clipped below the headers. A few sheets had red pen scrawls where the techs had stopped pretending the usual forms made sense.

Maya stepped in a moment after him. She looked like she'd slept maybe an hour—eyes slightly glassy, shoulders tight, jaw clenched the way EMTs clenched just to stay upright. She didn't acknowledge Graves, but she didn't have to. The air between them already carried enough strain.

Forensics Lead Maren stood at the projector with a remote in hand and an expression that didn't belong on someone who had seen everything twice.

"Detective. Raine. Thanks for coming on short notice."

Graves folded his arms. "You said you had findings."

"That's one word for it," Maren muttered.

A few techs exchanged uneasy looks. Someone adjusted the tray of evidence folders like they needed something—anything—normal to touch.

Maya glanced at the evidence board again. The temp logs on 24-117A bothered her; Graves saw it in her face. A single reading dipped lower than the rest by a margin that shouldn't have existed.

Maren nodded toward the table. "We'll begin with airway analysis from the Alder Street case."

Graves didn't sit. Maya didn't either.

The projector clicked, and the first slide filled the wall.

CASE 24-117A — AIRWAY INTERIOR (POST-MORTEM)

A close-up of the tracheal walls appeared, magnified—white crystalline ridges clinging to the inner cartilage rings like delicate frost growths.

Someone behind them swore under their breath.

Maren kept her voice level. "This is frost."

Graves' brow tightened. "Inside the throat?"

"Yes," she said. "Only inside. No frostbite on the skin. No freezing damage to external tissue. Ambient temperature at time of death was sixty-eight degrees."

Maya's breath stilled.

Graves didn't blink. "Explain the source."

"We can't." Maren didn't sugarcoat it. "There is no chemical agent. No cryogenic substance. Nothing environmental that matches this effect."

The projector hummed louder, overworking.

Maren continued, "This resembles an anomaly recorded in a small cluster of cases from 1911—warm rooms, cold bodies, frost only in airways."

Graves' jaw locked. He didn't want the historical angle. Not today.

A tech cleared his throat. "There's more."

Maren clicked the remote.

CASE 24-119C — RIB CAVITY INTERIOR (POST-MORTEM)

Internal tissue tearing with no corresponding external trauma. Pressure paths moving *inward,* toward the organs. Something had pulled, not struck. There was no mechanism for it—not one that made sense.

Maya's hand unconsciously tightened around her opposite elbow.

Graves didn't speak.

No one else did either.

The air felt denser now, like the room had gained weight.

Maren said quietly, "These are not isolated findings. The anomalies repeat across both scenes."

Graves' stomach dropped—not in fear, but in the sickening tilt that came when reality started to slip out of its lane.

"Detective," Maren said softly, "you'll want to see the next slide."

The projector clicked.

The next slide hit the wall with a cold, clinical brightness.

CASE 24-117A — SPINAL COLUMN ANOMALY

Maren stepped closer, tapping the pointed end of her pen against the highlighted region.

"This," she said, "is where things stop lining up with any known trauma profile."

The image showed the victim's cervical spine from the inside—vertebrae clean, ligaments intact, but the canal space narrowed as if something had pressed outward from within. Not crushed. Not snapped.

Pressed.

Graves squinted. "What kind of pressure does that?"

"That's the problem," Maren replied. "There's no external impact. None. No bruising. No swelling. No tool impression. Whatever caused this didn't touch the outside of the neck at all."

A murmur rolled across the techs.

Maya stared at the image, her shoulders rigid. Something inside her chest twisted. She'd felt that collapse with her own fingers—had felt the unnatural give of the cartilage, the hollowed quality beneath the skin.

Maren changed slides again.

CASE 24-119C — ELECTROMAGNETIC INTERFERENCE (BODYCAM)

A still frame appeared, split-screen from two responders' cameras: one normal, the other showing a half-second lag in the timestamp where the footage had captured the jogger's body. The image was subtly reversed in its motion, a frame folding in on itself before righting.

The tech operating the playback cleared his throat. "This isn't pixel corruption. We ran it through diagnostics. It's a temporal desync—like the camera tried to record two moments at once."

Another tech added, "No device malfunction. No heat damage. No RF spike. Nothing environmental."

Graves' skin prickled—not from fear, but from a deeper, quieter alarm that irritated him simply by existing.

"Could be a software glitch," he muttered.

The tech shook his head. "If it was software, it would show up at random. This only happens near the body. And only in a two-foot radius."

Maren clicked again.

COLD-ZONE LOG — CASE 24-119C

Temperature points overlayed a map of the jogger's chest cavity. One line dipped sharply—too sharply—to be ignored.

Maya stepped closer without meaning to.

The dip was identical to the one she'd seen inside the first victim. Identical.

Her throat dried.

Maren kept talking, unaware of the way Maya's eyes had gone distant. "These cold pockets don't make sense. They're isolated within the bodies or immediately around them. No surrounding environmental dip. No drafts. No HVAC malfunctions. The heat loss is localized to the tissue."

Graves exhaled through his nose. Hard. "Localized how?"

"Like something absorbed it," Maren said. "Directly. Efficiently."

One of the techs removed his glasses and rubbed his face. "I've been doing this twenty years. I've never seen thermal displacement inside a body without a source."

Maren clicked to the next image.

A side-by-side comparison: the jogger's rib interior tearing, overlaid with the Alder Street airway frost. Beneath it, a chemical analysis showing no external reagents.

"This is where we hit a wall," Maren said. "The injuries don't match any forensic category we have—accidental, environmental, homicidal, chemical, electrical. Nothing. If this is human-inflicted, there's no tool. If it's environmental, there's no cause. If it's biological…"

She trailed off, unwilling to say the word *impossible*.

Maya swallowed hard.

Graves stared at the screen until his eyes hurt.

One of the younger analysts on the back wall raised a hand hesitantly. "Detective… you should know this isn't the first time we've seen something like this."

Graves shot him a sharp look. "Meaning?"

The analyst reached into a folder and pulled a photocopied page—old, yellowed, water-stained.

"1978," he said. "Decommissioned refinery. Three bodies found inside a boiler unit. Internal frost, internal tearing, rib displacement with no external trauma. No perpetrator identified."

Maren's tone went flat. "We're seeing the same patterns. Down to the temperature variance."

Graves' pulse ticked once—hard.

He didn't want the connection. He didn't want *any* connection.

But the slide changed again.

INTERNAL DAMAGE — CROSS-EVENT CONSISTENCY

(Alder Street vs Jogger)

The overlay made the similarities impossible to ignore.

Internal collapse.

Internal frost.

Internal tearing.

Localized cold halos.

Zero external wounds.

Maya's breath faltered. Graves felt his chest tighten.

Maren lowered the remote. "Whatever is doing this… it's doing the same thing across both cases. Identical mechanisms. Identical signatures."

The room stayed silent for a long, suffocating moment.

Then Maren exhaled shakily.

"Detective… something is wrong in this county."

Graves didn't answer.

Because for the first time, he didn't know how.

When the briefing finally broke apart, it wasn't with the usual shuffling of papers and tired chatter. People left quietly, like they were afraid to say anything that might accidentally make the evidence real.

Chairs scraped. Gloves snapped off. A few analysts murmured to each other in low, shaken tones as they filed out, leaving the projector's pale glow humming against the wall.

Graves didn't move.

He stood there staring at the last slide—the overlay of internal-only trauma—his shoulders drawn tight like wire pulled too far. His jaw flexed and unflexed. He kept telling himself he was just thinking, just processing, just cataloging possibilities.

But he wasn't moving because he didn't trust his legs.

Maya lingered near the equipment rack, pretending to reorganize the secondary monitor cables. It wasn't subtle. Graves knew she was watching him, but he pretended not to notice. The last thing he needed was a medic reading how rattled he really felt.

The projector fan wound down with a soft whir. The room dimmed.

Graves reached for a folder on the table, but it slipped from his hand and fluttered to the floor. He muttered under his breath and bent to grab it.

As he straightened, something under the conference table hesitated—just a fraction of a second, just shy of perception. His own shadow had lagged behind his movement, the shape of his head and shoulders stretching, delayed, before snapping back into alignment like it had been tugged into place.

Graves froze.

His pulse punched once against the inside of his throat, sharp and ugly.

He didn't breathe.

The shadow was normal now. Perfectly normal. But he'd seen it. Clean. Unmistakable. No light flicker. No camera glitch. Nothing he could blame.

His mouth went dry.

Maya shifted in the corner of his vision, as if she'd sensed the change in him. "Detective?" she asked quietly.

Graves blinked once, slow. Too slow.

He forced himself to straighten, forced the stiffness out of his shoulders, forced his voice to come out even.

"Lighting's garbage in here," he said. Too fast. Too defensive.

Maya didn't challenge it, but her eyes sharpened slightly—not pity, not fear. Recognition. She'd seen him flinch.

He hated that.

Graves closed the folder harder than he needed to and set it on the table with a thud. "We're done here," he said. "They'll send us the full report."

He turned to leave, making sure his steps were steady. Controlled. Normal.

He did not look under the table again.

He did not look at the wall where his shadow had stretched wrong.

And he absolutely did not acknowledge the cold knot forming under his sternum, the one that felt nothing like fear and everything like impending collapse.

Behind him, Maya watched him walk out.

She didn't call after him.

She didn't need to.

The door swung shut behind Graves, leaving the forensic room dim and half-lit, the projector's fading glow still clinging to the wall.

Maya didn't move for a long breath.

She wasn't watching the door.

She was watching the evidence board.

Something in the layout tugged at her—something she hadn't had the space to really absorb during the briefing. She stepped closer, drawn forward the way a medic's instinct pulled toward the wounded.

CASE 24-117A — AIRWAY INTERIOR

CASE 24-119C — RIB CAVITY

SPINAL COLUMN COMPRESSION

Different victims. Different environments. Same impossible patterns.

She hovered a few inches from the thermal map overlay, scanning the numbers again. The faint dip in the center. The way the temperature had dropped only in the tissue. Not the air. Not the room.

Localized. Precise.

Something taking heat like a resource.

Her fingers brushed the edge of the display board as she leaned in—

A cold prickle swept across her forearm.

Sharp. Isolated. Gone in an instant.

She jerked her arm back and checked the wall vent beside the board. No airflow. No draft. No mechanical vibration. Just dead silence and still air.

Her pulse thudded once in her ribs, hard.

She stepped forward again, deliberately this time, watching her skin.

Nothing.

No cold.

No sensation.

Smooth, dead air.

But the moment she'd leaned in—directly over the cluster of readings at the center of the cold-zone dip—the temperature had pressed against her like a fingertip of winter.

She swallowed. Hard.

This was the same feeling she'd had kneeling over the first body. The same wrongness in the air. The same local absence of warmth. Not a chill. Not fear. A void.

The projector clicked one final time as its bulb cooled, the faint pop echoing through the room.

Maya turned toward the exit—then paused.

Across the far wall, the shadows cast by the evidence carts stretched a fraction too far. Not dramatically. Not unnaturally. Just... longer than they had any right to be under the fixed ceiling lights. When she blinked, they snapped back into their proper shapes.

No movement.

No flicker.

No cause.

Just wrong geometry settling into place.

Her throat tightened.

She backed away slowly, refusing to turn her back to the board until she was at the doorway. Even then, she hesitated—her pulse drumming an irregular beat she didn't trust.

Something was threading through these cases.

Something precise.

Something methodical.

Something that wasn't gone when the bodies were hauled away.

Maya stepped into the hall.

The forensic room lights hummed behind her.

And the cold stayed exactly where it had been—waiting.

Chapter 8 — Bloodline Fears

The call came just after dusk.

Maya had just gotten home, still wearing the same uniform shirt she'd sweated through at forensics, when her phone buzzed in her back pocket. The screen showed a name she'd been avoiding for weeks.

Clara.

For a moment, she froze—thumb hovering, breath locked somewhere between her ribs.

She almost let it go to voicemail.

Almost.

Then she heard the tremble in Clara's voice the second she answered.

"Maya? It's Lila."

A breath. A swallow.

"She's scared again. She keeps asking for you."

Something inside Maya tightened—old muscle memory, old instinct, the echo of a life that wasn't hers anymore but still lived in her bones.

"I'm coming."

Clara didn't have to say thank you. She didn't. She just exhaled with a softness that told Maya everything she needed to know.

The drive was short. Too short for Maya to fully rebuild the walls she'd spent years constructing.

The house was the same. The porch light still flickered. The paint still peeled. The same rust stain from the gutter still crawled down the siding. Seven years of memories crawled across her skin like file grit as she stepped out of the truck.

She knocked once.

The door flew open before her knuckles even dropped back to her side.

Lila hurled forward—small, shaking, barefoot—straight into Maya's arms. No hesitation, no question, just total collapse against the one person she still trusted when the dark felt too close.

Maya wrapped her arms around her automatically, breath catching. Lila smelled like shampoo and fear. The kind that clings to a child's skin.

"Hey," Maya whispered into her hair. "Hey, I've got you."

Lila didn't answer. She just clung harder.

Clara stood behind her in the hallway, worry carved into every line of her face. She looked like she hadn't slept in days.

"I'm sorry," Clara murmured. "She wouldn't calm down. She didn't want—"

Her voice cracked.

"She only wanted you."

Maya swallowed whatever rose in her throat—guilt, grief, something uglier—and nodded once.

"It's okay."

A lie.

"It's fine. I'm here."

They stepped inside together.

The moment Maya crossed the threshold, her skin prickled.

Cold.

Not environmental cold.

Localized.

Wrong.

The heater hummed in the vent. The thermostat on the wall glowed at a steady seventy-two. But a thin band of air across the hall brushed against Maya's arm like a cold fingertip.

She kept her face neutral. Lila didn't need panic. She needed solidity.

"Where were you when you got scared?" Maya asked gently.

Lila pointed down the hallway, her hand trembling. "My room."

Maya nodded, but her eyes flicked to the corner by the coat rack—where the light didn't quite reach. It wasn't dark. Not really. But the angle of the corner felt deeper, as if someone had taken a bite out of the geometry.

A shadow on the floor shifted when Lila moved.

Not much.

Not enough for someone untrained to notice.

Half an inch, maybe.

But it lagged.

Just a breath behind.

Maya's pulse jumped before she smothered the reaction.

"Come on," she said softly, guiding Lila toward the bedroom. "Show me."

Clara hovered behind them, arms folded tight over her chest, like she was trying to hold herself together.

Maya reached the doorway and stopped.

The air inside the room felt wrong. Not cold. Not warm. Just... emptied. Like the warmth had been scooped out of it and nothing was filling the space where it should be.

Lila clung to Maya again, her little fingers digging into the fabric of Maya's sleeve.

"It was here," she whispered. "Right here."

Maya knelt to eye level with her, brushing a piece of hair from Lila's cheek with a gentleness she didn't allow herself anywhere else in her life.

"You're safe," Maya said quietly. "I'm here."

Lila's eyes were wide, glossy with tears. "It keeps coming back."

Maya felt her stomach drop.

Her voice stayed calm. "Tell me what you mean."

Lila looked toward the far corner of the room, where the walls didn't meet cleanly. Where the angle seemed... deeper. Pulled.

She swallowed. Hard.

"It was watching me," she whispered.

Maya didn't move.

Didn't breathe.

"Lila," she said slowly, "what did you see?"

Lila's voice was thin, but sure.

"The same thing I saw when I was little."

Maya's chest tightened, and the room felt smaller.

"What thing?" she asked, though she already dreaded the answer.

Lila lifted a shaking hand and pointed to the corner—the wrong corner, the deep corner, the place where the walls didn't align with the house she remembered.

"The tall man," she whispered.

And the way she said it...

Not storybook.

Not childish.

Not imaginative.

Remembered.

Maya kept her expression steady, but something cold unspooled under her ribs.

"The tall man," she repeated quietly. "From when you were little."

Lila nodded—jerky, frightened, as if saying it out loud made it real again.

Clara leaned against the doorframe, rubbing her forearm with one hand. "My mom used to tell her it was the Cucuy. You know how she was with folklore. Scare-them-straight parenting."

Lila shook her head hard. "It wasn't the Cucuy."

The correction was instant. Automatic. Too certain.

Maya's stomach tightened.

She lowered herself to sit on the edge of the bed so she could look Lila in the eyes without towering over her. "Okay," she said gently. "Tell me what you remember."

Lila swallowed, gaze drifting toward that wrong corner like it still held gravity.

"I was seven," she whispered. "I got up at night because I heard breathing. Not Clara's. Not Grandma's. Something else. It sounded... hungry."

Clara flinched at that, turning her face away.

Lila went on, voice tightening. "I opened my eyes, and it was standing in the corner. The same corner."

Her hand trembled as she pointed.

"It wasn't a shadow," she said. "It had... shape."

Maya's pulse hitched.

"In what way?" she asked carefully.

Lila's face screwed up as she forced herself to remember. "Its head was bent forward like something was wrong with its neck. Like it couldn't hold it up. And its arms were too long. Almost to the floor."

The hairs rose on Maya's arms.

Exactly the proportions she'd seen on Alder Street.

Exactly the proportions from Vander's sketches.

"It was tall," Lila whispered. "But wrong-tall. Like it had more bones than it should."

Maya's breath stilled.

Clara let out a thin, helpless sound behind her. "Lila, baby—"

Lila shook her head. "Grandma said it was just the dark. Or a nightmare. Or the Cucuy trying to scare me. But I know what I saw. Its arms were... stretched."

Maya felt something shift in the air. Not temperature. Pressure. As if listening.

She leaned closer, pressing one hand lightly against Lila's back—not comforting, but grounding. "And you saw the same thing this week?"

Lila's chin trembled. Tears slipped down her cheek. "Yes."

"Where?" Maya asked softly.

"First time was in the hallway. Clara thought I was making it up. But it was standing by the bathroom. When I walked past it, my shadow didn't follow me right." Her voice cracked. "It bent. Like it was trying to reach it."

Maya's pulse thudded once in the base of her throat.

Shadow-lag.

Corner-deepening.

Early-stage recurrence.

Everything Vander had hinted at, wrapped in a child's vocabulary.

"And the second time?" Maya asked, voice threading thinner.

Lila wrapped her arms around herself. "In my room. I woke up because… because it was breathing again. Like before. Only closer."

Maya forced her face neutral. "Closer how?"

Lila pointed to the edge of the bed.

Right where Maya was sitting now.

Her finger shook with memory, not imagination. "It was standing there," she whispered. "Bent over me. Watching."

Clara covered her mouth with both hands.

Maya's throat went dry.

She had seen that same posture.

Felt that same posture over her shoulder at Alder Street.

A presence without form.

Weight without body.

But she couldn't say that.

She took Lila's hands gently. "You're safe right now. I need you to know that."

Lila looked at her with eyes too exhausted for her age. "No, Maya. It comes back. It always comes back."

And the worst part—the part Maya couldn't admit out loud—was that every part of her training, every clinical instinct, every forensic anomaly in the last week…

…told her the kid was right.

Maya eased Lila against her side, rubbing slow circles between her shoulder blades the way she used to when Lila was small and over-stimulated.

Clara paced once beside the dresser, arms folded tight. "She hasn't slept more than a few hours in days," Clara said, voice tense but controlled. "It's nightmares. It has to be."

There.

That was the real Clara.

The one who explained everything, even when she was scared out of her mind.

Maya didn't argue. She just looked around the room again, not with panic, but with the disciplined eyes of someone trained to read scenes.

Something was wrong.

Not supernatural.

Not mystical.

Just wrong.

The air near the corner felt... **thinner**, somehow.

Not colder.

Not warmer.

Just missing something.

A subtle absence where warmth should have been.

She reached a hand out slightly. Not enough for Lila to notice. Just enough to confirm a suspicion.

A two-foot span of "dead air."

No warmth.

No movement.

Just a hollow pocket in the temperature pattern.

Medical, not mystical — at least in the language Maya had available.

Clara noticed her pause. "What? You see something?"

Maya shook her head. "Just checking the airflow. Might be a bad vent."

Clara exhaled, relieved to have a rational answer to latch onto.

Lila, though, kept her eyes locked on the corner. Small hands clenched, jaw tight like she was trying not to cry again.

Maya lowered her voice. "Lila… look at me."

It took a moment, but Lila did.

"You're not crazy," Maya said gently. "You're scared. And when you're scared, your body notices things other people miss."

Lila's eyes glistened. "But it's getting closer."

Maya felt that land like a blow.

Not because she believed the words but because Lila did.

She brushed a thumb over Lila's knuckles. "I'm here. I'm not going anywhere."

Clara finally stopped pacing. "Is there anything— I mean—should I call someone? A therapist? Should we go to the doctor?"

There it was again: rational panic.

The kind that tries to fix fear with checklists.

"We can talk about that," Maya said, still keeping her tone level, "but for tonight, she needs calm. She needs to feel safe."

The house creaked — the normal kind of noise old houses make — but Lila flinched so hard Maya felt it through her ribs.

Maya pulled her closer.

Clara pressed her palm to her forehead. "God, I don't know what to do anymore."

"You're doing fine," Maya said. And she meant it.

She looked around the room one more time, slow, methodical.

The vent.

The bed.

The carpet.

The corner.

Everything was normal.

Everything was wrong.

Maya's throat tightened—not with fear, but with certainty:

Whatever was happening to Lila…

it wasn't just nightmares.

And something in this room still held the echo of that truth.

Lila finally drifted into a shallow, trembling sleep against Maya's side. Not real rest—more like exhaustion pulling her under in uneven breaths. Clara hovered near the doorway, arms wrapped around herself, watching them like she was afraid to blink.

"I'll stay until she's fully out," Maya murmured.

Clara nodded, relief fighting guilt across her expression. "I don't... I don't know what to do. She's never been like this."

Maya didn't answer. She didn't trust herself not to say something Clara wasn't ready to hear.

Instead, she eased Lila gently onto the pillow and stood. "I'll check outside," she whispered. "Just to make sure the yard's clear."

Clara exhaled shakily. "Okay."

Maya slipped out of the room, careful not to let the floorboards creak. The hallway lights were warm, steady. Normal. But she carried the image from Lila's story—the bent neck, the reaching arms—like a weight under her ribs.

She unlatched the back door and stepped onto the porch.

The air hit her first.

Cold.

Not weather cold—not the kind that slips off the ocean or settles in winter yards. This was directional, like stepping through an invisible band of chilled air. Her breath puffed white before she even realized she was exhaling.

The porch light spilled a weak circle across the grass. Beyond it, everything was dark. Typical suburban dark—houses spaced far enough that the streetlamps didn't quite overlap.

She scanned the yard.

Nothing moved.

The fence.

The shed.

The patchy winter grass.

All still.

Then the grass in the center of the yard shifted slightly—just a ripple, as if a faint breeze had passed.

But there was no breeze.

Maya's mouth dried. She took one slow, careful step off the porch.

At first, she thought her eyes were adjusting to the dark.

Then she realized the shape wasn't her imagination.

A **shadow** lay across the grass. Long. Too long. Like a smear from a tree branch stretching far past its real reach.

But there were no overhead branches.

And the direction was wrong. The porch light cast shadows *toward* the house, not away from it.

This one pointed straight at Lila's bedroom window.

Maya's pulse slammed once, hard.

She took another step, angling herself closer—not touching the shadow. She crouched, breath frosting the air in front of her. The shadow didn't distort with her movement. It didn't thin. It didn't soften at the edges.

It was as solid as spilled ink on the grass.

And it was **longer** than it had been a moment ago.

She straightened, scanning the fence line, the neighboring yards, the corners where ambient light failed.

Nothing there.

Nothing visible.

But the shadow was growing.

A slow stretch.

A crawl.

Her hand hovered over her radio before she remembered she wasn't on duty and didn't have it.

She forced herself back toward the house, keeping her body between the shadow and the window. She didn't look away from it. Not once.

When she reached the porch steps, something cracked—a sharp, brittle sound, like thin ice fracturing.

She looked down.

The dew on the grass had frozen in an arc around the stretched shadow. A clean semicircle of frost.

No temperature drop outside that boundary. Only inside.

A cold-zone imprint.

Like the ones Vander described.

Maya eased inside and shut the door quietly, locking it even though she knew a latch meant nothing to whatever had left that mark.

Clara hurried toward her. "Is something wrong?"

Maya forced her voice even. "Keep the curtains closed tonight. All of them."

Clara nodded, pale. "You saw something, didn't you?"

Maya didn't answer.

She didn't need to.

That shadow had been reaching.

And it had known exactly which window to reach for.

Chapter 9 — The Door Opens

The alley behind the convenience store smelled wrong.

Not the usual mix of rot, fryer oil, and spilled beer—this was metallic and sharp, a cold that carried weight, like air pulled from a morgue drawer. Ruiz parked the rig crooked across the back entrance and killed the siren. When Maya stepped out, the cold hit her first.

Not night-air cold.

Bone-cold.

A patrol officer stood near the dumpster, face pale and eyes darting everywhere but the ground. "Back here," he said, voice thin. "Juvenile. Unresponsive."

Maya followed the beam of his flashlight—and stopped breathing.

The boy lay half in shadow, half under the buzzing security lamp. His ribs were forced outward, bent into a wide, obscene bloom. The tissue inside hadn't been torn or spilled—it had collapsed in on itself, pulled toward a single point behind the sternum like a vacuum had opened inside his chest.

There was barely any blood.

What little smeared the asphalt had already thickened into a dark, gelatinous sheen, as if cooling too fast.

Ruiz swore under his breath. "What the hell..."

Maya knelt, her gloved hands steady out of sheer muscle memory. She touched the sternum.

Cold.

Deep cold.

Wrong cold.

Her fingertips hovered at the edge of the cavity. She angled her penlight, tracing the warped organs. The liver looked imploded. The pancreas was drawn tight to the spine. Threads of connective tissue clung like over-stretched webbing.

Not ripped.

Not cut.

Not chewed.

Drained.

Her stomach twisted.

A faint crackle—barely audible—rose from deep inside the cavity. She froze and leaned closer. It was the sound of cartilage adjusting under sudden temperature drop, tiny fractures forming in places cartilage should never fracture.

Ruiz took a step back. "Bodies don't do that, Maya."

She didn't respond.

Near the boy's head, his shadow smeared across the concrete at an impossible angle. His legs pointed one way; the shadow's legs stretched another, longer than they should've been, the arms bent at joints the real arms didn't have.

Her throat closed.

A different officer jogged in. "Detective Graves notified. He was already close. Maybe 2 minutes out."

Two minutes felt too long and barely long enough.

Maya forced herself to keep working. She checked for lividity, for any sign the body had been moved. Nothing matched anything she'd ever seen—not in calls, not in training, not in case studies whispered around trauma rooms.

She angled the penlight again—and noticed something else.

Frost.

A thin, delicate frost ring lined the inside of the cavity, so fine it could've been lace. She leaned closer. The crystals weren't random. They formed outward from a single point beneath the collapsed sternum.

A direction.
A flow.

Her pulse throbbed painfully in her neck.

She whispered to Ruiz, "Get a rectal temp."

He moved automatically, then froze. "It's… reading low. Too low. This can't be right." He adjusted, checked again. "Maya—it's thirty-two degrees. That's hypothermia territory. But he's been dead maybe fifteen minutes."

"Hypothermia doesn't collapse organs inward," she said quietly.

She looked back at the cavity—and saw something shift.

Not the body.
Not the ribs.

The **air** above the ribs rippled faintly, like heat distortion viewed backward.

Her penlight flickered.

A sudden hush fell over the officers behind her—radios, boots, voices—all going still at once.

A single, soft sound rose from deep inside the collapsed cavity.

A wet, slow suction.

Ruiz took an involuntary step backward. "No. No, no, no—"

Maya reached out—almost touched the cavity—then stopped, her fingertips inches from the frost-rimmed bone.

Something was still happening inside him.
Something finishing what had started.

Her hand shook.

An officer gagged behind them, retching noisily into the wall. Another backed away, hands on his knees, muttering, "Jesus Christ, Jesus Christ—"

Maya forced herself to focus, to document, to not let the panic around her pull her under.

"This isn't trauma," she said numbly. "This is extraction."

Ruiz blinked at her. "Extraction of what?"

She didn't answer.

She didn't know.

The security light buzzed louder. Its flicker crawled across the twisted shadow—elongating it another inch.

Her breath hitched.

And that was when footsteps pounded into the mouth of the alley—hard, fast, controlled.

Graves.

Still breathing heavy from the run. Still buttoning his coat.

He reached the tape, saw the boy—

—and stopped dead.

His jaw tightened.

His shoulders locked.

His eyes narrowed to a single, unwavering point.

"What am I looking at?" he whispered.

Maya didn't move. "You need to come closer."

He did.

Slowly.

He knelt beside her.

When his eyes found the ribs, his breath stuttered once. Just once. Barely perceptible—but she saw it. When his gaze slid to the shadow, he froze entirely.

The air thickened.

Graves swallowed and whispered, "This isn't possible."

Maya's voice came out thin. "It happened."

He didn't argue.

He didn't look away.

Because he couldn't.

Graves didn't move for a long time.

The alley noise went thin around him—radios whispering, boots shifting, some officer still quietly gagging near the wall—but he stayed fixed in a narrow cone of light and cold, eyes locked on the wreckage of the boy's chest.

Maya watched the way his pupils tracked the damage.

Not like a detective cataloguing evidence.

Like a man staring at a car crash and realizing his family's name is on the license plate.

He finally exhaled, a rough drag through his teeth. "Walk me through it."

Maya swallowed. Her tongue felt too thick in her mouth, her breath catching on the metallic tang of the air. "The ribs are bent outward. Force from inside the thoracic cavity. Organs collapsed, not ruptured. There's... frost along the interior." She angled her light again. The tiny crystals glittered. "No external wounds to match the internal damage."

"Blunt force?" he asked, but there was no conviction in it.

"Blunt force doesn't pull tissue inward," she said. "It crushes. This looks like... like something opened in him and sucked everything toward it."

A small, wet crack sounded again from inside the chest.

Graves' head snapped toward the cavity.

The sound wasn't loud. It was barely more than the sticky pull of two cold surfaces separating. But in the dead air of the alley, it landed like a gunshot. Ruiz flinched. One of the officers took two quick steps backward, boots skidding on damp asphalt.

"Reflex," someone muttered. "Just—post-mortem settling."

Nobody sounded convinced.

Graves shifted closer despite himself. The smell hit him—Maya saw it in the way his jaw tightened, the faint, involuntary twitch of his nostrils. Not rot. Not sewage. The sharp, too-clean stink of opened viscera cooled far below ambient temperature, like someone had dissected the boy in a freezer.

He leaned in until his gloved hand hovered a few inches over the frost-ringed bone. He didn't touch it.

"How old?" he asked quietly.

"Seventeen, eighteen maybe," Maya said. "Clothes suggest high school. Maybe a junior."

His gaze found the boy's shoes. One lace was broken. The sole of the right sneaker was scuffed hard, rubber peeled back where it had caught on rough ground. The kind of damage you got from trying to push yourself away from something you couldn't outrun.

Graves' throat moved in a slow swallow.

He shifted his focus to the boy's hands. Fingertips ragged. Two nails fractured halfway down the bed. Scrapes on the concrete where he'd clawed backward, leaving pale crescents of dust and skin.

He hadn't died suddenly.

He'd fought the air itself and lost.

Graves' voice came out lower. "Time of death?"

"Fifteen, maybe twenty minutes before we got here," Maya said. "But his core temperature... it doesn't match the interval." She glanced at Ruiz.

Ruiz held up the thermometer, his face still pale. "He's colder inside than the morgue cooler at county. Outside's still warm. That isn't environmental exposure. That's... something else."

Graves stared at him. "You're sure the reading's accurate?"

Ruiz gave a short, humorless laugh. "I checked twice. You want three?"

Graves looked back at the ribs.

For a moment, no one spoke.

The security light overhead buzzed harder, its filament whining like an insect caught in glass. The portable lamp flickered, then steadied. For a split second in the transition, the boy's shadow pulled sharper—limbs stretching longer, torso bending at a different angle than the body lying beneath it.

Maya saw it.

So did Graves.

His breath faltered again. "No," he whispered.

But the shadow didn't snap back.

It stayed wrong.

His rational mind lunged for an explanation. Faulty bulb. Warped angle. Camera artifact. Anything.

Except the cameras hadn't been reviewed.

Except he was looking at it with his own eyes.

"Raine," he said. "You seeing what I'm seeing?"

She didn't trust her voice, so she just nodded.

The silence behind them thickened. The gathered officers had picked up on it too—not the specifics, maybe, but the edges. The way the alley felt off-balance. The way their breath fogged heavier the closer they drifted toward the body.

One of the younger uniforms whispered, "It's like he... froze from the inside."

Graves' head turned sharply. "Keep your voice down."

The kid shut up immediately, but the words hung there anyway.

Maya couldn't unhear them.

Froze from the inside.

She checked the cavity again, forcing herself into clinical posture. The inner surfaces of the ribs were smooth, stripped of any residual fat that should've remained. A thin glaze of sheen clung to the bone, like moisture had been pulled tight across it and then flash-cooled.

Her mind supplied the only image it could find: a vacuum pump on a sealed line, sucking out fluid and air until the walls of the container bowed inward.

"Detective," one of the senior officers called from the edge of the tape. "We've got locals gathering at the front lot. Word's already getting out."

Of course it was. Kids talked. Phones existed. This boy had a life that had led him here, to this alley, to this obscene, opened cage of bone.

Graves stood up slowly, his knees cracking in the quiet. For a second, he swayed—not because of fatigue, but because the alley seemed to tilt around him, all weight pulled toward the open chest on the ground.

He dragged himself back into command mode by force.

"Expand the perimeter," he said. "I want the entire block sealed. Nobody cuts through this alley, nobody even looks back here unless they're on my list. Get the store manager. Pull every second of footage from every camera within a two-block radius. Street, parking lot, interior. Everything."

"Yes, sir."

"Canvass the houses backing onto this lot," he added. "Anyone who might've seen him come through. Anyone who heard anything. You see a porch light on, you knock."

Officers peeled away in pairs, grateful for an excuse to leave the epicenter of whatever the hell this was.

The alley felt emptier without them, but not less crowded.

Maya realized she was holding her breath. She forced a slow inhale, then wished she hadn't. The cold lodged deep in her lungs, a heavy, refrigerated ache. She couldn't shake the sense that the air she was breathing had passed through the ruined cavity a few minutes ago.

Graves glanced at Ruiz. "You stay on EMS protocols. No one moves the body until the ME gets here, but I want your observations documented in detail. Everything you've seen, everything you've heard, everything you've smelled."

Ruiz nodded, then hesitated. "Detective... I know what a bad scene looks like. I've been doing this for a long time." His eyes dropped back to the boy. "This isn't just bad. This is wrong."

The words landed like another temperature drop.

Graves didn't acknowledge them, but he didn't contradict them either.

He stepped back to Maya's side. "You said 'extraction.'"

She kept her gaze on the cavity. "That's what it looks like."

"Of what?" he pressed.

She shook her head once. "I don't know. Whatever it was, it wasn't something we can put back."

He stared at her for a long moment. There was a flicker in his eyes—anger, not at her, but at the fact that there wasn't a category for this. No box to drop it in, no form to attach it to, no suspect profile that fit.

The cold pressed harder against their faces.

Somewhere overhead, a vent fan on the convenience store roof clicked off. The sudden silence made the faint sounds from the body more obvious—the tiny creaks of cooling cartilage, the soft, almost inaudible shift of organs slumping into the vacuum their own structure had created.

Graves rubbed his forehead with the back of his wrist. "We get the ME's report, we get the footage, we get witness statements. There's a human explanation buried in this somewhere."

Maya didn't argue with him.

But when she glanced at the twisted shadow again, she knew he didn't believe his own words.

The shadow's arm still bent where no bone existed.

Its back still hunched at an angle the real spine couldn't match.

Its head angled as if looking down at the boy instead of lying with him.

"Detective!" a voice called from the alley mouth.

One of the canvassing officers jogged back in, chest heaving, cheeks flushed from the cold air.

Graves tore his gaze away from the body. "What've you got?"

"Neighbor on Willow Drive," the officer said. "Says he saw the victim about an hour ago. Kid was walking with someone."

Graves' posture sharpened. "Who?"

The officer swallowed. "He thinks it was a girl. Young. Lives a few houses down from him."

Maya's heart dipped sharply, like she'd stepped off an unseen curb.

Willow Drive.

Girl.

Young.

Her mind drew a line straight to a small house with a weak porch light and a kid who had already seen too much.

Lila.

The cold in the alley found a new place to settle—in the center of her chest.

Graves didn't miss the shift in her expression. "Raine," he said quietly. "You know who that is, don't you?"

Maya didn't answer Graves right away.

Her pulse thudded hard enough she could feel it in the tips of her fingers. The alley suddenly felt too narrow, too tight, like the cold was pressing in around her ribs.

Finally, she forced the words out.

"If the neighbor saw him walking with a girl," she said quietly, "I think it was Lila Mercer."

Graves' jaw tensed. "You're sure?"

"Yes." Her voice came out thin. "She lives right off Willow. Two blocks from here."

He processed that in a snap—eyes narrowing, expression shifting from confusion to command in the space of a heartbeat.

"She was the panic call from the other night," he said, mostly to himself.

"Yes."

"And she was… rattled then."

"Yes." Maya swallowed. "And she's been seeing things. Or—she thinks she has."

Graves didn't ask what that meant. Not here. Not with the body lying open behind them like a warning.

He tapped his radio. "Units Five and Nine—proceed to Mercer residence. Juvenile witness. Hold the perimeter. Do not question until I arrive."

Two quick chirps answered.

Maya could feel his attention shift to her before he even turned.

"You're going there," he said. "Because she'll talk to you."

Maya nodded, already stripping off her gloves.

"Raine," Ruiz said quietly behind her, "you want me to—"

"Stay here," she said. "Document everything. You're better at it."

Ruiz didn't argue. But worry carved at the lines around his mouth.

Maya stepped toward the alley's exit, but Graves stepped with her, stopping just long enough to catch her eyes.

"You're going to be straight with me the second I get there," he said. "Everything she says. Everything you see."

"I will."

He hesitated—not long, but long enough for her to see the hairline fracture in his composure. The place where logic didn't quite stretch over what he'd just witnessed.

Then he nodded once. Tightly.

"Go."

Maya turned and ran.

Her shoes hit the wet pavement hard, splashing through thin puddles, skidding once on a patch of frost that had no business being there this time of night. She cut through the back lot, past dumpsters rimed in thin white crystals, and slipped between two houses, breath burning in her throat.

The neighborhood was quiet. Too quiet.

Lights glowed behind curtained windows. Sprinklers ticked in the distance. A dog barked once, then stopped abruptly, as if someone had snapped a lid over the sound.

Maya kept running.

Her lungs hurt, her legs ached, but she didn't slow. She turned onto Willow Drive and saw Clara's house halfway down the block—porch light flickering softly, the same way it had the night Lila screamed.

Her chest tightened.

She climbed the steps and knocked hard—three sharp raps.

"Clara," she called softly. "It's Maya."

Footsteps inside. Quick. Uneven.

The door opened.

Clara stood there in her robe, eyes red, moving like she'd already been pacing for hours even though the night wasn't that old.

"Maya? What—"

"Where's Lila?" Maya asked. Her voice came out steadier than she felt.

Clara stepped back. "Living room. She's... shaking. She won't tell me why."

Maya entered without waiting for an invitation.

Lila sat curled on the couch, knees tight to her chest, blanket wrapped around her like armor. Her eyes were wide—too wide—tracking Maya the moment she stepped into the room.

"Maya?" Lila whispered. "Something's wrong. I—I don't know what, but—"

Maya sank to her knees in front of her.

"Lila," she said. "I need you to listen to me."

Clara hovered behind them, hands trembling.

Maya took a breath, steadying herself, because there was no gentle way to do this.

"The boy who walked you partway home," she said softly. "They found him. Behind the store."

Lila went still.

Every muscle. Every breath.

Still.

Maya braced for the scream.

It didn't come.

Instead, Lila's face crumpled inward in pure, collapsing grief. She let out a broken sound, small and sharp, and launched forward, burying her face in Maya's shoulder.

Clara gasped, covering her mouth.

"I'm sorry," Maya murmured, arms wrapping tight around the girl. "I'm so sorry."

Lila shook violently, sobs rattling her whole frame, the blanket slipping to the floor like she didn't even feel it.

Maya held her. Rocked her gently. Tried to shield her body with her own as the room seemed to dim around them.

Clara finally found her voice. "Oh my god. Oh my god, Maya—what happened? How—how did he—"

"They're still figuring it out," Maya said. "Clara... she may need to talk to the detectives."

Clara nodded through tears, wiping her face. "Whatever she needs."

Lila clutched Maya harder.

Outside, tires crunched gravel.

Patrol units.

Maya didn't move. Didn't look away from the girl in her arms.

But she felt it—the air shifting again. Thinning. Like something just outside the window had leaned closer to the glass.

Waiting.

Listening.

Drawn to the fear now blooming like a flare in the middle of the room.

Maya wrapped her arms tighter around Lila.

"It's okay," she whispered. "I've got you."

But the cold that slid along the baseboards told her something else entirely.

Lila was still shaking when the knock came.

Not loud. Not urgent. Just firm enough to announce authority.

Clara flinched. Maya didn't.

"It's the officers," Maya said quietly. "I'll talk to them first."

Lila's fingers tightened on her sleeve. Small. Desperate.

"I'm not leaving you," Maya added quickly. "I'll be right here."

Clara exhaled, wiped her cheeks, and headed for the door with the stiff, brittle motions of someone barely holding it together.

Maya listened as the hinges creaked open.

"Ma'am?" a voice asked—deep, controlled, professional. "We're with county PD. We need to confirm this is the Mercer residence."

"Yes," Clara said, voice frayed. "She's inside."

Footsteps crossed the wooden porch. Two shadows moved in the foyer—uniformed outlines cast against the wall by the porch light.

"Detective Graves is en route," one officer said. "He asked that we secure the scene and make sure she's not alone."

Maya stood, keeping one hand on Lila's shoulder. "She's not."

Both officers registered Maya, then the EMS jacket tied around her waist.

"You Raine?" the older one asked.

"Yes."

"Detective said you'd be here."

The younger officer scanned the living room. His eyes lingered on the hallway leading to Lila's bedroom—dark despite every other light in the house being on.

"This where she stays?" he asked.

Clara nodded. "Down the hall. Right door."

The officer flicked on his flashlight, aimed it down the hall, and froze almost imperceptibly.

Not from fear.

From confusion.

The beam thinned halfway down—like it passed through a curtain of air denser than the rest of the house. The light dimmed, regained strength, then dimmed again as it neared the bedroom door.

He adjusted the flashlight. Tapped the casing. Checked the beam.

It didn't change.

Maya felt the hairs on her arms rise.

"Electrical issue," the officer muttered to himself, even though it wasn't. "Probably the wiring."

He backed up a step.

The hallway seemed to darken a fraction further after he moved away, like it exhaled.

The younger officer shook his head and took out his notebook. "We'll get statements when the detective arrives. Until then, nobody leaves the residence."

Lila pressed herself against Maya's side, face streaked with tears, breathing in sharp little hits.

Maya tightened her hold.

Clara stepped closer, hovering—unsure whether to sit, stand, or collapse. "Do you want water? A blanket? Anything?"

Lila didn't respond.

Her gaze was fixed on the bedroom door.

The officers exchanged a look—quiet, professional, uncertain.

Then a car engine rolled to a stop outside.

Graves.

His boots hit the porch a moment later. Heavy. Purposeful. Controlled.

But as he stepped into the living room and saw Lila clinging to Maya, Clara's tear-streaked face, and the two officers standing rigid near the hallway, something in his posture shifted.

Not uncertainty.

Assessment.

"What happened?" he asked.

Maya kept her voice steady. "She's in shock. She needs a second. But… she can talk to you. Just not alone."

Graves nodded once. "Fine. We'll take it slow."

He crouched down—not close enough to crowd her, but near enough for her to see he wasn't asking her to shoulder this alone.

"Lila," he said quietly, "I'm sorry about your friend. I need to ask you just a couple of things. Nothing scary. Nothing you don't want to answer."

Lila swallowed, shaking again.

Her eyes flicked toward the hallway.

The shadow there seemed deeper than it had a moment ago.

Maya felt her spine lock.

Graves noticed her stiffen and glanced briefly at the darkened hall—but only long enough to register something he didn't like.

Then he brought his attention back to Lila.

"Did you see him after he left you?" he asked gently.

Lila shook her head hard. "No. He—he walked me to the stop sign. Then he went home."

"You didn't see anyone with him?"

Another frantic shake. Tears sliding fast again.

"Okay," Graves said softly. "That's enough for now."

He stood, exhaled slowly, and motioned the officers to step closer.

But before anyone could speak again, the porch light flickered sharply—just once.

The officers stiffened.

Clara jumped.

Lila buried herself against Maya's side, shaking so hard Maya had to wrap both arms around her to keep her steady.

Graves turned toward the front door, jaw tightening.

The flicker stopped.

The house went still again.

Too still.

Graves lowered his voice. "We're done here for tonight." He pointed at the two officers. "Stay posted until sunrise."

They nodded.

Maya didn't let go of Lila until her breathing slowed—until the tremor in her hands softened from panic to exhaustion.

Clara wiped her face again. "She can she sleep in my room tonight."

Maya said, "Keep the hallway light on. All night."

Clara nodded.

Graves didn't question it.

He just met Maya's eyes for a brief, sharp moment.

Not fear.

Recognition.

Something had shifted tonight—and they both knew it.

Without a word, he stepped out onto the porch, radio crackling softly as he walked into the waiting dark.

Chapter 9.5 — 1911, Coastal Oregon

The fog came in thicker than the tide that night—low, heavy, and wet enough to cling to Elias Harren's clothes as he trudged along the waterfront. The hour was late, but not unusual. Dock work kept men until after dark, and the wharf always stank of salt and old rope long after the lanterns were lit.

Tonight, though… everything felt off.

The fog didn't move right.

It didn't drift.

It *hung*, like wool soaked in seawater.

Elias wiped his sleeve across his mouth, tasting brine. Somewhere behind him, a gull shrieked once and then fell silent—cut off too sharply, as if something had swallowed the cry whole.

He paused.

The lamplight nearest him blurred into a pale smear. The next lantern—barely twenty paces away—didn't appear at all. Just a wall of white.

His boots thudded on the planks. The sound was quieter than it should've been.

Dampened.

"Hell," he muttered, pulling his coat tighter. "Fog like this'll kill a man."

Something breathed behind him.

Wet.

Slow.

Not a human sound—more like a bellows clogged with seawater.

Elias spun so fast his heel skidded on the boards. Nothing. Just fog. The kind that swallowed shape, motion, horizon. He could barely make out the pilings beneath his feet.

"Who's there?" he barked, voice cracking on the last syllable.

No answer.

He took a step back. The fog behind him *shifted*, not stirred by wind. A ripple in the white curtain, like a tall shape had been standing there without him noticing.

He blinked hard.

A silhouette stood deeper in the fog.

Tall.

Bent forward at the neck.

Arms too long for any man's proportions.

Elias's breath caught.

His body reacted before thought could.

He stumbled backward, boots scraping hard. The thing didn't walk toward him—it didn't need to. One moment it was ahead of him in the fog.

The next, the fog behind him pressed inward.

Something had **repositioned**, not moved.

A whisper-soft scrape brushed his collar. Cold—not the honest cold of weather, but a deep, biting cold—slid along his spine. He jerked away, terror surging so suddenly his vision tunneled.

"Stay back!" he shouted, voice breaking.

The fog split.

Not from wind.

From *something pushing out through it.*

Teeth appeared first.

Rows of them—outer ones wide and humanlike, bent slightly inward, inner ones needle-thin, vibrating with wet hunger. There was no jaw. No skull. Just a hovering mouth suspended in fog-thick dark.

Elias screamed.

But his scream never fully left his throat.

The teeth moved.

Not toward him—**into him**.

A white-hot spike of agony exploded in his neck as the inner needle-teeth pierced the back of his larynx from inside. Cartilage collapsed inward with a brittle crunch. His hands flew to his throat, grasping for wounds that didn't exist.

No puncture.

No tear.

No external injury at all.

But inside—

Something was feeding.

The first pull stole his breath completely. Moisture in his throat crystallized in an instant, frost spreading across the inner walls of his windpipe. His next gasp froze mid-inhale, turning to shards.

His knees buckled.

The mouth inside him tightened, pulling warmth, blood, air—everything. Each suction pulse dragged a thread of life out of him so sharply his vision strobed.

A crackle shot down his spine. Vertebrae twisted—not snapped, not broken, but **coerced** into a new shape from the inside out.

His shadow stretched unnaturally long across the wet planks, bending at angles his body didn't match—elongated, warped, wrong.

His final sound was a gurgling choke.

Then nothing.

The fog closed around his body, swallowing it into a pocket of impossible cold.

When the water lapped against the pilings, even the tide sounded muted.

The kill was done.

And the fog held its breath.

Constable Elias Hargreaves heard the whistle first—a sharp, panicked shrill from one of the dockhands still lingering near the waterfront tavern. He'd been making his rounds along Front Street, lantern in one hand, collar turned up against the fog's damp chill. The mist had swallowed most of the lamps hours ago, their glow smothered until the road looked more like a tunnel than a street.

Another whistle cut through the night.
Then shouting.

Hargreaves quickened his pace, boots thudding against the boardwalk. Fog curled around his legs, slick and cold. Not night-chill cold—**deep cold**. Wrong for the season. Wrong for the coast.

A pair of dockhands stumbled out of the mist toward him, faces pale as bleached canvas.

"Constable—down by pier three—" one choked.

Hargreaves lifted his lantern. "What happened?"

The younger man shook his head violently. "We heard... something. Elias Harren went to look. Didn't come back. Then we heard him shout."

"Shout what?"

"I—" the man swallowed. "I don't know. Only that it didn't sound right."

"Show me," Hargreaves said.

They led him down the planks. The fog thickened with every step, lantern glow shrinking to a faint gold halo. The air grew colder—cold enough that his breath puffed white, though the night itself wasn't near freezing.

Then he saw the shape on the boards.

Elias Harren lay on his back, limbs twisted awkwardly, head tilted at a sharp, unnatural angle. Hargreaves crouched beside him and pushed his lantern closer.

His stomach clenched.

Harren's throat had collapsed inward, the cartilage drawn into a tight concave curve, as though something had crushed it from within.

Frost clung to the skin along the right side of his neck in thin crystalline lines. His spine had rotated just enough to warp the way his coat sat—subtle, but unmistakable.

And the cold…it radiated off the body like a cellar vent in winter.

"What in God's name—" one dockhand whispered behind him.

Hargreaves didn't answer. He leaned in, hand hovering just above Harren's chest. Not touching—he didn't need to. The air was frigid enough.

He studied the boards around the body next.

Drops of condensation had frozen into tiny flecks—**ice** in fog-heavy humidity. And Harren's shadow, cast by the lantern-light, stretched far too long across the planks, bending at the torso in a way his body did not.

"Fetch the physician," Hargreaves said sharply.

The younger dockhand bolted, boots slipping on the slick boards.

Hargreaves stayed kneeling.

He'd worked this waterfront for twelve years. Seen men drown, fall from rigging, get crushed beneath cargo crates. He had never seen a man frozen on a warm night. Never seen a throat caved in without bruising. Never seen a spine twisted without a single mark on the skin.

A faint sound made him look up.

Along the row of houses facing the wharf, a door creaked open. A woman's face appeared in the gap—eyes wide, fear written plain. Beside her, half hidden behind her skirts, a child peered out.

A little girl.

She held a piece of charcoal in her hand, the smudges staining her fingers black.

Hargreaves straightened slowly. "Go back inside," he called gently. "There's nothing for you to see here."

The woman pulled the door wider just long enough to grab the child's wrist. In that instant, the girl lifted her drawing, as if showing him something important.

Hargreaves froze.

The figure on the paper was tall, with a neck bent sharply forward and arms that hung too long. Dark, slanted lines behind it suggested a shadow leaning over smaller figures.

Then the woman yanked the child inside and slammed the door.

Hargreaves stared at the house for a long moment, a cold heaviness settling into his gut.

Three children had drawn that same figure in the last week.

Three.

He turned back to Harren's body. The fog drifted in slow pulses around it, rolling and collapsing in ways that reminded him uneasily of breath.

Hargreaves tightened his grip on the lantern handle.

Something was hunting in this town.

By the time the physician arrived—coat half-buttoned, breath ragged from running—the fog had thickened again, curling low around the planks like a living thing. Hargreaves stepped back to give him room.

The physician knelt, pressed two fingers to Harren's neck, and immediately jerked his hand away.

"Cold," he whispered. "He's... chilled through."

"It isn't the weather," Hargreaves said quietly.

The physician didn't argue.

He only leaned closer, inspecting the throat. "Cartilage collapse," he murmured. "But no bruising. No exterior trauma. Never seen that." His eyes moved lower. "And the spine—good God."

Hargreaves waited.

The physician swallowed. "This wasn't done with hands. Or rope. Or any tool I know."

Hargreaves didn't answer. His gaze drifted past the physician, past the body, toward the narrow lane leading up toward the houses on Front Street.

The door where the child had stood was shut tight. Curtains drawn.

But a lantern flickered faintly inside, throwing a thin strip of light through the crack beneath the door.

He moved toward it.

The fog thinned slightly near the houses, but the air remained unnaturally cold—colder than any sea-mist he'd felt in his years here. Gravel crunched softly under his boots.

Halfway up the lane, he heard whispering.

Children's voices.

He slowed.

Two small shapes crouched beneath the overhang of a porch, sketching in the dirt with bits of charcoal. Their backs were to him. Their shoulders trembled—not from cold, but from the tight, frightened way children try to make themselves smaller.

Hargreaves approached carefully. "You two should be inside at this hour."

Both froze.

The older girl turned first. Her eyes were wide, rimmed red. She clutched the charcoal so tightly it stained her nails.

He crouched, gentle as he could. "What are you drawing?"

She hesitated. Then, silently, she pushed the dirt sketch toward him.

Hargreaves felt the hair rise on the back of his neck.

The drawing showed a tall figure—disproportionately tall—with a crooked neck that bent forward as if burdened by its own weight. Its arms dangled nearly to its knees. Behind it, dark lines suggested a shadow stretching across the ground, reaching toward two smaller figures drawn beside each other.

Children.

The younger child whispered, "It watches families."

The older shot him a warning look, but the words were already out.

Hargreaves swallowed. "Where did you see this?"

The girl pointed toward the fog-choked wharf.

"Out there," she said. "By the lamps. Mama said it was just fog. But fog don't lean."

The younger child shivered violently. "And its head was broken."

The girl slapped a hand over his mouth, eyes darting toward the houses. "Don't say that."

He nodded, muffled.

Hargreaves took the charcoal scrap from her fingers and examined the long, slanted lines marking the shadow. The proportions were wrong—deliberately wrong—as though the children had drawn what frightened them most honestly, without trying to make it human.

He stood slowly. "Both of you—inside. Now."

They obeyed at once.

The older girl grabbed the younger's hand and tugged him toward the porch. Before they slipped inside, the younger child turned back and whispered:

"It took the others in the fog."

The door shut.

The lane fell silent.

A gull cried out over the water—sharp and solitary—but even that sound seemed to falter halfway through.

Hargreaves exhaled, long and tight, and made his way back toward the wharf.

The fog was lifting in slow shreds.

But the cold lingered.

By the time Constable Hargreaves returned to his office, the fog had thinned into nothing. The night beyond his window was unsettlingly clear—moon faint behind thin clouds, the usual sea-hush returning in slow, uneven waves. It was as if the world had been holding its breath and finally let it out.

He lit the lantern on his desk, its flame wavering once before settling. The room felt too quiet. Even the ticking of the small clock on the wall sounded dulled, like it was reluctant to intrude.

He hung his coat over the chair and sank down heavily. His hands were still cold from the waterfront.

The ledger lay open where he'd left it—pages already full with notes from the past two weeks. Names. Dates. The sparse facts of disappearance after disappearance. Ten entries now in total.

He picked up his pen.

The nib hovered for a moment over the paper. What he meant to write first—cause of death, condition of the body, statements from witnesses—refused to come. His mind kept drifting back to the girl's drawing, the charcoal-smudged fingers, the way her voice had cracked when she said fog didn't lean.

He exhaled hard through his nose and put the pen down to steady his hand.

Then he wrote.

"The Reaper is not a man but a shadow that walks like one."

He paused.

Outside, a gull screeched once over the harbor—sharp, normal, alive. No muffling. No bending of sound. Just the ordinary night returning.

He dipped the pen again.

"Ten souls taken."

Another pause. He looked at the window. No fog. Just the black line of the far pier and the faint glow of lanterns that had been smothered only hours earlier.

"Then the fog lifted, and he was gone."

Hargreaves sat back.

The lantern hissed faintly, burning low. The office felt colder than it should have, but not with the unnatural cold from the docks—just the kind that seeped into old wood and older bones.

He reached into his coat and pulled out the small scrap of paper one of the children had shoved into his hand before darting inside. He flattened it gently against the desk.

A charcoal silhouette.

Head bent forward at an impossible angle.

Arms too long.

A shadow stretching out behind it like a second figure pulling itself free.

He clipped it to the ledger page.

Closed the book.

Blew out the lantern.

The room sank into darkness—ordinary darkness, soft and empty.

And outside, the night remained still.

Chapter 10 — Fear Rising

The candles came first—small flames trembling in the dusk, lined along the curb outside the convenience store like a makeshift warning line. By the time Maya arrived, the sidewalk was already swelling with people: parents clutching children, coworkers from nearby shops, a handful of teenagers pretending they weren't crying. Everyone stood too close together, as if proximity alone could keep whatever happened from happening again.

The air wasn't right.

It wasn't wind, or temperature, or anything environmental she could put her EMT training on. It was the stillness. The way sound didn't travel fully. The way breaths left mouths in thin, shaky threads—even though it wasn't cold enough for that. The storefront felt like it held the after-image of something awful, and the crowd could feel it without anyone naming it.

Maya exhaled slowly and scanned the perimeter. She wasn't technically on call, not for this, but dispatch wanted EMT standby for crowd anxiety, fainting, and grief responses. Normal things. Things she understood. She just wished her legs didn't feel like they were giving updates from deep inside her bones.

She found Lila standing near the curb, arms hugged tight around herself, gaze pinned to the candles like she wasn't sure they were real. Maya stepped up beside her.

"Hey," Maya murmured.

Lila didn't answer. She was shaking—minute tremors that traveled from her fingertips into her shoulders. Not from cold. From something else.

Maya shifted her stance subtly to put herself between Lila and the darkest corner of the building. She didn't know why she did it. Instinct, maybe. Or memory. Or the echo of the jogger's ribs pushing up under skin that should have held them in place—an image that kept replaying behind her eyes even when she blinked.

"Do you want to sit down?" Maya asked quietly.

Lila shook her head once. A small, jerky motion.

The candlelight jittered across her face, catching her cheekbones, the sheen of sweat near her temples. Behind her feet, her shadow stretched along the pavement—a thin outline pulled long by the streetlamp overhead. Except the geometry didn't make sense. The shadows of the people around them all leaned away from the curb, cast by the store's harsh fluorescent light spilling outward.

Lila's leaned toward her.

Maya stared at it for one beat too long before forcing herself to look away. Not now. Not here. Not with half the damn neighborhood around them.

A woman behind them set down another candle, the flame quivering as she stepped back. The shadow it cast was normal—long, straight, fleeing the light source in the exact direction it should.

Lila's shadow didn't adjust at all.

Maya swallowed. "Lila, how are you feeling?"

Another shrug. Another tremor.

The murmurs around them grew louder in the way fear does—quiet words piling on top of each other until they sound like a pressure system. Snippets drifted through the crowd: *"No one saw any-*

thing." "How does someone die like that?" "Kids aren't safe." "Why are the cops quiet about it?"

Someone farther back whispered, "This is the third one."

Maya's pulse kicked. She pretended she didn't hear it.

The vigil organizers handed out paper cups for candles. Someone prayed. Someone else cursed under their breath. A teenager lit a stick of incense and backed away quickly when the smoke curled oddly, rising in a thin, wobbling column before bending sharply left as if tugged.

Maya looked around. No breeze.

Lila's breath hitched.

Maya stepped closer. "Just breathe. You're okay."

A lie. But the only one available.

They stood there like that for a long moment. Lila trembling. Maya pretending she wasn't watching every shadow in her peripheral vision.

When the store's automatic door slid open for a customer trying to squeeze through the gathering, the brief blast of fluorescent white lit up the sidewalk perfectly evenly—and that's when Maya saw it again.

Lila moved a fraction—just a shift of weight, a tiny lean forward.

Her shadow didn't.

For the briefest heartbeat, it stayed where it was, stretched long and still. Then it slurred a half-inch and snapped back into alignment.

Maya felt her stomach hollow out.

"Lila," she whispered, "did you—"

Lila flinched at the sound of her own name. Her eyes jerked up, wide, glassy, terrified without understanding why.

Maya shut her mouth. Not here. Not in front of these people.

Someone sobbed near the curb. A man held his daughter tighter. A mother lit three candles in a row, her hand shaking too much to keep the flame steady.

Then Maya saw it on the far wall—just for a blink:

A shadow lag.

A man walked past the storefront, talking quietly to someone on his phone. His body moved in smooth, continuous motion. But his shadow—cast sharp and black by the overhead lighting—stumbled a fraction of a second before catching up, like a film reel missing a frame.

Maya blinked hard, convinced for a moment that her exhaustion was playing tricks again. But no—she'd seen this before. Her own shadow had done it. In her apartment. Behind her back. In that split second when Moxie hissed at the corner.

Lila swayed.

Maya snapped out of it and grabbed her gently by the elbow. "Let's step back," she said quietly. "Too many people. Too much noise."

Lila nodded weakly, but her gaze kept drifting back toward the store's entrance, toward the deepest patch of shadow along the wall, as if drawn there. As if something in that darkness was breathing her in.

The candles flickered all at once, a ripple passing through the line like a shared shiver. Someone muttered that it must be the wind.

There was no wind.

The cold near the entrance sharpened for a moment. Enough that Maya could feel it on her skin—a brief kiss of wrong-temperature air that didn't belong to this night.

She moved Lila another step away from the curb, heart thudding harder than she'd admit.

She kept her voice steady. "Stay with me, okay?"

Lila didn't answer.

Her shadow leaned toward her again.

Graves stood several yards back from the edge of the vigil, half in the light, half out of it, arms crossed tight against the evening air. He watched the crowd the way he'd watched crime scenes for years—looking for the one detail that didn't blend. But none of it blended. Not tonight. Not with the boy's death still soaking into the concrete like something the city wasn't designed to hold.

He'd already walked the scene earlier with Forensics, already heard the medical examiner's rough preliminary: fractured throat cartilage without external impact, ribcage misshapen from the inside, no signs of struggle, no meaningful trace. He kept replaying the words, trying to force them into categories that made sense. Human categories. But they slid around in his mind like loose pieces that refused to lock.

The vigil murmured behind him, dozens of soft voices blending into an anxious hum. Someone started crying harder. Someone else whispered a prayer.

Graves tuned it out.

He walked the few steps back to the exact spot where the boy had collapsed—right at the seam in the pavement where an old patch had been poured years ago. The memorial candles were just far enough away that the light didn't reach this patch properly, leaving it half-lit, half-dim. He crouched down, narrowing his eyes at the concrete.

No blood.

No drag marks.

No scuffing consistent with a fight.

Just the faint outline of where the boy's shoulder had pressed when he fell.

He exhaled through his nose. Something about the air felt... held. Contained. Like sound hadn't fully returned after whatever happened here.

A woman nearby cleared her throat and approached tentatively. "Detective... I—I saw something earlier, when he—when it happened."

Graves straightened. "Go on."

She wrung her hands. "I heard... I don't know. It sounded like someone talking, except it was... slow. Like words spilling through syrup." She shook her head. "I know how that sounds."

He paused, jaw tensing. "Anything else?"

Her eyes darted toward the store wall. "The echo was wrong. When he yelled, it was like the sound... stretched." She grimaced. "I didn't want to put that in the official statement. They already think I'm shaken."

"People saw a kid die," Graves said, voice flat. "Everyone's shaken." He waited.

But she was done. She backed away into the crowd, disappearing into the cluster of faces.

Graves pinched the bridge of his nose, then reached into his coat and pulled out his phone.

New folder.

He typed: **ANOMALIES.**

It felt stupid. Felt like indulging the very hysteria he fought against on every case. But the alternative—pretending the injuries were clean, pretending the witnesses didn't all describe some version of the same damned thing—wasn't working anymore.

He added the first notes:

- **Auditory distortion reported.**
- **Echo lengthened unnaturally.**
- **Localized cold zone persists.**

His thumb hovered.

Then he added another line:

- **Ribcage deformation inconsistent with known trauma mechanics.**

He stared at the last note for a long beat.

Someone behind him lit another candle. The small flare of light reached his peripheral vision—and something in the corner of his eye jerked against the rhythm of the flame.

He turned fast.

Nothing.

Just the wall.

Just the crowd.

Just the jitter of candlelight against the glass panes of the storefront.

He hated moments like this—those split-second flashes where his instincts registered something his logic refused to catalog. The jogger's ribs, Lila's description, Holt's panic, Maya insisting something felt off at every scene. It was too many little fractures, all pointing in directions he didn't want to follow.

He walked a few paces along the storefront, staying just outside the glow of the candles. One of the vigil attendees passed in front of him, head low, phone pressed to their ear. Their shadow stretched long across the wall—and stalled.

Just a flick of hesitation.

Barely half a breath.

But it stayed still while the person kept walking, then lurched to catch up like someone pulling a string too slowly.

Graves blinked sharply.

He turned his head toward the crowd. No one else reacted. No one else even looked.

His pulse thudded once, hard.

He backed up a step, then another, until he could see Maya across the vigil, one hand wrapped around Lila's elbow, guiding the girl gently away from the densest part of the crowd. Lila looked like she might collapse. Maya looked like she might bolt.

Graves pulled in a slow breath. The air tasted metallic.

He added one final line to the folder:

- **Visual distortion? Shadow latency? Investigate.**

The question mark was the only thing making the note survivable.

He locked his phone and pocketed it, but the pressure in the air didn't ease. The candles flickered again—too many at once, like a pulse under the concrete.

Graves didn't know what it meant.

Holt had drifted so far from the vigil that the candlelight barely reached him anymore. He stood near the edge of the parking lot, hands braced on the roof of his cruiser, head bowed like he was trying to breathe through a paper bag and couldn't find the opening.

The air back here felt even heavier.

A faint metallic taste clung to the back of his tongue—adrenaline, stress, something old and sour threading through his breath. The buzz of conversation from the vigil seemed distant, swallowed by a thickness he couldn't name. Every sound felt like it arrived a half-second late.

He wiped a shaking hand across his face.
"This isn't happening," he muttered under his breath. "You're just tired."

But exhaustion didn't make shadows behave wrong.
Exhaustion didn't make his living room lights fail in sequence.
Exhaustion didn't make something scrape along the ceiling.

He squeezed his eyes shut, but it only sharpened the vertigo. When he opened them again, the dim lot around him felt smaller—like the edges of the world had crept in while he was blinking.

A soft shift of motion flickered at the far end of the row. Holt's spine snapped straight. He stared at the space between two parked cars, breath shallow enough to hurt.

Nothing moved.

Nothing visible, anyway.

He swallowed hard. His pulse hammered against the base of his throat. He kept imagining the shape in his living room—that impossible smear of shadow sliding across the ceiling even under direct lamp light. He'd thought he hallucinated it. Part of him still begged to believe that.

The rest of him knew better.

A pair of teenagers wandered away from the vigil, their sneakers scuffing across the asphalt. Their shadows bobbed ahead of them—except one of the silhouettes dragged behind for the briefest instant, like it hadn't realized it needed to move.

Holt flinched.

The kids didn't notice. They laughed at something on a phone and kept walking.

Holt backed up until the cruiser bumper touched his legs. His chest tightened. He tried to steady his breathing—inhale, exhale—but each breath came thin, clipped, almost weightless. A cold prickle crawled across the back of his neck.

He wasn't alone.

Not in the way that mattered.

His hand drifted toward his hip automatically, fingertips brushing the empty spot where his holster would normally sit. He'd turned in his weapon after the discharge at his house. Protocol. Safety. Paperwork. He understood all of it. But right now, he felt naked without it.

Behind him, the store's automatic door slid open again. The momentary blast of bright fluorescent light spilled across the pavement—and Holt's shadow snapped sharp and deep at his feet.

He watched it carefully.

It watched nothing back. It just sat there, stretched wrong across the uneven concrete.

He waited.

Waited for it to twitch out of rhythm.

Waited for it to lag behind his movement.

Waited for it to reveal the thing he'd felt breathing down the back of his mind since the woods.

Nothing happened.

Then a passing car rolled through the intersection, headlights sweeping across the lot—and Holt's shadow elongated, stretched, hesitated—

His breath hitched.

The headlights kept moving.

His shadow didn't.

For one beat too long, it clung to the shape it had been before the light hit it. Frozen posture. Wrong angle. Then it dragged itself back into alignment like someone pulling a limp body across the pavement.

Holt's knees almost buckled.

He pushed away from the cruiser, sucking in air through his teeth. The buzzing in his ears deepened into something thicker—pressure, the same sensation he'd felt right before the scrape along his bedroom ceiling.

A weight settled on the atmosphere, subtle but unmistakable. Not a presence.

A focus.

His.

It felt like the air itself had turned its head toward him.

Holt took one step backward. Then another. His shoe caught the curb. He stumbled and caught himself on the metal railing by the trash bins, fingers whitening around the cold bar.

A very small sound whispered through the space between the cars. Not a footstep.

Not an animal.

Not wind.

More like the breath of a room adjusting to someone entering it.

Holt stared into the darkness until his eyes burned.

A car door slammed closer to the vigil, making him jerk violently. A woman hissed at her husband to be careful with the memorial flowers. Normal noise. Harmless noise. But it hit Holt like a gunshot.

He looked toward the vigil—toward the cluster of candles, the flickering light, the crowd cast in jittering silhouettes.

He looked back toward the cars.

Every nerve in his body felt strung tight as piano wire.

A faint pressure shift rolled across the back lot. Like the air moved around something that wasn't moving.

Holt whispered, "Stop. Please just stop."

He didn't know who he was talking to.

A ripple passed through a line of shadows cast against the pavement.

Not from the crowd.

Not from the lights.

Not from anything physical.

Just a synchronized… flex.

Like something unseen had adjusted its vantage point.

Holt's breath left him in a quiet, broken sound. His eyes watered. His legs shook so hard he had to brace both hands on the railing.

Whatever had followed him from his house… whatever had hunted him along his ceiling, through his hallway…

It was here.

Watching.

Waiting.

Not approaching.

Just learning him.

And Holt felt his own fear spike in a way that wasn't abstract anymore.

It was chemical.

Palpable.

A taste in the back of his throat.

The vigil's candles flickered again, a wave passing through the crowd.

Maya looked up sharply from across the lot, gaze flicking to Holt for a fraction of a second.

He couldn't move.

He couldn't blink.

He couldn't breathe without feeling like he was feeding something he couldn't see.

The pressure in the air thickened—not enough to name, not enough to scream about, just enough to make the shadows deepen at the edges of his vision.

A low, internal pressure tugged at the center of Holt's chest, subtle but steady, like something in the shadows was inhaling through him.

Chapter 11 — Missing Faces

Graves arrived at the precinct before sunrise, the sky still a washed-out gray that didn't feel like morning. The air in the squad room carried that strange unsettled quiet—the kind that came after bad news, before people figured out how to talk about it. He hadn't slept much. Holt hadn't slept at all, judging by the email time-stamps he'd sent overnight, each one shorter and more frantic than the last.

But Holt wasn't the first thing on Graves' desk.

A yellow slip sat at the center of it: **MISSING PERSON REPORT — PRIORITY: ELEVATED.**

He picked it up, scanned it once, then again more slowly.

Mark Bingham, 47. Last seen taking trash to curb. 11:13 p.m.

No signs of struggle.

Trash bin still upright.

Driveway undisturbed.

A nothing-case. The sort that usually wrapped itself up by lunch—someone drinking too much, someone sleeping at a friend's place, someone forgetting to call home. Still, something itched at him. He set the slip down and pulled up the digital file.

While the report loaded, his phone buzzed.

MISSING PERSON — SECONDARY REPORT.

Time-stamped two minutes ago.

He opened it.

Alicia Vasquez, 15. Did not arrive at school.

Last seen leaving home at 7:12 a.m.

Backpack still missing.

Phone off.

Neighbors didn't see her past the first intersection.

Two disappearances wasn't unusual for a city this size—not really. But Graves felt the same quiet pressure behind his sternum that he'd felt at the vigil last night. A sense that the air knew something he didn't.

He pushed back from his desk, grabbed a pen, and pulled the precinct map off the wall. He marked Bingham's home. Then Alicia's. Two red dots. Independent. Unrelated.

Except—

He marked the spot where the jogger died.

Then Kill Two.

Then last night's boy at the convenience store.

The dots formed the beginning of a curve—not a straight line, not random scatter. A subtle arc. Something widening, like a hand reaching outward from the woods one inch at a time.

He stood back, jaw tightening.

"Graves."

Vander's voice drifted from the hallway, low and gravelly in the early morning quiet.

Graves didn't look away from the map. "Two missing persons. Back-to-back."

"Yeah," Vander said, stepping inside. He held a stack of old folders and a leather-bound journal so worn it looked soft at the edges. "I figured you'd want these."

"I'm not jumping to conclusions," Graves muttered.

"Didn't say you were."

Graves set the pen down. "Trash bin untouched. No tire marks. No signs of movement. If someone grabbed Bingham, they did it without leaving a footprint."

"Or he didn't move under his own power," Vander said.

Graves didn't take the bait. "And the girl?"

"No tantrum history. Good attendance. No runaway signs. Family's terrified."

Silence hung between them for a beat.

Graves looked back to the map—just a simple precinct printout, nothing mystical about it—but the pattern tugged at him. A shallow crescent reaching outward from the first death site. A slow, deliberate widening.

He hated that he saw it.
Hated how natural it felt to draw the shape in his head.

He grabbed the folder for Bingham's case and flipped through it. No trauma. No noise complaints. No suspicious vehicles reported. Only one detail stood out: a neighbor said the street had been "weirdly quiet" around 11 p.m., like something muffled the wind.

He marked that on the map too.

"What's that?" Vander asked.

"Sound disturbance."

"Those are piling up."

Graves shot him a look. "You don't know that."

Vander lifted the journal. "Actually, I do."

Graves exhaled sharply and sat. "Give me an hour. I'll log both cases properly. Missing persons doesn't mean connected."

"Sure," Vander said, but the way he hovered told Graves he wasn't going anywhere.

The second missing-person report buzzed again on his screen, an auto-update from dispatch. No new info. No witnesses. Nothing.

Graves rubbed the back of his neck, the headache pulsing there like a steady, unwelcome heartbeat. He opened his private folder—**ANOMALIES**—and hesitated before adding anything.

Missing persons didn't belong with ribcage deformation diagrams and timestamp distortions.

He added them anyway.

The cursor blinked at him.

He wrote:

11A: early-morning disappearance.
11B: teenage disappearance.
Distance from prior sites = consistent arc.
Silence-zone witness noted.

He closed the file before he could think too much about what it meant.

He reached for his phone and sent a quick message to EMS, asking Maya to stop by when she got in—he needed clarification on her environmental notes from the convenience store death.

"Walk with me," Vander said.

Graves didn't bother arguing. He grabbed his jacket and followed him down the hallway, past the bulletin boards, past the break room where someone reheated coffee thick enough to chew. Vander moved with that slow, heavy certainty that meant he'd been thinking about this all night.

They stopped in one of the small interview rooms usually reserved for overflow cases. Vander set the stack of folders on the metal table and opened the top one.

"Before we talk theories," Vander said, "we talk history."

Graves rolled his eyes but didn't interrupt.

Vander laid out the first drawing—a charcoal rendering on brittle paper. A long, bent figure sketched in jagged lines, shoulders too narrow, arms sloping toward the floor. Human only in the vaguest sense.

"Pre-colonial," Vander said. "Local tribes reported shadow beings that appeared before unexplained deaths."

Graves folded his arms. "Folklore."

"Fine," Vander said. "Then how about this?"

He opened a leather-bound journal to a page filled with cramped handwriting. Dated **1793**. The entry described a settler who vanished on his way from the woods back to his cabin. The only clue: his wife hearing "a long breath that froze the air."

Graves looked at the words longer than he meant to.

Vander flipped to another sheet—this one a sketch from **1887**, showing a narrow hallway with an elongated shadow near the ceiling. Another from **1904** showing a cluster of houses with misshapen silhouettes along the walls.

Graves rubbed his jaw. "Shapes can mean anything."

"Then look at where," Vander said.

He slid a printed map over the table. Red pins dotted several decades of disappearance points. They weren't random. Not even close.

They formed a crescent.
Almost identical to the one forming now.

Graves swallowed but didn't speak.

Vander leaned in. "Someone—something—does this every few decades. It expands its hunting area before the worst of the cluster hits. You're mapping the early stage of the same curve. You just don't want to admit it."

Graves stared down at the map, not blinking.

Outside the interview room, a phone rang. A door closed. Someone laughed too loudly at something that wasn't funny.

Inside, the room felt smaller, the air thicker.

Vander slid another folder across the table, the paper catching on the metal lip as if the room didn't want it moved. Graves opened it without sitting down, bracing one hand on the back of the chair like he needed the anchor.

The first page showed a hand-drawn sketch—thick charcoal, uneven pressure. A tall, bent shape stood in the corner of a cabin interior, limbs too long, frame contorted like it had grown in the wrong direction. The shading around it was heavy, pressed deep enough to leave grooves in the paper.

"Southern tribes," Vander said. "Accounts from before the first settlements. Shadowed figures seen before unexplained vanishings. They didn't have a word for bodies that were never found."

Graves flipped the page with two fingers. The next image showed a narrow hallway, lantern-lit, with a stretched silhouette clinging to the ceiling. The accompanying notes, dated **1831**, described "a silent pressure" drifting ahead of the shadow, followed by several missing hunters.

He shut the folder halfway. "You're drawing lines between stories and a missing middle-aged man taking out the trash."

"I'm drawing lines between patterns," Vander said. "And your map is starting to look exactly like these."

Graves didn't answer. He lifted the journal, feeling the warped leather soften under his thumb. The ink inside was faded, but legible—terse descriptions of people vanishing mid-step, of cabins found empty with meals still warm, of families who swore they heard someone breathing in the corners before the disappearances.

He kept reading.

A page from **1887** described an incident in the neighboring county: three people missing, last heard screaming inside a barn. When searchers arrived, the barn was undisturbed—except for a cold layer of condensation on the interior walls. No frost. No ice. Just cold, in a warm summer.

Graves felt something click uncomfortably in the back of his mind. Cold that didn't match the air.

Cold that didn't linger naturally.

Cold like the one Maya kept circling in her reports.

Vander pulled out another document—photocopy of a 1920 newspaper clipping. The headline was blurred, but the illustration was clear enough: a distorted silhouette leaning at an impossible angle along a dirt road, trailing a figure whose feet weren't touching the ground.

"This one is exaggeration," Graves said automatically.

"Maybe." Vander tapped the margin. "But look at the reported symptoms of the area after the events. People hearing echoes in empty rooms. Sounds stretching. Corners darkening. Pets refusing to enter certain spaces. It's the same catalog of distortions your witnesses keep describing."

Graves kept flipping until he reached a page that made him stop cold.

A sketch—ink on brittle paper—of a long, narrow corridor. The shadow in it didn't stand or walk. It clung. Its head was angled downward, arms nearly scraping the floorboards.

1911 — 'The Hallway Shadow.'

Vander didn't speak. He didn't need to.

The proportions in the sketch matched too much.

Too precisely.

Graves swallowed, the back of his throat dry.

He turned the page. Another entry described bodies found "cold to the touch even under the midday sun."

Another spoke of ribs collapsed inward without impact.

Another described silence "as thick as snow" preceding a disappearance.

Maya's field notes came to mind—quiet details she had kept adding even when the evidence didn't support any explanation a detective could file: the cold halos, the sound drag, the wrong-angled shadows.

Vander laid out a final folder, this one thinner, its pages newer.

"These are the modern cases. Same symptoms. Same distortions. We've been looking at this thing through the wrong lens."

Graves bristled. "I don't believe in monsters."

"Neither did the people who wrote those journals," Vander said. "But their dead didn't care."

Graves turned the 1911 sketch over, staring at the edges where the ink feathered into the paper grain. The corridor depicted could've been anywhere—an apartment, an old house, a school hall. The proportions were what lodged beneath his ribs.

Too tall.

Too thin.

Bent in all the ways a body wasn't meant to fold.

He placed it on the table without looking at Vander.

"You're reading mythology into police work," he said. "Folklore doesn't solve disappearances."

"It's not folklore if it keeps happening."

Graves pushed away from the table, pacing once, twice. His footsteps sounded softer than they should have against the tile.

Vander opened his mouth to say something else, but footsteps echoed down the hall toward them—Maya's light, quick tread. She stepped into the doorway with a slim folder in hand.

Without looking toward the table, she crossed the small distance and handed the folder to Graves — the environmental clarification he'd asked for. He took it automatically.

As soon as she handed Graves the folder, her gaze drifted towards the papers spread across the table.

When she saw the 1911 sketch, she stopped moving entirely.

Her eyes narrowed, breath thinning. For a moment, she looked as if she were staring at something alive.

She didn't touch the sketch. Didn't step closer.

Just whispered, "Where did you get that?"

Vander answered, but Graves barely heard him.

He watched Maya instead.

Her face had gone pale—not with recognition of a drawing, but with the kind of recognition people had when they finally saw their nightmares on paper.

Her fingers tightened around the doorway frame.

A muscle in her jaw flickered.

She looked away last, like the image had weight she had to peel herself from.

The corridor outside flickered with a passing shadow as someone moved through the main office. Maya's head twitched in that direction, instinctively tracking the movement.

Maya stepped farther into the doorway, eyes fixed on the sketch as if the rest of the room had gone out of focus. Graves expected her to move closer, but she stayed rooted—shoulders tight, posture wound up like something behind her ribs had braced.

Vander didn't speak. He knew better than to break whatever was happening behind her expression.

Maya dragged her gaze away from the sketch long enough to force a swallow. "Who drew that?"

"A police artist," Vander said. "1911. Case file was mislabeled as a burglary until three more people vanished in the same boarding house."

She didn't look away from the page this time. "It's the proportions."

Graves felt something cold pass under his sternum. "What about them?"

Maya lifted one hand, hesitated, then pointed without touching the paper. "The arms. The set of the shoulders. That downward angle of the head. It's..." She cut herself off, biting the inside of her cheek. "It's not wrong."

Graves didn't like the way she said it.

Not unsure.

Not guessing.

Remembering.

Vander slid another sheet forward—an anatomical sketch copied from an autopsy log dated **1902**, the notes describing rib inward-collapse with no external blunt trauma. Beside it, he placed a modern diagram from the teen boy's postmortem packet.

Maya's breath stilled.

The skeletal distortions weren't identical, but they rhymed—same narrowing of the cage, same fractured larynx, same pressure signature.

Graves stared at the pairing longer than he meant to. "These are a century apart."

"Biology doesn't change much when it's perfected," Vander said quietly.

Graves shot him a look that said *not now*, but Vander only met it with a flat stare that carried decades of cases beneath it.

Maya set the clipboard down on the table. Her hand shook once before she pulled it back. "I need to see the rest."

Vander opened another folder without ceremony—photographs from the **1920 disappearance cluster**, each paired with witness statements. Sketches of elongated shadows, reports of silence "bending," whole households claiming the air in their stairwells felt "occupied."

Maya leaned over the table, scanning the notes, the margins, the hastily scribbled measurements.

Her jaw tightened.

Her eyes didn't blink enough.

She stopped halfway through one page. "Read this."

Graves moved closer, shoulder brushing the edge of her sleeve. The note described a body found near a barn: **severe internal cold despite ambient heat**, no external damage, no frost anywhere else. The wording mirrored Maya's own incident report from the convenience store almost line for line.

Vander tapped the page. "The same anomalies keep showing up. Different towns. Different decades. Same patterns."

Maya stepped back from the table like she'd brushed against a live wire. She pressed her palms against her thighs, steadying her breath. "Tell me you've tried ruling out environmental causes."

Graves lifted a brow. "First thing I did."

"And?"

"Nothing accounts for it."

He stopped himself before adding *yet.*

He didn't need to give Vander the satisfaction.

Vander picked up the 1911 sketch again, holding it out just enough for the overhead light to catch the dark charcoal strokes. "You've both seen shadows behave wrong at the scenes. You've heard witnesses describe distortions. This isn't new. It's just… resurfacing."

Maya's throat moved in a tight swallow. "No folklore?" Her voice was thin. "No monster stories? Just... resurfacing?"

"We're past folklore," Vander said. "This is documentation."

Graves braced both hands on the table, leaning his weight into them like the metal could hold everything he didn't want to say. He stared at the crescent of red pins on the map again—the slow outward sweep, the arc that didn't feel random anymore.

He didn't name it.
He didn't have to.

The door behind them creaked faintly as someone in the hallway passed by, their footsteps muffled, as if the air inside the room had thickened enough to swallow sound.

Maya's head twitched at the noise before she looked quickly away.

Vander sifted through the last of the documents, pulling a final sheet from the bottom of the stack: a translated report from a 1700s missionary describing "long shadows that hung from the rafters like wet animal hides," preceding several unexplained vanishings.

Maya stared at it for a long time. Not reading—absorbing.

Graves watched her jaw clench again, a muscle feathering just once. She didn't look at him. Didn't look at Vander. She kept staring at the drawing like something in it was looking back.

The room felt heavier, the edges cooling by a few quiet degrees.

Maya reached for the back of a chair, fingers tightening on the metal brace. She didn't sit.

She didn't need to.

The papers on the table were enough to keep her upright and unsteady in the same breath.

Chapter 12 — Mind Splinter

Holt hadn't slept in two days.

Not the dozing-in-a-chair kind of sleeplessness, but the rigid, electric sort where every muscle braced for something his mind couldn't name. He washed his face twice in the station bathroom, splashed cold water over eyes that wouldn't stay still, and stared at the mirror until the lights above it flickered—not enough to be a malfunction, just enough to make him blink too hard.

He dried his hands on the rough paper towel, breathing through the thin tremor running through his chest. The station air felt wrong again. Too still. Too tense. As though sound had thickened in the corners.

He stepped into the hallway.

Two officers talking near the vending machines glanced at him. One gave a small, tight-lipped smile. The other didn't bother hiding the look—pity edged with annoyance.

Holt's pulse flicked hard.

He walked past them and pretended he hadn't heard the whisper behind him.

"Watch your back, man."

Followed by the laugh.

His shoulders locked. He didn't turn. Couldn't. If he turned, he'd have to acknowledge the shifting shape he kept seeing in the reflection of the trophy case glass—his own silhouette, but wrong at the edges. Lagging half a second behind him when he moved.

He stepped outside into the cold morning air, but it didn't help.

The sunlight felt thin. Diluted. Like it wasn't reaching him the way it should.

Dispatch chatter bled through his radio, tinny and distant.

Holt swallowed hard.

His shadow stretched across the pavement in front of him. Nothing unusual. Except when he shifted his weight, the shadow seemed to settle into place a fraction late—just enough for his stomach to flip.

He closed his eyes.

It's nothing. You're tired. You're exhausted. Stop looking.

But that whispering sound drifted again—too soft to form words, too close to ignore. Coming from the empty space behind his left shoulder.

He moved quickly to his cruiser.

The interior smelled faintly of stale air and disinfectant. His hands gripped the steering wheel harder than necessary, knuckles whitening. He forced himself to breathe evenly.

Get through the shift. Just get through the shift.

His radio crackled.

"Unit 214, welfare check. Caller reports strange noises from abandoned duplex on Hathaway."

Holt's chest tightened.

Hathaway.

The word hit with a quiet, cold weight he couldn't explain.

He keyed the mic.

"214 en route."

His voice didn't sound like his own. Too thin.

He pulled away from the precinct lot and headed toward the address. The streets passed in a blur—the gray smear of morning light on windshield glass, the buzz of a distant transformer, the faint tremor of his own heartbeat thudding in his ears.

At a stop sign, he caught the reflection of himself in the side window.

His face looked drawn. Pale. Eyes hollowed out by something deeper than exhaustion.

Behind his head, just for a second, the background light dipped—as if something had leaned between him and the sky.

Holt jerked the wheel and blinked.

Nothing there.

Just morning.

Just quiet.

Just him.

He breathed through his teeth, forcing the air in and out. When the radio clicked again, he flinched.

"214, be advised: caller said there might be someone inside."

Inside.

A chill crawled up the back of his neck.

He turned onto Hathaway Road. The duplex sat near the end of the block—a squat, sagging structure with boarded windows and a sagging roofline. The kind of place kids dared each other to enter on Halloween. The kind of place that felt wrong even when the sun was up.

Holt parked. The air felt heavier the moment he stepped out of the cruiser. No wind. No ambient hum. Just a thick stillness that pressed against his skin.

He approached the door.

His keys jingled against his belt—too loud in the quiet.

Inside the duplex, something shifted. A faint scrape. Soft. Directionless.

Holt froze, breath hitching.

Not real. You're tired.

But his hand went to his holster anyway, the weight of the weapon grounding him just enough to move forward.

He stepped into the entryway. Dust coated everything—thick on the floorboards, clinging to the banister, settled into the gaps between warped planks. The air tasted old.

And beneath it…

Cold.

Not the winter kind. Something thinner. Emptier.

He swallowed and scanned the room, trying to steady his breathing.

At the far edge of the living room floor, a line of dust looked… disturbed. Not a footprint. Not an animal track.

A long, irregular scuff trailing across the surface.

Like someone had stumbled.

Or been dragged.

His throat tightened.

The house creaked—soft, almost apologetic.

Then the whispering returned, threading between the silence, brushing the inside of his skull.

Holt tightened his grip on the weapon, his breathing shallow, his pulse spiking hard enough that he felt it in his teeth.

Something moved deeper inside the duplex.

He stepped forward.

The second room opened into a narrow hallway, walls bowed slightly inward as though the house had been built around something that pushed back. Holt swept his flashlight across peeling wallpaper and empty doorframes. Dust motes drifted lazily in the beam, hanging in the air as if suspended on invisible threads.

His throat worked around a tight swallow.

The cold deepened as he stepped farther in.

Not the kind that prickled skin. This was the kind that settled *inside*—a thin, hollow temperature that felt like the absence of breath rather than the presence of winter. The air tasted metallic. Old. Wrong.

He kept moving.

At the end of the hall, a half-open door led into what might have been a living room once. The boards near the doorway were warped and split, the ceiling discolored in wide spreading arcs. On the floor, dust blanketed everything except for the single, elongated scuff trailing toward the back corner.

Holt crouched.

The mark wasn't sharp enough to be a typical print. The edges were blurred, uneven, as if a heel had slid or been tugged. The kind of mark someone made when they struggled to get up… or when they didn't.

His stomach flipped.

He forced himself upright.

Someone was in here.

That much he believed.

That much he could cling to.

The whispering brushed past again—soft, like someone muttering through fabric.

Holt spun, light sweeping across the walls.

Nothing.

Just the hollow shape of an empty house.

He stepped deeper inside.

The scuff trailed toward a shadowed corner where the ceiling dipped low. As he approached, the air shifted—just a fraction, a barely perceptible thinning—and a faint frost shimmered on one of the cracked floorboards. Not full ice. Not enough to crunch.

Just a silvered veil, like breath condensed and left behind.

He crouched again.

The cold radiating off the smear felt unnatural. Not like winter air sneaking in. Not like a draft.

Something different.

Something emptied.

Behind him, a soft exhale drifted through the silence.

Holt's spine locked.

The breath wasn't his.

Slow. Damp. Close.

He straightened too fast, heart banging against his ribs, flashlight trembling in his hand. The sound was behind him. No—beside him. No—everywhere at once.

He pivoted toward the hallway.

The floorboards whispered beneath something moving.

Holt drew his weapon before he processed the instinct, before training even caught up. The whispering blurred into a low, shuddering drag of sound that tunneled straight through him.

"Show yourself!" he barked, the command cracking at the edges.

The shadows didn't move.

The house didn't move.

But the breathing was closer now.

Right at his back.

He whipped around.

His flashlight beam quivered over the empty air, over walls and corners and warped floorboards. His lungs seized as the cold pressed in harder, tightening around his ribs like a band pulled too tight.

A floorboard flexed behind him.

He fired.

One shot.

Then another.

Then another—each one deafening in the confined space.

Splinters burst from the far wall. Dust shook loose from the ceiling.

The breathing stopped.

The house fell into a silence so deep it hummed.

Holt's arms trembled as he lowered the gun, adrenaline flaring hot and sharp through his veins. His heartbeat pounded in his skull, drowning out everything else. He swallowed hard and backed toward the doorway, every step measured, afraid to turn his back on anything.

Radio static crackled against his shoulder.

"214, status check. Shots fired reported—"

Holt forced himself to breathe.

"Suspect fled," he managed, voice frayed. "Requesting backup."

His throat felt thick around the lie, the words scraping on their way out. But they were the only explanation that didn't make something inside him split.

He stepped out into the hallway again, just far enough to keep the doorway in view. The silence clung to him like humidity, every hair on his arms raised.

Sirens wailed in the distance.

Holt didn't blink as the house watched him back.

The first cruiser screeched to a stop outside, tires spitting gravel. Doors slammed, boots hit pavement, and voices cut through the dead air—normal sounds, human sounds, loud enough to make Holt's lungs finally release.

He kept his gun trained down the hallway as two officers stepped inside, flashlights slicing through the dim.

"Where'd he go?" Officer Ramirez asked, eyes sweeping past Holt toward the back rooms.

"Didn't see him," Holt said. His voice felt scraped raw. "He was in here—I heard movement. Frost in the corner. Then shots. He bolted."

Ramirez nodded like it made sense. Why wouldn't it? Nothing in Holt's face suggested anything but a rattled cop responding to a threat. His breathing was too fast, his pupils blown wide.

Officer Dean moved past them, weapon raised.

"Clear down the hall," Dean called.

"Check upstairs," Ramirez said.

Holt swallowed, but the motion felt like dragging gravel down his throat. He forced himself to follow Ramirez into the main room again. The dust in the air still drifted, unsettled. Dean's flashlight swept up the staircase, catching tiny particles cascading from a cracked rafter overhead.

"Hold up." Dean angled his light downward. "Fresh disturbance."

Holt's stomach clenched.

The drag-scuff lay exactly where he'd seen it—long, uneven, carved into the dust like someone had been pulled or staggered across the floor. Dean knelt beside it, running a gloved finger along the edge.

"This isn't old," he said. "Dust line's too sharp. Someone moved through here not long ago."

Ramirez stepped in closer, examining the nearby overturned crate—its edge scraped across floorboards, leaving a fresh arc.

"Yeah," he agreed. "Somebody ran. Probably heard Holt coming in, panicked, tried to make for the back."

Holt didn't speak.

He didn't correct them.

Couldn't.

Because their explanation—the human explanation—was the only thing holding his mind together right now. If he challenged it… if he tried to put into words what really pressed against his skin in that room…

He might hear himself say it, and then he wouldn't be able to take it back.

Dean pushed open the back door. The hinges groaned.

"Rear exit's cracked," he called. "Could've slipped out."

Ramirez nodded. "Circulate the area. Maybe he ran through one of the yards."

More officers entered. More flashlights. More radios crackling with clipped updates. The normality of it all pressed against Holt like a weight—heavy, anchoring, suffocating.

He holstered his weapon with hands that still trembled.

Ramirez turned to him. "You good?"

Holt nodded before the question even finished.

Ramirez gave him a long, measuring look—something halfway between concern and something else. Something Holt didn't want to name.

"Get outside," Ramirez said quietly. "Catch some air."

Holt didn't argue.

He stepped back toward the entryway, his heartbeat still stuttering in uneven counts. The house felt smaller now, even with a half-dozen officers moving through it—like the walls had crept inward while he'd been alone.

Outside, the morning light should have helped.

It didn't.

The street felt too empty. Too still. The world too bright, but not warm. He dug his fingers into his hair, elbows resting on the cruiser's roof as he forced himself to breathe.

Dean stepped out behind him a moment later.

"You weren't wrong," he said. "Somebody was in there. That drag mark wasn't accidental."

Holt nodded without turning.

Dean clapped his shoulder once—a sharp, grounding pressure—and walked back inside.

The touch lingered long after the officer was gone, like Holt's nerves couldn't decide whether to register comfort or warning.

Behind him, the duplex loomed—quiet, sagging, vacant.

Graves arrived ten minutes later, striding under the crime scene tape with a look that wasn't quite anger but wasn't neutral either. Holt straightened when he saw him, pulse tripping into a faster rhythm. The other officers kept combing the duplex, voices drifting through the broken doorway in low, methodical calls.

Graves didn't speak until they were a few steps away from the tape, far enough that no one would overhear.

"Walk," he said quietly.

Holt followed him toward the end of the block, where a row of bare trees lined the sidewalk. The wind skimmed through the branches but didn't carry enough sound to break the tightness in Holt's chest. Graves stopped near the last tree, hands in his pockets, jaw tight.

"You want to tell me what happened in there?" Graves asked.

Holt kept his eyes on the pavement. "I heard someone inside. They were moving. I called it in."

"You fired three rounds."

"I—" He swallowed. "I thought someone was coming at me."

Graves didn't rush him. He waited, letting the silence hang between them in a way that made Holt feel like he should fill it, but he didn't have anything solid to offer. His mind kept replaying the breathing behind him. The cold. The way the air seemed to thin around his ribs.

"There was movement," Holt said finally. "You saw the floor."

"I saw the scuff, yeah," Graves replied. "And I saw the disturbed dust on the stairs. That's enough to justify your report. But I need to know if you actually saw someone."

Holt hesitated.

Graves noticed.

"I'm not looking to write you up," he added. "I need the truth so I can defend you if this lands on my desk."

Something flickered in Holt's chest at that—fear, gratitude, maybe both. He rubbed a hand over his face, the scrape of stubble grounding him just enough to force the words out.

"I didn't see him," Holt said. "Just the movement. The sound. It felt like—"

He stopped.

Graves waited again.

Holt shook his head. "It felt wrong."

Graves' expression didn't shift, but something in his posture tightened. Not disbelief. Not quite. More like he was trying to fit Holt's words into a box that didn't have the right shape.

"You're exhausted," Graves said. "That's not an accusation. It's what I'm seeing. You need rest."

"I'm fine."

"You're not fine."

Holt's jaw clenched, a flicker of heat rising under his skin. He looked away down the street, toward the duplex where the scuff mark stretched across the floorboards like a sentence no one could interpret correctly.

"I'm not making things up," Holt said, voice low. "There was some-one in that house."

"I didn't say you were making anything up," Graves replied. "But you're running too hot. You need to take tonight off."

Holt tensed. "I can finish the shift."

"You can," Graves said. "But I'm telling you not to."

Holt opened his mouth, then closed it again. The argument felt pointless. Heavy. Like it would take too much effort to push the words out, and none of them would land where he needed them to.

Graves exhaled, looking at the duplex. "Ramirez and Dean think someone slipped out the back. They don't think you overreacted." He paused. "Don't give them a reason to change their minds."

Holt nodded once. It felt mechanical.

Graves looked at him a moment longer, as if trying to read some-thing past the exhaustion. Then he turned back toward the house, lift-ing the tape to head inside.

Holt stayed where he was, the cold settling deeper around him as though it had followed him out of the duplex and refused to let go. The sounds of officers moving through the building filtered out onto the street—footsteps, radio clicks, low voices—ordinary noises that felt too far away.

He stood there until one of the units drove past, the brief wash of headlights sliding over him before fading into the gray morning.

Chapter 13 — The Five

The industrial block felt abandoned long before they reached it.

The streetlights along Briar Loop flickered in uneven pulses, not enough to fail, just enough to make the world twitch at the edges each time the bulbs dimmed. Maya drove behind Holt's cruiser, watching the brake lights shiver through the fog. Graves sat beside him, motionless except for the tiny muscle working along the hinge of his jaw.

The air temperature dropped the closer they got.

Not gradually.

In **steps**—like invisible thresholds carved into the street.

By the time they turned the last corner, frost had begun spreading across the inside of Maya's windshield despite the heater on full. She wiped a streak clear with her sleeve, but the glass chilled again immediately.

Up ahead the abandoned textile warehouse hunched against the fog, its concrete walls streaked black like something had burned inside it decades ago and no one bothered to clean the smoke out. Every window was either shattered or boarded over. What remained of the loading bay doors sagged inward, giving the building a posture that felt too low, too heavy, as if the structure remembered violence.

Holt pulled up near the warped entrance, stopping harder than he meant to. The cruiser rocked. He sat for two long seconds before opening the door, knuckles whitening around the handle. Maya parked behind him and stepped out into the cold.

Her breath fogged instantly.

Not thin mist.

A **dense, white plume** that unfurled from her mouth like steam off dry ice.

The early-morning air shouldn't have been anywhere near this temperature.

A thin metallic smell hit her next — not blood but something sharper.

Cold metal.

Freezer burn.

Old concrete.

A trace of rot that hadn't fully thawed.

Holt stiffened as he stepped toward the loading bay, one hand hovering near his holster. His shoulders rose and fell in uneven rhythm. Maya could hear his breathing from several feet away — too shallow, too fast, hitting the cold air like it hurt.

Graves joined him at the base of the ramp. "Caller reported five bodies," he said quietly, as if louder speech might disturb something. "No IDs. No suspects. No sounds since."

Maya glanced at the building again.

The darkness behind the warped doorway wasn't the natural kind. It didn't feel empty.

It felt **stunned**.

Like an animal that had just finished thrashing and left behind a silence that hadn't figured out what it was supposed to do next.

The cold deepened in a way that didn't feel like weather. It felt like air pulled from a deeper place and pushed into this one without warming first. She could feel it tightening around her jaw, seeping past the fabric of her uniform, settling into the space between her ribs.

Holt swallowed hard.

The sound was audible.

"You okay?" Graves asked, not looking at him.

Holt nodded, but it wasn't convincing.

They moved forward together.

Maya's boots crunched over a thin veneer of frost spidering across the concrete. Not a full freeze — just a thin film, but enough to give the ground a brittle texture underfoot. Her stomach tightened as they reached the doorway. The air inside the warehouse was darker, heavier, and the cold intensified fast enough she felt tears prick her eyes.

Graves raised his flashlight.

Holt lifted his.

Maya followed.

Their beams cut across the interior — rusted shelving collapsed in heaps, broken machinery, old drums corroded through at the bottoms, oil stains frozen into smeared black patches. Dust drifted in slow, lazy clouds that didn't seem to care about the law of gravity.

Holt's breath hitched.

The building smelled wrong inside.

The cold had held it all in place:

the metal, the mold, the faint sourness of stagnant water,

and underneath it — something faint but present,

a tone of **raw iron** that made Maya's throat close.

They moved deeper into the entry corridor.

The silence settled in thicker.

Not absence of sound.

Suppression of it.

Their footsteps landed too softly, absorbed too quickly, as though the air had no interest in carrying noise anymore.

Holt raised his light toward the open threshold leading into the main warehouse floor.

His jaw locked.

Maya saw the tremor in his fingers before she saw what he saw.

Graves stepped beside him, squinting into the dark.

None of them spoke.

They were only at the edge of the room.

But what lay inside the beam of Holt's flashlight was enough to let them know there was no version of this scene that would be manageable.

Maya felt her pulse spike so hard her vision sharpened around the edges.

They stepped forward together.

Graves' flashlight swept into the warehouse's open floor, the beam shaking as it hit the first shape on the concrete. Maya stopped moving.

The corpse lay half-twisted near a collapsed metal pallet, spine bent inward in a sickening arch that pulled the lower vertebrae into a compressed ridge. The lumbar column looked crushed from the inside—vertebrae sunk toward the canal, skin stretched too thin over the collapse. A dried, chalky white residue clung around a puncture track near the sacrum, flaking in uneven clusters like something had been forced out through a single point.

The man's face was frozen mid-scream—lips pulled back hard enough to crack, teeth exposed, eyes bulged and bloodshot from ruptured vessels. Frost ringed his lashes.

Graves lowered himself beside the body with a stiffness that wasn't caution—it was revulsion.

Holt's light drifted to the left, catching the second corpse.

This one had been torn open.

The ribcage wasn't cut or pried—it was **wrenched** apart. Several ribs bent outward in jagged arcs, snapped unevenly at their bases where the cartilage had given under brutal force. The sternum was twisted slightly off-center, rotated as though the upper torso had been turned while the spine resisted.

Parts of the internal organs had come partially free. A section of lung hung in a stiff grey arc, frozen mid-collapse. The liver was smeared across the floor in a heavy smear of dark brown-red, sticking to the concrete where it had frozen into a gelatinous layer. Coils of intestine protruded through a tear along the flank, frozen into a stiff contorted rope.

The corpse's hands were worn raw—the skin on the palms stripped in patches, fingertips cracked and bloodied, several nails torn off entirely. Scrape marks streaked outward from the fingertips across the concrete, as if the victim had been dragged or had tried to brace against something unstoppable.

Maya couldn't breathe through her nose; the air carried too much metallic weight, too much cold-soaked rot.

Holt stepped back a fraction, boots scraping against the frost-lined floor. His breath shook once—a sharp, involuntary hitch.

Graves stood slowly, his face set but pale under the warehouse's half-dead lights.

Maya's flashlight drifted farther into the room. The air got colder the deeper it reached into the dark—cold that clung like static, sharp enough to sting the inside of her nostrils.

Holt moved his beam slightly to the right. The light caught something thick and dark on the floor—blood frozen mid-drip, a line of it that had run from a ribbed steel beam overhead and hardened into a sharp, jagged spike partway down. The droplets suspended along its length were frozen in place, still perfectly spherical.

No sound carried in the space.

Their boots made contact, but the echoes died too quickly, absorbed into a deadened stillness that felt like the room didn't want noise in it anymore.

Maya forced herself forward.

Holt did the same.

Graves followed, jaw rigid.

They stepped deeper into the warehouse.

The cold thickened as they pushed deeper—sharp enough that Maya felt it in her teeth, like someone pressing ice cubes straight into her molars. Her breath fogged in heavy bursts, each exhale shaking more than the last.

Holt's flashlight slid across the floor and caught the third body.

His hand jerked violently.

The beam dropped.

He gagged—loud, wet, sudden.

The twisted corpse lay bent into a brutal corkscrew, spine torqued so violently the ribs had rotated around it. The skin along the back had split down the midline, opening in jagged, uneven tears that exposed vertebrae glistening with frozen marrow. The pelvis was rotated nearly ninety degrees from the shoulders—an anatomical impossibility that made the whole body look sculpted by a sadist.

Maya slapped a hand over her mouth as bile surged up her throat.

She didn't stop moving—just staggered sideways, bracing a palm against a rusted metal shelf. Her gag came out sharp and high-pitched, involuntary, a sound ripped out of her body rather than released. The cold air made the taste of vomit sharper.

Graves inhaled through his nose—wrong choice.

The smell hit him immediately.

A metallic stench of ruptured vessels mixed with the freezer-burn rot of internal organs exposed too long to open air. Beneath it all was something faintly sweet, like flesh that had cooled too fast for bacteria to keep up.

Graves doubled over, one hand braced on his thigh, coughing hard enough that his eyes watered. A deep gag tore its way up, harsh and violent. He forced it down with a series of shallow breaths that shook his shoulders.

Holt wasn't as lucky.

He turned away two steps and vomited onto the concrete.

It hit the floor with a wet slap that echoed strangely—too soft, too fast—but he didn't notice the acoustics. He stayed bent over, retching again, his whole frame trembling under the weight of it. Frost fogged from his lips as he choked the last of it out.

Maya forced her eyes back up.

The third body wasn't done.

A calf bone jutted through the skin, snapped outward in a near-right angle. The foot beyond it was rotated fully backwards, the boot half torn, laces frozen mid-whip as if they'd snapped while the leg was twisted. The victim's arm was bent under him unnaturally, elbow ruptured outward in a bloom of frozen blood that had spiderwebbed across the floor.

Maya gagged again—dry this time, throat constricting hard enough to ache.

Holt wiped his mouth with a shaking hand, eyes glassy. His pupils were blown wide, swallowing the whites. His breath came in sharp, icy bursts that shook his entire frame.

"We need..." Holt rasped, but he didn't finish.
He couldn't.

Graves straightened slowly—too fast would have tipped him over again—and forced himself toward the next shape on the ground. He wiped the back of his glove across his mouth, smearing moisture from either tears or sweat; in this cold he couldn't tell.

Maya followed him, jaw clenched so hard it throbbed.

The fourth corpse lay half-slumped against a collapsed table. This one didn't look like twisting or tearing.
This one looked like **explosion**.

Dozens—no, hundreds—of tiny ruptures spread across the torso and neck. Blood had burst from beneath the skin, freezing in black-red constellations that dotted the body in tight clusters. The chest cavity had collapsed inward in uneven folds, as though the internal pressure had snapped downward in a single catastrophic instant.

Maya's legs went weak.

She grabbed the corner of the table just to stay upright as a violent dry heave hit her—a wrenching, throat-straining convulsion that forced tears from her eyes. She squeezed her eyes shut hard, trying to steady her breathing, but the smell made it impossible.

The man's tongue protruded between broken teeth.
Blood vessels had burst inside it too—dark threads frozen beneath the surface.
The lower jaw was cracked on one side; frost had spread across the fracture line in delicate crystalline patterns.

A line of frozen blood trailed down his cheek—not dripped, not smeared.

Burst.

Thrown outward from inside before the cold seized it mid-flight.

Graves pressed a gloved hand to his stomach and bent slightly, swallowing against a rising heave. His breathing turned ragged, misting out in harsh, uneven bursts.

He steadied himself on sheer force of will.

Holt didn't look away. He couldn't. His eyes were locked on the ruined body with the wide, horrified focus of someone whose brain was trying to reject what it was processing.

His lips had gone pale.

His jaw trembled once, twice.

A harsh retch tore out of him again—nothing left to bring up, just the violent motion of a body recoiling from the world.

Maya wiped her mouth with the back of her wrist. Her throat burned. Her eyes wouldn't stop watering. Her pulse hammered against her ribs so hard she felt it in her fingertips.

The cold deepened as if responding to their breath—the frost thickening near the floor, crawling along the edges of debris in delicate crystalline veins.

The silence pressed on them like weight.

They weren't ready for what lay deeper inside.

They couldn't be.

But they kept moving.

Or rather—their bodies moved while their minds dragged behind, nauseated, numbed, and shaking.

And the cold got worse.

Much worse.

The deeper they went, the colder the air became — not like weather, but like stepping into layers of refrigerated deadness. Maya's lips felt numb. Holt's eyelashes had collected tiny beads of frost. Graves' breath came in harsh, broken bursts that sounded too loud in the suffocating quiet.

Holt's flashlight jerked as his hand spasmed.

The beam landed on the fifth body.

And Holt made a sound Maya had never heard from a grown man — a sharp, strangled grunt that cracked halfway into a sob before it broke apart into a gag. He doubled over instantly, hands braced on his knees, his back convulsing in violent heaves that wracked his entire frame.

Maya's knees went weak.

She clutched a rusted beam beside her as a wave of nausea surged so brutally it felt like her stomach was trying to claw its way up her throat.

The fifth victim wasn't arranged by violence.

The fifth victim looked **abandoned mid-suffering**.

Dragged.

Pulled.

Stopped.

Left.

The body lay half-on its side, half-twisted toward the wall, the spine visible through the torn skin along the back where cold had crusted the edges into brittle, frostbitten ridges. The vertebrae were discolored — not bloodstained, but **frost-burned**, the tissue around them collapsed inward as if something had gripped the torso and sucked the warmth straight out through the bone.

The legs...

God.

One leg was dragged so far behind the body that the pelvis had rotated out of alignment; the hip joint had separated with enough force to leave splintered bone dust scattered in a faint spray pattern behind it. The femur protruded, broken at mid-shaft in a jagged angle, marrow frozen into a pale, crystalline bloom around the exposed end.

Maya gagged again — violently — one hand slapped over her mouth, eyes squeezed shut as bile burned up her throat. Her body convulsed once, twice, almost folding her in half.

Graves wasn't doing any better.

He staggered back until his shoulder hit a steel pillar, the impact making a dull clang that seemed to vibrate through him. He bent forward, bracing one hand on his thigh, the other cupped over his mouth. A retch ripped out of him — deep, guttural, involuntary. Another followed.

He tried to breathe through it.

It made it worse.

Holt stumbled sideways, shoulder hitting a crate. He pressed his forearm hard against his mouth to muffle the sounds coming out of him. His throat worked in tight spasms as he dry-heaved again and again, each one harsher than the last.

Maya forced her eyes open.

The victim's left arm extended toward the floor — frozen mid-reach — fingers clawed toward nothing. The nails were torn. The skin along the fingertips shredded. Frozen blood rimmed each fingertip where the hand had scraped the concrete.

The hand had been reaching **away** from the direction the body had been pulled.

As if trying to stay.

As if trying to hold on.

As if—

Maya gagged again, stumbling back a step, elbow slamming into a rusted pipe.

Her vision blurred with tears she hadn't meant to shed.

She blinked hard, and the rest of the scene snapped into focus.

The victim's tongue…

It had frozen to the concrete.

A strip of it lay stuck to the floor — rigid, flat, pale. The remaining portion hung from the mouth, torn at the root, frozen against the teeth. The jaw was open wide enough to crack the joint on one side; the lips had split, exposing patches of gum iced over with frost crystals.

Graves choked on another dry heave, turning sharply away from the body and pressing his forearm to his mouth. He didn't vomit again, but his whole body shook with the effort of stopping it.

Maya staggered closer — not willingly, just because the others were behind her and there was nowhere else to go. Her light drifted over the victim's torso.

A pattern spread across the ribs — frozen blood fanned outward like wings on brittle bone. The abdominal cavity had partially collapsed; the organs inside shriveled from extreme cold, pulled inward as if the body had been drained of its internal heat fast enough to deform tissue.

Holt wasn't looking anymore.

He couldn't.

He was pressed against a support beam, shaking so hard the light in his hand jittered wildly across the walls. His breathing came in short, choking bursts, thick with panic and the lingering taste of vomit.

Maya crouched slightly, one hand gripping her own thigh to keep her balance as a wave of dizziness rolled through her.

Up close, the fifth body's face was the worst part.

The eyes had burst — not outward, not in gore, but inward.

Imploded.

Collapsed under pressure and cold.

What remained were dark, sunken cavities glazed with frost.

Her whole body shuddered.

Heat rose up her throat, swallowed by the ice in the air before it reached her lips. It felt like her stomach had been filled with boiling liquid and ice simultaneously — lurching violently, spasming under the assault of the scene.

She staggered backward, hand hitting the floor to steady herself, palm skidding across a patch of frozen blood that cracked under her weight.

Her breath fogged in frantic bursts.

Her pulse hammered in her ears.

Her stomach kept clenching violently, her throat tightening with another gag that barely stayed down.

Graves finally managed a breath deep enough to steady his voice, though it came out thin and ragged.

"—we need to get—"

He didn't finish.

He couldn't.

His throat closed on the words like they were something solid.

Maya's body was shaking uncontrollably.

Holt's light jerked again. He made another gagging sound — a full-bodied wrench that pulled his shoulders forward violently.

The cold deepened, sinking into their clothes, into their skin, into the joints of their hands until holding the flashlights felt impossible.

No one had any room left inside themselves for words.

And the worst wasn't the bodies.

It was the **sense** — subtle, unplaceable —

that the room hadn't finished settling

after whatever had happened in it.

That the air wasn't done reacting.

That the silence still held a shape.

That the scene had ended moments, not hours, ago.

And their bodies knew it

before their minds did.

The cold clung to them as they backed away from the fifth body — not as temperature but as weight, as if something in the room resisted letting them go. Maya stumbled first, her boot sliding on a patch of cracked frost. Holt caught her elbow, but his grip trembled, weak and unsteady, barely more help than gravity.

Graves didn't look back at the bodies.

He couldn't.

His jaw was locked so tightly it trembled.

They moved toward the doorway with no coordination, no formation, just three bodies trying to evacuate a scene their nervous systems were no longer built to withstand.

The deeper air of the warehouse pressed against their backs as they walked, sinking into their clothes like wet sand. Holt gagged again without warning — a violent, full-body wrench that bent him forward mid-step. Nothing came up. His throat was raw enough that the sound scraped.

Maya's hands wouldn't stop shaking, even once they reached the entry corridor. The flashlight beam jittered in spastic arcs along the floor. Each breath she took rasped in and out, cold enough that her chest ached, warm enough that nausea roiled with every inhale.

Behind them, one of the frozen droplets near the second body fractured under its own weight and hit the floor with a small, sharp *tick*.

Holt flinched so violently he struck the wall with his shoulder.

Maya jolted forward, pulse tearing through her veins like electricity. Every instinct screamed at her to run. Not walk. Not leave. **Run** the way prey runs when the brush behind it twitches.

Graves was already forcing himself toward the exit — posture rigid, steps uneven.

When the cold air finally broke into the warmer air outside, the shift punched them hard enough to make all three stop and gasp, like swimmers breaching the surface after being held underwater too long.

Holt braced a hand on the hood of his cruiser and gagged again — quieter this time, nearly silent, like his body had run out of energy to convulse with full force. Strings of saliva hung from his lips, catching on the cold wind before snapping.

Maya crouched down a foot away from him, not for support, not to help, but because her legs simply couldn't remain locked anymore. Her knees hit the concrete hard enough to jolt pain up her thighs. She bent forward, palms on the ground, breathing in huge, ragged pulls that left her dizzy.

The air outside should have helped.

It didn't.

The smell — faint but lingering — followed them out across the threshold:

frozen iron, ruptured tissue, the chemical tang of old machinery saturated with blood.

Graves staggered away from them, stopping near the police tape. He pressed both hands to his face and pulled them down slowly, trembling from unresolved adrenaline. His stomach clenched again — not enough to retch, but enough to tighten every muscle in his torso.

His voice, when it came, was barely audible.

"Jesus Christ..."

But the words didn't land.

They fell into the air like stones sinking through water.

Behind them, the news crews surged forward, cameras snapping as though the scene were nothing more than spectacle. Voices drifted from the crowd — low, horrified, speculative. Holt's name in a whisper. Maya's in another. Someone asking if the killer was still inside. Someone else pushing forward to film the door.

Holt wiped his mouth with the back of his hand, then again, as if trying to erase the taste of bile and cold. His breath wheezed in shaky bursts, too unsteady for speech.

Maya forced herself to stand, only to sway sideways. A paramedic she didn't know grabbed her arm to steady her. She didn't thank him. Her throat was still locked.

Her mind replayed the fifth body in violent flashes — the torn tongue adhered to the concrete, the frost-burned vertebrae, the hand reaching in the wrong direction — images burned so deeply she couldn't blink without seeing one.

Graves stared at the warehouse like he expected it to shift, or breathe, or produce another horror. His eyes were wide, pupils dilated, lashes rimmed with the frost that had clung to all of them inside. He wasn't speaking. He wasn't moving.

It was as if the warehouse had imprinted itself on him.

Holt straightened — barely — wiping his mouth again, gripping the cruiser door so hard his knuckles whitened. His breathing stuttered every few seconds, a violent hitch he couldn't control.

The wind shifted.

Maya didn't feel the cold.

She felt the **absence** of whatever had caused the cold.

Like the void left behind when a deep pressure lifts suddenly.

Inside the warehouse, frost crackled faintly as it continued to adjust to the air.

Across town, while the officers stood shattered and nauseated in the industrial lot, the local news cut live to a simple anchor shot:

"Breaking update — multiple fatalities discovered at a Briar Loop industrial site."

Lila watched the broadcast from her couch.

She stood too fast.

The remote fell to the floor.

Her breath hitched mid-inhale, caught in her chest like something had punched up under her ribs. The camera zoomed in on the warehouse's exterior — the boarded windows, the rusted siding, the sagging door.

Recognition hit her like blunt force.

Her legs buckled.

She dropped to her knees before she understood she was falling.

Her hands hit the carpet.

Her breath tore out of her in fast, uneven pulls.

The room tilted sideways.

A sound escaped her — thin, panicked, wordless.

Her mind flooded with a memory she hadn't asked for: the building's silhouette at dusk, the way the shadows around it bent in ways that didn't match the sun.

She stared at the screen, mouth opening and closing in small, shaky movements, as if forming words might burn.

When she finally whispered, it wasn't a thought.

It was a reflex.

A truth wrested out of the deepest part of her fear:

"I've been there…"

She didn't rise.
She didn't look away from the screen.
She didn't breathe properly for almost thirty seconds.

The broadcast continued.

And the fear—.

It sharpened.

Chapter 14 — Panic Heat

Dispatch had barely finished the sentence before Maya and her partner were already turning into the Briarview Market lot. *"Adult female, conscious, difficulty breathing. Possible fainting episode. Aisle 7."*

Third medical call in under an hour.

Maya grabbed her bag, dropped from the rig, and followed the anxious shoppers pointing toward the automatic doors.

Inside, the air felt strained—tight, uneven. People moved in jittery bursts or stood frozen in place, gripping cart handles hard enough to blanch knuckles. A few whispered to each other, the kinds of half-panicked, half-delusional threads people reached for when they didn't know what else to do.

Maya went straight to Aisle 7.

The woman sat on the floor, back pressed against the shelf, breathing in short, fast bursts that threatened to spiral. The shopping basket beside her had tipped, scattering groceries across the linoleum.

Her boyfriend hovered uselessly, voice shaking. "She said she felt dizzy. Then her chest got tight. She almost passed out—"

"I've got her," Maya said, kneeling.

The woman's skin was slick with cold sweat.

The air around them seemed ordinary.

Maya took her wrist. Fast pulse, unsteady. Panic physiology.

Small clusters of shoppers crowded both ends of the aisle, watching with wide eyes.

"Okay," Maya said softly. "Just breathe with me. Slow as you can."

The woman nodded, though her jaw trembled.

Then the **temperature around them dropped.**

A quick, sharp cold—tight and localized, hitting only the narrow span of floor where Maya knelt.

The woman's breath fogged.

The boyfriend recoiled slightly, eyes widening.

"What was that?" someone whispered.

The fluorescents above flickered once, then steadied.

Maya exhaled slowly, forcing her hands to stay steady.

She glanced past the boyfriend's shoulder.

A **silhouette** stood at the end of the aisle.

Tall.

Narrow.

Bent in a way that made her vision snag for a heartbeat.

It lingered—no more than a blink—then slipped backward into the shadow between an endcap display and the freezer unit.

Not a step.

Not a fade.

Just a shift—depth bending for a split second and then sealing over it.

A dog tied near the pharmacy counter let out a thin, panicked whine. Its claws scraped the tile as it backed against its leash, eyes fixed on the direction where the silhouette had been.

The cold thinned a moment later—quick, uneven.

The woman on the floor cried once, a sharp choke of sound. Her boyfriend wrapped both arms around her, shaking.

Maya steadied her breathing and checked the woman's vitals again. Still fast, but evening out.

Her breaths no longer fogged.

Maya rechecked the woman's pulse, keeping her movements steady even as a faint tremor clung to her fingers. The shoppers at both ends of the aisle hovered in a tight, uneasy hush—eyes fixed on the space behind Maya, then darting away as if they didn't want to hold the thought long enough to name it. She focused on the woman's breathing, on the familiar rhythm of the assessment, letting the routine settle into the strained quiet around them.

Maya barely had time to finish the transfer paperwork before the next call hit.

"Two individuals collapsed outside the Briarview Community Center. Possible panic episode. Multiple callers."

Her partner swung the rig to the curb. The area around the building looked like someone had kicked a hive—families clustered together on the grass, church members whispering fast, frantic prayers, people pacing with their phones clutched tight.

Fear had gravity now.

It pulled people into groups without their permission.

Maya knelt beside the two teenagers on the walkway. Both pale. Both shaking hard enough their teeth clicked. A third man leaned on a railing nearby, chest heaving like he'd lost a sprint.

"What happened?" Maya asked.

One of the teens swallowed. "We walked past the door and—it—it felt wrong. Like stepping next to a freezer in the dark."

His friend nodded quickly, hugging himself. "Then everything went cold. Really cold."

Their vitals matched panic physiology.

But the sweat on their skin had begun to bead into something that didn't match the warm afternoon.

Behind Maya, a knot of people argued — half swearing the place was cursed, others insisting everyone needed to leave.

Then the **temperature dipped.**

A tight drop, centered around the entrance.

The sunlight on Maya's shoulders stayed warm, but the threshold ahead of her rippled with a cold that did not belong to the day.

The teenagers gasped.

The man by the railing doubled over, gagging.

Maya turned her head toward the door—

—and the **doorframe deepened**.

Not visibly.

Not like an illusion.

Like the shadow inside the entry **pulled backward**, stretching the space an extra foot without the architecture actually moving.

For a split second, the interior looked farther away than it should have been—

as if someone tall had leaned back from the threshold just before she looked.

Then something **crossed the ground** near her.

A thin smear of darkness glided across the concrete —

too long, too narrow,

moving **against** the angle of the afternoon sun.

Maya blinked.

It was gone.

The cold tightened once, a short, sharp contraction —

and then let go.

Noise surged back.

People talking too loudly, as if covering something they didn't want to admit they'd noticed.

Maya steadied one teen's breathing, then checked the man leaning on the railing.

Pulse racing.

Skin clammy.

Fear spiraling.

She kept her focus on the work, on the steps she could control, but the doorway behind her felt heavier now — as though whatever had brushed against the threshold had not fully retreated.

Across town Graves had just finished signing off on an overnight report when the PD radios started turning ragged around the edges.

Not loud.

Not chaotic.

Just wrong.

Officers were speaking faster than usual, stepping on each other's transmissions, asking for backup on calls that didn't normally need more than one patrol unit.

"10-56, unknown disturbance on Oakview—crowd forming—request another unit."

"Copy that. Two subjects down in front of the community center—EMS en route—crowd is agitated."

"Briarview Market reporting another collapse. Manager says people are refusing to enter Aisle 7."

"Multiple calls coming in about 'freezing air'—unknown source—advise?"

That last one made Graves tighten his jaw.

He stepped out of his office and into the bullpen just as two officers came through the rear entrance, both looking more rattled than they should have over routine disturbances.

"You two just back from a call?" Graves asked.

The older officer nodded, rubbing the back of his neck. "Group of teenagers at the community center. Two of 'em went down hard. Crowd got jumpy. People swore the doorway was cold enough to see their breath."

"Any environmental cause?" Graves asked.

"Nothing measurable," the officer said. "Sun was out. No breeze."

The younger officer muttered, "People kept moving like something was behind them."

He immediately regretted saying it. Graves saw it in his face.

"So… what? Everyone in town's suddenly hysterical?" Graves said.

No one answered.

He walked to the front windows. Through the glass he could see residents beginning to cluster on the station steps—not panicked, not loud, but drawn by something they couldn't explain. A man stared at the building like he expected someone inside to speak for him.

A woman clutched her coat closed even though the afternoon was warm.

Another radio call came through:

"10-50—caller reporting someone standing in her hallway—officers on scene found nothing."

Graves closed his eyes for a beat.

Rumors were spreading faster than he could put out fires.

He grabbed his jacket and headed through the lobby. As he pulled open the station doors, the murmur outside lifted into a low, uneasy swell.

Not a crowd.

Not a mob.

Just residents gathering in small knots, whispering the same questions, the same fears, the same half-formed impressions that had begun at the grocery store and community center and were now rolling through town like an unseen tide.

Graves stepped onto the top stair and watched all of it.

The shifting glances.

The held breath.

The way people kept checking shadows without meaning to.

Inside, radios kept crackling.

Outside, the street felt one degree tighter.

Nothing dramatic.

Just a town bracing against something it couldn't see.

Holt tried to steady his breathing as he turned onto Pinehurst. The neighborhood didn't feel right. Houses stood too still, the kind of stillness that made his shoulders tense before he understood why. Even the air felt thinner here.

Dispatch repeated the welfare check:

"Caller reports heavy breathing in an empty hallway. No signs of forced entry. No visible subject."

Holt swallowed. His pulse thudded higher than it should have.

"Unit 14 en route," he said into the mic. His voice didn't sound like it belonged to him.

He pulled up to a narrow house with sun-faded siding and a porch light still burning even though it was full daylight. A man stood in the yard hugging himself, staring at the door as if waiting for it to exhale.

"You the one who called?" Holt asked.

The man nodded too quickly. "It was behind me," he stammered. "Not footsteps. Breathing. Deep. I turned around—nothing."

"Anyone else inside?"

"No."

Holt motioned him back and stepped to the door.

Crossing the threshold felt like stepping into a different temperature entirely — a tight ring of cold wrapped around the back of his neck and slid down to his shoulders, sharp enough to make him flinch.

He steadied his flashlight and swept it ahead.

Entryway: still.

Living room: empty.

Kitchen: untouched.

He moved down the hall.

The air grew heavier the farther he went — not colder, not warmer, just thick, as though the walls were leaning in a fraction too close.

Halfway down, a soft scrape whispered above him.

Holt jerked the beam upward.

A strip of darkness hung from the ceiling —

thin, elongated, drooping downward like a length of shadow suspended in the air.

Not moving.

Not swaying.

Just *there*, inches lower than the ceiling should have allowed.

Before he could react, the darkness **dropped farther**, lowering toward him like a slow, deliberate sink of weightless fabric that tugged the air with it.

Holt's lungs clenched.

He stumbled back a step—

—and the ceiling shadow **snapped upward**, vanishing into the seam where plaster met wood.

Holt's flashlight flickered in his hand.

He didn't get a chance to breathe.

A new pressure built behind him.

The wall to his right darkened.

Not the whole wall —

just a rectangular patch of shadow that deepened, then **pressed outward**, bowing in as if something large leaned against it from the other side.

The drywall flexed a millimeter.

Just enough for the eye to catch it.

Just enough to make Holt's stomach drop.

A cold rush swept across the hallway floor, crawling over his boots and up his calves like a rising tide.

His chest tightened —

not panic, not exertion —

just a sudden inability to take a full breath, as if the hallway air had thickened around him.

He tried to inhale.

It caught halfway.

A low, dragging inhale whispered through the hall —

not from ahead,

not from behind,

but from **everywhere** the walls touched.

Holt staggered backward until his shoulders hit the doorframe, forcing himself upright even as numbness crept into his fingers.

The wall-shadow **pulled back** into its corner.

The last of the cold thinned along the floorboards.

Sound rushed back.

The caller's voice cracked from outside. "Officer—? Officer, are you—?"

Holt pushed through the front door, pulling air into his lungs too fast, chest heaving with sharp, uneven breaths.

The man stared at him, pale and shaking.

Holt managed a steady tone only by habit, not because anything felt steady.

"The house is clear," he said.

The man didn't believe him.
Holt wasn't sure he believed himself.

A faint tremor lingered along his spine all the way back to the cruiser —
like something had reached for him
and let go
only when he stepped outside.

Chapter 15 —
Breathing Below

Maya killed the siren before she pulled onto Alder Creek Lane. The street was dark—too dark for a neighborhood where porch lights usually stayed on. Only one was lit now: a dim yellow glow spilling from a small two-story house near the end of the block.

Holt was already out of his cruiser, posture tight, one hand hovering near his sidearm. Maya grabbed her kit and jogged toward him.

The homeowner—a woman in her late forties—stood just outside the front door, arms wrapped around herself, shaking hard enough that her teeth clicked. Her slippers were damp from the lawn. She kept glancing over her shoulder toward the house as if expecting something to follow her out.

Holt spoke first. "Ma'am, you said on the call you heard someone breathing in your basement? Someone you think might be injured?"

The woman nodded quickly—too quickly. "It didn't sound right. It wasn't… normal breathing. It was slow. Heavy. Like somebody trying to catch their breath after—"

She broke off, eyes darting toward the open doorway. "Please. I don't want to go back in there."

Maya stepped closer. "You didn't see anyone? Just heard it?"

"Yes. Right behind the basement door. I thought—" Her voice cracked. "I thought someone fell. Or passed out. I don't know."

That was enough.

Possible intruder.

Possible medical crisis.

"Okay," Maya said quietly. "We'll check. You stay out here where it's safe."

The woman clutched the edge of her robe and nodded, lips trembling.

Holt's eyes flicked to Maya—he waited for her confirmation. She gave a single nod.

They stepped inside.

Cold hit them immediately. Not the soft edge of night air from an open window—this was sharper, more concentrated, like stepping into a room left refrigerated for hours. Maya inhaled reflexively, the chill tightening the inside of her nose.

The thermostat on the wall read sixty-eight.

The air felt closer to fifty.

Holt's flashlight clicked on with a metallic snap. "I'll take point," he muttered.

Maya stayed a few steps behind him, kit held tight at her side. This wasn't the first home where someone thought an injured intruder was hiding, but something about the stillness here made her shoulders draw inward.

The living room looked untouched.

The kitchen was dark, chair half pulled out.

A half-finished mug of tea sat cooling on the table.

Everything felt paused.

Holt stopped in front of a narrow door tucked along the hallway. The frame looked older than the rest of the house—swollen wood, paint cracked along the edges.

"This it?" he asked.

From the doorway, the woman's shaky voice answered, "Yes. That's the basement."

Holt tried the knob.

It resisted.

Not locked—just sticking, like pressure on the other side pushed the wood outward by the smallest fraction.

He leaned his weight into it. The latch gave with a muffled thud, and the door creaked open an inch, exhaling a deeper cold that rolled over Maya's hands, numbing her knuckles.

Holt stiffened.

"You good?" she murmured.

He didn't answer, but he took another breath and pushed the door fully open.

A black rectangle yawned beneath them.

The top stair disappeared into shadow.

Maya clicked her penlight on and stepped up behind him. "If someone's down there and they're hurt, we need to get eyes on them."

Holt nodded without turning. His shoulders were rigid, breath shallow.

They stood at the top of the steps, the cold spilling out in a steady, breathless draft, as if the basement exhaled without stopping.

Maya adjusted her grip on the rail and followed Holt down the first stair.

The basement door sucked a draft inward as soon as Holt opened it the rest of the way. The cold rolling up the stairs had weight to it—heavier than upstairs, almost damp. Maya tightened her grip on the railing and followed Holt down the first step.

The wood creaked under their feet.

Not loud—just sharp in the stillness.

Her penlight's beam hit the basement wall and stopped abruptly, swallowed by the corners in a way that made the room feel narrower than it was. She swept the light slowly, letting her eyes adjust between flashes of illumination and darkness.

Holt's breathing was off.

Too fast.

Too shallow.

She could hear it over the quiet hum of the water heater.

"Stay behind me," he murmured.

His voice shook around the edges.

Maya moved one step at a time, her boots pressing into air that felt several degrees colder with each descent. Halfway down, she paused to steady her footing—the air near her shins had a faint, prickling bite, as if a draft crawled upward from the floor.

The last few steps opened into a wide, unfinished space. The concrete floor was bare. Boxes lined the far wall. A laundry sink stood crooked near the pipes.

Nothing moved.

But the stillness was wrong.

Basements always carried some low-level noise—settling wood, distant plumbing, the refrigerator upstairs. But here, the silence pressed against her ears, thick enough that she kept trying to swallow to clear it.

Holt's flashlight jerked as his hand trembled. The beam swept across stacks of holiday decorations, an old exercise bike, a plastic bin half full of tools.

Maya called softly, "If someone's down here, we need you to answer us."

Only their own breathing came back.

Maya edged farther in, sweeping her light low. A trail of dust near the water heater looked undisturbed—no footprints, no dragging signs. Nothing to mark a person being here at all.

But the cold lingered in an odd way.

Not diffuse.

Centered.

Like it held to one part of the room more than the others.

Holt seemed to feel it too; he shifted his weight, favoring the wall as though keeping distance from the open floor.

"What do you hear?" she whispered.

He didn't answer. His eyes stayed locked on the far wall.

Maya took another step. The cold deepened around her calves—a gradual thickening, not a temperature drop, like the air at that height had a different density entirely.

She aimed her light toward the far end of the basement.

Something faint shifted there—

not movement,

not sound,

just the sense of the dark settling differently, as if the room was holding its breath.

Maya exhaled slowly, listening.

Nothing.

Just the quiet.

The kind of quiet that had weight.

Behind her, Holt's breath stuttered.

She turned her head toward him—but his eyes weren't on her. They were fixed on the wall across from them, pupils blown wide, chest rising and falling too fast.

He whispered, "Do you see that?"

Maya's pulse kicked once, hard.

She followed his gaze and narrowed her light on the far wall.

The shadows there didn't settle cleanly.

They clung a half-second too long before shifting, as though something behind the wall breathed slower than the room around it.

Holt's breath hitched.

"Do you see that?" he whispered.

Maya didn't answer. She stepped beside him, angling her light from a different direction. The beam caught the wall, brightened the concrete, pushed the dark back—

—and the darkness **moved** just a fraction behind it, lagging as though reluctant to follow.

Just a **delay**, subtle but unmistakable, like the wall's shadow was thinking before it responded.

A soft scrape whispered across the floor—
too faint to be footsteps,
too steady to be settling boards.

Holt flinched back hard enough to rattle the metal shelving behind him. His flashlight jittered across the ceiling, beam jumping with the tremor in his hand.

"Something's in here," he said, voice cracking. "Something's—"

The next breath he tried to take collapsed halfway.

His chest pumped shallow, frantic, like his lungs couldn't decide how to fill. He pressed a hand to the wall to steady himself, fingers digging into the concrete block as if trying to anchor his body in place.

Maya reached for him. "Holt—"

But Holt shook his head fast, eyes locked wide on the far wall. His pupils swallowed most of the color, leaving only two dark circles staring into a darker patch of basement.

The cold dipped sharply, not everywhere—
just in a tight radius around Holt's legs.
A narrowing band, like the floor itself had turned colder beneath him.

His throat clicked as he tried to swallow.

"I can hear it," he whispered.

Maya held still, breath caught in her own chest.

She didn't hear breathing.

But the air around them had changed.

It pressed in at a different angle, thinner on one side, thicker on the other, as though the basement's quiet had shifted its weight.

Holt backed toward the stairs, one slow step at a time, never turning away from the wall.

The shadows **lagged again**—
a beat out of sync with the motion of Maya's flashlight,
a stuttering delay that made her skin crawl.

"Holt," she said softly, "go."

He didn't wait for her to say it twice.

Holt turned and stumbled up the stairs, boots striking the wood too fast, breath tearing in sharp, broken bursts. By the time he reached the landing, the banister clattered under the force of him grabbing it.

The basement swallowed the sound he left behind.

Maya stood alone on the concrete floor, the quiet deepening around her—
a heavy, expectant kind of stillness
that felt like the room had just emptied
when nothing had moved at all.

The cold around her legs pulsed once—
a faint contraction, subtle enough she might have missed it if she hadn't been standing so still.

The basement didn't feel empty.
It felt paused.

She swept her penlight toward the far wall again, slow and steady, watching for anything out of place. The beam cut across stacks of boxes, the laundry sink, the concrete blocks. Nothing moved.

Then the breathing stopped.

Not gradually.
Not fading.

Just—
gone.

The silence that followed had weight to it, like the basement had filled with too much air and not enough sound. Maya's nostrils stung with the cold as she inhaled, careful and shallow, trying to pick up anything she'd missed.

Her light jittered once as her grip tightened. The shadows on the far wall held their shape a second longer than expected before settling. She took a step back, eyes darting between the corners and the center of the room.

The cold shifted again—
not spreading,
just lifting a little from the floor,
as though whatever pressed it downward had loosened its hold.

"Holt?" she called up the stairs.

She heard him somewhere near the living room—boots scraping, breath ragged, the muffled sound of him bracing himself against something.

"I'm here," he managed. His voice was thin.

Maya scanned the basement one more time. Her light found nothing. No movement. No drag marks. No sign of anyone.

Still, the room felt wrong.

She climbed the stairs slowly, one hand on the rail, her penlight angled behind her until the last possible step. The cold receded a little more with each rise, thinning into the natural chill of unfinished wood and concrete.

At the landing, she paused, letting her eyes adjust to the softer light coming from the hallway.

"Holt," she said gently.

He stood with both hands on the wall near the doorway, trying to steady his breathing. Sweat had beaded along his hairline despite the cold.

"You okay?" she asked.

He nodded once, not trusting his voice.

Maya stepped aside to give him space.

He pushed past her toward the living room, shoulders hunched, head down.

Only after she turned away from the basement did the last piece of movement occur.

A long, stretched shadow—
one she had illuminated moments earlier—
peeled itself a fraction off the concrete wall,
lifting with a slow, reluctant drag,
like a strip of darkness pulled free from something it had been resting against.

It paused—
floating a finger's width off the surface—
then slid back into place,
settling flat a beat behind the rest of the room's shadows.

Maya didn't see it.

She only felt the last thread of cold lift off her spine as she stepped fully into the hallway, closing the basement door behind her.

Chapter 16 — Wounds That Match

Graves hadn't finished his first cup of coffee when the fourth missing-persons alert hit his terminal.

The first had come in at 5:42 a.m.

A grocery clerk who never made it home after locking up for the night. The store cameras showed him walking across the lot. They didn't show him reaching his car.

The second pinged an hour later.

A retiree who walked the same route every morning for twenty-two years. His dog was found circling the sidewalk, leash dragging across the concrete.

The third landed at 7:18 a.m.

A seventeen-year-old whose friends swore they saw him leave the parking lot after early practice. He never arrived at first period.

The fourth broke whatever thin illusion of routine Graves had been clinging to.

A night-shift nurse who'd clocked out at the hospital at 6:03 a.m. Her badge was still in her scrubs pocket. Her car never left the lot.

No struggle.

No sign of flight.

No witnesses.

Just absence.

Graves logged each report automatically, fingers moving before his thoughts caught up. By the time he pulled the precinct map down from the wall, the morning light had barely reached the windows.

He marked the locations one by one, red ink bleeding slightly into the paper where he pressed too hard.

Four new points.

Neatly spaced.

Too neatly.

He stepped back a few feet.

The arc expanded.

Not wildly.

Not jagged.

Smooth.

Deliberate.

As if something were growing outward in quiet, widening breaths.

He didn't trust the feeling crawling up his spine, so he forced himself to check the geometry again. The distances between the vanishings sat almost equidistant from the older sites. The pattern held even when he tried to approach it from another angle.

A deeper unease tightened beneath his ribs.

He pushed the pins in more firmly and drew a slow, shallow curve connecting the fresh marks to the earlier ones. The line curved outward from the woods, the same direction the early kills had pushed before everything spiraled.

It looked like expansion.

Methodical.

Patient.

Predictable in a way nothing about this case had the right to be.

He didn't say the word pattern.

He didn't have to.

The map said it without permission.

A knock hit his doorframe.

Officer Weller leaned in. "Another family's here asking if you've got updates on the hospital disappearance."

Graves nodded without looking up. "Tell them we're coordinating with hospital security and the sheriff's office."

Weller hesitated. "Sir... that's four in two days."

"Log it," Graves said. The words came out flat. "All of them go in the same folder."

He closed the precinct door after Weller left and exhaled through his teeth. The air in the office felt tight, like someone had shut the vent without telling him.

He checked the clock.

7:41 a.m.

Four disappearances in that span should have felt chaotic.

They didn't.

They felt arranged.

He turned back to the map.

The crescent widened again when he connected the grocery clerk's dot.

Widened further with the nurse.

Graves swallowed once, jaw tightening.

Whatever was happening wasn't slowing.

It wasn't scattering.

It was... escalating.

He didn't let himself finish the thought.

He picked up the phone and requested the forensic updates still pending from the industrial building scene. His voice stayed steady, but something inside him wasn't steady at all.

The map waited behind him, the curve unmistakable, widening like the slow pull of a tide he couldn't see but could feel in his teeth.

And the morning kept going.

The call from the lab came just after nine.

Graves didn't ask questions over the phone; the tone in Harrow's voice was enough. He left the squad room, crossed the lot, and walked the short block to the forensic wing behind municipal operations.

The morning had warmed, but the building's interior felt colder than it should have — the kind of refrigerated morgue chill designed for stainless steel, sealed drawers, and air that never moved unless a vent forced it.

Harrow waited by one of the examination counters, a tablet under his arm, a printed folder beside him. He didn't bother with small talk.

"We completed the trauma comparisons you requested," he said. "You need to see them yourself."

Graves stepped to the counter. Harrow set the folder down and opened the first panel — modern autopsy photos aligned beside the archival images Graves had asked the lab to pull from storage.

It took a full second for the images to make sense.

The rib fractures weren't just similar.

They were exact — the same angle of outward flare, the same distortion along the cartilage, the same unnatural bend as though something had expanded inside the thoracic cavity with sudden, violent pressure.

Harrow tapped the archival side of the page.

"Oregon case, 1911," he said. "Victim three."

He tapped the modern side.

"Warehouse victim two."

The fractures lined up as if one image had been printed over the other.

Harrow flipped to the next comparison.

"Cold halos," he said.

Three of the warehouse victims had shown a ring of localized frostbite along the sternum and upper abdomen. The archival photo beside it — a century old, yellowed at the corners — showed the exact same ring, same shape, same feathered radius of thaw along the edges.

Graves tried to speak, but his voice caught behind his teeth.

"Environmental temperatures wouldn't produce that."

"They didn't," Harrow said. "Ambient readings at the warehouse were low, but not low enough for patterned frostbite. And the distribution here—" He pointed to the archival photo. "—is identical."

He turned to the third set.

Modern tissue samples — photographed under magnification — were shown beside historical slides. Both displayed micro-lacerations along organ surfaces, tiny tears arranged in irregular arcs. When Harrow zoomed closer on the modern slide, Graves saw the same pattern repeated: vacuum-force collapse that looked like suction damage without an implement.

"These micro-tears were verified with electron microscopy," Harrow said. "They're not artifacts. They're real. And they match two archived cases from 1934 and 1952."

Graves swallowed hard.

The edges of the counter felt too sharp beneath his palms.

"Any possible equipment overlap?" Graves asked. "Shared pathology methods? Contaminated slides?"

"No," Harrow said. "Every archival sample was independently preserved, catalogued, and stored. Chain of custody is intact. Nothing overlaps."

He slid a final transparency across the counter — an alignment overlay Harrow had printed for personal verification. On one layer: modern rib fractures. On the other: the 1911 case.

Stacked together, the fractures matched like traced outlines.

The room seemed to tilt a fraction.

"This isn't coincidence," Harrow said quietly. "And it isn't a copycat. These injury signatures are identical in a way that shouldn't be possible across generations."

Graves didn't answer.

He couldn't.

For a moment, the only sound was the distant hum of the ventilation system pushing cold air through steel ducts.

Harrow closed the folder. "All files are uploading to your secure directory."

Graves nodded once, mechanical, then turned toward the hallway.

The lights overhead buzzed faintly as he passed beneath them.

It wasn't the noise that stayed with him —

it was the way the photographs kept replaying behind his eyes, modern ribs bending in the same impossible shape as ribs broken a century before.

Graves didn't go back to his office right away. He walked the precinct halls once, twice, as if the movement might settle the pressure gathering beneath his ribs. It didn't.

By the time he reached the squad room again, he already knew who he needed.

He called Maya first.

"Can you come to the station?" he asked. "I need you to look at something from your side of things."

She didn't ask what. She just said, "On my way," and hung up.

Then he called Vander.

The historian answered on the second ring, sounding like he'd been awake for hours already, which didn't surprise Graves. "You said to call if anything matched the old clusters," Graves said. "I have material you need to see."

There was a pause. Not excitement. Not fear. Just quiet recognition.

"I'll be there in twenty."

Now that he knew there were patterns, he flagged several earlier interviews for routine follow-up — standard procedure whenever a case widened. Graves sent the notices out before heading to one of the small briefing rooms.

He cleared a table—just steel, laminate, and a humming overhead fixture that flickered once when he turned it on. He set the forensic photos down first. Printed out, the trauma looked even worse. More real. More impossible.

Maya arrived moments later, still in her EMS jacket, hair pulled back tight, the look of someone who'd been running calls since dawn. She closed the door behind her and approached the table without waiting for an explanation.

"You said you needed my notes," she said.

Graves pointed to the first panel. "The warehouse victims."

She studied the frost halos first, her brow tightening. "These rings match what I saw on the man from the earlier cold-call—the one in the apartment hallway." She traced the edge of the frost pattern with her finger without touching it. "Same radius. Same thinning around the edges."

"What about the rigidity?" Graves asked.

Maya nodded slowly. "The stiffening we saw didn't match the time-of-death window. Not even close. And... the shadow displacement at a couple scenes..." She stopped herself, jaw flexing. "Well. You know."

He did. And he didn't.

Before he could respond, Vander stepped into the room, carrying a satchel so worn it looked like it had survived three decades of bad weather. He nodded once to Graves, then once to Maya, then set his materials on the table with quiet purpose.

"You said the wounds matched?" Vander asked.

Graves slid the modern photos toward him.

Vander didn't sit. He stood over the table, leaning just close enough for the overhead light to catch the lines in his face. The archival scans he pulled from his satchel were carefully sleeved in plastic—handwritten dates at the corners, yellowed edges preserved under transparent film.

He placed the 1911 image beside the modern one.

Maya's breath caught sharply. Graves wasn't sure if she'd meant for the sound to escape.

The rib fractures lined up.

The same outward flare.

The same internal distortion.

The same anatomical collapse that no known injury mechanism could produce naturally.

Vander didn't speak for several seconds. He only lowered another sheet—a disappearance map from an early twentieth-century cluster. Red dots traced an arc along the edge of a wooded area, expanding outward in smooth, deliberate spacing.

Maya stared at it, then at Graves' current precinct map pinned on the wall behind him.

"That's the same curve," she said quietly.

"It is," Vander murmured.

Graves felt something cold settle behind his sternum. Not environmental cold. Not supernatural. Just the realization of impossible repetition.

"Look at this," Vander said, sliding forward a third archival photo—this one from 1934. It showed the same frost-ring pattern Maya had just identified on the modern victim. "Same trauma. Same environmental signature. Same geographic widening pattern."

Graves couldn't deny what sat in front of him.

Not coincidence.

Not misfiled records.

Not a copycat mimicking century-old injuries.

Something was repeating itself with mathematical precision.

He braced his hands on the table and leaned in, jaw tight.

"What you're showing me..." he said quietly, eyes locked on the overlay Vander had matched against the modern photo, "...shouldn't exist."

There was no argument.

Not from Maya.

Not from Vander.

The briefing room held only the hum of the fluorescent light and the impossible truth laid flat across the table between them.

Vander unfolded one last sheet—a hand-drawn journal entry, dated 1907, the ink browned with age. The sketch wasn't graphic, just a rough outline of a human torso with ribs flared outward in the same unnatural shape they had just seen in both the warehouse victims and the 1911 case.

He laid it beside the modern photograph.

The match was immediate.

Perfect.

Wrong.

Maya pressed her fingertips lightly against the edge of the table, not touching anything, just anchoring herself. "This isn't variation," she said softly. "These aren't different injuries. They're... the same."

Vander nodded. "Across decades. Across locations. Across environmental conditions." He tapped the old map he'd brought—another crescent widening outward from a central cluster of disappearances. "Even the spacing holds."

Maya moved closer to Graves' precinct map, eyes narrowing. "These two vanishings..." she said quietly. "They fell along here." She traced the most recent points with careful precision. "And they're spreading the same way." She glanced back at the archival map Vander had placed beside it. "The exact same way."

Graves' jaw tightened. "There were four more."

She looked sharply at him. "Four?"

"This morning," he said. "All of them."

The room felt tighter around them—not colder, not darker, just smaller, like the air itself had drawn in.

Graves stood absolutely still.

His gaze moved between the images—modern ribs, century-old ribs, frost halos separated by generations, shadow-distorted sketches recorded before electricity reached half the town. None of it drifted. None of it varied. None of it reflected the kind of chaotic spread violence usually carried.

It was steady.

Predictable.

Methodical.

Vander set down his final piece of evidence: a short ledger of names from the early 1900s case cluster. Nine in total. Each marked with the same injury notations.

"This is how far it went before the last recorded surge," Vander said quietly. "Nine."

Maya looked back at Graves' map. "We're at six."

Graves didn't answer.

He didn't look away from the evidence.

The pattern wasn't subtle anymore.

It wasn't speculative.

It wasn't something he could dismiss as misinterpretation or folklore or coincidence stretched too thin.

It was repeating.

His jaw tightened once, a small involuntary movement he couldn't stop. When he finally spoke, his voice held no edge, no performative disbelief, no attempt at skepticism.

Just the flat, inevitable truth.

"This isn't human."

No one argued.

Vander didn't move.

Maya didn't blink.

The evidence stayed where it was, cold and silent under the fluorescent lights.

A faint draft brushed across the briefing table—not cold enough to register, not strong enough to draw attention, just a whisper of air that didn't belong in a closed room.

None of them noticed it.

They were all staring at the maps.

Chapter 17 — Three Myths, One Maw

The briefing room had barely settled after Maya and Vander finished comparing the historical crescent map to the modern one when movement in the doorway made Graves turn.

Carla stood there—shoulders tense but held together, one arm around Lila as if shielding her from a room she didn't fully understand. Lila stepped just inside, backpack strap twisted in her fingers, eyes lowered almost to her shoes.

"Detective Graves," Carla said quietly. "We got your follow-up notice. It said you needed to talk to Lila again."

Graves nodded, straightening. "Thank you for coming in."

Carla exhaled once, a steadying breath, then guided Lila farther into the room.

Only then did Lila lift her gaze.

Her eyes landed on Maya.

The shift was immediate—a small, startled intake of breath, the way someone reacts when finding the one steady thing in a place that feels foreign. She moved toward Maya without thinking, as if the sight of her pulled her forward.

Maya stepped around the table. "Hey," she said softly.

Lila didn't smile. Didn't speak. But the terror in her posture eased by a fraction.

Carla brushed Lila's shoulder and looked toward Graves. "We weren't sure what this was about. The notice didn't say." She tried to sound firm, but worry crept around the edges. "Just that she needed to come in."

"It's routine," Graves said. "We're revisiting everyone from the initial interviews."

Carla nodded and stepped back enough to give Lila space.

Graves motioned them inside. Vander closed his journal with deliberate care but remained where he was, observing without intruding.

Lila sat slowly, pulling her backpack onto her lap like a barrier she wasn't sure she needed. Her hands stayed wrapped around the strap.

Maya took the chair beside her.

For a long moment, Lila didn't speak. She only stared at the table, jaw clenched tight, as though holding something far heavier than the room around her.

Finally, she whispered, "Is this… about him?"

Graves didn't push. "It's just a follow-up," he said. "You don't have to talk about anything you're not ready for."

Lila shook her head—not in refusal, but in something closer to dread. "I don't… I don't want to talk about that night."

Maya leaned in slightly. "Then don't start there."

Lila swallowed hard. Her fingers tightened.

"I didn't tell you everything," she said softly.

Carla went still.

Maya's voice stayed steady. "What didn't you tell us?"

Lila lifted her eyes, and the look in them was older than she was, worn down by years of trying not to remember.

"It's been happening since I was little," she whispered. "Before the boy. Before all of this."

Vander's posture shifted—sharpening, but silent.

Graves stayed where he was, letting her speak.

Lila's breath shook once. "You have to promise you won't think I'm lying."

Maya didn't even blink. "I'm listening."

Lila nodded, small, fragile.

And then she said it:

"It wasn't the first time I saw it."

Lila didn't look at Graves when she said it.

She looked at Maya.

Her voice stayed thin, almost weightless. "It was… a long time ago. I was little. Maybe six. I don't remember the exact age."

Carla's hand lifted to her mouth again, fingers trembling before she forced them down.

Maya kept her expression steady, neutral but open. "Take your time."

Lila nodded once, though it didn't make speaking any easier. "It happened at the hospital first. When my uncle was dying." She swallowed, throat clicking. "I remember being in the hallway with my mom. I wasn't supposed to go in the room, but the door wasn't closed all the way."

Carla's eyes squeezed shut.

Lila's breathing hitched—just once. "The machines were beeping. I remember that. And someone said he didn't have much longer." She stared down at her shoes. "And then I saw something move next to the bed."

Maya didn't move.

Vander's head tilted slightly, the way someone adjusts to hear a particular frequency.

Graves stayed very still.

"It was tall," Lila whispered. "Bent over. Like it was leaning down toward him. I thought it was a nurse at first, but the shape was wrong." Her fingers twisted the backpack strap until her knuckles whitened. "The head… it was too low. Like it was looking at him without bending its knees."

Carla's breath escaped in a soft, pained sound.

"I told Mom there was someone in the room," Lila said. "But when she looked, no one was there. She told me I imagined it." She swallowed again. "I tried to believe her."

Maya didn't speak. Didn't comfort. She let Lila keep going.

"It didn't happen again for a while," Lila said, voice drifting as if she were following the memory down a long hall. "Not until the hallway at home."

Carla shifted—a protective, helpless reflex.

Lila pressed on. "It was late. I'd gotten up to use the bathroom. I didn't turn the light on because I didn't want to wake anyone. And when I stepped into the hall…"

Her voice lowered even further.

"…the shadow at the end wasn't right."

Maya's spine tightened, but she didn't interrupt.

"It was stretched," Lila said. "Too long. Too thin. Like it didn't fit the shape of the wall." She lifted her eyes finally, meeting Maya's. "And it was facing me."

The room went still.

Graves didn't blink.

Vander's hand hovered above his journal, not writing—just listening.

Lila's voice cracked for the first time. "I froze. I couldn't breathe. I remember trying to scream but nothing came out. And then it…" She shook her head. "It leaned. Just a little. Like it was looking down the hall at me. But nothing else moved. Not the lights, not the air, just the shadow."

She wiped her face quickly with the back of her sleeve, embarrassed by the tears.

Maya reached out but didn't touch her, giving her the choice.

Lila took the gesture and leaned in slightly, like a plant reaching instinctively toward warmth.

Carla's voice broke into the quiet. "I thought she was having night terrors," she said softly. "She was terrified. For months." Her voice thinned. "I never saw anything. I thought she'd had a bad scare at the hospital and it stayed with her."

Lila shook her head. "It wasn't a dream."

No one in the room doubted her now.

She drew one unsteady breath and continued. "And then... then came the Cucuy warnings."

Vander's attention sharpened instantly.

"My grandma used to tell me stories," Lila whispered. "About a shadow that followed kids who were scared. I thought she was just trying to keep me from wandering at night. But she said it always looked bent. And it didn't make sense at the time, but she said: 'You'll know it's close when the shadow isn't yours.'"

Maya's jaw tightened.

Vander finally wrote something down—one single line, slow and deliberate.

"And then what?" Maya asked softly.

Lila looked between the three adults, as if deciding whether to continue.

Her voice trembled. "I think... I think it's the same one."

She lifted one hand and pointed downward—toward the floor, toward the memory that had brought her here.

"The thing that was with my uncle. The one in the hallway. The one Grandma warned me about."

A shiver ran up her shoulders.

"And the one that followed the boy."

Maya steadied her.

Carla swallowed hard.

Vander closed his eyes once, as if the pieces had clicked into place exactly where he feared they would.

Graves stared at Lila with an expression he had never worn before:

Not disbelief.

Not skepticism.

Not dismissal.

Recognition.

Lila's last words hung in the briefing room like a draft that had slipped under the door.

Carla blinked hard, once, twice—her expression tightening in a way that had nothing to do with belief and everything to do with fear she refused to name.

"Honey..." she said cautiously. "You've had nightmares like this. You told me about shadows after Javier died. You were grieving. You were scared. That's all this is."

Lila shook her head. "It wasn't a nightmare."

Carla took a step closer, voice firmer now, the tone of a mother trying to re-ground a child spiraling into memory. "Sweetheart, these things feel real when you're small. And when you're upset. It doesn't mean they *were* real."

Lila's fingers dug into the backpack strap. "I wasn't small in the hallway. I was ten."

Carla's jaw tightened—just a flash of anger at herself, not at Lila. "And you were barely sleeping then. You remember? The panic attacks? You were seeing shapes in every shadow. I stayed up with you half the night for weeks."

Maya watched the exchange with careful stillness.

"Mom, this wasn't a panic attack," Lila whispered.

Carla forced a soft, soothing tone she didn't feel. "Baby, you're remembering fear. Fear gets mixed up over time. Shadows look strange when we're upset. Kids remember things wrong. Adults do too."

Lila's breath hitched.

Carla turned toward Maya—not confrontational, but desperate for backup. "Maya, please—tell her it was just trauma. She trusts you."

Maya's throat tightened. She didn't answer.

Carla's face changed—bewilderment crashing into the silence. "Why aren't you saying anything?"

Graves stayed still.

Vander didn't even blink.

Carla's pulse stuttered visibly in her neck. "You can't seriously be—Maya, she's a child. She's been through hell this week. She's terrified. She's remembering shadows from years ago. That's all."

Lila lifted her eyes, trembling but certain. "It's the same one."

"Lila." Carla's voice broke, but her denial didn't. "Shadows can look bent. Lights distort. Hallways—and hospitals especially—can make things seem off. Your mind fills in the rest. That's what happens in nightmares."

"It wasn't a nightmare," Lila said again. Soft but steady.

Carla pressed her lips together. "Then why didn't you tell me? If it was real, if it was happening again, why wouldn't you say something?"

"Because you didn't believe me last time."

Carla flinched as if struck. "Because you were a child waking up screaming about shadows leaning at you! What was I supposed to think?" Her voice wavered. "I thought you needed comfort. I thought you needed to feel safe."

Lila wiped a tear with the cuff of her sleeve. "It leaned again."

Carla's breath trembled. "No. No, sweetheart. You're scared. You're mixing things up. Anyone would."

Lila's voice cracked. "It was at the fence."

Carla's eyes filled. "It was dark. You were upset. That's all."

"It was at the end of the street last night."

Carla shook her head immediately, too quickly. "No. Absolutely not. You didn't see anything. You couldn't have. You're telling a story your mind made out of being terrified about that boy. That's what this is."

Lila whispered, "I know what I saw."

Carla's hands trembled, but she clung to her disbelief like a life raft. "You had a horrible week. You're grieving someone who was kind to you. Your mind is trying to make sense of it. Shadows, fences, shapes—our brains connect things that aren't connected."

She looked around the room—desperate, pleading, confused at the silence.

"Somebody say something," she whispered. "Please."

But Maya only tightened her grip on Lila's hand.

Graves' jaw clicked once.

Vander's gaze tracked every word Lila spoke with unnerving focus.

Carla felt the shift in the room but didn't understand it—and would not accept it.

Her voice dropped to a raw, trembling denial.

"Lila… these are nightmares. Nothing more."

Lila finally met her mother's eyes.

"They're not nightmares," she said. "They never were."

The room stayed silent after Lila's last words—silent long enough that the hum of the fluorescent light grew loud enough to feel like pressure.

Carla shook her head again, slower now, disbelief hardening into something brittle. "Lila… honey, listen to me. You're exhausted. You've barely slept since—since that night. Fear can make the world look wrong. It doesn't mean it *is* wrong."

Lila stared at the table. "It was there."

"No," Carla whispered, as if saying it softly might make it true. "Sweetheart, no. You saw a shape. A person. A shadow. Something explainable."

Lila didn't answer.

Maya did. Her voice stayed steady, but there was weight under it. "Carla… she's not describing a nightmare."

Carla looked at her sharply, wounded. "Don't you start. She trusts you. You can't feed into this."

"I'm not feeding anything," Maya said. "I'm listening."

Carla's jaw clenched, trembling with the effort not to scream or cry or both. "And what exactly are you hearing?"

Maya didn't answer that. She couldn't—not without saying something Carla wasn't ready to hear.

Vander finally leaned forward—not imposing, not interrupting, just shifting his weight enough to speak without crowding anyone.

"Lila," he said carefully, "did you notice anything else? Before the fence? Before last night?"

Carla cut in immediately. "No. She didn't. She hasn't. She's been home—she's been with me. She hasn't seen anything."

Lila's shoulders hunched. "I didn't tell you everything."

Carla froze.

Vander continued, gentle. "You said it happened in the hallway. And in the hospital. But was there something… more recent?"

Lila nodded once, barely.

Carla took a small step back, confusion flickering across her face like static. "More recent? When? Lila—when?"

Lila's voice thinned to a whisper. "A few nights before the boy died."

Carla's hands rose reflexively to her hairline, gripping her scalp as if she could hold reality still. "No. No, you didn't say anything. You would have told me. You always tell me when you're scared—"

Lila shook her head.

Carla's breath cracked open. "Why didn't you tell me?"

"Because you'd think it was another nightmare."

Carla's eyes filled, denial colliding with hurt. "I'm your mother. You tell me things like that. You *should.*"

Lila examined the strap of her backpack, voice soft and small. "You wanted it to be nightmares. So I let you believe that."

The blow landed—clean, quiet, devastating.

Carla's throat closed. She turned away, hands on her hips, blinking hard as if she could rearrange the last decade of parenting by force of will.

Graves didn't interrupt. He couldn't. His composure had thinned to something taut and brittle, like he was holding back more thoughts than speech.

Vander watched Lila with the focus of a man who had seen this pattern before—

in journals, in case files, in children grown old before their time.

He didn't soften his voice or sharpen it.

He asked a question that mattered.

"Lila… when you saw it near the fence—was it facing you? Or the house?"

Lila's eyes drifted toward Maya, then down to her own knees.

"It was facing my window," she whispered.

Carla spun back, eyes wide. "No. No, you're not telling this right. You saw a shadow from the streetlight, or the neighbor's cat, or—"

"Mom," Lila said, barely audible. "It leaned again."

Carla stopped talking.

The denial didn't leave her face—but it wavered, just enough to show the fear underneath.

Vander exhaled slowly, the sound too measured to be casual.

Graves finally spoke, voice low. "Lila… this thing you've been seeing… how long has it been happening?"

Lila's voice thinned. "Since before the hospital. Before Javier. Before we moved. I think…" She swallowed. "…I think it's always been there. And I didn't know until it got closer."

Carla whispered, "Stop. Please. Stop."

Lila's tears finally spilled over.

Maya reached for her hand again. This time, Lila clung back hard.

Vander watched the two of them, a single line digging deeper between his brows.

Graves stared at Lila with a look he hadn't worn once since the boy's body was found—

not skepticism,

not discomfort,

but a dawning, nauseating realization of something that couldn't be unlearned.

Carla, still clinging to the last logic she had, pressed the heel of her palm to her forehead.

"This is because she misses him," Carla whispered. "It's grief. It's trauma. Kids see things when they're hurting. They connect things that aren't connected. This isn't real. It can't be real."

Lila wiped her cheeks with the cuff of her sleeve.

"I know what's real," she said softly. "I've known for years."

No one corrected her.

No one reassured Carla.

No one told Lila she imagined it.

Because for the first time in her life—

she was saying it in the only room in the world where it *was* real.

Chapter 18 — Holt's Last Night

Holt had pushed his couch against the front door hours ago, jamming it into the frame until the legs scraped deep grooves into the hardwood. Every lamp in the apartment burned. The television hissed static he couldn't remember switching to. His phone lay on the coffee table, screen cracked from where he'd dropped it earlier.

He sat on the floor with his back against the far wall, knees pulled up, breath sawing unevenly in and out. Sweat soaked through the collar of his shirt despite the cool air drifting from the vent above him.

He couldn't stay still.

Every few seconds his eyes flicked toward the hallway—
to the dark seam at the end of it
to the bathroom door he'd triple-checked
to the thin line of shadow under the bedroom frame that didn't look the same length every time he blinked.

He'd tried to tell himself none of it meant anything. He'd tried to listen to the rational part of his brain, the part that still knew how to talk like a cop, how to explain things away.

But the rational part was losing its grip.

His chest tightened hard enough to make him shove a fist against his sternum. His breathing came too fast, and then too shallow, and then stalled completely for two horrible beats before returning in a sharp, panicked gasp.

"Stop," he whispered. "Just... stop."

He squeezed his eyes shut.

It didn't help.

The darkness behind his eyelids pulsed once—
a low, heavy push like something large shifting its weight in a room he couldn't see.

Holt's eyes snapped open.

He grabbed his phone with a shaking hand and fumbled for the camera. The screen blurred as he lifted it, the lens catching the trembling of his fingers. He didn't start recording because he felt brave. He started recording because he didn't trust his own senses anymore, and he needed something—anything—to confirm what was real and what wasn't.

The hallway light flickered once.

Just once.

Barely.

But his breath punched out of him like he'd been struck.

There was nothing visible in the hallway. No movement. No sound.

Still, Holt lifted the phone higher, zooming in on the dark shape at the far end of the carpet runner. The edges of the shadow along the baseboard looked wrong—too sharp on one side, too soft on the other, like it hadn't formed at the same time as the rest of the room.

"Don't," he whispered to himself. "Don't look at it. Don't give it anything."

His hand wouldn't lower.

A cold pulse rolled through the apartment. Not winter cold. Not open-window cold. A tightening, internal cold that pressed into his ribs from the inside, the way panic sometimes clawed up the throat before a person realized they were afraid.

The phone camera's exposure jumped, the screen whitening for a fraction of a second as though the sensor tried to compensate for a temperature drop it couldn't understand.

Holt's breath stuttered again.

He wiped his face with the back of his hand, smearing sweat down to his jaw. The air tasted metallic. He didn't know why. He didn't want to know.

Another flicker.

Not the lights this time.

A shape at the far end of the hallway pulled back a fraction, like a retreating silhouette—but only for a blink, only for a single stuttering frame of motion. Then it was gone. Or had never been there.

The phone trembled so hard it nearly slipped from his grip.

"Just stop," Holt whispered again, voice cracking. "Please. Stop."

He slid down the wall until he was half slumped on the floor, the phone angled upward toward the hallway without meaning to. His breathing turned ragged, uneven, his ribs expanding too fast and then hitching.

He closed his eyes for half a second—

—and something shifted in the corner beyond the bathroom door.

A soft, dragging inhale that wasn't his.

Holt's whole body jerked. His eyes snapped open.

The hallway was empty.

But his pulse hammered so violently it made his vision blur, and the air felt wrong again—thinner near the ceiling, thicker near the floor, as if the room had been rearranged around him when he blinked.

His thumb slid over the phone screen, smearing sweat across the glass.

He didn't know if he was recording his last night or trying to convince himself he wasn't already inside something else's hunting ground.

He only knew he couldn't look away.

And the hallway—
that narrow stretch of darkness at the far end of the carpet—
seemed to breathe with him.

Or against him.

He couldn't tell which.

The lights steadied again, but Holt didn't trust them. He pushed himself upright, joints stiff, and backed toward the living room without taking his eyes off the hallway. His phone stayed raised in front of him, screen glowing against the dark.

The air tasted colder. Not sharply—just enough that every breath scraped a little at the back of his throat.

He tried to swallow. It didn't go down clean.

A soft tap sounded behind him.

Not loud. Not sudden.

Just a gentle, deliberate bump against the windowpane.

Holt spun, camera jerking wildly.

Nothing outside.

Just the streetlight haloing the empty lot across from his building, the branches of the elm tree shivering in the wind—
except the wind wasn't blowing.

He focused the camera on the glass. His heartbeat thudded against his ribs in uneven, painful pulses.

A thin lace of frost touched the lower corner of the pane. Not spreading. Not receding. Just resting there, delicate and wrong.

Holt wiped the sweat from his forehead with a shaking hand.

"Don't," he whispered to no one. "Don't come in here."

His voice sounded too thin, too small in the apartment.

He turned back toward the hallway.

The dark shape at the end had changed.

Not much. Barely a shift. But the shadow near the bathroom was deeper—denser—like the light couldn't quite reach it now, even though the bulb overhead burned steady.

Holt's breath stuttered in his throat.

He raised the phone higher, zooming in. The pixel edges stuttered, catching some interference he couldn't name. Then the image steadied, showing only stillness.

The hallway didn't move.

But Holt did.

He stepped backward again, bumping into the side table. A framed photo rattled—him and Graves at a precinct barbecue two summers ago, laughing at something Holt couldn't even remember now.

He nearly dropped the phone.

The air thickened.

Not everywhere—just behind him. A subtle weight, as if someone stood too close, leaning over his shoulder, breathing in very slowly.

Holt couldn't turn around.

His diaphragm spasmed. His breath hitched halfway through the inhale, chest seizing like his lungs couldn't expand fully.

"No," he whispered. "No—no—"

A cold thread slid along the back of his neck, thin as a fingertip tracing downward.

He gasped and staggered away from the wall, clutching the phone like it was the only thing anchoring him to the room.

The hallway deepened again.

A patch of shadow near the floor pulled inward for a second—
as if something drew breath from inside the dark—
then relaxed back into place.

Holt's knees nearly buckled.

He aimed the camera down the hall again, hands trembling so badly the frame jittered in sharp, nauseating pulses. The lens caught a flicker—something tall, something bent—
and then the exposure blew out in a wash of white.

When the picture returned, the hall was empty.

Holt's mouth had gone dry. He tried to steady his breathing, but every inhale felt jagged, and every exhale shook on its way out.

He backed toward the kitchen, desperate for distance, for space, for anything but the narrowing tunnel of the hallway.

The cold followed him.

Not a draft. Not the vent.

A slow, constricting pressure around his ribs tightening with each backward step like hands settling beneath his sternum.

His vision pulsed once, black at the edges.

He braced his free hand against the refrigerator handle to steady himself. The metal burned with cold, far colder than it should have been.

The phone slipped in his grasp, almost falling.

He caught it just in time, fingers clenching so tightly the joints ached.

Something scraped along the carpet in the hall.

Soft.

Dragging.

Measured.

Holt froze.

He didn't breathe.

He didn't blink.

He raised the phone again with deliberate slowness, angling it toward the darkness.

The camera's autofocus jittered, struggling.

Then the image sharpened.

And the shadow near the floor was closer.

Just a few inches.

But closer.

Holt's breath collapsed entirely.

His vision blurred at the edges.

His pulse hammered loud enough he could hear it in his teeth.

The apartment felt too small now, too tight, every wall leaning in by degrees.

Something in the hallway inhaled.

A long, slow draw of air that didn't sound like lungs at all.

Holt choked on his own breath, knees nearly giving out as he stumbled backward—

—and the recording caught the first delicate veins of frost beginning to creep along the lower half of the lens.

The frost-webbing thickened over the corner of the screen, branching slowly, silently, the way ice crawls across a winter window—but the apartment wasn't cold enough for that. Not by a mile.

Holt didn't notice the pattern fully. His eyes were locked on the hallway, on the impossible slow shift of shadow he could feel more than see.

His breath wouldn't come right.

Every inhale hit a wall halfway down, chest tightening, diaphragm trembling in short, shallow spasms that left him lightheaded and shaking. Panic should have launched him into motion—should have sent him bolting for the door—but the weight in the air held him still.

Held him **there**.

He tried to exhale through pursed lips, tried the grounding trick the precinct therapist had once taught him, but the air felt syrupthick. Heavy. Wrong. Like the room was breathing with him and **against** him at the same time.

The soft dragged scrape sounded again.

Closer.

Holt jerked the phone up, angling the camera down the hallway. The screen flickered—one brief stutter—then stabilized.

The dark near the bathroom door had deepened, massing around the frame like a spill of ink. The edge of it curled inward, a slow folding motion that shouldn't have been possible in still air.

His throat constricted.

"Stop," he rasped, barely audible. His vocal cords felt too tight. "Please—stop—"

Nothing moved.

But something **waited**.

His legs wobbled as he backed farther into the kitchen, bumping into the counter hard enough to jolt the phone. The video lurched, angle tilting just enough to catch the far right edge of the hallway floor—

—where a shadow didn't match.

Not length.

Not shape.

Not direction.

His own cast backward from the overhead light, stretched long behind him.

But the second one—the mismatched one—leaned forward.

Toward him.

Holt's stomach dropped, a sudden, violent freefall that left bile climbing his throat. He tried to swallow it back, but his body wasn't responding cleanly anymore. Muscle tremors shivered up his arms, down his spine, into his jaw.

He braced himself against the counter again, breath breaking in sharp, uneven bursts.

A low hum filled the air.

Not electrical. Not mechanical.

A vibration.

So faint he could feel it in his teeth before he heard it. A resonance that made the roots of his molars ache, a pressure that built behind his eyes like a migraine blooming too fast.

His vision shuddered.

He blinked hard, but the blur didn't clear. The hallway swam, edges softening while the dark at the far end grew sharper.

He forced one step sideways.

Then another.

His knee buckled on the third.

The phone slipped from his grasp and clattered against the tile, skidding to a stop near the kitchen doorway. The camera faced upward now, recording Holt from below—his heaving chest, his trembling arms, the sweat shining across his face.

Behind him, the hallway stretched like a throat.

The camera caught a ripple.

Just one.

A stuttering dip in the shadow pooled beneath the bathroom door. That was all.

But Holt saw it.

He choked on a gasp, palms slamming flat on the counter as if the anchoring might keep his ribs from collapsing inward. His chest burned. His throat seized. The cold around him intensified, tightening like invisible bands around his torso.

His breath tore out in a high, thin whine.

He tried to speak—Graves' name, maybe, or Maya's—but nothing rose past the pressure crushing his windpipe.

The camera on the floor kept recording.

It caught the frost climbing now, branching across the lens in jagged white lines. The digital image fractured, pixel edges glitching in staggered patterns. The air shimmered faintly above the floor, the way heat might distort—but inverted. Wrong.

Holt dropped to his knees.

His hands slapped the tile, fingers splayed, nails scraping helplessly. His breath came in broken gasps, chest hitching, diaphragm spasming like his body was forgetting how to breathe.

A soft inhale.

Not his.

Not anywhere near him.

Everywhere around him.

His vision ghosted at the edges.

The apartment dimmed, the shadows swelling, thickening, reaching—

—and Holt's final conscious thought wasn't a word.

It was a sensation.

Something standing inches behind him, drawing breath through the space where his warmth used to be.

The camera recorded the sound of his body hitting the floor.

The frost finished its bloom.

The screen went white.

Holt didn't show for roll call.

By 7:12 a.m., his radio checks were already late.

By 7:18, still no response to phone or text.

By 7:24, a welfare knock was authorized.

Two patrol officers reached his apartment at 7:31.

They hammered the door, called his name, waited.

Nothing.

On the second shoulder hit, the lock gave.

A thin, refrigerated draft slid out—wrong for a heated unit, wrong for any home that had held a human body overnight.

"Police!"

Silence.

They cleared the living room, weapons raised.

The cold worsened toward the kitchen—concentrated, directional, like it had traveled through the space instead of filling it.

One officer reached the doorway, saw the body, and keyed his radio with a stiff hand.

"Dispatch, we need EMS at 412 North Alder. Adult male unresponsive. No forced entry. Officers on scene."

Maya caught the call while heading back to station quarters. She changed course immediately.

She arrived two minutes later.

Both officers stepped aside as she approached, neither willing to re-enter the kitchen.

"He's in there," one said quietly. "We didn't move him."

Maya crossed the living room.

The cold thickened around her ankles first—an unnatural band of chilled air at floor level—as if she were stepping into the wake of something that had passed through minutes earlier.

She entered the kitchen.

Holt was slumped sideways against the lower cabinets, one shoulder wedged awkwardly against the refrigerator. Legs folded under him in a position no natural collapse would produce. His face was locked mid-panic—eyes half-open, jaw clenched hard enough to tremor in death.

Maya dropped beside him.

She reached for the carotid.

The artery **collapsed** under her fingers.

Not firm.

Not resistant.

Collapsed—tissue giving like soaked paper, the vessel flattened as if something had hollowed it from the inside.

Her stomach turned.

She tipped his chin gently, enough to check the airway.

Frost clung to the back of his throat—delicate, branching, arterial shapes like glass fractures spreading across soft tissue.

The same impossible cold-pattern she had felt on more than one body these past weeks — different scenes, different circumstances, but always the throat going cold first.

She withdrew her fingers slowly, breath unsteady.

Something shifted behind her.

Not sound—pressure.

The corner shadow near the fridge **lengthened**, stretching across the linoleum in a thin, warping line before snapping back into place. It didn't behave like a shadow at all—more like an afterimage left by something that had been standing there, something tall.

Residual imprint.

Fresh.

Maya's pulse hammered in her throat.

She scanned Holt again, forcing herself to complete the assessment:

– His lips bore faint suction bruising at the corners.

– His chest showed early rib-flare distortion—arcing outward under the skin, not fully bloomed but unmistakable.

– His sternum was rigid in ways that didn't match early postmortem intervals.

– His abdominal cavity felt sunken beneath intact skin, like the organs beneath had partially collapsed inward.

Interrupted.

Half-finished.

Like whatever had happened to him started… and then pivoted.

Her vision blurred for a moment—hot, then cold.

The refrigerator's shadow twitched again, stretching up the wall instead of sideways.

Maya forced her hand to steady as she reached for her radio.

"EMS confirming—Officer Holt is deceased. Scene is secure. Requesting coroner and PD supervisor on priority."

Her voice didn't match the way her lungs felt—like they needed twice as much oxygen as they were getting.

She stayed kneeling beside Holt because that was procedure.

But she didn't look at the corner again.

Not after the shadow peeled upward, stuttering once—

as if something tall had just stepped away from the wall

and slipped out before anyone arrived.

Chapter 19 — The Hollowed

The call came in at 3:47 p.m.

Not a welfare check.

Not a medical complaint.

A child's voice, thin with shock, telling dispatch she had found her mother "sitting weird" in the living room and she wouldn't answer.

Maya was already two blocks away on a lift-assist return when the alert hit her unit tablet. She froze mid-step outside the rig. The address punched the breath out of her chest.

Carla's house.

She didn't remember getting back behind the wheel.

She didn't remember the turn onto Sycamore.

Only the way her pulse hammered against her ribs—hard, mechanical, wrong.

The street looked normal when she arrived. Sunlight. Lawns. Cars. A dog barking somewhere too far away to matter. For a moment Maya felt the absurd hope that dispatch had mis-typed the number, that the universe had made a clerical error.

Then she saw Lila.

The girl was standing in the driveway, arms wrapped around herself so tightly her fingertips were white, her backpack dropped at her feet. A neighbor hovered uselessly behind her, trying to ask questions she wasn't hearing.

Maya didn't even put the rig in park before she was out the door.

"Lila—hey—hey, I'm here."

Her voice cracked on the last word.

Lila didn't run to her.

She didn't speak.

She just lifted her trembling hand and pointed toward the open front door.

Maya felt the world tilt.

She forced herself forward, every EMT reflex pushing against the dread rising up her spine. She wanted to take Lila in her arms and run the other direction. She wanted to scream at the neighbor to shield her, to shield all of them. She wanted this not to be the call she had been dreading for weeks without letting herself name it.

But she walked.

Every step toward the house felt heavier than the last.

The carport was open.

Carla's car was there.

Groceries still sat in the passenger seat, a bag tipped over, apples rolling against the floor mat.

Nothing dramatic.

Nothing violent.

Just… wrong.

Maya crossed into the kitchen.

The air hit her instantly—cooler than it should have been. Not freezing. Not the predatory cold she had learned to fear. This was subtler, thinner, like the echo of something that had already passed through.

The fruit bowl on the counter was overturned. One chair was angled slightly away from the table.

That was the only sign of anything out of place.

"Carla?" she called, though she already knew she wouldn't hear an answer.

Her shoes felt too loud against the tile as she moved deeper into the house, past the counter, past the doorway that led into the living room. The stillness became palpable—dense, as if sound itself didn't want to cross the threshold.

Lila hadn't followed.

Good.

God, that was good.

Maya steadied her breath and stepped fully into the living room.

She stopped.

Carla sat on the sofa. Upright. Head resting lightly against the cushion. Legs tucked to one side as though she had just shifted to get comfortable. Eyes closed.

Peaceful.

Too peaceful.

Maya's throat closed.

She couldn't move.

Couldn't breathe.

Her hand twitched toward her radio, but she couldn't make herself lift it—not until she understood what she was seeing. Not until her mind caught up with the thing her nerves were already screaming.

Carla looked exactly as she always had—hair pulled back, soft sweater, one hand relaxed against her thigh.

Nothing violent.

Nothing broken.

Nothing that should have stopped a heart.

But the room felt hollow.

Soundless.

Shallow, like depth had been carved out of the air.

And Maya hadn't touched her.

Hadn't reached the horrifying truth.

She swallowed hard and took one shaking step closer.

Something in the room changed.

The light shifted—not brighter, not dimmer, just subtly warped, as though the shadows along the far wall had lengthened a fraction in her peripheral vision.

Not enough to name.

Enough to notice.

Enough to dread.

Maya forced herself to speak, quietly, as if volume might alter the reality of the scene.

"Carla… I'm here."

Her voice came out thin and paper-dry.

Carla did not move.

Maya closed her eyes for one second.

Just one.

Then she opened them again and crossed the final feet toward the sofa.

She didn't touch her.

Because some part of her—some deep, terrified instinct—already knew what she would feel when she did.

Maya stepped closer, her breath tightening as she took in the stillness of the room. The overhead light hummed faintly, too bright against Carla's unmoving silhouette on the sofa.

She knelt beside her.

Up close, the wrongness thickened.

She reached for Carla's wrist.

The moment her fingers touched skin, her pulse stumbled.

Cold.

Not the faint cool of poor circulation.

Not room-temperature stillness.

A deeper cold—quiet, settled, unnatural.

Maya pressed gently along the forearm.

Something beneath the skin shifted—too soft, too empty, as though the internal structure had loosened or vanished entirely. Her throat tightened. She lifted Carla's chin with two fingers, meaning only to open the airway—

—and the tissue yielded.

Not violently.

Not with force.

But with the weightless collapse of something that no longer had the integrity of living anatomy.

A thin exhale escaped Maya without her meaning it.

She angled her penlight toward the mouth.

Frost.

Delicate, crystalline branching tracing the back of Carla's throat, feathering outward like arterial cracks in ice. Not thick, not dramatic—just a fine pattern forming an impossible map across tissue that should have been warm.

Her hand trembled.

She pulled back, inhaled once, slow, anchoring. Then she shifted, pressed two fingers lightly beneath Carla's jaw.

The cartilage beneath the surface felt wrong. Bent—not shattered, not displaced—just warped, as though pressure from inside had forced the ribs outward and left the throat struggling to follow.

A hollow thump of dread hit low in Maya's chest.

She lowered her hand to Carla's sternum.

Even through clothing, she could feel it: the faint inward sink, the unnatural flexibility, the impression of space where solidity should have been.

Her breath hitched.

Not again.

Not someone this close.

Not like this.

Maya pulled back a fraction, staring at Carla's face—the peacefulness of it, the impossible serenity, the way her posture remained upright though her body had nothing inside it to hold that posture anymore.

It wasn't a collapse.

It was placement.

Positioning.

Deliberate.

Her eyes burned. She blinked hard. Once. Twice.

Then she forced herself to stand, fingers trembling at her sides as she looked toward the hallway—toward the living room, toward the front door, toward anywhere she could steady herself—but the house felt too small, as if the air itself had been pressed down into something dense.

Her heartbeat climbed into her throat.

She swallowed it back down.

And stepped farther into the kitchen, because she had to, because she couldn't let herself turn away, not now, not with Lila's backpack still sitting by the door, not with the sofa angled so neatly toward the window, as though Carla had been placed there to watch something she would never see.

Maya braced one hand against the edge of the coffee table, steadying herself. The room felt subtly wrong—quiet in a way that didn't match the neighborhood outside, as if the air had been rearranged while no one was watching.

She forced her breathing to even out and stepped closer to the sofa.

Carla's posture hadn't changed.

Upright.

Centered.

Hands resting loosely in her lap.

Too composed for what the body beneath the skin had become.

Maya crouched again, letting her eyes adjust, tracing details she hadn't processed the first time.

Carla's shirt had fallen slightly open at the hem when Maya lifted her chin earlier. Now, with the angle of the overhead light, the contour of her abdomen caught the faint illumination—

—and the shape was wrong.

Too flat in some places.

Too concave in others.

A subtle inward bowing where firm anatomy should form gentle rise and fall.

Maya lifted the fabric a little higher.

Her breath stopped.

The skin was pallid but intact. No incisions. No trauma. But beneath it—beneath the thin give of the abdominal wall—there was only cavernous emptiness. A hollow chamber where organs should have been resting against one another in warm, dense silence.

Her vision tunneled for a second.

She lowered the hem with shaking fingers and rose slowly to her feet. Not because she was done—she wasn't—but because kneeling in front of Carla made the room tilt.

She stepped back.

The living room came into view again: the coffee table, the framed photo of Lila from a school field trip, the lamp Carla always left on low in the corner.

And then—

A shape on the far wall.

Not a shape.

A shadow.

Carla's shadow.

But wrong.

Stretched upward at an angle that didn't match the position of her body. One arm elongated unnaturally along the plaster, tapering toward a point higher than the lamp's height. The torso widened, then thinned, as if pulled by competing directions before settling into something broken.

Maya stared, breath locked.

It didn't move.

Didn't flicker.

Didn't behave like shadow at all.

She took one step toward it.

The angle wasn't possible.

No light source in the room could have cast this shape.

Not from the sofa.

Not from the lamp.

Not from anything in the house.

Her throat tightened.

She reached out with one unsteady hand and touched the wall just outside the distorted silhouette.

The plaster was cold.

Not cool.

Cold—like metal left outside in winter, sharp enough to sting the pads of her fingers.

She jerked her hand back.

A soft crackle of frost broke where her fingertip had touched.

Her breath trembled out of her in a shaky exhale.

She turned back toward Carla—and for the first time felt the reality settle in her bones: whatever had done this hadn't just taken her apart inside. It had stayed long enough to leave an imprint. A presence pressed into the geometry of the room.

The air seemed to tighten around her shoulders.

Maya swallowed hard and forced herself toward the hallway—not to flee, but because her legs needed movement or she would collapse right there on the living room floor.

She made it only two steps before her balance faltered. Her hand hit the wall.

The cold radiated through it.

Not fresh.

Not fading.

Lingering.

She pulled her hand away and closed her eyes.

Then reopened them, because she couldn't afford not to look.

Carla sat exactly as before.

Too still.

Too placed.

Maya's breath stuttered once, and her vision blurred—not from tears, but from something deeper, a shock that lived lower than grief and older than fear.

She steadied herself.

And the house stayed silent, as if holding whatever had happened inside its walls too tightly to release.

Maya forced herself back toward the sofa.

She had to check again—protocol, habit, denial, she couldn't tell which—but her legs felt unsteady, like the floor under the carpet had gone soft.

She crouched beside Carla one more time, her breath shallow as she lifted the hem of the shirt.

The hollow beneath the skin hadn't changed.

No organs.

No density.

Nothing but a cold, impossible space.

Her fingers hovered there, not touching, afraid to feel that collapse again.

A sound drifted through the room.

Not a creak.

Not a settling board.

Something lighter.

A faint shift of air—like the tail end of breath moving through a place where no one was breathing.

Maya's head snapped up.

The shadow on the far wall had changed.

Not dramatically—no lunge, no movement—but the elongated arm had thinned, the taper stretching a fraction farther down the plaster. Just enough that she knew she wasn't misremembering the shape from moments ago.

Her pulse hammered against the hinge of her jaw.

She rose to her feet slowly, as if an abrupt motion might provoke something she couldn't see.

The living room felt smaller now, every corner deeper than it should be. The air held a tension that clung to her ribs.

Her gaze swept the room.

Carla's slippers still sat near the coffee table. One sock had slipped halfway off her foot. A glass of water on the end table had a ring of condensation collecting at the bottom.

Ordinary things. Normal things.

But the temperature around them didn't match the world outside.

She stepped back toward the hallway.

Her boot slid.

She looked down.

A thin frost line traced across the hardwood floor—so faint it could have passed for dust, but crystalline when the light hit it. It ran straight from the living room toward the back sliding door, a delicate seam like something cold had been dragged or had passed through the room in a deliberate line.

Her chest constricted.

She followed it with her eyes—not with her feet—up to the doorframe and the glass beyond.

Outside, the backyard was still.

Nothing moved.

But the frost line ended right at the threshold, as if whatever left it had stopped there before vanishing.

Maya swallowed, throat tight, heat stinging behind her eyes.

She didn't cry.

She couldn't.

She backed up until she reached the sofa again, bracing a hand on its armrest to steady herself.

Carla sat unmoving.

Unaware.

Gone.

And Maya felt something inside her crack—

—not loud,

not breaking all at once,

but the slow fracture of something that had been holding her together far longer than she realized.

She knelt beside the sofa, one hand gripping the cushion to keep it from shaking.

Her breath came in shallow pulls.

"Carla…"

It was barely a whisper, barely sound at all.

No answer.

Only the faint hum of the refrigerator down the hall and the almost inaudible tick of the living room clock.

She wiped at her eyes once—quick, rough—then stood, forcing herself upright because collapsing now would mean she might not get back up.

Her gaze returned to the distorted shadow on the wall.

It hadn't changed again.

It just waited there, impossible, frozen in a posture no living person could cast.

A mark.

A remnant.

A thing left behind.

Her hands curled into fists without her thinking.

Not in anger.

Not entirely.

In refusal.

In the instinctive recoil of someone who had seen too much and still not enough to understand what she was supposed to do next.

A floorboard creaked behind her.

She spun.

The house was still empty.

But something in the far hallway—some depth of shadow where the light should have reached—looked a shade darker than before. Not moving. Not changing. Just present.

Maya backed toward the front door, eyes never leaving that darkened stretch of hallway.

When her hand found the doorknob, she twisted it, the metal cold under her palm.

She stepped outside.

Only then did she allow herself to breathe fully.

The door shut behind her with a soft click.

Maya stood on the walkway, hands shaking, breath refusing to settle. The cold she'd carried out of the house clung to her skin in a thin, stinging layer she couldn't rub away. The world outside felt wrong—too bright, too normal for what was inside.

Two patrol cars turned onto the street and rolled to a stop at the curb. Doors opened. Officers stepped out.

Graves was among them.

He saw her first.

"Maya," he called, already moving toward her with a fast, direct stride that told her he'd read everything he needed from her posture alone.

She didn't answer.

Her eyes were locked on the living room window— on the warped shadow imprint she could still see stretched across the far wall.

Her pulse spiked again, hard enough to blur her vision.

Graves reached her. "Maya. Talk to me."

She didn't look at him. Couldn't.

The distorted shadow seemed to lean in the glass, a wrong angle against the plaster, elongated and bent like something reaching.

Her breath hitched sharply.

Graves followed her stare but from where he stood, he saw nothing unusual—just the dim wash of the interior lights.

"Maya," he said again, firmer now. "Stay with me."

But she took a single shaky step toward the porch.

Graves' hand closed around her arm. "No. Stop."

She tried to pull free, grief and shock tightening her muscles in an unfocused surge. "I can't leave it there—"

"You're not going inside." His grip tightened as she twisted again. "You know you can't."

"I have to—" Her voice cracked. Her gaze darted back to the window, to the thing on the wall. "It shouldn't still be in there. I can't just—"

"Maya." His tone cut through her, steady and grounding. "Look at me."

She didn't.

She lunged toward the porch.

Graves grabbed both her arms, pulling her back before her foot hit the first step. The restraint wasn't violent—just firm, necessary, the only thing keeping her from running straight into the room where Carla's hollowed body still sat.

"Let me go—" She choked on the words.

"No." His voice dropped lower. "I'm not letting you go in there."

She struggled once more, then sagged forward under the weight of everything—shock, grief, the impossible wrongness still clinging to her muscles like cold.

Graves shifted his hold, bracing her upright as her knees threatened to buckle.

Behind them, an officer guided Lila toward a cruiser, murmuring something soft. Lila didn't look away from Maya, her eyes wide, shaking.

Maya couldn't look back.

She couldn't look at the house either.

A breath shuddered out of her as Graves tightened his hold just enough to keep her standing.

"You're alright," he said quietly. "I've got you."

It wasn't true.

Nothing was alright.

But she didn't collapse, and she didn't run back toward the door, and she didn't tear her hands open on the plaster trying to destroy the shadow imprint that shouldn't exist.

She stood in Graves' grip, shaking, breath stuttering, the world tilting beneath her.

The house behind them stayed silent.

And through the living room window, the twisted shadow remained on the wall—
unmoving,
impossible,
a lingering mark of something that had fed quietly, efficiently, and left nothing living behind.

Chapter 20 — The Broadcast

Maya signed her name in the blank line and stared at the curve of the penstroke like it belonged to someone else.

The form sat centered on the conference table between her and Graves, stacked on top of the others they'd been working through since she'd walked in barely an hour after sunrise:

TEMPORARY EMERGENCY GUARDIANSHIP — MINOR.

Her signature looked too steady for how she felt.

Graves flipped the page, the paper sounding too loud in the small room. The fluorescent light above them hummed with the same faint, metallic note every station light carried, but today it pressed against Maya's skull like a headache already forming.

"We still need this section," Graves said quietly. He tapped the next block with his pen. "Household contacts. Anyone who might seek placement."

Maya shook her head. "There isn't anyone," she said. Her voice was rough, like it had been scraped down overnight. "It's just her."

Graves absorbed that, then marked **none** and initialed the line.

He was quieter than usual—less clipped, more deliberate.

Grief had its own gravity, and he could feel hers even if neither of them named it.

Beside his elbow sat a second folder, thicker, its top sheet branded with a fresh Records stamp:

ARCHIVE RETRIEVAL — 1978 CLUSTER

and beneath it, in handwritten pencil:

For Vander — possible match geometry.

Graves had called Vander the moment the file arrived, just after seven.

He hadn't said why; he didn't need to. Vander understood the tone.

"Medical section," Graves said. "Any ongoing concerns?"

"She's healthy," Maya answered. "Nightmares. Panic. But nothing diagnosed."

"I can note acute stress from bereavement. It'll push this through faster."

Maya nodded once. Her throat felt thick.

Graves filled in the line without looking at her.

The office clock ticked loud enough to mark each second. Somewhere down the hall, a printer cycled and stopped. Phones rang and cut off. Normal station noise. None of it felt normal.

"School contacts?" Graves asked. "We need someone authorized for pickup. Emergency list."

"I'll handle it," Maya said. "I'll talk to her counselor myself."

He checked the box.

Maya reached for the next page, hands steady in a way her chest wasn't.

She could still hear Lila's voice from last night—thin, shredded, desperate.

She's all she has left now.

And what terrified Maya more: **Maya might be all Lila has left too.**

A soft knock pulled both their eyes to the door.

"You said to come straight to you."

Vander stood in the hallway with a worn satchel over one shoulder and a slim archival box tucked under his arm. The box edges were frayed, the tape label yellowed nearly to beige. He looked like he hadn't slept, but that wasn't new—some people carried the weight of old history like a second spine.

Graves let him in. "You made good time."

"You didn't sound like it could wait," Vander replied, stepping inside. His gaze flicked to Maya for the briefest moment—saw the forms on the table, saw the top line, saw the reason—but he didn't comment. He only nodded to her with a gravity that didn't require words.

Before he could set the archive box down or open his satchel, another voice cut in from the doorway.

"Lieutenant?"

Officer Weller stood there, one hand braced against the frame. Not breathless. Not panicked. But tight around the mouth, the way people looked when they had to say something they didn't fully understand.

"What is it?" Graves asked.

Weller jerked his chin toward the hallway. "You're gonna want to see this. It's on every local station. They're running a segment on the disappearances—live map, the whole thing. People are crowding the break room."

Graves' expression didn't change, but something in the room shifted—air tightening, not cold but close.

Maya pushed her chair back and stood; the legs scraped against tile. Vander adjusted his grip on the satchel strap.

"We're not done here," Graves said to Maya, voice low but steady. "But this takes priority."

She nodded.

Together they followed Weller out of the conference room and down the hall toward the break room, where the low, unsettled murmur of gathered officers grew louder with every step.

The break room was already full when they reached it.

Half a dozen officers stood motionless around the mounted TV, the usual lunchtime chatter gutted out of the air. A few chairs had been dragged aside. Someone had turned the volume up too loud, so the newscaster's voice carried through the room in sharp, clipped bursts.

"...police have not confirmed any link between the disappearances, but online analysts are pointing to a repeating geographical shape—"

The screen showed a map of the town, zoomed out enough for the industrial district to sit like a dark block near center. Little red dots pulsed one by one. Then lines traced between them in a slow arc, forming a curve that Maya recognized before she understood why.

Vander stepped closer without waiting for permission, eyes locked on the screen. The color drained from his face in a way Maya had never seen.

Graves moved beside him, arms folding tight across his chest. His jaw clicked once as he set his weight forward.

A reporter appeared on-screen—wind in her hair, microphone trembling slightly. Behind her, the industrial district's outer warehouses sat in the morning haze. The station logo ticked in the corner.

"...residents are expressing concern as GIS overlays show the vanishings following a distinct crescent pattern—"

The map reappeared.
This time with contour shading.

Maya blinked, her breath catching a fraction too high. She knew those streets. She'd driven them all week. Every call she'd run in the last several days sat along the shaded sweep the graphics department had unknowingly highlighted.

Her ribs tightened.

One of the officers muttered under his breath, "What the hell..."

Another whispered, "I've never seen anything like that. Not natural."

The newscaster continued, her voice stretched thin by the feed's compression.

"...community forums describing unnerving phenomena—power flickers, strange audio distortions, and isolated cold pockets reported even during midday. Local residents say shadows have been appearing 'longer' or 'out of sync.' Officials deny any threat but have issued a reminder to remain indoors after dark until further notice—"

Maya's stomach twisted.

Cold pockets.

Shadow lag.

People feeling watched.

Every detail lined up with the EMS calls she'd run—breathing-noises reports, dark corners that seemed to move, cold that settled only around terrified people, not rooms.

She felt Vander exhale beside her.

It wasn't relief.

The feed cut to a still image—an enlarged version of the map, crescent-shaped, unmistakable.

A shape that widened exactly the way Graves had marked on his wall.

Exactly the way Vander had shown them in the archival cases.

The newscaster continued, almost mechanically now.

"…though authorities have released no official statement regarding the mapped pattern, social media speculation continues to escalate. Some users are calling it a serial killing arc. Others claim the shape matches several historical disappearances dating back over a century—"

Vander lifted a hand toward the screen, stopping just short of touching it.

"That is the same geometry," he murmured. "Down to the spacing."

Graves didn't speak.

Didn't blink.

Didn't look away from the screen.

The reporter returned, standing in front of an industrial fence. The camera glitched once—just a brief ripple across the pixels. The audio warped a moment later, stretching the vowel in her sentence into something hollow.

Maya stiffened.

She'd heard that distortion before.

In a basement.

In hallways.

In the moments just before the cold tightened.

A hush spread through the break room as the reporter continued speaking, unaware of the glitch.

"...residents advised to travel in groups... report any suspicious activity... police increasing patrols..."

Behind her, in the far back corner of the camera frame, a shadow bent a half-inch too long under a streetlamp and snapped back into place.

Someone in the room whispered, "Did you see that?"

Another officer stepped closer to the screen, squinting.

The reporter kept talking.

Her breath fogged.

Just once.

A soft cloud dissolving in warm daylight.

The room fell silent enough that Maya could hear someone swallow.

Graves leaned in slightly, eyes locked on the screen.

The reporter didn't seem to notice the breath mist.

Or the glitch.

Or the distortion tugging faintly at the edges of her shadow.

"...more after the break," she finished, and the feed cut to a commercial with a muted insurance jingle.

The room exhaled a low current of unsettled voices. Chairs scraped. Someone stepped aside to get a clearer view of the frozen map on the screen. Radios clicked on and off as dispatch chatter bled through the hallway.

Graves shifted forward first.

"Come on," he said, voice tight. "We're not done."

He moved toward the doorway, already in motion.

Maya and Vander followed.

The hallway outside the break room felt tighter than it had minutes ago. Officers were moving faster now—small jolts of activity, clipped conversations, the restless shift that ripples through a precinct when something hits the air wrong.

Graves didn't slow.

He cut through the hall toward the briefing room they'd been using, his stride sharp enough that Maya had to match it. Vander followed close behind, clutching the leather satchel against his ribs the way he always did when something was turning in his head.

"Graves," a passing officer called, tapping the radio on his shoulder. "You seeing this? Phones are blowing up."

"I'm aware," Graves said without breaking pace.

When they stepped back into their room, the hum of the overhead fixture buzzed a fraction louder than before—barely perceptible, but enough that Maya's shoulders tightened. The air wasn't cold. Not even close. But the *room* felt off. Compressed by the noise coming from the rest of the station.

Vander shut the door behind them.

"Fear response," he murmured. "Collective. It's predictable, given—"

"Save it," Graves said. "We don't have time for theory right now."

He dropped into his chair long enough to drag the precinct map toward him, sliding aside the paperwork scattered across it. The map—still marked with the red pins from earlier in the week—looked different to him now, and Maya saw that shift in his expression before he even spoke.

He wasn't skeptical anymore.

He wasn't cautious.

He was scared, whether he'd admit it or not.

Vander moved around the table and set down a folded page—one of his archival cluster maps. He pressed it flat beside the precinct map, lining its arc up with the red curve marking Harrowgate's disappearances.

The shapes met.

Not perfectly.

But too close.

Maya exhaled through her teeth. She thought she was prepared for this. After Holt. After the basement. After the warehouse. She wasn't.

"That's a ten-case curve," Vander said softly. "Oregon, 1911. Same spacing. Same outward progression. Same pause before escalation."

Graves' jaw set hard. "We're at eight."

Maya looked sharply at him. "Unofficially."

He didn't argue.

Outside the door, another wave of voices rose— dispatch radios, overlapping calls, the frantic beat of something spiraling in real time.

Graves checked the doorway, then turned back to them. "We need to get ahead of this before the whole town goes into free-fall. Whatever's happening out there,"—he jerked his chin toward the hall—"it's just the start."

A thud hit the far end of the corridor. Someone swore.

Another burst of chatter flared from the watch sergeant's radio.

Maya felt her pulse kick.

Not from cold.

Not from proximity.

But from something she hadn't felt since the vigil night:

A sense of pressure building somewhere else—away from the station, gathering weight.

"Graves," Vander said, his voice tightening, "you need to see the 1978 file. If the arc is this far along—"

A sharp knock hit the door before he could finish.

Graves moved first.

He opened it to find Officer Weller, flushed and breathing too fast.

"Sir—" Weller swallowed. "You need to come to the watch desk. Now. Someone just brought in footage. It's... you need to see it."

Graves didn't question it.

He stepped into the hall.

Maya followed, already bracing herself.

Vander gathered his satchel and came after them.

And the three moved toward the front of the station, the sound of voices rising around them like the start of a storm pulling itself together.

They didn't know what they were about to see.

But they kept moving toward it.

The watch desk was already surrounded when they reached it—dispatchers, two patrol officers, a sergeant leaning forward with his palms braced on the counter. None of them were talking. The room wasn't loud anymore. It was too quiet.

A small TV sat on the end of the desk, volume low but unmistakable.

A news anchor's voice cut through the silence:

"—authorities have yet to comment on any connection between the disappearances, but residents are growing increasingly concerned as new details emerge—"

Graves stepped closer.

"Start it from the beginning."

Weller rewound the segment and hit play.

The screen flickered to a still image: a town grid. Streets flattened into clean white lines. Neighborhoods rendered in pale blocks. At first glance, it was nothing but a map.

Then the red markers appeared.

Not one at a time—

but all at once, lighting the screen like punctures.

Maya's breath caught in her chest.

Eight.

Every one of them marked.

The anchor continued:

"—when plotted together, the disappearances form a striking pattern. A crescent-shaped sweep beginning near the industrial district and expanding outward over the last two weeks—"

The camera cut to a crime analyst, gesturing at the overlay behind him.

"These aren't random," he said. "The spacing is too consistent. The curve—right here—shows clear progression. If another disappearance occurs, statistically speaking, it will fall along this arc."

A ripple went through the officers around them—
a hush,
a subtle shift of dread,
the kind that tightens shoulders without anyone noticing.

Beside Maya, Vander leaned in slightly, eyes narrowing at the display. Not surprised—just grimly recognizing what he already knew.

"That curve," he murmured, "is almost identical to 1911."

Graves didn't speak.
He was watching Maya.
Not the screen—
Maya.

Because she'd stopped breathing for a beat too long.

The anchor's voice continued, steady and oblivious to the way the precinct was tensing around every syllable.

"Residents have reported strange occurrences across Harrowgate. Flickering streetlights, sudden cold drafts, and unexplained power outages—though police stress there is no evidence linking these events."

Maya felt the skin along her arms lift.
Not cold.
Just fear moving through too many people at once.

The screen shifted again—
this time to doorbell camera footage.

A porch.
Nighttime.
A frame-gray street behind it.

"—several videos submitted to the station show unusual shadow distortions. Experts attribute these to compression artifacts—"

The footage played.

In the corner of the yard, a shadow elongated across the lawn not stretching with the camera movement,

not matching any object in the frame.

Someone behind Maya whispered, "What the hell…"

Another clip.

A parking garage.

A woman walking to her car.

Her shadow lagged half a second behind her steps.

Lagged.

Maya's pulse jumped.

She felt it—her body remembering the basement's delay, the warehouse's bloom, the shape peeling away from Holt's wall.

The anchor kept talking, but the words had dissolved into a hum.

Beside her, Vander whispered, almost to himself, "Phase eight viewing artifacts… showing up on public footage…"

Graves shot him a warning look.

Not here.

Not out loud.

The final graphic filled the screen:

a bold red crescent—

the exact shape they had drawn themselves, hours earlier, days earlier—

Now broadcast to tens of thousands of people.

And fear—real, palpable—rolled across the station like a pressure wave.

Phones started ringing behind the desk.

Three at once.

Then five.

Dispatch radios crackled.

Multiple officers reached for incoming calls at the same time.

Maya felt the room tightening, the air shifting with the collective spike of panic pouring in from outside the station.

Graves lowered the volume, turned toward her and Vander.

"This changes everything."

A sergeant hurried up from the hallway, a printout in hand. "Lieutenant—PD lines are backed up. People are calling about cold spots, shadows in hallways, silhouettes outside windows—half of these are probably panic, but—"

He didn't finish.

Behind the desk, another phone began to ring.

Then another.

Then three more.

Maya looked at Graves.

Graves looked at Vander.

And Vander, very quietly, closed the worn satchel at his side.

Not because he was done.

But because something was beginning.

Graves straightened, grounding himself.

"Maya," he said, voice low but firm, "finish the placement forms. I need you here, not in Operations."

He was already turning, striding toward the hall as dispatch phones and radios erupted behind him.

Vander closed his satchel—not in departure, but in tension—then looked to Maya. "Go on," he murmured. "He'll need those papers done before anything else."

Maya drew a steadying breath and stepped back from the watch desk.

One last look at the TV—

at the crescent glowing red against white,

at the shape a news station had thrown into the world without understanding what it meant—

Then she turned and moved toward the conference room, the rising noise of fear-swollen calls chasing her down the hall as the station braced for the night ahead.

Vander followed a few steps behind, silent, carrying the weight of maps and centuries in the bend of his shoulders.

Chapter 20.5 — 1978, West Texas

The first disappearance didn't make the news.

In a town that baked under oil-field sun and coughed dust when the wind shifted, people vanished sometimes. They ran off. Took jobs in Midland. Hitched rides they shouldn't have. Nobody thought much of it when **Ricky Hall**, age nineteen, didn't show up to his shift at the Texaco.

His coworker said Ricky had walked across the gravel lot, keys in hand.

The camera above the pumps showed him passing under one buzzing light.

He never reached the next one.

The second disappearance came three days later.

A **divorced mother of two**, leaving the night shift at the refinery cafeteria, crossed the employee lot toward her truck. A security guard saw her silhouette break the floodlight—just a blink of motion—then nothing. The guard walked out, expecting she'd crouched to tie a shoe or dropped her purse.

The gravel was smooth.

The driver's door untouched.

Her lunch pail still on the ground, upright.

By the time the third disappearance hit the dispatch logs, the night-shift operator—a woman named **Janet Pierce**, tired-eyed and meticulous—started making little pen marks on a folded county map she kept taped beside her rotary phone.

She didn't do it for any reason.

Habit, maybe.

Pattern-seeking boredom in the low hum of midnight hours.

Each red dot landed a little farther west, curving softly around the rusted shell of the decommissioned refinery that had been rotting on the edge of town since '62.

She didn't think anything of it.

Days stretched hot and longer.

The smell of heated metal settled over the streets.

The refinery loomed like a burned-out ribcage against the horizon.

Then **Case Four** went missing.

A schoolteacher, headed home before sunrise. Her Chevy was found gently idling on the shoulder of County Road 6, driver's door open, the interior still warm. Music played from the radio—some AM preacher murmuring about sin and redemption.

Her purse sat neatly in the passenger seat.

Her thermos lay in the middle of the road as if someone had placed it there and stepped backward into the dark.

Janet marked the fourth dot.

She looked at the slow, bending sweep forming along her map.

A crescent, faint and accidental.

The kind a person saw only out of the corner of their eye.

Two days later came **Case Five**.

And this time, they found a body.

They found him at the edge of the old drainage culvert behind the shuttered livestock auction—**Case Five**, though nobody called him that yet. His name was **Terry Cole**, thirty-four, former roustabout, part-time mechanic. A man who could lift an engine block by himself and drank Lone Star from sunup on Saturdays.

The deputy who found him vomited in the dust.

Terry was sitting upright against the concrete lip of the culvert, back pressed to it as though he'd simply leaned there to rest after walking too far in the heat. His boots were still on. Sunglasses hanging from the collar of his shirt. His hair stirred a little in the hot breeze.

From a distance, he looked asleep.

Up close, everything was wrong.

His chest had collapsed inward—not caved by blunt force, but **drawn**, as though something inside had emptied. The ribs were bowed inward in sharp, unnatural angles, cartilage warped and bending beneath the skin. His sternum had folded slightly, pulled into a shape no human body formed on its own.

Both lungs had deflated and flattened into dark, rubbery folds.

His tongue was bitten through.

His eyes were open but sunken deep, as if pulled backward in their sockets.

There was no blood.

Not on him.

Not on the ground.

Not anywhere.

Just a faint, dark stain on the inside of his shirt where fluid had leaked downward in an irregular line, thick and glossy, like something had melted rather than spilled.

His spine, from the base of the neck to mid-back, arched in a way no accident could produce—half curled, half extended, like the body had been forced forward and backward at once.

The medical examiner would later write that the damage resembled "**pressure inversion**"—a term he used once and never again. A single page filed, then boxed, then forgotten until years later.

Janet heard the call come in over the radio.

Her fingers tightened on the pen she still held from her overnight shift.

When she marked Terry's location on the map, the fifth dot slid cleanly into the curve forming along the refinery's northern edge.

She didn't understand what she was seeing.

She only stared, throat dry, as if the heat had thickened the air.

That afternoon, the local AM station broke from country music to run a caller's shaky story:

"He ain't the only one gone missin'. Folks hear someone breathin' in the corners of their trailers. Like somethin's watchin' when the lights go out."

The radio host laughed nervously and dubbed it:

"The Shadow Man Summer."

People chuckled.

Then locked their doors.

Three days passed.

Then **Case Six** vanished walking home from the feed store.

Then **Case Seven** was found — not far from the refinery.

And his body was worse.

Much worse.

Case Seven turned up where the dirt road met the service track behind the refinery—where the cracked asphalt dissolved into pale dust and thornbrush. A teenager found him while riding his bike home from fishing the reservoir. The boy pedaled back to town so fast his chain snapped on Main Street.

Deputies reached the site before sundown.

The body lay half in the brush, half on the open ground, one arm stretched forward as though it had been reaching for something just beyond the weeds. His name was **Eldon Price**, fifty-eight, a retired pipefitter who still carried himself like a man who worked steel.

What was left of him didn't look like steel had anything to do with it.

Eldon's torso was **hollowed** in a way the sheriff's office had no language for.

Not torn.

Not eaten.

Not surgically altered.

Emptied.

As though something had drawn everything inward—muscle, organ, connective tissue—leaving the cavity smooth and slack beneath his shirt, the fabric collapsing over an impossible absence. His ribcage bowed backward, flared in a wide, unnatural fan, the ends of the cartilage bent into shapes that looked pressed, molded. His lower ribs were pulled almost horizontally, as if something had gripped from within and stretched them outward before letting go.

His jaw hung open.

Not from decay.

From dislocation.

Both sides.

The angle was grotesque—an "O" shape pulled wide, teeth exposed, the mandible forced down and to the sides as though something massive had forced its way past his lips without breaking the skin around them. Dried saliva crusted the corners of his mouth in long, brittle strands.

His spine was curved into a sharp arc, pelvis slightly lifted from the ground, as if his body had been pulled upward by the chest and dropped. No footprints. No drag marks. No disturbance in the dust.

A single line of moisture stained the earth beneath him—a thin, dark streak, drying at the edges, viscous in the center.

The medical examiner would write later that the damage resembled "extreme internal pressure variance" but offered no theory. The term was underlined once. Never again.

When word spread, people stopped going out after sunset.

Someone's porch light flickered for the first time in years.

A dog refused to cross its own threshold.

Three callers told the AM station they'd woken to the sound of someone breathing in their trailers.

Janet marked Eldon's location on the map.

The curve deepened—sweeping wide around the refinery like a slow, deliberate arc drawn by a hand that didn't care who saw.

Two more vanishings followed in the next forty-eight hours.

Case Eight.

Case Nine.

No bodies.

No witnesses.

Just two more spaces where people had been—and then weren't.

Janet added both red dots.

The crescent neared completion.

A shape was forming.

Not random.

Not scattered.

Controlled.

Something had been moving through that town all summer, and whatever it took next would complete the line Janet didn't know she was tracking.

She didn't sleep her next shift.

She waited.

Three nights later, another man was simply gone.

His truck sat in the drive, dust untouched.

His coffee pot was still warm when his sister came by in the morning. The front door locked from the inside.

A single work boot lay tipped on its side near the sofa, like he'd stepped out of it mid-motion.

No sign of struggle.

No sign of leaving.

Just absence—quick, clean, and final.

The refinery sat silent in the heat, a rusted husk against the horizon.

The phones stopped ringing at the dispatch desk.

The radio show callers stopped talking about breathing in their trailers.

The anomalies ceased as abruptly as they'd begun.

Janet folded the map.

Put it in a drawer.

And never marked another dot.

The summer ended.
The heat broke.
The town kept its silence.
It would take years before anyone saw that crescent again.

Chapter 21 — The Deathwatcher

Maya set the last page of the guardianship packet flat against the table and drew the pen toward the signature line. Her hand didn't shake, but her chest felt tight, like every breath she took had to pass through something weighted. The conference room lights hummed overhead, steady and sharp.

Vander stood on the other side of the table, the worn satchel open beside him and the archival box already unpacked. He had spread several documents across the laminate surface—maps with browned edges, photocopied sketches, and a handful of grainy photographs that looked older than the building they stood in.

He wasn't speaking.

He was waiting.

Maya finished the signature and set the pen aside. Her fingers hovered for a moment before she pulled the packet toward her and slid it into the completed stack.

Vander reached for one of the photocopies and turned it so it faced her—a woodcut print, its ink uneven and dark. The figure in it was long, thin, bent at the neck, its arms dragging close to the ground. Not a scythe. Just bone and shadow carved into a wrong shape.

"I've seen versions of this across different regions," Vander said quietly. "Different names. Different eras. The posture never changes."

Maya looked at the print without touching it. The shape dug at something old in her memory—something from childhood, whispered warnings that didn't feel like stories anymore.

She kept her voice low. "El Cucuy looked like this in the drawings my grandmother used to keep."

Vander nodded once. "Spain's Reaper carvings match it too. And the shadow-figure accounts from the border towns in the fifties. They all describe the same silhouette."

Maya didn't want to look at the next page, but her eyes went to it anyway—a blurred security photo from some decade long gone. A figure in the corner of a hallway, too tall to be a person, its head bending toward the floor like it was listening.

She felt her throat tighten.

A footstep sounded at the doorway.

Graves walked back in, the weight of the precinct still on his shoulders. His sleeves were rolled higher than before, as if the last twenty minutes had been spent putting out fires in every direction. He closed the door behind him, shutting out the rising noise from the watch desk.

"Dispatch is overwhelmed," he said, not bothering to sit. "People are calling about everything—shadows, power flickers, cold in places that shouldn't be cold. Half panic, half something else."

His attention shifted to the documents on the table.

"What am I looking at?" he asked.

Vander slid another page forward—an annotated journal entry from centuries earlier. The handwriting was cramped, the ink browned at the edges. A rough sketch marked the margin: a long-limbed figure crouched in a corner.

"Different parts of the world," Vander said. "Different languages. Same body shape. Same behavior patterns described. Watching in corners. Standing in doorways. Breathing heard but not seen."

Graves scanned the pages, brow tightening. "These are myths."

"Stories," Vander corrected. "But consistent ones."

Maya watched Graves take in the sketches and old woodcuts. His skepticism had cracked days ago; what was left now was something quieter, heavier.

"Everything circles the same thing," Vander said, lowering his voice. "Different names for it, but every legend calls out the same posture. The same way it stands. The same way it leans. The same way it waits."

Graves didn't argue.

He reached for the Reaper print, tracing the outline with his eyes—the bent head, the dragging arms.

Maya glanced at the old image, then at the grainy photo Vander had set beside it. The match was too close. Too clean. Too familiar to ignore.

Her stomach knotted.

She had seen that same posture in a basement.

In a warehouse.

Behind Holt.

Footsteps echoed in the hallway—someone moving fast toward the watch desk again.

Graves set the print down and straightened.

"Keep going," he told Vander. "I need the rest of this."

He stepped toward the door.

Maya pushed the next stack of completed forms toward the edge of the table, ready to hand them off when he returned. She didn't look away from the sketch until she had to.

Graves opened the door.

Noise waited on the other side—phones ringing, radios popping, voices rising in sharp, clipped bursts.

He started down the hall.

Vander lifted another document from the archive box.

Maya slid the next sheet toward her, but her eyes kept drifting to the spread of materials Vander had laid out. The conference room felt smaller now—not from cold, just from the weight of what was sitting between them.

Vander opened the archival box fully and lifted out a thin binder bound with brittle thread. He set it beside the woodcut print and flipped it open with careful fingers. The pages inside were copies of older texts—some typed, some photographed, some barely legible.

"These are pre-colonial accounts," he said, keeping his voice low. "Different storytellers. Different regions. But the descriptions repeat."

He angled the book so Maya could see.

One page showed a charcoal sketch: a figure hunched in a doorway, head hanging low enough that the chin almost touched its chest. The arms dragged long, like ropes brushing the floor.

"The posture appears again and again," Vander continued. "Not always drawn well, but always the same structure. Long limbs. Bent head. Watching."

Maya's breath tightened. Her grandmother's voice flickered through her mind—warnings she'd dismissed as superstition. Don't stand in dark hallways. Don't look too long at corners. Don't let the Cucuy see you first.

"What about the breathing?" she asked.

Vander turned another page.

A handwritten column of notes covered half the sheet. Translated excerpts lined the other side.

Children hearing breathing in empty spaces.
Adults feeling watched in doorways.
Cold that pressed close only when fear did.

"They described it the same way," Vander said. "Always near. Never speaking."

Maya felt her throat tighten, and she forced her eyes back to the guardianship packet so she could keep moving. She filled in the next line—Contact for educational liaison—then initialed the margin.

The door opened.

Graves stepped back inside, closing it firmly behind him. His expression hadn't softened; if anything, it had sharpened, the kind of look he wore when something had shifted just outside the lines of procedure.

He came to the table, bracing one hand on the edge as he looked over the spread of sketches and old prints.

"What is all this?" he asked.

Vander turned the binder so Graves could see the charcoal figure.

"Documentation," he said. "Five hundred years of it. Across continents."

Graves leaned closer. His eyes moved from the woodcut print to the hallway sketch to the blurred photo. The match was clear enough that he didn't bother pretending otherwise.

"That shape," Graves said quietly. "It's the same damn shape people talk about here."

Maya didn't answer. She didn't need to. Every call she'd run in the last week, every basement, every terrified person—she had heard versions of these stories from the people who lived them.

Graves shifted his gaze to Vander. "You said there were patterns."

"There are," Vander replied. "But the stories came first. People saw something. They described what they could. Myths are just the pieces left over after memory erodes."

Graves' jaw locked for a moment.

He turned slightly, not sitting, just bracing himself with both hands on the back of a chair.

"Does any of this tell us how to stop it?" he asked.

Vander didn't answer right away. He lifted one more page from the binder—a translated passage from a centuries-old folktale. The text was faded around the edges, like it had been pulled from a book that hadn't been opened in decades.

"It tells us how people survived it," Vander said. "Not why."

Maya marked another line in the packet, her pen steady even as her chest tightened.

Outside the conference room, the precinct buzzed—dozens of phones, too many voices, the kind of activity that didn't come from routine.

Graves straightened.

"Keep going," he told Vander. "I need to know everything we're dealing with."

He stepped toward the door again, already turning back into the chaos of the hallway.

Maya finished the next signature block, but her attention kept drifting toward the table where Vander was laying out more documents—carefully, almost reverently, the way someone might handle bones.

He opened a second folder, this one containing photocopies of much older pages. Ink faded to brown. Edges warped. The sort of paper that carried its own smell.

"This one," Vander said, sliding it toward her without interrupting her work, "is from Iberian plague records. Fourteenth century."

Maya didn't lift it fully—she glanced sideways while her other hand filled another line on the guardianship form.

The illustration showed a figure standing behind a farmhouse doorframe. Long arms hanging low. Head bent forward. No visible face. Just darkness where the face should've been.

Her chest tightened. Not from cold. From recognition.

"I grew up hearing stories like that," she murmured. "Not that picture—just… the shape."

"The same shape," Vander said. "Different century."

He slid another copy next to it. This one wasn't drawn—it was a woodcut. The posture identical. The angles identical. Shoulders pitched forward; arms unnaturally long.

Graves came back into the room then—not rushing, but moving with the momentum of someone walking out of one emergency into the next. He shut the door behind him and took a slow breath that didn't quite settle.

"They've got more footage coming in," he said. "Doorbell cams. Garage feeds. Some with… distortions."

He didn't finish the sentence. He didn't need to.

His gaze dropped to the table.

"What am I looking at?"

Vander didn't answer immediately. He slid the woodcut closer, letting the overhead light catch the carved lines.

"Every culture describes its own version," he said. "Different names. Different stories. But the anatomy never changes."

Graves studied it for a long beat.

Then another.

"This is the same thing people here call the hall-walker," he said quietly. "The one in the local legend."

Maya's hand froze halfway down a signature line.

Her grandmother's voice echoed again. Don't stand in the hallway after midnight. Don't look into corners too long. If the hall-walker bends to look back, you run.

"This is the same story," Vander said. "Stripped to bone. Passed down, distorted, retold. But the creature is always the same shape."

Graves set his hands flat on the table. Not shaking. Just steadying. He scanned the assembled images—modern CCTV stills, medieval carvings, colonial drawings—each one capturing the same silhouette in a different era.

"People treat these stories like superstition," he said. "Like something you scare children with."

"Because they don't know they're describing an animal," Vander replied. "Not a spirit. Not a demon. A creature that's been here longer than the stories themselves."

Maya felt her throat tighten again. She finished the last line of the page and flipped to the next form.

"How many sightings?" she asked.

Vander tapped the stack beside him—the one he hadn't opened yet.

"As many as you'd expect when a thing knows how to stay just out of sight."

Graves exhaled slowly. His eyes were on the binder, but his thoughts were somewhere else—tracking, mapping, trying to turn myth into something he could hold.

The hallway outside the conference room flared with a sudden burst of radio chatter, too quick and too layered to make out. The precinct had shifted again—not loud, not panicked, just tighter, a collective breath pulled too high.

Maya initialed another line and pushed the completed page aside.

Vander lifted yet another document—a colonial-era record written in cramped cursive across uneven lines.

"Listen to this," he said, voice low. "This was written in 1694. New Mexico territory. A monk documenting the deaths in a high desert settlement."

Graves stepped closer.

Maya looked up.

Vander read:

"...the children spoke of a tall watcher who bent low to breathe upon the fearful. Those who felt the breath did not rise again with the morning sun."

The room tightened around the words.

Maya's pulse climbed—

not because of cold.

Because she'd heard that exact phrasing once before, from someone who didn't know ancient stories, who didn't know myth, who only knew what she'd seen.

Lila.

Breathing in corners.

Breathing behind her.

Breathing in the dark.

Maya set her pen down.

"This isn't mythology anymore," she said.

"No," Vander murmured, turning the page. "It never was."

The next document was already waiting under his hand.

Maya leaned in.

Graves did too.

Vander unfolded the next sheet with the same careful precision he used on autopsy photos. This one wasn't an illustration—it was a page of field notes, ink pressed hard enough to scar the paper.

"1712," he said. "Spanish mission records. Northern frontier. A friar documenting unexplained disappearances."

He slid it forward so Graves and Maya could read.

The handwriting was jagged, hurried:

"...the figure was seen again in the long corridor. Bent of head. Arms reaching near the floor. Shadow wrong-shaped even by lanternlight. Children refuse to sleep. Those who witnessed it feel watched for days..."

Maya's eyes drifted to the next sentence, written darker than the rest:

"...and when fear grew in the household, the cold returned."

Her chest tightened.

Not because the room was cold—it wasn't.

But because she'd heard that exact combination before.

Fear first.

Cold after.

Not the other way around.

Her pen hovered above the guardianship form, the unfinished line waiting, but she couldn't look away from the text.

Graves' jaw flexed once, the way it did when something in his mind clicked into place even if he wasn't ready to admit it.

Vander continued, voice steady:

"This predates electricity. Predates modern thermometers. They didn't track temperature. They tracked *fear.* They noticed the sequence."

Graves scanned the page again. "Fear spikes first."

"Always," Vander said. "Then the cold arrives. Then the vanishings accelerate."

Maya swallowed once, the sound dry and thin.

"That's exactly what's happening now," she said quietly.

Graves didn't answer.

But he didn't have to.

The station outside the conference room had been growing louder by the minute—overlapping calls, more feet in motion, radios pinging with clipped bursts of chatter—but beneath it all was that same squeezing tension Maya had felt at the vigil, in the warehouse, in Holt's apartment.

Fear swelling.

Cold following.

Vander reached into his satchel again.

"You should see this next one," he murmured. "It's the earliest depiction I've found."

He placed a stark, hand-drawn charcoal rendering on the table.

A narrow hallway.

A figure rising from the darkness at the far end.

Bent forward.

Head angled down.

Arms dragging low.

No face—just the implication of one leaning closer.

The charcoal strokes were rough but unmistakably consistent with the CCTV silhouettes from Harrowgate.

Graves stared at it so long Maya thought he hadn't blinked.

"That's the hall-watcher," he said under his breath.

"That word didn't exist when this was drawn," Vander replied. "But yes. Same posture. Same anatomy. Same behavior."

He turned the rendering so the light caught the shading on its shoulders—long, curved, sloping in an arc that matched the shape Maya had seen peeling off Holt's wall.

"Every region gives it a different name," Vander said. "The Tall Man. The Hall-Watcher. El Cucuy. The Reaper. Shadow People. But the core description never changes."

Maya's breath left her in a thin exhale.

All the names she grew up hearing—stories whispered to scare kids into behaving, legends meant to keep people away from dark corners—they weren't about different things.

They were all the same thing.

Every culture had been describing a single predator.

Graves steadied both hands on the table, bracing like the movement helped him stay anchored.

"Show me how far back this goes."

Vander opened the archival box.

The papers inside were older still—brittle, yellowed, some with torn edges that looked like they'd been rescued from fire or rot. He spread them out in sequence:

• a medieval parchment depicting a bent shadow moving across a monastery wall

• a 16th-century missionary account of a "tall darkness" stalking the edges of a sickened village

• a colonial-era death ledger noting "lungs collapsed inward without wound"

• a 19th-century folk sketch labeled *the corridor lurker*

The progression wasn't random.

It was evolution.

Recognition echoing across centuries.

Maya stared at the spread of papers, her chest tightening with every similarity she saw.

"It always does the same thing," she said. "Every cycle. Every culture."

Vander nodded slowly. "Because it's not adapting to us. We are adapting our stories to *it*."

Footsteps pounded down the hall outside—an officer shouting for someone to pick up Line Four, another yelling to clear space near the watch desk.

The noise pressed against the conference room walls.

But the three of them stayed where they were—leaning over centuries of warnings that no one had ever taken seriously.

"We're not dealing with a legend," Vander said softly.

He lifted the oldest image, held it between them.

"We're dealing with the thing that *made* legends."

Maya's pulse thudded harder.

She finished the last signature on the page in front of her.

And Vander was already reaching for another file.

Maya slid the next form toward herself, the paper whispering against the table. Her hand hovered over the signature line, but she didn't pick up the pen yet.

Across from her, Vander laid the next archival photo flat, smoothing its curled edge with quiet, practiced care. The woodcut beneath his fingertips showed the same impossible posture as all the others—tall, bent, arms dragging low—but rendered in ink so old it had browned like dried blood.

Graves hadn't moved since Vander's last words.

He stood at the table's edge, arms folded tight, jaw set in a way that made the tendon along his neck stand out. He wasn't looking at the paperwork now. He wasn't looking at the photos either.

He was watching the two of them.

Watching the pieces finally settle into the shape he'd been refusing to name.

Maya picked up the pen. Her signature slid across the line—clean, even—nothing like the tremor sitting under her ribs.

"One more page," she murmured, mostly to herself.

Vander closed the photo he'd been studying and reached for another sheet from the archival box. But this time, his movements slowed. He wasn't exhausted. He wasn't uncertain.

He was finishing.

Putting away only what was safe to leave.

He tucked the last folder into his satchel, pressed the clasp shut, and let out a breath that didn't quite steady him.

"That's all I can show you today," he said, his voice low but sure. "The rest… I'll bring tomorrow."

Graves gave him a single, short nod—permission to stop, permission to leave, permission to breathe.

Vander returned that nod, then looked to Maya. Not sympathy. Not reassurance. Just recognition. A quiet understanding that they were all standing inside something none of them could step out of now.

He lifted the satchel strap onto his shoulder and slipped out of the room without another word.

The door clicked closed behind him.

The hum of the overhead fixture settled into the silence he left.

Maya finished the final line, pressed the pen to the table, and exhaled slowly. The stack of papers sat complete in front of her—official, unavoidable, carrying the weight she hadn't allowed herself to feel until now.

Graves stepped forward and slid the forms toward himself.

"I'll get these filed," he said. His voice wasn't clipped anymore. It was steady in a way that made it clear he was holding his own fear down with both hands. "Placement becomes active as soon as Records logs them."

Maya nodded once. Her throat tightened but didn't break.

Graves looked at her for a long moment.

"You should go home," he said quietly. "Rest while you can."

He didn't mean sleep.

He meant: **before it gets worse.**

He gathered the paperwork, squared the edges out of habit, and walked out toward Records, the folder tucked under his arm.

Maya remained still for a few seconds, the room stretching around her like it needed the silence to finish changing shape.

Then she stood, collected her things, and followed him out—not to catch up, not to ask anything—

just because nothing in the conference room felt like it belonged to the world she had woken up in yesterday.

Chapter 22 — Lights Out

The diner was running louder than usual for a Thursday night—forks clattering, a kid banging his heels against the vinyl booth, coffee machines hissing steam into the humid air. Every table was filled. The smell of grease hung thick enough to taste. Maya stood just inside the door, uniform shirt damp with sweat from the ambulance bay, trying to ignore the dull pulse behind her eyes. Her shift wasn't over—she had stopped only long enough to refill a coffee she didn't need and maybe pretend the world wasn't falling apart outside.

A server brushed past her with a tray, muttering an apology. Something about her motion snagged wrong in Maya's peripheral vision—her shadow dragged a fraction slower than her body, the lag so slight it could've been nothing. Maya forced herself not to look twice. Everything in her life felt one second behind lately; maybe her eyes were too.

She slid onto an empty counter stool. The Formica was warm under her palms.

"Refill?" the server asked.

"Please." Maya rubbed her jaw. "Extra strong."

He nodded and turned toward the coffee pot. Another flicker—his silhouette didn't pivot with him right away. It jerked a beat late, like a puppet catching up to its strings.

Maya's breath hitched before logic shoved the fear down. **Shadow-lag was real**, yes, but not here, not now, not in a building full of people. She stared at the chrome napkin holder in front of her instead, forcing her mind back to work. Back to the paperwork Graves had pushed into her hands. Back to Lila and the way she clung to Maya's sleeve earlier like touching her was the only thing keeping the world in place.

Her radio crackled, then dropped into dead static. She lifted it, frowning. No signal. In a diner with perfect coverage?

A low hum crawled across the ceiling—fluorescent tubes rattling in their fixtures. A woman in the booth nearest the door looked up, annoyed.

"What now?" she said to no one, shaking her head.

The hum deepened, then wavered into a throbbing vibration. The overhead lights dimmed just slightly, enough to feel rather than see. Conversations slowed. Chairs stopped moving. It was the kind of shift that made the air feel heavier, as though the room had drawn in a sharp breath and held it.

A toddler in a high chair slapped his palms against his tray and then froze mid-motion, wide eyes staring toward the far corner of the diner. His little chest expanded on a trembling inhale. He whimpered, turning his head toward his mother, but his gaze kept snapping back to the dark where the restrooms were.

A silence pocket had formed so cleanly there that it swallowed even the kitchen noise.

Maya's fingers tightened around her radio. "Did anyone else feel—"

The lights pulsed.

Just once.

And went out.

Not a fade. Not a flicker.

A drop.

Black swallowed the diner whole.

Someone gasped sharply—then the room plunged into a vacuum of sound. The kind of silence that didn't feel empty, but **occupied**.

For one heartbeat, Maya sat perfectly still on the counter stool. Her eyes couldn't find shapes. Couldn't find edges. Couldn't find where the room ended. Everything felt too close. Too thick.

Then someone screamed.

Not a long scream.

Not even a full one.

It cut off halfway through the first exhale, strangled into a wet choke.

A fork clattered across tile.

Something heavy hit a table.

Maya shot to her feet, hand instinctively going to the trauma shears on her belt. Her pulse slammed against her ribs as bodies shifted blindly around her, people reaching for one another in the dark.

"Everyone stay where you are!" she shouted, voice tighter than intended. "Don't run—just stay low!"

But panic had already taken the room.

A chair toppled. Glass broke. A man cursed loudly as he tripped over something or someone on the floor. In the black, his voice cracked into a terrified sob.

The **cold** arrived like a punch.

A wave of temperature collapse rolled through the diner so fast Maya felt her skin prickle with needles. Her breath came out in a pale fog. Someone whispered, "Why is it freezing?"

Another scream ripped through the dark—this one high, wet, and suddenly cut short.

Emergency lighting sputtered once from behind the counter, then snapped on fully—a narrow red strip casting the room in blood-warm glow.

And the diner was no longer just chaotic.

It was broken.

To Maya's left, a man lay slumped sideways in a booth, head dangling unnaturally. His throat was **inverted**, the airway crushed so precisely it looked carved inward. Frost clung **inside** the collapsed wound. His eyes were wide, as if the last thing he saw was something he couldn't comprehend.

Closer to the kitchen, a woman was half-folded over the juke-box—her body bent backward, ribs spread open like someone had forced both hands into her chest and **bowed the cage outward** without breaking the skin. The shape of her torso was wrong. Too open. Too hollow.

Behind the counter, a cook lay on his side, apron soaked through. The left flank of his body dipped inward, soft tissues eaten out in a smooth crescent, incomplete but grotesquely efficient.

People screamed. Someone retched violently. A teenager in a letterman jacket tried to crawl backward under a table, one shoe slipping in something dark smeared across the tile.

Maya's mind snapped into EMT mode, even as cold gnawed at her bones.

"Anyone conscious, call out!" she shouted.

A sob came from her right. A whispered "help" from her left.

Then—

A phone flashlight blinked on in a shaking hand near the center of the room.

It illuminated nothing at first.

Then the screen **glitched**, fracturing into static, the image fracturing into blocks. For a single frozen frame, the lens caught something at the restroom hallway—

A silhouette.

Tall.

Bent.

Limb stretching at an angle no joint should allow.

And then the frame collapsed into black static.

Someone screamed again, shrill enough to scrape Maya's nerves raw.

"Stay down!" Maya yelled. "Don't run, stay where you are! We'll get you out—just stay low!"

The red emergency strip guttered again—hard—throwing a smear of bloody color across the diner. The shadows it cast weren't behaving. They didn't stretch from people. They stretched **toward** them.

The temperature kept dropping. Fast. Too fast. Maya could feel the cold punching through her uniform, kneading into the marrow of her hands. A woman's breath billowed out beside her in such a dense plume it looked like smoke from a split lung.

Then something thudded under a booth so violently the entire table jumped an inch.

A man screamed—one of the truckers near the front. He stumbled backward, knocking over chairs, hands clamped around his own throat. Maya ran toward him—fast—only for him to collapse on his side. His airway was already **gone**, crushed from the inside, the flesh around it **wrinkled inward** as though pulled through a collapsing pipe. White crystals webbed the cavity.

Someone else shouted, "Help him—please—help him—"

Maya checked, but the man wasn't breathing. The cold radiating off him was strong enough to sting the backs of her fingers.

A sound tore through the dark—

A **long, low dragging** sound.

Not like something being pulled.

Like something **pulling itself**.

The emergency light flickered hard, and for a split flash Maya saw the floor shift—no, **the shadows** on the floor shifted—sliding under tables like they were hunting in the open.

A server near the counter lurched forward, suddenly choking. His feet lifted off the tile for half a second before he was thrown down so brutally that one of his knees buckled sideways with an audible crack. Maya sprinted toward him, but she wasn't fast enough. His back arched unnaturally, spine jerking in staccato spasms, and then something inside his torso **collapsed inward**—a soft, obscene fold-ing sound that sucked the breath out of the man next to him.

Maya landed next to the server on her knees, hands flying to his ribcage. It had caved inward as if something had **bitten through bone from the inside**, pulling it toward the organs instead of away from them. The sternum hadn't broken; it had **bowed backward**, smooth and precise.

He was still warm.

He had been alive seconds ago.

A plate whirled across the floor, spinning so fast the ceramic whis-tled before shattering against the wall.

Someone screamed behind her.

Then another voice—raw, breaking: "It's in the dark—oh God—no—"

The cold smashed deeper. Maya felt it latch onto her lungs in a way she had never felt before—like inhaling knives. Her breath fogged so violently she couldn't see past it for a second.

She wiped her mouth, turned—and froze.

At the farthest booth, a woman was half on the floor, head twisted at an angle no neck could tolerate. Her hair stuck to the wall where something slick had hit it. Her torso had been opened without a tear—**the skin stretched thin over a hollowed side**, muscles drawn inward like pulled taffy. Her mouth was wide, still trying to scream.

Not eaten.

Collapsed.

Folded toward nothing.

A man lunged from behind the counter, tripping over a wet smear—blood—and fell face-first. Before Maya could shout, the shad-ows under the counter **compressed** toward him, a tight, focused movement that made no physical sense.

He screamed—cut short as his chest hit the tile and **flattened**. Not crushed. Flattened. His ribcage didn't break outward; it **imploded**, the cartilage popping in a rapid, wet sequence that sounded like bones inhaling.

Maya staggered back a step, hand slamming against a booth to steady herself. She could taste copper on her tongue.

"Move!" someone shrieked. "It's coming from—"

The emergency light blinked hard again—

And something **skittered across the ceiling** so fast the tiles flexed downward, dust raining onto Maya's shoulders. Claws—no, not claws, points—pierced the paneling for a split moment, dragging a jagged path above the diners' heads.

A child screamed—a sound so thin and high it cut straight through the chaos.

Maya bolted toward it.

Under a booth, a boy no older than six was curled around himself, face frozen in a silent wail. His tiny body shook so violently his sneakers tapped the tile in rapid, panicked beats. The cold around him was the deepest yet—his breath fogging so thickly it clung to his eyelashes.

"Hey," Maya kneeled down, swallowing back the panic clawing at her throat. "I've got you, okay? I'm right here. Look at me."

He didn't blink.

He wasn't looking **at** her—

He was looking **past** her, over her shoulder, into the dark.

She didn't turn.

Couldn't turn.

If she turned, she wasn't sure she'd keep moving.

"Come on," she whispered, sliding her hands under him. "Come on—we're moving."

The emergency light sputtered again—harder—flickering in jagged, violent bursts that made shadows strobe across the boy's face like claws closing in.

Maya lifted him. His body was trembling so violently she nearly dropped him.

A tray launched from the pass window at their backs—and slammed into the opposite wall with bone-jarring force.

The man under the next booth twitched—once—then his entire spine **snapped downward**, compressing into a shape that looked like he had been folded in half at the waist from inside the body itself. His last exhale came out in a thin, bubbling hiss.

Maya gripped the boy tighter and rose, boots sliding across something slick and cold.

The red strip light flickered so hard it buzzed like a dying insect.

The diner plunged back into darkness as the glow failed, the black swallowing everything in front of her while she stepped forward with the child in her arms.

The darkness didn't settle.

It **shifted**.

Maya could feel it moving around her—not wind, not air displacement, but pressure. Like the black itself had weight. The little boy in her arms convulsed in another tight shiver, his fingers digging into her uniform with enough force to hurt.

Somewhere ahead, glass shattered.

Not like a cup falling.

Like something had **punched** through it.

A man cried out—raw, wordless—followed by the sound of something heavy hitting the wall hard enough to make the entire diner shudder. Maya crouched instinctively, shielding the boy, her breath fogging so thick it curled around her face like smoke.

The emergency strip light surged back for a heartbeat.

One heartbeat.

It was enough.

The diner's interior lit up in a smear of red—and every corner was filled with bodies that hadn't been bodies seconds ago.

A woman near the entrance was pinned upright against the coat rack, her spine bent backward until her head hung limp against her own shoulder. Her ribcage had been forced open in two places, cartilage spread almost delicately, as if something had pressed outward from inside and then simply left her there, arranged.

A cluster of teens near the windows huddled together, sobbing, but Maya's eyes snapped to the one slumped forward in their midst—his chest sunken so sharply that his sternum nearly touched his spine. His friends didn't even know he was dead yet.

At the far booth, a man's legs stuck out, twitching faintly—his torso was wedged beneath the table, spine twisted in a spiral like something had gripped his shoulders and **wrung him**.

The red light faltered.

Maya moved.

She didn't think. She didn't look behind her. She grabbed at the nearest overturned chair to steady herself as she slipped on a smear of blood made slick by the cold. The boy whimpered, a choked little sound pressed against her collarbone.

A sound tore across the ceiling—

A rapid scatter of impacts

—like many thin limbs tapping in sequence, moving far too fast.

Chunks of plaster fell. A ceiling tile snapped in half and dropped beside Maya with a sharp crack, dust raining down like gray ash. She looked up.

Nothing.

But something had been there.

The cold intensified again—tightening around her ribs like a hand.

Half the remaining diners began screaming at once.

The emergency light snapped back on.

This time it didn't flicker.

It **strobed**.

The bursts of red fire lit the room in violent flashes—each long enough to reveal a different piece of hell.

FLASH—

A man clawed at his own throat, eyes bulging as his windpipe collapsed in a silent crush, like an invisible fist squeezing until cartilage compressed into itself.

FLASH—

A server tried to crawl toward the kitchen. His shadow lagged behind him by almost a full second, stretched too tall, twitching in ways his body didn't.

FLASH—

A woman fell backward over a table, landing with a thud. Frost fanned outward from under her body, blooming across the tiles like veins of ice.

FLASH—

Something slammed into the ceiling above Maya again—this time hard enough that she felt the shock through the floor. The boy in her arms screamed.

FLASH—

A man at the counter was jerked sideways, slammed spine-first into the metal napkin dispenser. His torso buckled like a paper cup crushed in a fist. His legs spasmed once, then dangled uselessly off the stool.

FLASH—

Shadows along the far wall bent sharply inward, as if the darkness were being pulled through a narrowing gap.

"Maya!" someone shouted—she didn't know who, didn't look. Her world had narrowed to the screaming child in her arms and the brief red strobes mapping out where she could step without falling or slipping or dying.

She ducked low, cradling the boy tighter as another body fell from somewhere above, hitting the tile so close she felt blood mist her cheek.

The cold rolled again, a suffocating wave that made her lungs ache.

Then the red strip light failed a second time—
the glow collapsing inward
and the black swallowing the diner whole.

Maya shifted her grip on the child and stepped toward the only place she hadn't seen bodies stacked—
toward the far end of the room, where a thin slit of pale light seeped

under the exit door

and the screaming didn't sound as thick.

The pale line under the exit door brightened—just for a second—as something outside passed through the glow of approaching headlights. Maya shoved forward, the boy clinging to her, his breath coming in thin, terrified whimpers against her neck. The air inside the diner felt heavier with every step, pressure thick enough to make her ears ring.

Behind her, something hit the floor hard—so hard the impact tremored through the tiles. A table leg snapped with a sharp wooden crack. Someone screamed. Someone else choked mid-word. A metallic dragging sound scraped across the ceiling like something too long and too jointed was repositioning itself directly above the remaining survivors.

Maya didn't turn. She kept moving toward the only hint of light left in the building.

The cold surged again—so intense her vision blurred around the edges. Frost traced itself across the tile in branching veins, racing outward from a point behind her. The boy in her arms convulsed once, fingers digging into her uniform.

Closer. Just a few more steps.

Then, for several seconds, the entire diner fell into a silence so absolute it felt wrong—pressure dropping out of the air, oxygen thinning. Maya could feel her heartbeat in her teeth.

A wet exhale sounded somewhere in the dark.

Not close.

Not far.

Just *there*.

Her legs nearly buckled, but she forced one foot forward, then another.

Outside—

sirens.

Growing louder.

Blue light flickered across the front windows in fractured pulses. The boy in her arms tensed at the sound, burying his face against her collar.

Maya forced herself another step forward.

A heavy shudder hit the far side of the diner—something falling, something dragged, something shifting its weight in the dark. She didn't turn. Couldn't. The pressure around her lungs felt like it was trying to squeeze her breath out of her body.

Then—

The front door exploded inward in a burst of cold night air.

Flashlights slashed through the dark, beams jerking as officers pushed inside.

Shouts overlapped—sharp, panicked, human:

"Police—hands visible!"

"Is anyone alive in here?"

"Fan out, check the corners—watch your sectors!"

The overhead fluorescents sputtered in the same instant, buzzing angrily as they fought to rewarm. One tube lit. Another. The whole room stuttered into a flickering half-light that showed just enough—

—and all the shouting stopped.

Tables overturned.

Blood sprayed across the walls.

Bodies bent into shapes that did not belong to living anatomy.

Ribcages crushed inward.

Spines twisted.

Frost drifting from collapsed throats.

Shadows misaligned from the bodies that cast them.

One officer staggered sideways, hand clapped over his mouth. Another lowered his weapon without realizing it, eyes glassing with shock.

A rookie backed into a coat rack, breath stuttering too fast to be useful.

Maya blinked against the sudden light, tightening her hold on the little boy. He clung to her, shaking.

A paramedic hustled through the doorway behind the officers, skidding to a stop when his brain finally registered the scene. His gaze snapped to Maya—not because he'd known she was there, but because she was the **only uniformed responder standing upright**.

"Jesus—Raine?" he breathed, voice cracking. "Give him here—I've got him."

She handed the boy over, fingers numb, breath still fogging faintly from the cold.

"You injured?" someone yelled from behind the counter, but the voice was raw, barely steady.

Maya shook her head, once. "There are survivors. They need help."

She stepped away from the doorway—into the chaos of lights and bodies and the living—and moved toward the next person who hadn't stopped breathing yet.

Chapter 23 — The Archivist Falls

The university's Special Collections wing always felt a little too old for the rest of the campus—older wood, older air, older silence. Vander pressed the intercom button with one hand while the other tightened on the strap of his satchel. His pulse beat quicker than usual under his thumb, something close to anticipation humming through him.

The lock buzzed and clicked open.

He stepped inside.

The smell settled around him immediately: old paper, dust warmed by decades of flickering fluorescent lights, the faint metallic tang of antique ink. The overhead fixtures hummed in uneven tones, each bulb emitting its own wavering frequency. Vander paused beneath the first light, listening to the dissonance as if the room were tuning itself wrong.

"Back room's yours," the night librarian muttered without looking up. She swiped her keycard across a stack of returns and disappeared through a side doorway. "If the alarms chirp, ignore them. Breaker's been acting up."

Her footsteps faded quickly.

The hallway to Special Collections stretched ahead in a long carved-out lane between towering shelves. Motion-sensor lights flicked on in delayed intervals—one overhead, one several feet ahead, another that sputtered twice before staying lit. Strips of shadow pooled in the gaps.

"Old wiring," Vander whispered to himself, though the empty acoustics made the words feel thin.

His footsteps clicked too sharply across the tile. No students studying late. No distant printers. No voices. Just the sterile echo he associated with morgue corridors Graves had shown him early in the investigation—spaces that swallowed sound and waited for it to come back wrong.

He reached the locked cabinet where restricted materials were preserved. Through the glass, the ledger sat on its shelf, leather cracked and faded, its crest worn into an indistinct bruise of ink. Dust coated the metal trim around it.

He keyed in the access code.

A soft chirp.

The latch released.

He reached inside.

The moment his fingers closed around the ledger's spine, a faint static prickled across his skin.

He stiffened.

The reports had mentioned effects like this—equipment cutting out, radios dying, dust lifting in strange patterns on the pavement. He'd seen the photos, the margins Graves had underlined, the notations of unexplained cold pockets and electrical disturbances.

The ledger had no reason to hum.

He set it on the reading table gently.

He opened to the first page. The brittle paper crackled like frost-split branches. Inked folklore lined the margins: early accounts of shadow figures in old port towns, joint distortions in bodies found in the late 1600s, references to "night-walkers" described by sailors who never agreed on what they'd seen. Nothing he hadn't cataloged before.

He turned the next page.

His breath caught.

A ribcage sketched in meticulous ink—bowed outward, ribs strained but not snapped. Force applied along the inner arc. The configuration matched an old coroner sketch Graves had shown him last month—pressure points that didn't follow any anatomical logic.

He turned another.

A spinal column imploding inward, vertebrae drawn as if pulled toward the body's midline. The same concave collapse he'd seen in the alley photographs. Graves had traced the shape over and over, calling attention to the unnatural symmetry.

A cold shiver crept along Vander's arms.

He flipped again.

Temperature-drop notes. References to breath crystallizing. Shadow elongation drawn in six different hands. Maps of crescent-shaped arcs across continents. Cases spread hundreds of years apart with identical trauma signatures.

And then—

Ten small marks arranged in a curved line.

Ten deaths.

A repeating arc.

At the bottom corner of the page, nearly lost to age, a cramped line of handwriting:

"The ninth comes where fear breaks."

Vander leaned closer, heart pounding in his ears. He didn't understand the phrase, but he knew its weight. The timing. The cycle. The warning that had been waiting for someone patient—and terrified—enough to read it.

He reached into his coat for his phone to photograph the page.

The screen stayed black.

He tapped again.

Nothing.

Another tap.

Still nothing.

The motion-sensor light at the far end of the aisle blinked out.

Vander froze.

A second fixture died.

Then a third.

Darkness advanced down the row in measured intervals, swallowing the stacks section by section.

"Come on," he whispered to his phone, tapping it again.

Still dead.

He lifted his eyes toward the exit. The red glow of the emergency sign cast a warped, bloody halo across the tiles.

The air pressure shifted.

Not wind.

Not movement.

A tightening.

As if the hallway itself were bearing down on him.

Vander stepped back—instinct, small and controlled—until his spine pressed against the tall shelving. The metal vibrated under his weight, followed by a low groan.

The sound didn't come from him.

Something impossibly tall had moved along the back of the shelves. The vibration in the metal still trembled faintly, as if settling from contact.

A thin stream of vapor escaped Vander's mouth—white, brief, sharp.

Cold.

Sudden.

Localized.

The exit sign flickered.

A single, pulsing stutter of red.

Vander's pulse slammed hard against his ribs. He reached blindly for the ledger, for his bag, for anything with weight—anything that felt real.

Somewhere in the dark behind him, a tall shape shifted its weight. No sound.

No breath.

Just the faintest suggestion of presence.

His own breath hitched.

"…no."

The darkness pressed closer, heavy and deliberate

The lights over the reading table flickered once—hard—bathing the ledger in a tremor of yellow. Vander drew a slow breath, trying to steady the shake in his fingers. The cold in the room had deepened by a subtle but unmistakable degree, the kind that didn't belong in a building with sealed windows and an always-too-warm HVAC system.

He dragged the ledger a little closer.

The sketches on the next page were even more detailed than the last. Inked angles mapped the force vectors of a ribcage distortion. Scribbled notes in three different handwritings circled the inward bow of a spinal collapse. Margin annotations described temperature anomalies in cramped, archaic English. The lines were almost frantic—whoever recorded them had been trying to capture something that defied their language.

Vander set a palm on the page to keep it flat. The paper felt colder than the table beneath it.

He swallowed.

He turned another page.

Here, the sketches changed style entirely—less anatomical, more geometric. Crescent arcs marked across hand-drawn maps of Europe, South America, the northern U.S. regions. Each arc contained ten small notches. Always ten. Always in the same curve.

Vander followed the arc with his fingertip.

Ten kills.

One cycle.

Over and over again.

And each historical cluster showed the same forensic signatures:

— collapsed airway without external trauma

— ribcage distortion without tearing

— abdominal depressions without penetration wounds

— localized cold zones around newly dead bodies

Graves had noted the exact same patterns on his legal pad.

Vander's pulse throbbed. He flipped to the next page.

It didn't contain imagery.

It contained confirmation.

A meticulous list of years and cities—Lisbon, Antwerp, Temuco, Halifax, New Orleans—each followed by a short line of text written in an increasingly unsteady hand: "ten marked," "ten hollowed," "cycle complete," "arc holds."

Vander's stomach twisted.

He flipped again.

That was when he found the page he'd only skimmed earlier—the one he'd recognized instantly but hadn't been ready to face.

The handwritten arc.

Ten marks drawn at precise intervals.

And in the lower right corner, almost invisible under age and fading ink:

"The ninth comes where fear breaks."

His chest tightened. He leaned closer, tracing the marks with his eyes. The handwriting wasn't decorative—it was cramped, urgent, like a warning carved in haste.

A faint vibration tremored beneath his fingertips.

He jerked his hand back.

The ledger stayed still. But the table under it... no, not the table. The *floor*, maybe. Or the shelf behind him. Or—

A soft metallic click echoed from the aisle behind him.

Not a footstep.

Not a book shifting.

A lock.

The kind of small mechanical sound a door makes when it closes itself.

Vander turned his head slowly. The far end of the aisle had grown darker, even though the nearest emergency fixture still cast a weak red glow down the hallway. The shadows between the shelves looked deeper now, like they had thickened.

He looked back at the ledger.

The page with the ten marks trembled again—barely—a whisper of movement like a breath passing over it.

He pressed his palm to it to keep it down.

Cold bit into his skin.

He pulled his hand back fast, wiping the frost-mist off on his coat. His pulse surged in his ears, a dull pounding that made the silence around him feel thinner, stretched like a membrane about to split.

He reached inside his coat for his phone again on instinct—dead. Still dead.

He set his jaw and leaned over the ledger, bringing it closer to the edge of the table. The lighting overhead dimmed another notch, buzzing low like something straining inside the wiring.

He slid the ledger slightly toward him, hesitated, then hooked his fingers under the bottom corner of the page with the arc.

If he couldn't photograph it, he needed to remove it.

The paper resisted at first, stiff from age. Then it tore—slowly, jaggedly, the sound too loud in the quiet.

He froze mid-tear.

A light at the opposite end of the row blinked out.

The next one followed.

And the next.

Darkness advanced down the aisle in a clean, predatory sequence, eating the room fixture by fixture.

Vander kept tearing, breath shaking. The page came free with a final brittle rip.

The lights over the reading table flickered again—once—twice—

The ledger's remaining pages rustled without any movement of air.

Vander's breath fogged sharply in front of him.

He gripped the torn page in one hand, his other hand braced on the table edge.

Something brushed the far end of the shelving.

Tall.

Slow.

Just enough contact to make the metal complain.

Vander stepped backward.

Just one step.

The next light died.

And he moved again, page clutched tight in his hand as the darkness closed in behind him.

The next light died with a soft electric pop, and the aisle ahead dropped into a fuller, heavier dark. Vander backed away from the table, one hand braced against the shelf, the torn ledger page crumpled in his other fist. His breathing sounded too loud. Too sharp. The shadows between the stacks didn't look like absence—they looked *occupied*.

He took another step.

A cold draft slipped across the back of his neck.

Not airflow.

Not circulation.

Something colder than the room, colder than the building, colder than anything mechanical could produce.

He swallowed hard and turned toward the faint glow of the emergency exit sign at the far end. The red block of light distorted across the floor, stretching into a long warped smear.

Another fixture blinked out.

A shiver climbed his spine.

He pressed the ledger to his chest, hand shaking. The leather felt colder now, as if the chill were seeping into it. He started down the aisle, moving slowly at first, then faster as another light flickered above him.

A soft creak sounded to his right.

Not wood.

Not shelves.

Something taller than the shelving shifting its weight.

He froze.

His breath clouded into a thin white plume.

The air pressure changed again—dropping suddenly, like oxygen had been sucked out of the space around him. His ears popped. His eyes watered. The silence thickened into something physical, something that pressed against his skull.

Vander's chest tightened.

He forced himself to take one step toward the exit.

Just one.

Something brushed the top of the shelving behind him with a long, slow drag.

Metal vibrated. The entire row tremored.

He staggered forward, gripping the ledger page tighter, heart pounding so loudly he swore it echoed off the stacks. His vision flickered at the edges—not from fear, but from the cold that was settling deep into his lungs.

He moved again. A second step. A third.

Then—

A shadow at the end of the aisle folded inward like a hinge bending the wrong way.

The emergency sign flickered.

The silence collapsed in on itself.

Something huge shifted behind him—

—and hit him from the back with a force that felt like the air itself had turned solid.

Vander's body lifted off the ground.

He didn't even hear himself hit the opposite shelf. The impact knocked every ounce of air out of him in a single brutal expulsion. The ledger flew from his grip, slamming open on the floor. The torn page remained crushed in his hand.

He tried to inhale.

A sudden pressure clamped around his throat—sharp, crushing, inward.

A wet collapse.

A splitting pinch of bone and cartilage crushed into itself.

No sound came out.

Not even a gasp.

His knees buckled as whatever held him released. He hit the floor hard, his skull bouncing once against the tile. His vision scattered into starburst fragments.

The silence changed—thickening, concentrating.

A second pressure slammed into his sternum. Ice exploded outward from the point of impact, spreading across his chest like frost climbing a windowpane. His muscles seized. His vision tunneled.

He tried to crawl.

His right arm jerked forward; his left dragged weakly underneath him. His legs didn't respond. Something inside his lower spine folded inward, a brutal concave crush that felt like vertebrae collapsing toward each other.

He couldn't breathe.

He couldn't call out.

All he could do was move his hand—just barely—dragging the torn page beneath him as the cold closed around his ribs like a tightening vise.

A shape blocked the emergency sign for half a heartbeat.

A long, crooked silhouette bending at an angle no joints should allow.

Then it withdrew into the stacks.

Silent.

Efficient.

Gone.

Vander's vision blurred.

He pressed the torn page to his chest with the last of his strength.

His fingers stiffened.

His breath stuttered.

The cold deepened until it felt like his bones were turning brittle.

And he kept moving—just enough to pull the page tighter against his body before the dark overtook everything else.

The frost held him in a quiet the building didn't deserve. Thin white veins stretched outward from Vander's chest, branching across the tile like roots searching for warmth that wasn't there.

His hand stayed locked around the torn ledger page.

No breath.

No movement.

Just that faint, impossible cold radiating from the point of impact.

Minutes passed in a silence that felt too heavy for a university archive.

A distant door buzzed.

Soft footsteps approached—hesitant, casual at first. The night librarian rounding the corner from her break.

"Lights… why are they—?"

She stopped speaking.

Her steps slowed.

A faint scrape of her shoe against the tile.

Then she saw him.

At first, she didn't scream. She made a small sound—barely a syllable—something caught between breath and disbelief. Her books slid from her hands, scattering across the floor with soft, uneven thumps.

"…sir?"

It wasn't a real question. It was an instinct.

She took one step closer.

The frost caught the dim light in brittle blue-white cracks.

She clapped a hand over her mouth and stumbled backward, hitting the wall with enough force to jolt the emergency phone. Her trembling fingers searched for the receiver, knocking it off once before catching it properly.

"H-hello—? Please—Special Collections—there's—there's a man, he's—he's frozen—he's not—please send help—"

Her voice broke.

She slid down the wall until she was sitting on the tile, knees pulled to her chest, shaking violently as the line clicked dead.

Silence settled again.

Not total, but close.

The sirens began faintly, far off at first, then growing louder, echoing between brick buildings outside. The librarian pressed herself against the wall and didn't move until red and blue flashed through the high windows.

"Police!" a voice called down the hall. "Ma'am—stay where you are!"

Boots thundered toward her.

Officers swept past, their flashlights slicing through the dim corridor and into the reading room.

A low curse.

A sharp inhale.

Someone muttered, "What the hell...?"

They didn't touch the body. They didn't touch the ledger. They only stepped in enough to confirm one thing.

"Dispatch, scene secured," one officer said quietly into his radio. "EMS needed. This is… not normal."

"Copy," dispatch replied. "Unit responding."

———

Maya reached the hallway seconds after the officers gave clearance. The cold hit her first—the kind that crawled straight through fabric and bone. She tightened her grip on her trauma bag and stepped into the reading room.

Her breath fogged instantly.

And then she saw him.

"Vander?"

It wasn't a whisper. It was air leaving her lungs in a single broken exhale.

She crossed to him fast, but her steps slowed the moment she saw the shape of his back, the inward collapse of his spine, the frost blooming across his chest.

Her knees hit the tile beside him.

She checked for a pulse she already knew wasn't there. Her gloved fingers hovered for a moment over the bent angle of his ribs, the cold still radiating from his sternum.

Her throat tightened hard enough to hurt.

An officer stepped closer, voice low.

"There's something in his hand. We figured you should look before we touch anything."

Maya forced her breath steady.

She leaned in and examined Vander's frozen grip, teeth clenching as she eased her fingers under his stiffened knuckles. Frost cracked softly as she coaxed the page free.

The paper slid loose with brittle resistance.

She held it up toward the nearest beam of light.

A crescent arc.

Ten small marks.

A cramped line of handwriting bending with the curve.

Her stomach dropped.

Her hands tightened around the page.

One officer murmured, "What the hell does that mean?"

Maya swallowed once, the answer forming not in words but in a cold pressure behind her ribs.

"It means," she said quietly, "you need to bag this. Right now."

The officer sealed the page into an evidence sleeve. Another stepped farther into the room, radio buzzing at his shoulder, calling for detectives and command staff.

Maya rose slowly, breath still visible in the air. She looked down at Vander's body one last time, the frost, the impossible violence, the silence pressing in from every direction.

Her jaw tightened.

She stepped into the hallway.

The cold didn't disappear behind her.

It followed her into the corridor, riding the air like residue.

She adjusted her bag on her shoulder and kept walking—because stopping wasn't an option anymore.

Chapter 24 — The Breakpoint

By morning, the town felt thinner—like the air itself had been stretched too far overnight.

Screens lit up across kitchens, break rooms, patrol cars, and convenience store counters as the first major leak hit social feeds. It wasn't a single clip. It was a chain—stitched uploads, mirrored angles, pixelated zooms. The diner blackout was everywhere.

A teenager's shaky phone footage led most of the threads. The lights died; someone screamed; shapes blurred across the dark. Then the frame fractured—jittering static, warped geometry, shadows that leaned in the wrong direction. When emergency lighting flared back on, bodies lay collapsed across booths and tile in a pattern no one could explain.

Some commenters insisted it was doctored. Others pointed out the timestamp matched scanner archives. Arguments flared and multiplied, dozens deep within minutes.

The next leak was worse.

A truncated segment from the **first responder's bodycam**—the early case the department had tried to bury under "equipment malfunction." Only thirty-three seconds made it online, but it was enough:

A man stumbled into frame, breath thinning in rapid, shallow pulls as though the air around him had been scooped out. A brief cold flicker washed across the camera—sharp, unnatural—and the audio dropped into a flat electrical hum. Then the collapse. Sudden. Wrong. The geometry of the frame bent just slightly as he hit the ground.

Commenters slowed the clip to forty percent speed, circling distortions in red: angles that tightened, corners that folded inward, a booth edge bending at an impossible margin between frames.

"What artifact makes someone's breath vanish like that?" someone wrote.

Another user stitched the diner clip beside the bodycam segment. In both, a shadow at the edge of frame seemed to move *before* the person did—a fraction of a fraction, barely visible unless viewed frame-by-frame.

Theories ignited instantly:

"Gas leak hallucinations."

"Riot-control experimental tech."

"No—this is something else. Look at the geometry."

A man watching the videos in his apartment felt a sudden cold flicker across his forearm—brief, like the sensation of opening a freezer door too close to skin. His next inhale caught shallow in his chest. He rubbed his arm, replayed the clip, confused and uneasy.

On a conspiracy forum, someone overlaid all confirmed incidents on a digital map—the early bodycam case, the missing persons clustering across downtown, the diner. The dots curved subtly, unintentionally forming a crescent. Another user traced the arc with a shaking stylus.

"Nah, coincidence," someone replied.

But then more users added locations.

And the line became clearer.

Fear-density rose in pockets around town—clusters of people watching the same leaked videos, arguments turning frantic, breath catching in shared moments when multiple viewers noticed the same distortion.

In the EMS station break room, Maya passed a coworker's phone and froze—not at the imagery, but at the sharp, brief tightness under her sternum. A second-long hitch in her inhale, just like she'd felt at multiple scenes. Not cold. Not frost. Just that pressure.

She pushed through it. She didn't want to watch the clip again.

Outside, a group gathered under a bus stop awning, replaying the diner angle over and over. As panic rose among them, the hum of the powerline overhead shifted pitch—dropping into a low, uneven vibration that made a few people glance up nervously.

A rumor began spreading within half an hour:
someone online claimed the police were "hiding something tall in the footage."

No proof.
No silhouette.
Just the wrongness caught in pixels.

The town inhaled—sharp, uneven, uncertain.

By noon, the police department tried to seize back control with a hastily assembled press conference. Uniforms crowded behind a folding table under harsh office lighting, microphones tangled together in a mess of cables. Reporters pressed tight against the rail, phones raised, lenses fixed.

Captain Ruiz stepped to the mic.

"The circulating videos are under review," he began. "We are coordinating with state investigators. There is no confirmed link between—"

A reporter cut him off.

"Then why do the timestamps match your own dispatch logs?"

"That information is still being evaluated."

Another voice rose immediately:

"What about the respiratory distress noted in multiple EMS reports?"

Ruiz stiffened.

"We can't verify those claims."

"But the victims' breath disappears mid-frame," someone else shouted. "Explain that."

A ripple moved through the crowd. Several people leaned closer, breath catching just briefly — shallow, incomplete inhales, the kind that left a moment of pressure in their chests. A few rubbed at their throats without quite knowing why.

Ruiz tried again.

"There is no evidence of any... unusual assailant behavior."

"Then what crushes a ribcage from the inside?"

"What makes shadows move before the person does?"

"What's causing the distortions in the video?"

Questions collided over one another, the noise rising, the control slipping. Officers exchanged glances behind the barricades — they could feel the shift too. The crowd wasn't just angry; it was afraid. Compressed. Breathing unevenly.

Maya watched from the edge of the lot, leaning against her rig between calls. She could feel the tension layering through the crowd — the same thin-air sensation she'd felt at several scenes. Not frost. Not feeding cold. Just the subtle oxygen-thin pressure that always crept in when fear pooled too densely.

A woman near the front gasped in a single sharp inhale, blinking fast as though her lungs hadn't taken enough air. Maya saw it. The fear-feeding signature — brief, shallow, gone before anyone could register what they'd felt.

Inside her kitchen, Lila watched the livestream on her tablet. When the shouting peaked, the hallway behind her seemed to tighten by a fraction — the shadows pulling subtly toward the far end, like depth had shifted without light changing. She pressed a hand to her sternum. Her breath narrowed, shallow and uncertain.

She stepped backward until her shoulders hit the refrigerator.

The sensation faded.

But the panic didn't.

Outside the precinct, the press conference broke down completely. Ruiz abandoned the podium. Officers tried to separate the crowd, voices rising above fraying tempers. Someone shouted they were being lied to. Someone else started crying. A man bent forward, hands braced on his knees, breath thin and rapid.

The air felt wrong again — not cold, not freezing — just too light, as if the atmosphere had thinned in isolated pockets.

Maya retreated toward her rig, eyes scanning for anyone in medical distress. No collapses. No visible injuries. Just panic stacking on panic, amplifying itself.

Her phone vibrated.

A text with a city extension but no saved contact name:

Raine. Call me.

—Graves

Her pulse spiked.

She stepped into the cab, shut the door against the crowd noise, and dialed.

He answered halfway through the first ring.

"Maya," Graves said. His voice was strained, the edge she'd only heard once before — at the first impossible death they'd worked together. "Can you come in?"

She sat straighter. "What happened?"

A long exhale on the other end — not relief, not steadiness. Something cracking.

"Just get here," he said. "Please."

He hung up.

Maya stared at her phone, the last word echoing harder than it should have. Graves never said *please*. Not like that.

Outside, the crowd surged again.

A reporter shouted something unintelligible.

Shadows shifted as a cloud crossed the sun.

Maya grabbed her keys, swung out of the rig, and started toward the building.

Graves wasn't in his usual bullpen corner when Maya arrived. The station felt off the moment she stepped inside—voices sharper, footsteps quicker, the entire building moving with the twitchy rhythm of people pretending they weren't afraid.

An officer pointed her toward the investigative wing.

"He's in the conference room. Been in there awhile."

Maya thanked him and headed down the corridor. The lights above hummed in an uneven pitch, brightening and dipping in small pulses. Not flickering—just straining, like the building was holding its breath.

She pushed open the door.

Graves stood over a long table, both hands braced on its edge, shoulders tight. Papers covered the surface—crime-scene notes, missing persons lists, timestamp logs, stills from the diner blackout, and in the center, sealed inside an evidence sleeve, the torn page Maya had pulled from Vander's hand.

He didn't look at her right away.

"Close the door," he said.

She did.

Only then did he lift the torn page by its sleeve, holding it up to the overhead light. The inked arc curved gently across the brittle yellow paper. Ten small marks dotted the line at near-perfect intervals. Someone—long before any of them—had written a note beneath the arc in cramped handwriting.

Graves kept staring at it like it might shift.

Maya stepped closer. "You got it logged in already."

He nodded, jaw tight. "Came in about an hour ago. Evidence tech brought it straight to me."

His voice wasn't steady.

She'd never heard his voice do that.

Graves set the page down and reached for a map beside it—one with pins marking disappearances, strange deaths, and emergency calls stretching back over several months. Another sheet held the diner positions. A third held incident coordinates from older files Vander had compiled.

He pulled a straight-edge ruler across them, lining up clusters.

The arcs overlapped.

Not perfectly, but close enough that the pattern was undeniable.

Maya exhaled through her nose, slow. "You think Vander knew what he was marking?"

"I don't know what he knew." Graves dragged a hand down his face. "But whoever wrote this—" he tapped the torn page "—was tracking something we've been stumbling into blind."

He reached for another file, flipping through injury reports with trembling fingers.

"Look at this," he said. "Internal compressions with no external trauma. Collapsed airways with no bruising. Vertebral torque without fracture displacement. It doesn't make sense."

He looked up at her then.

"It *can't* be a person doing this."

Maya stiffened.

For a moment her lungs tightened—not panic, not cold, but a thin-air pressure blooming at the base of her throat. She swallowed against it and stepped closer.

"Okay," she said quietly. "If it's not a person... then what? A group? Some kind of coordinated attack? Tech we don't know about? Gas? Pressure waves?"

Graves shook his head. "Nothing we have explains the geometry distortions. Or the respiratory events. Or the shadow displacement."

He tapped a diner still.
The one where the emergency lights had just come on, showing the collapsed bodies.

"Look at the way her shadow bends," he said. "Before she falls. Before her body moves. Shadows don't do that."

His breathing hitched, barely perceptible. Maya heard it anyway.

"Whatever's doing this," he said, "it's operating outside anything we can classify."

"Graves," Maya said, voice low, "I felt something at the library. It wasn't cold like the diner. Just... thin. Like my lungs didn't know what to do for a second."

He looked at her sharply.
"And outside," she added. "Today. In the crowd. Same thing."

He nodded slowly. "Fear events. High-density panic."

He didn't look relieved. He looked sick.

"The more afraid people get, the more… whatever this is seems to react."

Maya's pulse thudded in her ears. "So fear's feeding it."

He didn't deny it.

He didn't confirm it either.

He just slid the torn page toward her and whispered, "We're running out of time to understand this."

A soft electrical tap came from the light panel overhead—just a tiny noise, but both of them looked up instinctively. The fluorescent tube brightened too sharply, washed the room in pale glare for a moment, then settled back to normal.

The air thinned again for a heartbeat.

Not cold.

Just pressure.

Maya steadied herself with a palm on the table.

Graves closed the ledger page carefully back into the evidence sleeve.

A knock hit the door—an officer, breathless, eyes wide.

"Graves," he said. "You need to hear this. Another… incident. Dispatch wants you immediately."

Maya and Graves exchanged a look.

Not confirmation.

But understanding.

They moved.

Maya stepped out of the conference room with Graves beside her, both moving quickly down the hall. Officers hurried past in tight clusters, eyes wider than they meant to show. Phones rang in short, clipped bursts. Someone down the corridor argued with a supervisor in a low, tense whisper.

The building felt tense in a way she couldn't name.

At the end of the hall, a patrol officer intercepted Graves, breath unsteady.

"Detective—there's another call. Residential. It's bad. They want you on-site."

Graves absorbed the words silently, jaw tightening. He nodded once and headed for the exit.

Maya followed, but slowed when she saw him stop abruptly at the bottom of the steps. He wasn't looking at her. He was looking at the street.

A line of storefront windows across the road held reflections that didn't match the movement of the people walking past them—shadows pulling a fraction longer behind their owners, lagging half a beat before snapping back into alignment. No one on the sidewalk seemed to notice, but it made Maya's breath catch in a thin, uneven pull.

Graves exhaled slowly, a strained sound.

"Dispatch should call you soon," he said, still watching the street. "If it's the same address, we'll both end up there."

She nodded.

A car horn blared at the intersection as a traffic light blinked twice and shifted too quickly, throwing drivers off rhythm. A few pedestrians hesitated mid-step, confused, touching their throats like something had pressed against their breathing for an instant.

Maya steadied herself.

The lights along the block dimmed in a brief wave—just a sweep of lowered brightness moving from one pole to the next, subtle enough to dismiss if she hadn't seen this kind of distortion before.

She forced her focus back to Graves.

"What did the officer tell you?"

His eyes flicked toward her. "Possible injury. Unverified circumstances."

He hesitated. "They didn't say much else."

Which meant whatever details existed weren't meant for EMS channels yet.

Before she could respond, her radio buzzed with a clipped burst of static. She adjusted the knob. The dispatcher's voice broke through—strained, words dragging in and out like the signal was trying to hold together.

"Available units respond to Lexington Terrace. Possible medical. Callers... unclear..."

The transmission wavered, then stabilized just enough to give co-ordinates.

Maya didn't need more.

She jogged toward her rig.

Across the street, one of the storefront reflections shuddered—the shadow inside the glass leaning a fraction outward before falling back into place as if nothing had shifted at all.

People walked on, unaware.

Maya climbed into the rig, shut the door, and turned the key. The engine caught, vibrating beneath her hands. Her breath came thin for a second—just long enough to feel the pressure settle in her chest—before easing again.

She pulled out of the lot.

Ahead, the block-length line of streetlamps dropped in brightness one after another, a soft descending ripple guiding her toward the turn that would take her to Lexington.

She accelerated into it.

Chapter 25 — Dragged Back

Maya turned onto Lexington Terrace with her headlights cutting a narrow path between rows of darkened houses. No porch lights. No movement. The entire block felt hollowed out, as if sound itself had withdrawn.

Two patrol cars were parked crookedly along the curb up ahead. Their lights rotated in slow, muted pulses that didn't seem to reach the houses around them. Two officers stood near the walkway of a narrow single-story home, both of them with their hands on their knees as though bracing themselves from something they couldn't steady.

Maya killed the engine and stepped out.

Cold bit the skin of her neck immediately—not a night chill, not weather. This was a sharper kind of cold, the sort she had felt only a few times in her life and never this strong. Her breath tightened on the inhale.

Graves pulled in seconds later, his unmarked sedan rolling to a hard stop. He climbed out without shutting his door fully, eyes fixed on the house as if listening to something inside it. He joined her at the foot of the walkway, jaw clenched.

One of the officers straightened when he saw them.

"We didn't go farther than the hall," he said, voice unsteady. "Temperature drops the second you cross the threshold."

Maya frowned. "Gas leak?"

He shook his head too quickly. "Gas doesn't do… this."

He gestured toward the open door.

A faint current of air drifted outward—thin, colorless, but carrying a cold so abrupt it made Maya's ribs tighten. Her breath fogged instantly. The officer's fogged as well.

Graves flicked on his flashlight. "What about the caller?"

"Line went dead," the second officer said. "Screaming first, then nothing."

Maya stepped forward. The cold deepened as soon as she crossed the doorway. It wasn't just temperature—it was pressure. The kind that stole half a breath before releasing it.

Her boots cracked something beneath them.

She lowered her light.

A delicate network of frost webbed across the entryway floorboards, tracing thin, branching lines as though something had moved through the hallway and left the cold behind in its path. The frost wasn't uniform—some strands looked thicker, others splintering into needle-fine filaments.

Maya crouched, her gloved fingers hovering just above the ice. The cold radiating off it stung even without contact.

Graves stepped in beside her. His breath plumed into the dark with every exhale. He angled his flashlight down the hallway.

The frost trail continued inward, branching left and right before converging again, like whatever caused it had paused, shifted direction, then committed to one path.

The house was silent. Too silent. No hum of appliances, no settling wood, no far-off traffic. The kind of silence that felt pressed down over the space, held in place.

Maya swallowed and rose.

"Hallway," she said quietly.

Graves nodded.

The two officers stayed near the doorway, unwilling or unable to take another step inside.

Maya and Graves began down the hall, their lights cutting through the cold, their breaths fogging in fast, uneven bursts. The frost thickened underfoot, each step sounding like glass cracking in slow motion.

Farther ahead, the darkness of a room opened on the right.

The frost trail ran straight toward it.

Maya lifted her flashlight higher and moved faster.

Graves moved ahead of her without hesitation, his flashlight cutting a hard line through the dark. His shoulders were rigid, each step measured, deliberate. Whatever he saw in the frost, whatever he felt pressing against the air, he didn't acknowledge it aloud—he just pushed forward, jaw locked.

Maya stayed just behind his left shoulder, close enough to catch the slight tremor in his breath each time the temperature dipped further.

The hallway narrowed as they approached the open bedroom. The air felt compressed here, heavy enough that Maya had to force her lungs to cooperate. Frost clung thicker to the floorboards, spreading in uneven sheets that cracked sharply beneath Graves' boots.

He paused at the doorway, raising his light slowly.

"Stay behind me," he murmured, low enough that only she heard it.

Maya nodded, though her pulse hammered so hard she wasn't sure he could have missed it.

Graves swept the beam across the room.

The victim lay on the floor near the foot of the bed—half turned, limbs slack, body contorted in a way no fall could ever produce. His ribs had been bent outward from inside the chest cavity, flared into jagged, uneven arcs like something had pushed—or pulled—through them. Frost radiated from the wounds in brittle patterns, clinging to fabric, carpet fibers, and the victim's skin.

Maya's breath stalled.

Graves took a slow step inside.

Another.

Then another.

"Sir?" His voice was steady, though she could hear the strain under it. "Can you hear me?"

A shaky inhale rose from the victim's throat—thin, ragged, almost absent. Maya felt it more than heard it, the faintest draw of air pulling at the space around them.

She moved to Graves' side automatically.

He extended an arm to bar her from rushing in.

"Let me clear it first."

She froze, every muscle tight.

Graves swept the corners with the flashlight—first high, then low, then across the bed, behind the nightstand, along the closet door. The frost patterns were strongest here—thin white veins branching outward from the victim's chest, creeping across the floor in delicate, fractal lines.

"Clear enough," Graves said, though his tone held no real confidence. His arm lowered. "Go."

Maya dropped to her knees beside the victim, gloves numbing instantly from the cold radiating off his body. Her breath fogged with each exhale as she leaned over him.

The man's eyes fluttered.

His chest rose barely a centimeter.

The cold pulsed outward in faint waves, like the last remnants of whatever had been here moments earlier.

"Hey," Maya whispered, leaning close. "Stay with me. You're not alone."

His lips moved without sound.

Graves circled behind her, flashlight steady, watching the room, the corners, the doorframe. The two officers hovered at the hallway entrance, refusing to come any closer.

Maya examined the wounds—organs partially displaced, torn free but not removed. Jagged trauma along the rib edges. The pattern wasn't random. It never was.

The temperature dipped again—sharp enough that Maya's lungs seized for half a second. She pressed a hand to her chest, fighting the sudden tightness.

Graves stiffened.

The air in the room shifted.

It wasn't a sound.

It wasn't a breeze.

It was something subtle and immediate—a feeling of space contracting, of the edges of the room folding just slightly inward.

Then, from the corner behind her, something creaked.

The closet door.

Just an inch.

Just enough to move in a room where nothing else dared.

Maya froze.

Graves raised his flashlight toward the sound, muscles coiling.

The victim took one more thin, broken breath.

The closet door eased farther open.

Graves angled his flashlight toward the closet, arm sweeping back in front of Maya in one sharp motion—instinctive, protective, absolute. His shoulders tensed beneath his coat, every line of him tightening as the temperature in the room dropped another several degrees.

The victim's breath guttered in a thin, rasping thread behind her. The sound barely made it into the air before dissolving there, like the room itself was swallowing it.

Another creak.

This one deeper.

Lower.

As though something inside the closet had braced a weight against the door and shifted it.

Graves leaned forward, jaw tight, raising his light a fraction higher.

The shadows inside the closet **contracted**.

Not from movement.

Not from the flashlight.

From something pulling them inward, folding them toward a center point Maya couldn't see.

Her breath caught—shallow, jagged.

She tried to inhale again, but the air wouldn't fill right.

A line of darkness split down the middle of the closet's interior.

Not a door.

Not a crack in wood.

A **crease** in shadow.

Then the crease widened.

And something forced itself through.

The first thing that emerged didn't look like a limb. It looked like **an outline breaking**, like the shape of a shoulder peeling itself loose from another dimension. It was wrong in a way her brain immediately rejected—sharp where it should have been rounded, narrow where structure should have required width.

The arm came next.

Long.

Too long.

It dragged something wet behind it—shadow-thick, viscous, clinging to the doorframe. The substance pulled upward as though trying to crawl back toward the thing that had birthed it.

The forearm bent in two places.

Two joints—one where it should be, one where it absolutely should not.

Maya's stomach lurched.

The flashlight beam hit the emerging torso and dimmed around it, as if the light itself lost courage. Whatever passed for its surface wasn't skin—it was shadow with weight, swallowing brightness and revealing flashes of anatomy underneath only when the angle hit just right:

A ribcage shifting in slow, grinding pulses.

Bone pushing outward against something pressing from within.

Cavities opening and collapsing like wet apertures beneath stretched darkness.

The neck unfolded last, slow and deliberate, curving outward at an angle so sharp Maya felt her own neck ache as if in sympathy.

The head hung forward, heavy, bent low—not with gravity but with intent.

Where features should have been, there was nothing but **a hollow recess**, an indentation that looked deeper than the light could reach.

The room **dipped inward** around it.

A pressure shift.

A collapsing of distance.

The creature—whatever it was—didn't step into the room.

It **arrived**, collapsing the space between itself and the victim in an impossible stutter of movement that punched air out of Maya's lungs.

The victim's body jerked violently.

His back bowed.

A sound tore from him—wet, broken, cut short by the force lifting him upward.

Graves locked his grip around Maya before she even felt herself moving.

She screamed—raw, involuntary—as the victim's limbs scraped across the frost-hardened carpet, leaving streaks of melted ice in his wake. His head lolled backward, mouth open in a silent shape of terror that would never be completed.

The thing pulled him against its torso.

Not cradling.

Not holding.

Absorbing.

The victim's chest caved in on itself with a crunch that echoed through Maya's teeth. Frost burst outward in a web of crystalline fractures.

"NO—NO, LET ME GO—" Maya thrashed, nails tearing at Graves' sleeve.

Graves dragged her backward, boots digging grooves in the frost. "Maya—stop—Maya, STOP—!"

She didn't hear him.

Her eyes were locked on the impossible shape pulling the man into the closet's darkness, limbs bending in grotesque angles as the body disappeared inch by inch into the shadow-space behind the doorframe.

The head—the hollow, featureless head—tilted slightly toward her.

Not with eyes.

Not with a gaze.

But with **recognition**.

Her scream broke into something ragged and animal.

The door snapped shut with enough force to shake dust from the ceiling.

The walls shuddered.

For three full seconds after the closet door slammed, no one in the room breathed.

Then the house exhaled.

A faint shift—barely perceptible—moved through the air, like the pressure inside the walls loosened just slightly. The cold didn't vanish, but it eased enough that Maya could drag in half a lungful of air. Her knees hit the floor the moment Graves released her waist, palms skidding across the frost.

The victim was gone.

There was nothing left but the smear of melted ice where his body had been.

Maya pushed herself toward the closet, fingers clawing at the carpet, but Graves caught her arm again—hard this time, pulling her back before she could lay a hand on the door.

"Stop. Maya—stop."

His voice cracked against the strain of holding her.

"No—he was alive—he was still—" Her words broke into jagged breaths. The cold had left her throat raw, and every inhale stung.

"He's gone."

Graves forced the words out like they cost him something.

Behind them, one of the officers stumbled into the hall, hand braced against the wall, eyes wide and unfocused. The other whispered a string of curses under his breath, flashlight shaking so violently the beam jittered across the ceiling.

Maya's vision blurred.

Her mouth tasted metallic.

It wasn't just shock—it was recognition, the old fracture cracking open inside her chest, memory hitting so fast she couldn't brace for it.

The helplessness.

The too-late arrival.

The feeling of something being taken right out of her hands.

Graves pulled her to her feet. She sagged against him, not because she wanted support but because her legs refused to hold her. Her breath wouldn't deepen; the air still felt thinned, as if the house hadn't fully reset.

"We have to leave the room," Graves said quietly. "Now."

He guided her backward, one step at a time. The officers followed, boots crunching over the frost. The crackling sound felt obscene in the settling silence.

Halfway down the hall, the temperature shifted again—warmer, only by a degree or two, but enough to tell them whatever had been here was no longer close.

The frost on the walls began to bead and melt.

One officer checked his bodycam automatically, hands still trembling. The screen glitched, static bleeding over the image. Then a single frozen frame appeared, warped at the edges:

A stretched silhouette bent over the victim.

A dark arc pulling the man backward.

The room skewed in impossible angles around the shape.

The officer's breath hitched sharply, and he snapped the device shut, face going gray.

Maya didn't look.

She didn't trust herself to.

Graves kept an arm around her as they reached the entryway. Her boots slipped once on the melting frost, but he steadied her without comment. The officers gave them space, neither daring to speak.

Outside, distant sirens were already rising across the city—multiple directions, overlapping, building toward something larger. Something spreading.

Maya blinked hard, pulled free of Graves' grip, and forced her legs to move on their own.

"I'm fine," she lied.

She wasn't.

She pushed past him and stepped out onto the walkway, breath fogging in the night air. The world outside felt too bright, too loud, too normal after the weight of the bedroom.

A fresh siren rounded the corner.

Maya squared her shoulders and started toward it.

Chapter 26 — City of Dark

Maya kept both hands tight on the wheel, but they wouldn't stop trembling. Every blink brought the same flash—the closet door flying open, the wrongness pouring out of it, the ribs folding outward as the body vanished into a depth that shouldn't have existed.

She forced her eyes back to the road.

The city still held its usual glow. Porch lights. Windows. The steady amber of streetlamps lining the blocks ahead. Normal enough that, for a moment, she almost believed she could hold herself together long enough to get to the precinct and tell Graves everything before the images in her head took root.

Air pressed oddly against her ribs. Each breath felt like someone tightening a band across her chest before letting it ease.

She reached for her phone, needing to hear Lila's voice more than she needed to understand why her lungs felt unsteady.

The call clicked through on the second ring.

"Hello?" Lila sounded tired, relaxed—soft pieces of an ordinary evening.

"Hey," Maya said, swallowing. "I'm heading to the precinct. Just checking on you."

"You okay?" Lila asked.

Maya opened her mouth.

A sharp metallic pop cracked in the distance.

The streetlamps ahead of her went dark, one after another, in a straight collapsing line. The block beyond them blinked out next. And the next.

Darkness swept toward her, fast and heavy, swallowing the city block by block.

"Maya?" Lila's voice tightened. "The lights here just—everything went out."

Maya's breath caught halfway down her throat. "Listen to me. Stay inside. Don't go near the windows."

"What's happening?"

Another transformer blew somewhere over the rooftops—white sparks cutting the night before everything dropped back into deeper darkness. A low groan rolled through the neighborhood as circuit after circuit failed in a chain reaction.

Static fuzzed through the phone.

Lila's inhale stuttered. "I hear something outside."

Maya's decision locked into place.

"I'm coming home," she said. "Right now."

"But—don't you have to—"

"I said stay inside."

The line cut out completely.

Maya turned onto her street, headlights sweeping across familiar outlines that no longer felt familiar at all. Houses were silhouettes, windows black squares, yards disappearing into a pitch so deep her headlights barely carved through it.

Her dashboard lights dimmed for a long blink. A faint ripple of cold brushed her arms, followed immediately by another breath catching sharply in her chest. She forced it through, fingers tightening around the wheel.

Her house came into view.

The front door was open a few inches.

Lila stood framed in the slice of light from Maya's headlights, backpack slung over her shoulder, breath trembling in shallow pulls she couldn't seem to steady.

Maya braked hard and stepped out fast.

"Lila!"

Lila ran straight to her. Maya folded her arms around her, holding her tight as Lila pressed her face into her shoulder, shaking.

"I'm here," Maya whispered. "Come on. We're going to the precinct."

A siren wailed somewhere in the distance—thin, broken, swallowed by the dark around them.

Maya helped Lila into the cab, shut the door, and circled back to the driver's side. She pulled onto the street, steering toward the faint glow of the precinct's generator lights cutting through the blackout miles ahead.

The drive toward the precinct cut through a city that no longer looked like itself. Maya's headlights glided over abandoned intersections, stalled cars, and people moving in frantic silhouettes along the sidewalks—some shouting, some waving their arms at anyone who might stop, most just trying to run toward somewhere with light.

Lila kept both hands clamped around her backpack straps, shoulders tight, eyes fixed on the windshield. The glow from the dash lit her face in pale, trembling lines.

Maya reached over and squeezed her knee once. "You're okay. Stay with me."

Lila nodded, but her breath came fast and uneven—not panic exactly, more like she couldn't get enough air past a point just behind her sternum. Maya felt a faint, matching snag in her own lungs a second later—a thin-air pocket passing through the cabin, subtle but unmistakable.

The blackout had changed the air itself.

Ahead, the precinct rose out of the dark like the last lit building in the world. Backup generators pushed out a faint, stuttering glow through the windows—too dim to be comforting, bright enough to draw every desperate person left on the street.

Maya pulled into the lot, joining a mess of patrol cars left at crooked angles. People crowded near the entrance—some crying, some yelling at officers, some just staring at the dark around them as if waiting for it to move.

She helped Lila down from the rig. The girl immediately stepped closer, almost shoulder-to-shoulder, her breath trembling again. A pressure shift rolled through the air—weak, quick, enough to make Maya's inhale falter before she forced it all the way.

Inside, the precinct was chaos.

Phones rang nonstop.

Dispatchers clashed voices with officers demanding updates.

Two civilians shouted at each other over a rumor that the blackout was spreading statewide.

Children cried in a cluster along one wall while a young officer tried to hand out water to calm them.

Maya guided Lila through the narrow pathways between people and desks. Lila's steps were hesitant, like she expected the floor itself to pull out from under her. Her gaze caught on every shadow, tracking places where the emergency lights didn't quite reach.

"Maya."

Graves' voice cut through the noise as he pushed through the hallway toward them. He looked exhausted and wired all at once—jaw tight, shirt half-untucked, hair disheveled from rushing out of the house and straight into the blackout chaos.

His gaze snapped to Lila first, then to Maya. "You got caught in the grid collapse?"

"Picked her up on the way," Maya said. "Wasn't leaving her alone in that."

Graves nodded once—no argument, no second thought. He stepped closer, lowering his voice under the noise around them. "Call volume's blown up. We've got reports from half the city about… disturbances. And we're down to generator power."

A woman screamed somewhere deeper in the building—not from injury, but from raw panic. Lila flinched hard, clutching Maya's sleeve. Her breath stuttered again, chest rising in a shaky half-inhale she couldn't finish.

Maya crouched slightly beside her, rubbing a hand along her shoulder. "You're safe. Just breathe with me."

Lila nodded, but her eyes kept darting to the corners where the light bent strangely across the floor. The shadows there lingered too long, stretching when no one moved near them.

Maya felt her own lungs tighten again—a thin ripple of cold brushing her arm, followed by a quick pressure drop that made the hairs on the back of her neck rise.

Someone else felt it too; an officer near the entryway gasped and braced a hand against a desk, blinking like he'd gone dizzy for a second.

More voices rose from dispatch. Someone yelled for everybody nearby to listen.

Graves jerked his head toward the bullpen. "Come on."

Maya tightened her grip on Lila's shoulder and steered her forward through the frantic bodies, toward the cluster forming around dispatch.

The precinct lights flickered once overhead.

The dispatch room pulsed with overlapping noise—phones ringing off their hooks, officers shouting over each other, civilians demanding answers no one had. A dispatcher waved them over, eyes rimmed red.

"Just listen," she said, hitting the speaker on an incoming call.

A man's breath tore through the room—fast, broken, running on blind adrenaline.

"It's—on the roof—"

crackle, warp

"—went over the whole street—wasn't walking—wasn't—"

The sound shredded into a warped hum, like the call itself buckled.

The dispatcher muted it and immediately queued the next recording.

A woman whispered so softly it barely registered over the chaos. "It stretched across the alley. The light didn't hit right. The shadow—shifted."

A crash. Something falling.

"I don't know what direction it moved. It wasn't—"

The call cut out.

Lila flinched hard, fingers digging into Maya's sleeve. Her breath caught mid-inhale, trembling. Maya felt a matching hitch in her own lungs—a faint cold ripple brushing her arm before tightening the air around her ribs.

Another dispatcher flagged them down as an officer hurried over, clutching a tablet to his chest.

"This came in from a cruiser," he said, swallowing. "Just—watch."

Graves angled the screen.

The bodycam feed jittered violently, the timestamp stalling and then skipping ahead as the officer moved into the blackout. The street was barely visible, lit only by headlights and the orange smear of a distant fire.

For a moment, nothing.

Then the footage fractured.

Frames stretched sideways, tearing at the edges. A smear of darkness rippled across the top of the image—not a shape, not even a silhouette. Just a distortion, as if the lens dragged a piece of shadow with it for a heartbeat too long.

Lila made a soft sound—barely a breath escaping her.

"That's happening everywhere," the officer said. "None of the cameras can focus on it."

Before Graves could respond, the air shifted—soft at first, then sharp.

Ceiling tiles trembled, not from impact, but from **pressure**. A low groan rolled across the rafters, the kind that didn't sound like weight but like the building's structure bending a degree too far in the wrong direction. Dust drifted down in faint, drifting sheets.

Every emergency light flickered in a single, uneven pulse.

Maya's breath seized halfway. A cool ripple slid along her spine as she forced air into her lungs. Officers around them inhaled sharply, hands bracing on desks or walls as if the room had tightened.

Lila pressed both hands to her sternum, eyes wide, trembling. "It's close," she whispered, voice thin and breaking.

The rooftop camera feed on a wall monitor flickered on. The image twisted—pixelation collapsing inward, then blowing outward again. For a fraction of a second, the darkness along the roofline rippled and bowed, the shadows bending out of sync with the building beneath them.

Then the monitor went black.

Someone screamed near the front entrance—short, sharp, swallowed immediately by the noise rising through the building.

Dispatch consoles erupted again. Calls overlapped. Voices shouting about alleys pulling open, rooftops blurring, something moving too quickly to see but leaving wrongness in its wake.

Maya tightened her arm around Lila, pulse hammering.

The building felt like it was bracing—walls tightening with every breath.

The bullpen was falling apart under the flood of noise—phones ringing nonstop, dispatchers clashing over overlapping calls, civilians crowding the inner walls while officers tried to restore some kind of order. The emergency lights stuttered again, stretching shadows across the floor in long, bending streaks.

Maya held Lila close, feeling the girl's breath hitch in thin, uneven pulls. Another mild ripple of cold brushed against Maya's arm, followed by the familiar tightening in her lungs. Several officers stiffened at the same time, hands bracing on desks.

Graves stepped toward her, lowering his voice under the chaos. "I still need your statement from the house," he said. "You didn't get a chance to file anything."

Maya nodded, jaw tight. "I know. I was trying to   "

She glanced around the room. No one could hear anything over the noise. There was no desk left free. No officer not already drowning under calls.

"I haven't had the chance."

"I get it," Graves said. "Tonight's turned into—"

Maya's radio crackled violently against her hip, cutting him off.

A sharp two-tone EMS alert sounded, loud enough to slice through the entire bullpen.

She grabbed the handset automatically.

The dispatcher's voice came through thin with interference:

"EMS Four, priority response. Fairview Apartments. Multiple callers reporting injuries and screams. No response on call-back. You are the closest available unit. Acknowledge."

Maya's stomach tightened.

"EMS Four, en route," she said, her voice steady by force alone.

Graves turned toward her instantly. "Fairview's two blocks out," he said, grabbing a patrol radio from the desk. "I'm going with you."

Before either of them could move, a sergeant approached—older, calm, the kind of presence that cut cleanly through panic. Her eyes went first to Lila, still gripping Maya's sleeve.

"If you two are responding," the sergeant said, steady and firm, "she stays here. We've got personnel assigned to civilian safety under the generator lights."

Lila's fingers tightened. "Please don't—"

Maya crouched, taking her shoulders gently.

"Lila, listen to me. You stay with them, where it's bright. Don't move unless they tell you to. I'll be back."

Lila's breathing grew shallow and fast, air catching in the same tight stutter Maya had felt herself. Tears gathered, but she nodded.

The sergeant extended a hand. Maya watched Lila take it—hesitant, trembling—and let herself be guided toward the cluster of civilians under the brightest lights.

Another pressure shift passed through the bullpen—soft cold brushing Maya's wrist, breath tightening in her chest. Officers reacted in sync, inhaling sharply as the air thinned for a moment.

Graves met her eyes. "We move now."

Maya grabbed her kit.

The emergency lights flickered again, shadows bending long along the tile before snapping back.

Together, she and Graves pushed through the precinct doors into the blackout outside as new distress calls erupted behind them.

Chapter 27 — Frozen Screams

Sirens wailed somewhere distant, swallowed quickly by the blackout as Maya and Graves cut through the dark street. The generator lights from the precinct cast only a weak glow behind them, leaving most of the block drowned in shadow. The rig's doors clattered when Maya pulled one open, her breath rising in a thin, unsteady plume from the cold still clinging to her lungs.

Graves scanned the street as he keyed his radio. "Fairview units, status?"

Only static answered him—static laced with a low pulse that rattled the casing in Maya's hand.

Another frequency cut in:

"—multiple callers—eight bodies—frost—she's still scream—"

crackle

Silence.

The radio hissed softly, like breath dragging across the speaker.

Graves exchanged a look with her. No question left to ask.

Maya climbed into the rig. Graves took the passenger side, slamming the door hard enough to make the mirrors shake. The moment she turned the key, the engine coughed and caught, dashboard lights flickering against the windshield.

They sped toward Fairview through a street that looked strangled by its own darkness. Vehicles sat abandoned at odd angles—doors open, hazard lights clicking in uneven rhythms. A bus sat half-on the curb, its interior lit only by a dying emergency bulb. Something inside had knocked a row of seats sideways. Graves didn't look long.

The radios flared again.

"Unit seven, we heard—"

"—stairwell—something—moving—"

"—freeze on the walls—he—he stopped breathing—"

Voices overlapped and dissolved.

A harsh, subharmonic pulse surged across every channel at once. Maya winced as the vibration lanced through her skull.

"Jesus..." Graves muttered, hand tightening around the dash.

They turned onto Fairview. The apartment building loomed ahead, its windows dark except for a handful flickering as if the lights inside were struggling against something unseen. The front entryway glass was fogged from the inside—thick condensation clinging to the pane.

Maya felt the first stab of breath restriction before she stepped out of the rig. A cold pressure settled against her sternum, tightening her inhale without any drop in temperature outside.

She forced a slow exhale and grabbed her med kit.

Graves took the lead up the stairwell, gun drawn, flashlight cutting a thin beam through the dark. Maya followed close, the air growing heavier with each step. A soft crackling reached them—like ice crystals forming and fracturing.

When they reached the third-floor landing, the sound deepened. Frost slid in branching lines across the hallway drywall, forming delicate trees of ice that reached outward in sharp angles.

Maya's breath fogged again. This time the cold wasn't fear.

This had happened **seconds** ago.

"Stay behind me," Graves whispered, not looking back.

A scream tore down the corridor—raw, high, desperate—then cut so abruptly it sounded like the voice had been crushed mid-syllable.

Maya flinched. Graves surged forward.

Her heartbeat hammered against her ribs as she ran after him, frost cracking beneath their shoes. Somewhere deeper in the building, something scraped against linoleum—long, quick, too smooth to sound like any human movement.

They rounded the corner toward the sound.

The deeper they moved into the corridor, the colder the air clamped around Maya's skin. No breeze. No draft. Just an abrupt, crushing chill that wrapped the hallway like a sealed freezer. Frost coated the walls in uneven plates, some curled outward like hooks made of glass. When her glove brushed one, it stuck for half a second before snapping free.

Graves' flashlight trembled in his grip.

The first body lay sprawled across the tile.

Maya stopped short. Her breath punched out of her in a small, cracked sound she couldn't hold back. The man's ribcage had been **forced outward**, bone split into jagged prongs that turned his chest into a frozen, gaping bowl. Organs had spilled across his torso in thick ropes of red and violet, some mid-spill, frozen into glossy, bulbous shapes that clung to his skin like crystallized flesh.

Steam still curled faintly from where warm tissue met the freezing air.

A metallic, hot-copper scent hit her nose—thick, sharp, burning in the back of her throat.

Graves staggered one step, hand pressing over his mouth.

They pushed forward because stopping felt like it would break them.

The second body slumped against the wall a few feet ahead. The spine gaped open between the shoulders—vertebrae cracked apart, fluid frozen into pale streaks that ran down the wall in long, ribbed trails. A spray pattern arced upward and outward, captured mid-flight as a sheet of thin, curving ice.

Maya crouched because reflex demanded she check for warmth. Her glove stuck to the frost-coated tile, resisting her pull for a beat.

The skin beneath her fingers still radiated heat.

Her stomach flipped, her breath jolting in a shallow, fast series of inhales. She stood too quickly and nearly stumbled.

Graves' voice came thin, tight. "Maya… this is seconds old."

They reached the third body—if it could still be called that—near the intersection.

Limbs were scattered across the tile, torn free at the joints with violent force. The torso had ruptured open entirely—flesh spread in thick, torn ribbons that had frozen in mid-collapse. Blood streaked across the floor in dark, glossy swaths, still warm enough at the center to bead instead of crystallize. The wall behind bulged outward, cracked through the studs, as if something had hurled the body into it with enough power to bend the building.

The copper smell here was overwhelming.

Maya gagged, clapping a hand over her mouth, eyes watering hard.

A tremor rolled through the flooring—small, but deep enough to feel in bone. The frost around the first body split down the center, a brittle crack echoing through the corridor.

Maya's next breath stuttered, shallow and uneven.

Then came the sound.

A glide across linoleum—smooth, fast, controlled. No footsteps. No rise or fall of weight. Something moving with frightening precision through the dark.

Graves raised his gun, shoulders tight, hands shaking.

"Maya—on me," he hissed, voice frayed at the edges.

She followed, boots crunching through frost thick enough to break under each step, her pulse hammering hard enough to blur her vision.

Ahead, the emergency lights trembled—shadows stretching in long, trembling lines across the frost—

before collapsing back in a sudden jolt.

A metal door slammed deeper inside the building, the frame rattling.

Graves broke into a run.

Maya went after him.

They followed the hallway toward the source of the slammed door, frost cracking under their boots. The cold tightened again—sharp enough that Maya's breath broke into short, uneven pulls she couldn't slow. Her fingers tingled inside her gloves, numb at the tips.

A soft, rhythmic tapping echoed through the ductwork above them. Not metal shifting. Not settling. A pulse, faint and spaced irregularly, like something brushing against the vents as it moved past.

Graves slowed, gun angled forward.

Maya felt the floor vibrate—a low tremor that traveled up her legs, settling in her knees. Then the frost on the wall beside her shivered in thin, brittle patterns, splintering outward as if reacting to pressure from inside the sheetrock.

She forced air into her lungs, the inhale tight and stinging.

A sound came from the right—barely audible over the static of her own breathing.

A voice.

Small.

Choked.

Graves swung the light toward a half-open bathroom door.

Maya reached it first.

Inside, the room was colder than the hallway. Frost crept along the sink and wrapped the edges of the mirror, obscuring the glass with cloudy white. The shower curtain had collapsed inward, clinging to the tub like it had been pulled taut and then released.

A young woman sat curled in the bathtub, knees drawn to her chest, arms wrapped around her shins. She shook uncontrollably, breath hitting in thin, rapid gasps that kept catching in the top of her throat.

Her eyes tracked Maya's movement before her head did.

Maya lowered herself slowly, hands open, voice soft despite the pounding in her chest. "We're here. Can you move?"

The girl tried to speak. Only air came out.

Then a fractured whisper.

"It… moved wrong."

Maya leaned closer. "Tell me what you saw."

The girl pressed the back of her head against the tile, eyes unfocused, hyperventilating through the cold.

"The hallway... stretched," she managed. "It... kept shifting. It was close, then... somewhere else. Too fast."

Her voice broke. A thin sob escaped.

Maya felt another cold ripple slide under her skin. Her lungs tightened again, breaths coming too shallow.

Graves scanned the ceiling, the corners, the hallway beyond the door. His light jittered once as it passed the mirror. The frosted surface didn't reflect the beam cleanly—it bent it, warping the glare into a smear that slanted sideways for a heartbeat before snapping back.

Maya lifted the girl's arm. "We have to move. Now."

The survivor nodded, but her legs shook violently as she tried to uncurl them. Maya slid an arm under her shoulder and helped her upright. Her skin felt like ice, her breath short and stuttered.

A sudden pop of air pressure cracked behind the wall—sharp enough that the mirror quivered in its frame.

Graves flinched, then grabbed the radio clipped to his vest. Static pulsed through it in staggered waves, the speaker vibrating like something pressed against it from the inside.

Maya didn't wait. She guided the survivor toward the hallway.

The lights flickered again, stretching shadows across the frost in thin streaks that trembled like they were trying to pull away from the walls.

A metallic scrape rolled through the corridor ahead—smooth, fast, gliding.

The survivor whimpered, collapsing against Maya.

Graves stepped into position ahead of them, raising his weapon, breath shaking.

"Keep moving," he said.

Maya tightened her grip on the girl and followed him into the corridor's fractured light.

Maya's grip on the survivor tightened as they moved, the girl's knees buckling with every other step. The hallway felt wrong—an off-kilter heaviness that pressed against their bodies, like the air had thickened into something that clung to skin and bone.

The emergency lights flickered in uneven pulses. Each flash stretched the shadows along the frost-coated walls so far they thinned into tremoring lines, then snapped them back with a violent jolt that rattled the glass in nearby frames.

A sharp pulse surged through Graves' radio, loud enough to make him flinch. The speaker vibrated in his hand, filling the corridor with a low-frequency warble that crawled up Maya's spine.

"Jesus—" Graves muttered, adjusting his grip. "It's hitting every channel."

Behind them, somewhere on the lower floors, a scream tore through the building—high, desperate, and ending so abruptly it sounded like something had cut the voice out of the air.

Maya felt the survivor seize in her arms, body curling inward in panic.

"We're almost out," Maya whispered, forcing steadiness she didn't feel. Her own lungs strained against the pressure, breaths short and sharp. Her heart pounded hard enough she felt it in her fingertips.

As they reached the connecting corridor, Graves' flashlight beam skittered across the wall—and the shadows on that wall **moved first**. A fire extinguisher's silhouette slid a fraction sideways, stretching into a thin smear, before the extinguisher itself seemed to catch up a heartbeat later.

Maya froze. Her breath snagged painfully in her chest.

The survivor whimpered, hiding her face against Maya's jacket.

Graves forced himself to look away. "Don't stop. Go."

They pushed forward.

To their right, an open doorway revealed two more victims on the floor. One lay curled in on themselves, mid-collapse, the skin along the spine split open in a deep, jagged breach. The other sprawled face-down, both arms torn from the sockets, blood still slow-moving in dark, syrupy lines along the tile.

Maya didn't look for long. Her body reacted before her mind could—throat tightening, stomach clenching so hard her knees weakened. She swallowed hard against the sting rising into her mouth.

Another pressure shift hit the corridor.

The lights dimmed, shadows stretching outward as if something on the far end of the hall had taken a slow breath inward.

The cold rippled through Maya's ribs. Her next inhale barely made it halfway.

"Move!" Graves snapped, voice breaking.

They reached the stairwell, but even here the air pressed against their lungs. Frost crept along the railing, forming thin crystalline webs between the bars.

The survivor's legs gave out. Maya caught her before she hit the floor, dragging her upright with effort.

Graves shoved the stairwell door open, checking the landing. The distortion in the lights had spread here too—brief flickers bending the edges of the hallway outside the stairwell like heat waves, except cold.

More screams erupted somewhere below them. Then silence. Then another warbled pulse through Graves' radio.

"Come on," he said, voice hoarse. "We're getting out of this building."

They descended fast, Maya half-carrying the survivor, Graves sweeping corners even though every corner felt like it was tightening around them.

On the first floor, the main lobby flickered in and out of weak emergency light. A trail of frost cut across the tiles in branching lines, leading toward a darkened hallway they didn't dare check.

They burst through the front doors into the night air. Cold—but normal cold. Breath came easier for a moment as Maya eased the survivor into the back of the rig.

When the doors slammed shut, the sound echoed longer than it should have—like the night was stretching it.

Maya climbed into the driver's seat. Graves slid into the passenger side, chest heaving.

The radio erupted with a new cluster of calls:

"—screaming on Carson—"

"—entire block power surge—"

"—someone's down—multiple—"

Another warbled pulse cut them off.

Graves looked at Maya, face pale, shaken in a way she'd never seen.

"This isn't stopping," he said.

Maya gripped the wheel tighter. "I know."

A fresh scream burst across the radio—close, too close—followed by a crash of something heavy hitting metal.

Maya started the engine.

Chapter 28 — Graves' Stand

The precinct lobby looked different when Maya and Graves pushed back inside—too bright, too loud, too crowded. People pressed shoulder-to-shoulder against the inner walls, their voices rising in broken waves as officers tried to hold the chaos together. The generator lights flickered overhead, casting short, stuttering pulses that stretched the shadows along the tile one moment and snapped them tight the next.

Lila spotted Maya instantly. She broke from a cluster of civilians and ran to her, breath coming in fast, panicked bursts. Maya caught her, the girl's arms locking around her waist, trembling hard enough that Maya had to brace her weight.

Graves scanned the room—fast, assessing, jaw clenched. Two officers were arguing with a man near the front desk who was sobbing uncontrollably. A mother sat with her back to the wall, clutching her son, both of them shaking. Someone else was vomiting into a trash can; another was trying to pry open the locked front doors before a sergeant hauled him back.

A faint vibration ran through the floor. It traveled up Maya's legs and into her ribs—a low, bone-level hum that made her breath catch. Lila felt it too; she flinched, face burying deeper against Maya's jacket.

Graves didn't flinch. He straightened.

"All right!" he barked, voice rising over the noise. "Everyone away from the perimeter! Move toward the center of the room—keep the walls clear!"

Officers reacted immediately, corralling people inward. The civilians resisted at first—crying, panicking, demanding answers—but the trembling in the walls convinced them faster than orders did.

A cold draft slipped under the front doors. Not a normal gust—Maya felt it slide over the floor, thin and directional, brushing across her ankles and climbing her shins like a rising tide. Her lungs tightened again, and she drew Lila closer.

Graves grabbed two officers near the entrance. "Barricade those double doors. Tables, desks, file cabinets—whatever isn't bolted." They moved fast, hauling furniture into place.

Another rumble passed through the building, this one stronger, making the overhead lights flicker in a jagged strobe. Shadows stretched across the lobby in long trembling lines, pulled toward the street-facing windows before collapsing back into place.

Maya's pulse kicked hard against her sternum.

Graves' voice cut through her panic. "Maya—get her to the back. Away from the glass."

Maya lifted Lila, guiding her toward the cluster of survivors now gathered near the center of the lobby. The girl wouldn't let go of her, fingers dug tight into Maya's jacket.

"It's okay," Maya whispered, though her own voice shook. "I've got you."

A new burst of shouting broke near the front:

"Something moved outside!"

"I saw it—by the cars—"

"No, the shadow—look at the shadow—"

Maya looked instinctively.

The window glass jittered in its frame as if pressure outside surged and dipped. The faint glow of distant generator lights across the parking lot warped for a heartbeat—stretching sideways before snapping back.

Graves moved closer to the front, scanning the doors, his hand resting near his weapon.

The lights dimmed again—twice in rapid succession.
Each pulse made the shadows on the far wall deepen, pulling inward by inches, as if something outside had leaned into them.

Maya felt it—inside her lungs again—a tightening like the air had thinned enough to steal half her breath. She braced her free hand against the nearest desk, steadying both herself and Lila, who whimpered when the cold brushed her bare wrist.

People began crying louder.

Officers tried shouting instructions over the panic, but the whole room seemed to pulse with an internal pressure, rising and falling in uneven waves. Maya saw one of the fluorescent bulbs overhead stretch its glow along the ceiling before flickering back to normal.

The wrongness crept closer.

Graves stepped back from the window, face shifting—not fear, not disbelief, but a grim, quiet certainty.

He turned toward the tables and cabinets he'd spread with files earlier. Pages fluttered as another cold draft slipped into the lobby, lifting the corners and scattering a few across the tile.

He walked toward them with a hard set to his jaw.

Something important had just settled in him.

Graves swept the scattered pages back onto the table with a sharp motion, hands shaking hard enough that a few sheets slid to the floor. He grabbed a marker from the desk, uncapped it with his teeth, and dragged thick lines across the precinct map—marking each kill cluster Maya and the responding units had reported over the past week.

The crescents formed quickly. Too clean. Too deliberate.

He froze, marker hovering over the last unmarked stretch of town.

Maya approached slowly, Lila clinging to her hip, breath still stuttering from the pressure shifts rattling through the building. The pages on the table trembled as another cold draft pushed under the doorframes, lifting edges and skittering loose sheets across the tile.

Graves exhaled through his nose, long and unsteady.

"It's closing in," he said quietly—more to himself than to anyone in the room. "Every cluster… every timing… it's boxing the whole damn town."

He set the marker down, the tip clicking against the desk as he reached for another stack of reports. Vander's notes lay open nearby, pages wrinkled from being gripped too tightly. Graves flipped through them with fast, jerking movements, stopping on a page marked with a fading photograph of an older crime scene—victim placement forming a rough arc.

Then another.

Then another.

His throat tightened visibly as he lined the old arcs beside his own.

"Maya…" His voice cracked. He swallowed, starting again. "It follows the same shape every time."

She didn't speak. She didn't need to. The lines on the map spoke for him—curving inward like a trap that had nearly closed.

A sudden flicker rolled through the lobby, the lights dimming to a thin red pulse before snapping back. The shadows along the far wall leaned—subtle at first, then with a slow, dragging pull toward Graves. Lila whimpered against Maya's shoulder; Maya felt her shaking increase, breath skipping in rapid, uneven bursts.

Graves didn't look away from the wall. Not this time.

He braced a hand against the desk, fingers whitening as he gripped its edge. "It's choosing someone. It always does near the end." His voice was rough, scraped thin by realization.

A stack of reports lifted slightly from the table as another cold draft crept beneath the door. A page fluttered free and drifted toward him, brushing his boot before settling on the tile.

Graves stared at it.

Then he turned one slow inch toward Maya, eyes hollowed but steady.

"Get her back into the inner room," he said, nodding toward Lila. "Away from the glass. Away from the walls."

Maya swallowed hard. "Graves... what are you doing?"

He didn't answer at first. His gaze moved across the room—over the barricades, over the terrified civilians, over the officers trying to keep themselves together. His chest rose on a deep inhale that shook at the top.

Then he said, "Someone has to keep its attention."

Maya felt her stomach drop.

Lila pressed closer, breath hitching, as if she understood the shape of his words even without their full meaning.

Graves picked up the ledger notes again and closed them with a firm snap. The sound echoed across the lobby, louder than it should have been.

The shadows on the wall stretched another inch toward him.

Graves began gathering equipment without another word—flares, flashbangs, spare magazines. He moved like someone who'd already accepted the outcome, hands steady now in a way that made Maya's chest tighten.

He checked each item by touch, not sight.
Metal clicked. Velcro snapped. Fabric rustled.
He wasn't prepping for a fight—he was preparing to draw something away.

Maya set Lila down for only a moment and moved toward him. "Graves, stop." Her voice wavered, cracking around the edges. "You don't have to do this."

He didn't look at her. He slid a flashbang into his vest pouch, then another. "It's already watching the building."

Another cold pulse swept through the lobby—this one sharp enough that Maya gasped. The breath caught halfway in her throat, her lungs tightening until she coughed. Beside her, Lila folded in on herself, arms wrapping around her ribs as she fought to inhale.

Maya pulled her close again, one hand on the back of her head, whispering reassurance she didn't feel.

The lights flickered—longer this time. Shadows pooled under chairs and desks, stretching toward the front doors in thin, trembling threads.

Graves finally lifted his eyes to Maya.

"It's drawn to the edge of the pattern," he said. "Every time. Someone steps forward. Someone it fixates on." He adjusted the strap on his vest. "It's not random."

Maya shook her head, tears burning hot behind her eyes. "You saw what it did tonight. You go out there, you—"

She couldn't finish.

His expression softened for just a breath. "I know."

Lila made a small, strangled sound. Maya looked down. The girl clung harder, knuckles white, breath fluttering too fast to control. Her gaze stayed fixed on Graves as though something in her body had already chosen fear for her.

Another pressure-pop rolled across the ceiling tiles, rattling the vents. A few civilians screamed. Officers steadied each other with shaking hands.

Graves stepped forward and placed a hand on Lila's shoulder. She stiffened under his touch, eyes widening in a mix of instinct and terror.

"You stay with her," he said quietly to Maya. "No matter what happens."

Maya grabbed his wrist, fingers digging in. "You're not walking out there alone."

"You can't follow me," he replied, voice low, steady. "If you're with me, it'll take all of us. That's not happening."

He glanced at the far wall—at the shadows that now leaned toward him as if the room itself were tilting.

He inhaled once, deep, steadying himself.

"I won't let it get her," he whispered.

For a moment, Maya thought she might collapse. Her knees weakened; her breath stuttered. She tightened her grip on his wrist, desperate, panicked.

Graves gently pulled free.

He cupped the back of Maya's head with a rough, shaking hand and drew her into a brief, urgent embrace. She clung to him with one arm, Lila locked against her side, their breaths tangled between them.

Then he stepped back.

Another flicker. Another cold surge tightening their lungs.

Graves looked at them one last time.

The generator lights flickered again—hard enough that the entire lobby dipped into a moment of reddish dimness before snapping back. People screamed, ducking, shielding their children. Officers braced against desks, weapons drawn but trembling.

Another cold pulse swept the room, compressing the air so sharply Maya's next inhale stalled. Lila gasped against her, a thin, broken sound, fingers clawing at Maya's jacket.

The front doors shuddered.

Once.

Then again—subtle, but undeniable.

A low vibration hummed through the floor, rattling the pens on the front desk and sending a thin crack spidering up one of the frosted outer windows.

Graves took a step toward the lobby entrance.

Maya moved fast, intercepting him, Lila held tight against her side. "Graves, please," she rasped. Her voice was raw, pushed through lungs that wouldn't pull enough air. "Don't walk out there. Don't leave us."

He paused, and for a heartbeat the weight of his fear showed—deep, human, crushing. But the resolve behind it didn't bend.

He touched Maya's arm, thumb brushing once along her sleeve. "I want you both alive when this is over."

A sharp thud hit the exterior wall—like something had struck metal or concrete with enormous force. Several civilians screamed; officers stumbled as another pressure wave rolled through the building, warping the shadows along the baseboards into long, trembling streaks.

The distortion crawled toward Graves.

Lila cried out, burying her face against Maya's chest, clutching fistfuls of fabric. Her breath came in short, rapid bursts, body shaking violently.

Maya held her tighter, then reached out toward Graves again, tears blurring her vision. "You don't have to do this," she whispered.

His expression shifted—grief, love, acceptance, all in one fractured moment. "I do."

He turned to the closest officer. "Keep the civilians centered. No one near the doors. If anything breaches, fall back to the evidence hall." The officer nodded through tears, jaw locked against panic.

Graves unlatched the first barricade table. Another officer ran up to help, but Graves waved him off. "I've got it."

Maya's heart slammed so hard she thought she might drop. "Graves!" she shouted, her voice breaking.

He didn't look back.

He slid the last cabinet aside, clearing a narrow path to the doors. The glass shook again—tiny vibrations that rippled through the web of frost along its edges.

Inside the lobby, people were sobbing openly now. Someone dropped to their knees and prayed. Officers yelled for everyone to stay behind the central line of desks.

Lila pulled away from Maya just long enough to scream, "Don't go!"

Graves' shoulders flinched—but his steps didn't stop.

He reached the entrance.

A thin line of cold crept under the door, crawling across the tile toward him, brushing over his boots like a beckoning draft.

He placed his hand on the door's crash bar.

Maya surged forward a step, Lila dragging with her, both of them trembling.

"Graves—"

Her voice fractured completely.

He looked at her one last time.

One final, anchored moment—his eyes saying everything his words hadn't.

Then he pushed the door open.

Night slammed into the lobby—dark, heavy, wrong.

A pressure wave rippled through the room, scattering papers, rattling desks, stealing half the air from Maya's lungs.

Graves stepped outside.

The door swung inward behind him.

Chapter 29 — Warm Fear

The night swallowed Graves the moment the precinct doors slammed behind him. The sound echoed down the empty street, stretched thin by the cold air until it faded into nothing. He took three steps forward, then another, forcing his boots to scuff louder than they needed to. Every scrape was meant to draw attention. Every breath fogged instantly, crystals breaking from the exhale and drifting like ash.

The temperature dropped fast.

Frost cracked across the asphalt in branching lines that spread beneath his feet, delicate at first, then thickening into jagged ridges. Streetlights along the block flickered in uneven pulses—white, then dim amber, then white again—each flash bending the shadows on the ground into long, trembling streaks.

He kept walking.

The air tightened in his lungs as if pressure had folded around his chest. He forced sound up through his throat anyway.

"HEY!"

His voice echoed off the brick facades, harsh and desperate.

"You want someone—take me! Do you hear me?"

No wind carried the words. They just dropped into the cold and vanished.

A deep silence settled around him, dense enough that even his heartbeat felt muted. Graves swallowed, the inside of his mouth already stiffening from the cold. A thin layer of frost spread across the back of his sleeves, creeping higher each time he exhaled.

He walked farther down the block.

The darkness pressed close—thick, heavy, unmoving. The streetlights flickered again, longer this time, and the shadows along the buildings elongated toward the center of the road. They stretched in slow, incremental pulls, like the night was breathing downward.

A pressure wave rippled across the pavement.

Graves staggered. His knees nearly buckled under the sudden shift. The lights flickered in response—short bursts of pale illumination that lit the frost spreading across the entire street.

His breath crystallized so completely it fell in tiny shards that tinked softly against his jacket.

He shouted again, voice cracking from the cold and adrenaline. "HEY! I'm right here!"

The sound bounced back at him from the dark storefronts, warped at the edges, like something in the air had bent it.

He stopped walking.

The cold tightened once more—harder, deeper—and the shadows at the far end of the street began to stretch inward, narrowing the darkness into a funnel that pointed directly at him.

His chest rose fast. Too fast. Every inhale caught halfway, like the cold air refused to let his lungs expand.

The frost on the asphalt shimmered under the trembling streetlights.

Another pressure ripple rolled down the block—stronger now.

Graves squared his stance.

"Come on," he said through chattering teeth. "Come on."

The street held its breath.

The quiet broke in a single, uneven pulse.

A tremor rolled across the pavement, shallow but unmistakable—like the street had taken a breath beneath him. Graves shifted his weight, boots scraping over the frost as he steadied himself. His fingers tightened around the grip of his gun, the metal already burning cold against his skin.

Another flicker passed through the streetlights.

The shadows nearest him twitched—just a fraction—lagging behind the lights' return before sliding back into place. Then they stretched again, inch by inch, all leaning toward him as if drawn by a slow, steady pull.

Graves' mouth went dry. His exhale came out ragged, a thin plume of crystals drifting off his lips before shattering silently against his jacket.

A cold sweep slid behind him. Not wind—pressure. His lungs tightened. He turned fast, raising the gun, breath shredding in his throat as he scanned the empty block.

Nothing moved.

But the air felt crowded.

A second sweep passed to his left, brushing the side of his neck with a burst of cold so sharp it cut through muscle. Graves flinched violently, shoulder jerking as he pivoted that way too, gun aimed, heart pounding hard enough to shake his arms.

His breath broke again—short, unsteady, half-swallowed.

Something circled him.

He felt it—not a presence he could see, but shifts in the air that bent around him in slow arcs, passing from one side of the street to the other. Each sweep stole more warmth from his body, leaving his chest tight and burning with the effort to draw even a shallow inhale.

His flashlight flickered once in his free hand.

Then died.

Dark swallowed the space where the beam had been.

Graves' pulse hammered in his ears. His fingers trembled around the trigger. The cold crawled deeper, numbing the tips of his ears, the bridge of his nose, the corners of his jaw. His breath came shorter now, catching at the top of his chest like something inside resisted expanding.

He forced his voice up anyway.

"You stay away from them!" He swallowed, voice cracking. "Do you hear me? I'm right here!"

The words bounced back at him, warped by the thick air—bending, flattening, as if the street itself distorted the sound.

A faint scrape drifted from behind—smooth, gliding, fast.
He spun again, nearly slipping on the frost.

Another pressure wave rolled across the pavement—strong enough to make the frost jump in tiny crystalline bursts around his boots.

Shadows along the storefronts bent inward, all converging toward the spot where he stood.

His breath seized completely for a beat—no air moving, no sound—and panic surged up his spine, raw and electric.

He sucked in a thin, burning gasp.

His vision blurred at the edges.

"Come on," he whispered through clenched teeth. "Come on."

A final cold ripple swept the street, sharper than the others—so sharp Graves nearly dropped his weapon as his arm spasmed.

The darkness in front of him trembled.

The last tremor hadn't finished rippling when the cold slammed into Graves' chest.

He staggered backward, one hand clutching at his ribs as the temperature inside him dropped so fast it felt like his lungs had turned to stone. His breath shattered in his throat—thin crystals bursting against his tongue. His eyes watered instantly, tears freezing at the corners.

A crushing pressure clamped around his chest.

He fired.

The gun kicked hard in his hand—once, twice, three times—but each shot vanished the instant it left the barrel, swallowed by the collapsing dark. No ricochet. No impact. Just the muffled thump of recoil and the hollow echo of spent casings hitting the frost.

The cold surged deeper.

His heart lurched, then hammered wildly, each beat slower than the last.

His knees buckled. He dropped to one hand, palm burning from the frozen pavement.

Warmth tore out of him in a sudden, violent rush.

His breath didn't fog anymore. It spilled from his mouth as a thin stream of white vapor that froze mid-air and drifted downward in brittle flakes.

A crushing force wrapped around his torso—tightening, tightening—compression so brutal his back arched involuntarily. His gun slipped from numbing fingers, clattering against the asphalt before sliding across the frost.

Graves choked on a sound he couldn't force out.

Something gripped his throat.

An invisible clamp—solid, cold, powerful—closed around it. His windpipe compressed, cartilage creaking under the pressure. His vision blurred. Blood roared in his ears as the cold slid upward, locking his jaw, stiffening the muscles in his neck.

His feet left the ground.

He realized it only when his boots brushed the air, toes scraping the frost with no weight beneath them. His hands clawed at the empty space around his throat, fingers digging into nothing he could grasp.

His chest seized.

His heartbeat faltered.

A rapid internal freeze ripped through him—lungs crystallizing from the inside out. His mouth opened on instinct, but air wouldn't enter. His breath hung suspended, trapped behind ice forming deep inside his ribs.

The pressure at his throat tightened again.

A sickening crack echoed down his spine as cartilage gave way. His legs jerked once, then again, then stiffened in mid-spasm. His vision narrowed to a single frozen tunnel—the fractured glow of a distant streetlamp bending sideways.

Frost bloomed across his chest from beneath the skin, spidering outward in pale, branching lines.

His body convulsed a final time.

Then the crushing force deepened with one brutal snap.

He dropped.

The impact sent a hollow thud through the pavement, ice crystals spraying outward in a thin ring around his body. His limbs twitched once, reflexive and fading. Frost spread rapidly beneath him, radiating in spirals from his chest cavity.

A pressure wave tore down the street—rattling windows, bending every shadow toward the center of the block.

The air itself recoiled.

Inside the precinct, every light flickered at once.

Some went dim. Some surged bright. Others snapped off entirely for two full seconds before stuttering back in a wash of red and white. Papers lifted from desks, caught in a cold draft that tore through the lobby in a sudden, concussive burst.

Lila screamed.

Maya dropped to her knees beside her, arms wrapping tight as the girl's lungs seized. Lila's entire body locked in a violent tremor, breath wheezing out in thin, panicked gasps that never reached full inhale. Her hands clamped over her ears.

"Maya—Maya—"

Her voice broke into raw fragments, no words forming.

Another pulse rattled the windows—deep, heavy, rolling through the building like a shockwave. Officers stumbled. A few civilians collapsed to the floor, covering their heads as if expecting impact.

Maya's breath caught sharp in her chest.

She knew.

She didn't need a radio call. She didn't need confirmation. Something inside her—the same instinct that had kept her alive through every impossible hour—twisted hard enough to steal air.

Graves was gone.

She stood in a single motion, grabbing her kit. Lila clung to her leg, panic-stricken, but Maya pulled free gently, breath shaking.

"I'll be right back," Maya whispered, though the words barely left her throat.

Lila's eyes widened further, tears streaking fast across her cheeks. Her head shook in frantic, tiny movements.

Maya cupped the back of her head and kissed her hairline once before handing her into the arms of a waiting officer. "Stay with her," she told him. "Do not let her out of your sight."

He nodded, terrified.

Maya ran.

The front doors slammed open under her shoulder, and the night hit with a blast of frozen air that cut straight through her clothes. She stumbled out onto the pavement, boots sliding across a thin sheet of frost already forming on the steps.

The street ahead glowed faintly under failing lights—sections blinking in and out. The cold was worse here—deep, penetrating, enough to sting her lungs with every inhale.

"Maya, wait!"

An officer shouted behind her, but she was already moving.

Her breath puffed in ragged bursts as she sprinted across the lot. The shadows along the buildings twitched with delayed motion—lagging a split second behind her steps, then snapping back. A faint ringing filled the air, high and brittle.

She turned onto the block where Graves had gone.

And stopped.

Frost coated everything—cars, asphalt, brick, even the edges of street signs. The temperature drop had frozen the moisture in the air itself, turning it into a drifting haze of silver particles that clung to her eyelashes as she pushed forward.

Halfway down the street, a dark shape lay collapsed against the pavement.

Her body moved before her mind caught up.

She reached him fast, sliding the last few feet on her knees. Her gloves brushed his coat first—stiff with cold—then she pulled him toward her, turning him onto his back.

Her breath broke.

Frost spiraled across his chest in branching lines. His throat had caved inward, bruising and crushed cartilage visible through the thin crust of ice spreading along the skin. His mouth hung slightly open, a thin trail of frozen vapor suspended before it—a breath stopped halfway.

His eyes were half-closed, lashes dusted with white.

"Graves..."

Her voice shattered instantly.

She pulled him into her lap, hands trembling violently as she tried to wipe frost from his face. Her palms burned with cold; she didn't stop.

"Graves, come on—"

The words cracked, breaking apart.

Her tears hit his jacket and froze on contact.

Footsteps approached behind her—officers calling her name—but they sounded far away, swallowed by the cold that smothered the street.

Maya bent forward until her forehead touched his.

Her breath hitched hard enough to choke her.

Another pressure shift rolled along the block.

A soft metallic echo drifted between buildings—distant, distorted.

Maya lifted her head—not because she expected him to wake, but because the night itself seemed to shift, as if the world had tipped slightly toward the next horror waiting for them.

She tightened her grip on him once, then forced herself upright.

She had to move.

Chapter 30 — Marked

The precinct doors slammed open as Maya stumbled inside, breath hitching from the run, frost still clinging to her clothes. Every head snapped toward her—the officers, the handful of civilians, Lila.

Lila froze.

She didn't need words.

She didn't need an explanation.

One look at Maya's face was enough.

A sharp, thin sound tore out of her—a broken inhale that scraped the back of her throat. She backed away from the bench so fast her heel slipped on the tile. Her hands flew to her chest, fingers digging in as if she could stop her ribcage from collapsing.

"Lila—" Maya reached her, but the girl recoiled, breath spiraling out of control before Maya could even touch her.

The panic hit like impact.

Lila's knees buckled, and she dropped into Maya's arms, shaking violently. Her breath fractured into short, shallow gasps—too quick, too thin, barely pulling any air at all. Maya pulled her in tight, one arm around her back, the other against the crown of her head.

"It's okay—breathe with me—breathe—"

But Maya's own voice trembled. She tasted salt before she realized she was crying too.

Lila shook harder. The overhead lights crackled—one bulb buzzing so sharply the sound cut across the room like a blade. Shadows along the walls lagged half a beat behind movement, smearing in brief, sick distortions before snapping back.

An officer stepped forward, startled. "What the hell—?"

Maya didn't look up. She held Lila tighter, rocking her slightly, trying to anchor her body against the spiraling panic overtaking her.

Lila's breaths came faster, shallow and sharp, barely drawing air. Her fingers curled into Maya's jacket, knuckles white, nails scraping fabric.

"Maya—"

Her voice broke on the single word, strangled and terrified.

"It's okay. I've got you," Maya whispered, though her voice cracked on the last syllable.

But Lila wasn't hearing her—not fully.

The girl's eyes were wide, unfocused, fixed on nothing in the room. Tears poured fast down her cheeks, breath shaking so violently her whole frame jolted with each inhale.

The fluorescent tube above them flickered again—one long, stuttering buzz that rattled the metal housing. The air felt thin, tight, as if the room were being squeezed from the outside.

"Easy—easy—stay with me," Maya breathed.

But Lila's chest kept seizing, each inhale shorter than the last.

Her pupils tightened.

Her breath broke.

A memory hit her so hard her whole body jerked.

Lila clutched her temples as if something inside her skull were pulling apart. Her breath hitched in short, panicked bursts—each one tighter, sharper, almost swallowed.

"I've seen it," she gasped. "I've seen it—I saw it—"

Maya held her shoulders, grounding her. "You told us before. The hallway. The hospital. It's okay. You're okay."

But Lila shook her head violently, hair sticking to her tear-wet cheeks. "No—no, not like this. I didn't—I didn't remember all of it."

Her voice cracked on the last word.

Another flicker rippled across the ceiling. The fluorescent tube buzzed, dimmed, then sharpened into an overbright glare before settling into an uneasy pulse. A stack of papers lifted on a nearby desk—just an inch—before falling back in a scatter.

Lila's eyes squeezed shut.

And the memories surged forward.

"I was eight," she whispered, shaking harder. "At my abuela's house. She told stories—Cucuy stories—and I laughed, but…" Her breath stuttered. "That night, something stood in the doorway. I thought it was my uncle, but it didn't move right. It stayed too long."

Her fingers curled into fists.

"And in the hospital—after the accident—I woke up, and the curtain around my bed was shaking. But there was no air vent near it. It moved anyway." Her voice thinned. "I thought it was just fear. Just grief."

Maya felt her stomach twist.

Lila wasn't rambling—she was aligning.
Each memory sharpening, edges matching, pieces clicking into place under the weight of late-cycle proximity.

Lila pressed a trembling hand to her chest, breath staggering. "And—and the hallway… that night when the lights went out… I saw a shape at the other end. It leaned. It touched the floor before the rest of it. I thought I imagined it."

The tube above them flicked again—quick, stuttering pulses that made the shadows along the far wall bend out of sync.

Lila opened her eyes. The pupils were blown wide, shimmering with panic.

"It was the same thing," she whispered. "Every time. Every place. The same shape. The same feeling. It wasn't stories. It wasn't fear. It was real."

Her voice faltered.

She sucked in a ragged breath.

Then another memory hit—so fast her shoulders jerked as though struck.

Lila's breath hitched, sharp enough to sound painful. She curled inward against Maya, fingers knotting in the fabric of her jacket as another memory tore to the surface—stronger, clearer, threaded with the same cold dread she had felt as a child.

"It came back," she whispered, shaking so hard her teeth clicked. "After we moved. After the hospital. I—I woke up one night and the air in my room felt wrong. Heavy. Like something was watching from the corner."

Maya held her tighter. "Lila, listen to me—"

"It wasn't just once," Lila choked out. "It kept happening. I'd hear the floor creak, just one board, the same one every time. I'd look, but the dark wouldn't... stay still." Her breath fractured. "I tried telling people. No one believed me. They said it was trauma. Nightmares."

Her body jolted with a sudden, violent tremor.

"But it wasn't." Her voice broke on the words. "It wasn't night-mares."

The lights above them stuttered—three rapid pulses that made the shadows along the wall fall out of rhythm again. A desk chair rolled an inch as air pressure shifted, pushing inward from the hall.

Maya lifted her head, scanning behind them, heart pounding.

Lila's panic surged again, breath tearing in thin, uneven gasps.

"I didn't know it was the same thing," she said, voice thinning into a whisper. "The stories. The hospital. The hallway. My room. I thought they were different. I thought I was losing my mind."

Her fingers spasmed, clutching at Maya's sleeve.

"But it was all the same. It was always the same." Her voice cracked. "It watched me for years."

Maya's throat tightened, a raw ache forming behind her ribs. She didn't interrupt—not when Lila finally lifted her face from Maya's shoulder, tears running unchecked down her cheeks.

Lila swallowed hard, voice trembling.

"It marked me."

The words landed like impact—quiet, but undeniable.

A pressure ripple moved through the precinct—not sound, not temperature, just a tightening of the air that made the walls seem to pull inward for a fraction of a second. A pen rolled off a desk nearby and clattered to the floor.

Lila flinched.

Her eyes darted toward the inner hallway, pupils dilating as if she felt something shift far beyond what anyone else could sense.

Her breath stalled.

Maya guided Lila into one of the smaller interview rooms, closing the door behind them to muffle the noise of the panicked precinct. The overhead light buzzed faintly, its glow uneven, casting unsteady bands of brightness across the cramped space.

Lila curled onto the bench, arms wrapped tightly around herself. Her breaths came in thin, shaky pulls—still too quick, still too shallow. Maya crouched in front of her, hands light on her knees.

"Slow," Maya whispered. "Match me. In and out."

Lila tried. The inhale faltered halfway.

"I didn't understand," she whispered. "All those years… I thought I was just scared. I thought I was broken."

"You're not broken," Maya said, voice shaking. "You were a kid. You did what you could."

Lila squeezed her eyes shut, tears slipping free. "But it kept finding me. Every house. Every room. Every time the lights went out." Her voice thinned. "I thought I was safe here. I thought—maybe—it was over."

Maya swallowed hard past the ache rising in her throat. She brushed Lila's hair back gently, though her own hands trembled.

"You are not the reason this is happening," Maya murmured. "Do you hear me? This isn't on you."

Lila shook her head, small and quick. "Graves died because of it."

Maya's breath stuttered—but she didn't look away. She forced her voice steady, even while the truth twisted inside her.

"Graves died protecting us," she said softly. "That was his choice. His heart."

Lila pressed her palms to her eyes. "It won't stop. I feel it. Even now—I feel it."

A low hum rolled through the walls—subtle, almost like the building adjusting its weight, but too rhythmic to be structural. The fluorescent light flickered once, shadows dragging sluggishly across the room before snapping back into place.

Maya looked up sharply.

Lila's breath hitched. "See? It's closer."

Maya moved onto the bench beside her, pulling the girl against her chest, arms wrapping around her shoulders with a fierce, protective hold. "You're not alone," she whispered into her hair. "You're not facing this alone. I'm here. I'm not going anywhere."

Lila clung to her, shaking, sobbing in muffled bursts against Maya's jacket.

A soft vibration trembled through the floor—barely there, like something distant testing its reach.

Maya lifted her head, eyes narrowing, jaw tightening. A cold certainty settled beneath her ribs.

It wasn't finished.

And it wasn't wandering blindly.

It was searching.

Maya tightened her hold on Lila, breath unsteady but resolve hardening with each beat of her heart.

The fluorescent light flickered again—brief, sharp—before steadying.

Maya turned her head toward the door, listening.

Chapter 31 — What It Left Behind

The fluorescent light steadied overhead, its last flicker fading into a low, electric hum. Maya held Lila against her chest, the girl's trembling breaths warming the fabric of her jacket. She kept her eyes on the door, pulse beating hard enough to throb in her throat.

The room felt suspended—like everything was waiting.

Lila shifted weakly in her arms, a small, fractured sound slipping out as if her lungs were still trying to remember how to breathe. Maya loosened her grip just enough for the girl to settle back into the rigid plastic chair, her own hands lingering on Lila's shoulders until she was sure the girl wouldn't fall.

Only then did Maya step back.

Not far—just enough that Lila wouldn't see her face break.

Her spine hit the wall beside the metal table, breath shaking as the pressure in her chest finally cracked loose.

Images flooded up too fast to block.

Graves lying in the street.

Frost blooming across his chest.

His throat collapsed inward.

The weight of him going slack when she lifted him.

Her breath hitched into a sharp, soundless gasp. She pressed her palm hard against her mouth, shoulders trembling as she fought to stay quiet for Lila's sake.

The fluorescent tube above them buzzed—hard.

Light stuttered, dimmed, surged bright again.

A loose evidence form on the table slid a few inches, shifting in a sudden, restless sweep of air.

"Maya?"

Lila's voice was small, raw, frayed by everything she'd already endured.

Maya didn't turn immediately. She wiped her face with the back of her hand, tears cold against her skin. Her fingers shook when she lowered them. She forced herself to draw a breath deep enough not to break on the exhale.

"I'm here," she managed, though her voice wavered.

She turned toward Lila, trying—failing—to keep her expression steady. Lila watched her from the chair, legs drawn up, hands twisted in the hem of her shirt, eyes huge and shimmering.

Maya pushed off the wall, breath unsteady but moving. She took one step toward the table, breath catching as the light overhead trembled in a thin, uneven flicker—pulling her into the next moment whether she was ready or not.

Another tremor rolled through the light fixture—subtle, a thin vibration that buzzed along the metal housing before falling still again. Maya's eyes tracked it automatically, breath still uneven as she fought to steady herself for Lila's sake.

But the sound…

That faint, wavering buzz…

It struck something buried.

A hallway.

A hospital floor.

Her brother's last night.

The memory hit without warning, sharp enough to make her grip the edge of the table for balance. The interview room dissolved for a moment, replaced by the polished linoleum of a late-night pediatric ward. Her younger self standing barefoot outside a dim room. Machines humming softly. Nurses whispering. Her brother asleep and fading.

And at the far end of the hallway—

A light that flickered twice.

A shadow stretched across the floor, reaching from a corner too far from the bulb to cast anything that long.

Its edges trembled in a slow, delayed motion before settling.

She had told herself it was exhaustion.

That she'd imagined it.

That grief had carved shapes into the dark that weren't really there.

Her breath faltered now, here in the interview room, as the old panic rose like cold water inside her chest. She pressed a hand against her sternum, fingers splayed, trying to swallow the pressure gathering beneath her ribs.

Another flicker in the present—

the overhead light dimming for a heartbeat before resuming its uneven glow.

The shadow under the table lagged a moment behind the motion of her hand.

She squeezed her eyes shut as another memory clawed its way forward—a moment she'd nearly erased:

Waking in her childhood bedroom at twelve years old.

The air heavy.

A corner darker than it should've been.

Her breath coming short and shallow, as if something pressed down on her lungs.

A shape that felt tall even without seeing it.

She had pushed it away for years.

Filed it under nightmares.

But now—

Now the pieces aligned too cleanly.

Too perfectly.

Her fingers tightened on the table edge until her knuckles blanched.

She wasn't just failing people now.
She had missed the signs long before tonight.
Long before this cycle ever began.

Her breath hitched again, sharp as a stab.

The fluorescent light hummed in a strained, wavering note—then steadied.

Maya opened her eyes, chest aching as another memory began to surface, rising fast and unavoidable from the place she had buried it.

The next memory rose faster than she could brace for it.

Maya's vision blurred again—not from tears, but from the sudden rush of something hot and sharp behind her eyes. She gripped the edge of the table with both hands as another buried moment tore free.

She was sixteen.
Alone in her room.
The house quiet except for the ticking in the hallway thermostat.
And there—
in the corner near her dresser—
a patch of darkness that felt too thick, too weighted, as if it leaned forward slightly with each unsteady breath she took.

She remembered freezing in place.
Chest tight.
Hair rising along her arms without a draft to justify it.

Now, standing in the interview room, the echo of that pressure tightened her ribs all over again. Her lungs fought to expand against it, drawing in only shallow fractions of what she needed.

The overhead light flickered in a short, sharp pulse.

Lila startled in her chair, fingers curling into the fabric of her shirt. Her wide eyes fixed on Maya—sensing more than she understood.

Maya swallowed hard, but her throat resisted, feeling constricted by an ache that had nothing to do with the room's temperature.

She pressed a shaking hand against the wall.

Another moment slammed into her—

She was twenty-two, waiting outside an ICU room.

Her brother gone less than an hour.

The hallway lights dimmed briefly from a surge somewhere in the building.

And for a breath—one single breath—

she thought she saw something move against the far wall.

Something tall.

Something angled.

Something that shifted a hair too late after the light returned.

She had never told anyone about that flicker.

Never admitted she'd felt watched in that hallway.

But now—

now the shape's edges felt familiar.

The same unnatural stretch.

The same pressure she felt tonight.

The same breath-stealing weight.

Her pulse hammered unevenly.

A new tremor rolled across the light fixture above them; the glass hummed, shadows beneath the table stuttering in a delayed smear before snapping back.

Lila's breath hitched. "Maya…?"

Maya met her gaze—and for the first time, she didn't push the memories away. She let them rise, one after another, each one sharpening into a pattern she could no longer deny.

This thing hadn't entered her life tonight.

Or this year.

Or even with the cycle.

It had brushed close before, hidden in places she'd been too young, too shattered, too grief-stricken to recognize.

Her heartbeat throbbed once—hard enough to sting.

Another tremor buzzed faintly in the walls, subtle but crawling along the floor like static.

Maya straightened slowly, breath unsteady as a new understanding locked into place.

She hadn't been imagining those moments.

Not any of them.

The truth pressed in around her, undeniable.

Maya pushed herself off the wall, lungs tight but steadying. The panic didn't vanish—it settled differently, sinking beneath her ribs as something heavier and sharper took its place.

Lila watched her from the chair, curled in on herself, eyes red and swollen. She looked small. Too small for everything the night had already taken from her.

Maya crossed the room and knelt beside her.

Not rushing. Not trembling now.

Just present.

Lila lifted her head, breath catching. "It's getting closer," she whispered. "I feel it. Every time the lights—every time the room—" Her voice broke. She dug her fingers into the fabric of her shirt to keep them from shaking.

Maya took her hands gently, guiding them down from her chest. "You're not imagining any of this," she said softly. "And you're not facing it alone."

Another flicker rippled through the light above them—brief, jittered, a stutter that smeared the shadows a beat behind Lila's movement. The air tightened for a split second, a pressure shift that brushed both of them like a silent warning.

Maya didn't flinch this time.

She tightened her grip on Lila's hands. "It's been near us for a long time," she murmured. "Longer than we understood. But it doesn't get to take you. Not now."

Lila's breath wavered. A tear spilled down her cheek.

"I'm scared," she whispered.

"I am too." Maya's voice cracked, but she didn't look away. "And we're still going to face it."

The fluorescent tube hummed in a low, strained vibration.

Maya rose slowly, brushing her palms against her thighs to steady herself. Her knees trembled—but her spine did not.

She scanned the small room—the table, the chairs, the harsh overhead light—each corner a reminder of how little stood between them and whatever waited beyond the door. Her fear pulsed once, heavy—but this time it didn't steal her breath.

She crossed to the door, still keeping Lila in sight, her fingers hovering near the handle. Not to leave—
but to be ready.

The light flickered again. Shadows jittered in delayed motion beneath their feet.

Maya drew in a slow, controlled breath, feeling resolve settle into every aching part of her chest.

Whatever waited outside, whatever the night still intended—
She would meet it standing.

Chapter 32 — The Tenth

The fluorescent light above them steadied, its last flicker fading into a strained, uneven hum. Maya stood at the interview room door, her hand hovering near the handle, Lila close behind her—breath trembling, fingers twisted into the fabric of Maya's sleeve.

Maya drew a slow breath, letting resolve settle beneath her ribs.

Her radio crackled.

A burst of static ripped through the speaker, loud enough to make Lila flinch and press herself fully against Maya's side.

"—St. Brigid's—male screaming—"

"—blood on scene—caller dropped—"

"EMS, respond immediately—"

The transmission fractured again, scraping along Maya's nerves.

Lila gasped, clutching Maya's arm with sudden, panicked strength. "Don't—don't leave me—please—"

Her knees buckled. Maya caught her at the shoulders before she hit the floor. Lila shook violently, breath breaking into shallow, uneven pulls.

Maya's stomach twisted. She couldn't leave Lila like this. But the call wasn't optional—someone was alive at St. Brigid's, or had been seconds ago.

She tightened her grip on Lila, steadying her. "I have to take that call," she said softly, voice thin but certain. "There's someone hurt."

Lila whimpered, shaking her head, holding tighter.

Maya pressed her palm against the door and opened it.

The hallway erupted with noise—voices raised in panic, radios glitching, civilians crying, the generator rumbling in a strained pulse. Light flickered down the corridor, shadows dragging behind motion in slow, jittered streaks.

An officer nearly collided with them, skidding to a stop when he saw Lila clinging to Maya, barely able to stand.

Maya had to raise her voice to be heard. "I've been dispatched to St. Brigid's. I need to go."

The officer's eyes flicked from Maya's radio to Lila's collapsing posture to the chaos flooding the precinct.

He swore under his breath. "We don't have anyone free to stay with her. We're drowning out here."

Lila pressed her face into Maya's sleeve, trembling so hard her teeth clicked.

The officer's expression tightened. He stepped back, making room.

"Take her with you," he said. "We can't keep her safe here tonight."

Lila's grip tightened further. "Don't leave me," she whispered, voice cracking.

Maya swallowed hard, looping an arm around her shoulders. "I'm right here," she murmured. "Come on—we're going together."

They moved through the chaotic lobby, weaving past frightened civilians and exhausted officers. The lights flickered again—hard enough to smear every shadow across the floor.

The glass doors at the front rattled in their frames.

Maya pushed them open.

Outside, the blackout swallowed the street. No wind. No sound. The air felt thin—pulled inward, pressing tight around her lungs.

Lila stiffened beside her, breath hitching. "It's close," she whispered.

Maya loaded her into the rig's passenger seat, then climbed in behind the wheel. The engine caught on the third attempt. She drove toward St. Brigid's, the church rising ahead like a hollow silhouette against the dark.

She parked at the curb.

The silence around them felt absolute.

Maya stepped out of the rig, her hand closing around the door frame as the air compressed in a sharp, breath-stealing pulse that pushed her forward into the dark ahead.

The church loomed above them—its steeple a jagged silhouette carved out of the blackout sky, windows black and hollow. The front doors hung slightly ajar, one hinge trembling in a faint, uneven shiver that didn't match the stillness around it.

Maya rounded the rig and helped Lila down from the passenger seat. The girl's legs wobbled beneath her, breath catching in quick, uneven pulls. She clutched Maya's sleeve with both hands, eyes locked on the dark mouth of the church.

Maya scanned the area—no movement, no voices, just a silence wound tight enough to press along her ribs.

Her radio hissed once, then faded.

They stepped toward the doors.

The moment Maya crossed the threshold, sound changed. Each footstep landed as if swallowed mid-air, returning with a faint, delayed smear that trailed behind them like an echo struggling to keep pace.

Lila's grip tightened.

A crushing sweep of cold clamped down on the air, tightening around Maya's lungs until her breath thinned to shallow, scraping inhales. Frost crawled across the nearest floorboard in branching lines, spreading toward the nave's center.

Lila's whole body trembled. Maya wrapped an arm around her to steady her.

A hymn book on a nearby pew glazed over in seconds, ice blooming across the cover in delicate crystalline veins. The cold pulsed through the church, sinking deeper with each step they took.

The darkness between pews thickened in layered pockets, shifting with their movement—shadows dragging behind each step before snapping back into shape.

Somewhere deeper inside, water dripped.

Then a second drip landed out of rhythm, as if the sound passed through a warped pocket of space.

A metallic tang seeped into the air—sharp, stinging, marked by the frozen bite of blood. Lila gagged, pressing a hand to her mouth as they moved farther down the aisle.

A jitter of movement caught Maya's eye—shadows along the far pews bending briefly in a warped angle before straightening again.

Her heartbeat hammered hard enough to make her vision pulse.

She stepped forward.

Then again.

A shape lay ahead on the floor, just emerging from the dark—a form sprawled across the center aisle, frozen in a way her mind struggled to interpret.

Maya steadied herself and moved toward it.

The shape in the aisle sharpened as Maya stepped closer, frost spiraling outward from it in violent bursts—jagged, branching fractures that spread across the floorboards like impact waves. The air pressed inward, constricting her breath until her knees nearly gave out.

Then her vision cleared.

And she froze.

This wasn't a body.

It was the **remains of a life unmade**.

The ribcage had been forced apart with such immense strength that the bones no longer curved—they had been **pulled into spears**, stretched thin at their tips, frozen into glasslike sharpness. Several ribs had splintered entirely, each fracture widened into long, webbed cracks filled with ice.

The chest cavity lay completely hollow.

Not scraped.

Not carved.

Scooped clean, as though the organs had been lifted out in a single, seamless extraction. The interior walls had frozen into mirrored surfaces that reflected warped fragments of the pews around them, bending the images into impossible angles.

The spine had been removed from its natural line.

Pulled forward.

Twisted.

Its vertebrae formed a spiraled tower rising several inches from the floor, as if something had wound it upward, rung by rung, until the column resembled a corkscrew of bone and frost. Thin, tendril-like strands of frozen nerve fiber trailed from the exposed channel, stretched into translucent filaments that fluttered with each pulse of cold air.

The head rested several feet from the torso, turned halfway toward the ceiling. The jaw had been forced open so wide the hinge had shattered, leaving the mouth stretched into a rigid, silent scream. Frost clung to the tongue and inner throat, forming crystalline needles that pointed outward. One eye had collapsed inward, frozen into a sunken pit; the other stared glassily, rimmed by frost that radiated outward like a shattered halo.

The arms had been contorted backward, bones pulled into elongated arcs, each limb twisted so violently it looked as if they had been folded and refolded without breaking cleanly—only stretching. Muscle fiber hung in ribbon-like sheets from the shoulders, frozen mid-tear.

The legs lay splayed at opposing angles, the pelvis nearly sheared apart from the torsion. One femur had been drawn forward until it pierced through the skin, protruding in a long, frozen spike that steamed faintly in the cold.

And around the entire scene—

a perfect ring.

Frozen blood had exploded outward in a single circular burst, droplets suspended on the air before freezing mid-flight. They hung several inches above the floor, fixed in space like a halo of crimson shards.

Lila's breath snapped.

Then her body crumpled.

She collapsed to her hands and knees, heaving, sobbing, her fingers clawing at the floor as if trying to grip something solid in a room turning inside out. A high, broken scream tore from her chest, cutting off into choking gasps. Her eyes squeezed shut, tears freezing on her cheeks in tiny, crystalline streaks.

Maya staggered beside her, hand slamming against a pew as her vision whited out at the edges. Her pulse hammered so violently she felt each beat shudder through her skull. Her mouth flooded with the metallic taste of adrenaline and bile.

The church reacted.

The pews groaned—not from wood strain but from something deeper, as though sound vibrated through the structure itself. Stone along the walls cracked in thin, jagged lines that crept outward like fractures in a frozen lake.

Shadows spiraled around the body, pulling into a vortex so dense the floor beneath it flickered out of true alignment. Lines bent. Corners elongated. The air shook in low, vibrating pulses that rattled Maya's bones.

Her vision doubled—

then tripled—

as the shadow vortex twisted, each layer of darkness slightly out of sync, delayed by a fraction of a second.

The cold deepened, crawling up her spine in a sharp, biting climb that reached the base of her skull and locked her jaw.

She forced herself forward anyway.

Her hand lifted—shaking so violently she barely recognized it as hers—and hovered over the spiraled vertebrae.

The air around the bones throbbed.

Something unseen brushed against her knuckles—
a pressure like breath without warmth, without wind, without anything human.

The floor beneath her feet trembled.

Lila clung to Maya's arm when she tried to stand, fingers trembling so violently they slipped against her sleeve. Her breaths came quick and shallow, each one scraping through her throat. Maya steadied her, though her own hands shook hard enough to blur the edges of her vision.

The vortex around the corpse spasmed once—
a violent twist of shadow folding inward—
and then collapsed to a single point beneath what remained of the body.
The cold surged outward in a crushing wave that struck Maya's legs and rolled across the nave, rattling the wooden pews in a low, groaning tremor.

Then the church fell still.

Silence pressed against her ears.
Only the faint cracking of ice along the floorboards broke the stillness, the sound delicate and horrifyingly final.

Maya forced herself to look again.

Every trauma signature she had seen across the entire cycle had converged here:
the hollowed cavity,
the shattered throat,
the spiraled spine,
the drained channels,
the frozen arc of blood suspended midair.

Every pattern.
Every mode.
Every cycle note Vander had recorded.
All of it—here.
Unmistakable.

Her heart lurched.

This wasn't a precursor.

This wasn't a stage.

This was the end of the feeding cycle.

The tenth feed.

The final one.

Behind her, Lila whimpered—a thin, broken sound. Maya turned and saw her staring at the far corner of the church, where the shadows sagged in a heavy, unnatural fold, as if the darkness itself had weight. A faint shiver rippled through the pocketed black, disturbing the edges of the pews.

Lila's voice cracked. "It's done feeding."

Maya felt the words settle in her chest like sinking stone.

The Maw no longer needed food.

No hunger drove it now.

What came next had nothing to do with survival—

only fixation, instinct, and whatever purpose it carried into the dark.

Lila pressed closer, trembling so violently her teeth knocked together. "Maya… it's looking for me."

A pulse tremored through the nave—soft, rhythmic, like a heartbeat shuddering through the church walls. Frost crept another inch along the floor.

Maya grabbed Lila's hand, pulling her toward the doors. "We're leaving. Now."

The air pushed back against them, thickening as they moved, as though the church itself tried to keep them inside. Each step cracked the frost beneath their feet, sharp and brittle.

Maya hit the doors with her shoulder. The wood groaned, warping around the hinges as if something on the other side pressed inward. She shoved harder until the distorted frame gave way and the night air rushed in.

Outside, the dark felt charged—alive, humming with the weight of something that had just completed its final ritual.

Lila stumbled down the steps, clinging to Maya. Her breath broke into ragged gasps, eyes wide and unfocused.

"Maya," she whispered, voice splintering. "It's finished. And now it's coming."

Maya pulled her forward into the night.

The night swallowed them as soon as they cleared the bottom step. The air felt heavier out here—dense, charged, humming with something that hadn't existed a moment earlier. Lila stayed pressed against Maya's side, shuddering so violently Maya could feel it through both of their coats.

They moved fast across the patchy walkway toward the rig parked beneath the dead streetlamp. Frost cracked under their shoes in brittle snaps, each one echoing too sharply in the stillness.

The blackout wasn't silent.

It *listened.*

Maya yanked the passenger door open and lifted Lila inside. The girl folded against the seat, arms wrapped around her ribs, breath quivering.

Maya circled to the driver's side, slid in, and slammed the door. Her fingers barely felt the keys as she shoved them into the ignition.

"Please," she muttered, voice trembling. "Start."

She turned the key.

The engine clicked—

a thin, metallic tick—

then sagged into a dull, compressing whine, like the sound was being dragged downward into the floorboard.

She tried again.

No turnover.

No cough.

Only a soft pulse rolling through the dashboard lights—an unnatural dimming that rose and fell in slow, suffocating waves.

Lila's voice cracked. "Maya."

Maya lifted her eyes to the windshield.

The street wasn't the street anymore.

Shadows along the pavement jittered in layered motions, each one out of sync with the next, like multiple silhouettes moving at slightly different times. The sidewalk on the opposite side of the road bent inward, angles pulling toward a point just beyond the darkness. Storefront windows bowed subtly, their reflections warping as though the glass were softening.

A vibration crawled through the rig's frame.

A deep, low thud rolled under their feet—too heavy to be distant, too controlled to be random. Maya felt it pulse through the steering column and settle cold against her wrists.

Lila grabbed her arm with both hands. "It's looking for us."

Maya didn't try the ignition again.

Something in the air told her the rig wasn't just dead—

it was being *suppressed.*

She shoved the door open and pulled Lila out, keeping one arm locked around her as they stumbled back onto the street.

The ground trembled once—

a shallow quake that sent small cracks splintering through the frost at their feet.

The darkness ahead shifted.

Not movement—

but *migration.*

Shadows folding, funneling, dragging the edges of the street into a narrowing corridor as if the night were shaping a path with only one direction.

Maya tightened her grip on Lila.

"We're moving," she whispered. "Stay with me."

The air thickened—

a pressure wave rolling toward them.

Maya pulled Lila forward, forcing their bodies through the tightening dark as the street warped around them.

Chapter 33 — Last Corner

Maya kept Lila's hand tight in hers as they pushed deeper into the blackout. The night pressed heavy against their faces, thick with cold that settled along the skin in uneven bursts. The only illumination came from distant backup lamps—thin, scattered points that flickered irregularly along the street like exhausted fireflies.

The town had gone quiet.

Too quiet.

No engines.

No voices.

No hum from the grid.

Only the rasp of their footsteps and Lila's uneven breathing broke the stillness.

Maya scanned the street ahead, trying to make sense of the patchy light. Shadows pooled at the ends of the block in uneven shapes, shifting slightly each time her eyes refocused. Depth felt hard to judge; corners receded too quickly, then too slowly, as the dark swallowed any stable point of reference.

A faint tremor rolled beneath the pavement—subtle, more sensed than heard.

Lila jerked, stumbling into Maya.

"What is it?" Maya whispered.

Lila pressed a hand against her sternum, breath catching in sharp, panicked pulls. "Feels like pressure... here."

Maya steadied her, one arm firm around her shoulders. She'd seen people react like this during high-stress calls—breathing patterns tightening, bodies responding to changes in temperature and fear faster than conscious thought could catch up. But Lila reacted with startling precision, flinching each time the air shifted in barely perceptible waves.

Lila swallowed hard. "It's moving."

"Then we keep going," Maya said, guiding her forward.

They turned onto a narrower block where the buildings leaned close, their upper stories lost in the blackout sky. Without streetlights, the angles looked different—edges blurring, corners sinking into deeper pools of shadow. Maya's eyes strained with each step, depth perception fighting the low contrast.

A cold brush swept along her ankles like a sharp draft cutting across the street. Lila gasped and nearly went down. Maya caught her under both arms, pulling her upright.

"I'm here," she murmured. "Stay with me."

Far ahead, emergency lights flickered—steady enough to silhouette the outline of the old school, dim enough that everything between them and the building remained drowned in murky, shifting dark.

Maya pulled Lila toward that faint glow.

Behind them, something shifted in the far end of the street—a weighted thump, soft but deliberate, absorbed by the thick air instead of echoing. Lila tensed, fingers digging into Maya's sleeve.

"It's closer," she whispered.

Maya tightened her grip and pushed them forward, forcing their bodies through the uneven darkness toward the only place left with light.

They moved into a stretch of road where the blackout thickened, swallowing what little definition the street still held. The last hints of distant light faded behind them, leaving only faint reflections in window glass and the dull orange blink of a malfunctioning transformer several blocks away.

Every surface caught the light differently, enough to suggest shapes but never long enough to confirm them. Depth warped with each step as Maya's eyes strained against the uneven dark.

She tightened her grip on Lila and pushed their pace.

Cold shifted across the street in abrupt pockets—brief sweeps of dense, chilled air that clamped against their skin. Each time the temperature dropped, Lila jerked as if startled by something just out of sight.

"Left," Lila whispered, tugging at Maya's arm.

"Tell me."

"The air changes faster on the right," she said between shallow breaths. "Feels like something's pushing through."

Maya didn't hesitate. She followed Lila's pull and cut left between two rows of shuttered storefronts. The narrow block felt deceptive only because the blackout hid any reliable point of reference—structures rising tall on both sides, their rooftops merging into a dark mass overhead.

A flicker stirred at the far end of the street.

just a quick distortion in the shadowed area beside a lamppost, a momentary shift where the light should have been flat and still. Maya's heart kicked hard against her ribs. She clutched Lila closer and kept moving.

A metal crash broke through the silence—sharp, echoing, the unmistakable slam of a dumpster against brick. The sound ricocheted off the enclosed street, rippling along the pavement.

Lila gasped, her whole body tightening. "It's using the darker spots," she whispered, her voice cracking.

Maya didn't answer, but she didn't need to.
The pattern was forming:
small disturbances where visibility collapsed, pockets of cold sweeping across their path, shifts in shadow just outside clear focus.

The creature was repositioning with intention quiet, efficient, exploiting every gap the darkness offered.

Another faint vibration rolled through the pavement, subtle but steady. Lila's fingers dug into Maya's arm.

"It moved again," she said, barely audible.

Maya kept her eyes forward.

Ahead, an emergency light flickered above the school's side entrance—thin, weak, but steady enough to mark their destination. Lila faltered, legs shaking under her weight.

Maya caught her around the waist and urged her forward. "Almost there. Stay with me."

The vibration deepened, coursing up through the soles of their shoes.

Maya pulled Lila across the intersection, the school's faint glow growing clearer with each hurried, uneven step.

The school finally rose ahead of them, a broad shadow outlined by a thin scatter of emergency lights. Each bulb flickered at its own pace—slow, weak flashes that cast narrow strips of illumination across the empty parking lot.

Maya kept Lila close, guiding her toward the gate. The cold shifted across the pavement in rolling pockets, brushing over their legs and ribs with uneven force. Lila flinched each time the air tightened, fingers locking around Maya's sleeve.

They crossed into the lot.

The pavement seemed to waver under the unsteady lighting—shadows thickening, thinning, then thickening again. Maya narrowed her eyes, trying to keep her focus steady.

Lila stopped suddenly, breath catching in her throat.

Maya leaned toward her. "Show me."

Lila raised a trembling hand toward the far corner of the building. Her arm shook so hard the gesture wavered, but the direction was clear.

Under one of the flickering lights, the pavement dipped into a dense patch of shadow. The light stuttered again, and the darkness shifted—just a thin, drifting change in depth, like something had moved through the space faster than the eye could track.

Lila pressed herself to Maya's side. "It's moving around us."

Maya tightened her grip and pushed them forward.

A hollow clatter echoed from the side of the building—sharp metal striking metal, then settling. The sound vibrated through the lot, carrying a tone that prickled across Maya's scalp. She didn't turn toward it; she didn't need to. Lila's grip had already confirmed the direction of the disturbance.

Ahead, the emergency lights nearest the entrance blinked in a short sequence—left, center, right—then repeated, the timing uneven but deliberate enough to make Maya's pulse spike. The air trembled with each flicker, a faint pressure brushing across her ribs.

Lila stumbled, knees buckling. "It's getting closer."

Maya caught her, lifted her weight, and pushed harder toward the doors.

The double glass entrance shimmered under the weak lights. Reflections shifted across the surface—narrow bands of brightness stretching and compressing as the bulbs pulsed overhead. Maya reached the door and pulled. The handle felt rigid from the cold, but it swung open with a jolt.

A tremor rolled through the pavement behind them—slow, heavy, steady enough to feel through their shoes.

Maya pulled Lila inside

The door closed behind them with a muted clack, sealing out the windless dark of the lot. Inside, the school corridor stretched ahead in a thin line of emergency lights—small, rectangular panels spaced too far apart to give any real depth. Each light hummed faintly, their glow low and uneven, leaving long patches of shadow between them.

Maya kept Lila close, one arm secure around her as they moved deeper inside. The air carried a faint chemical scent—floor polish, dust, something metallic beneath it that clung to the back of the throat. Their footsteps landed softly on the tile, the sound swallowing itself before reaching the far end of the hall.

Rows of lockers lined both sides, their metal doors reflecting the emergency lighting in warped, stuttering bands. As Maya passed, the reflections lagged just slightly behind her steps, stretching for an instant before snapping back into place.

Lila tightened her hold around Maya's arm. Her breath trembled in quick, shallow bursts. "Something's ahead."

Maya slowed, guiding her toward the center of the hallway where both walls felt equally distant. Her eyes adjusted again and again, trying to pull detail from the shadows. Corners groaned under the shifting temperature—metal expanding, contracting, settling—every sound amplified by the long corridor.

A locker door down the hall creaked, then eased open a few inches. No slam. No second sound. Just a gradual shift, slow and steady, until it hung in a silent drift.

Lila whimpered softly. "It passed through here."

Maya kept moving.

The next emergency light flickered overhead—once, twice—each pulse flashing across the walls in narrow sheets. The shadows beneath the lockers deepened during each flicker, spreading in thin lines that crawled outward across the tile before retreating when the light steadied.

The pressure in the air thickened. Maya felt it along her ribs first, then her spine, a subtle weight settling against her breathing. Lila pressed closer, clinging hard enough that her nails caught in Maya's sleeve.

As they neared the intersection where two hallways crossed, the lighting shifted again—three quick pulses in staggered rhythm. Lila's breath hitched with each one, her body reacting an instant before Maya processed the changes in brightness.

Maya paused only long enough to orient herself. The gym lay through the next hall, past the double doors at the far end. Open space. Brighter lights. Fewer corners.

She guided Lila forward.

The tile under their feet vibrated in a shallow wave, subtle but steady, rolling down the hallway like pressure traveling through the floor. Locker doors trembled in response, hinges clicking softly.

Lila lifted her head, eyes wide. "It's close."

Maya's grip tightened.

They kept moving—faster now—toward the final stretch of hallway where the gym doors waited in the dim glow ahead.

The hallway narrowed as they pushed deeper into the school, the emergency lights thinning until only a faint spill reached the tile beneath their feet. The air pressed against their skin in slow waves, each pulse sliding up Maya's spine before settling like a weight behind her ribs.

Up ahead, the gym doors loomed—broad panels of reinforced wood framed by metal that reflected the dim light in fractured streaks. With each step, the reflections shifted, sliding across the surface as if the lights in the hall were struggling to settle on one steady angle.

Lila's knees weakened again. Maya caught her around the waist, pulling her close enough that she could feel the girl's breath shaking against her arm.

"It's right behind us," Lila whispered, voice thin.

Maya didn't look back. She felt the change before she heard anything—the faintest vibration passing through the tile, rolling toward them in steady pulses. The sound followed a moment later, a low, soft thrum that pressed along the hallway walls and hummed through the vents overhead.

The lockers lining the corridor reacted first. A few doors rattled, hinges clicking in short bursts. Then another vibration moved through the floor, sharper this time, enough to make several locker handles tremble as if brushed by a passing draft.

Lila clutched Maya's sleeve. Her breath stuttered. "It's lining up."

Maya pushed them forward.

As they neared the gym, the overhead lights flickered in a three-beat pattern—front to back, then back to front—casting the hallway in alternating stretches of brightness and thin shadow. Each flicker tightened the air, squeezing Maya's lungs until her breaths fell short and fast.

The pressure came again—this time from both sides of the hallway, subtle ripples traveling along the lockers as if something large shifted its weight on the far side of the walls.

Lila's fingers dug into Maya's palm. "It's choosing an approach."

Maya gripped the gym door handle and pulled. The metal felt chilled, stiff from the cold that had seeped into the building. The door hesitated, then gave way with a low groan, opening into a vast, dim space washed in the thin glow of emergency floodlights mounted high in the rafters.

The lights inside flickered once—broad beams stuttering across the empty bleachers.

Maya stepped through, pulling Lila with her.

Behind them, the hallway vibrated in a long, rolling tremor that traveled straight through the soles of their shoes.

Maya tightened her grip as they crossed the threshold into the gym.

Chapter 34 — When Light Fails

The gym swallowed them whole.

Emergency floodlights mounted high in the rafters burned with a dull, uneven glare—broad white cones stretching across the polished floor in long, overlapping pools. Each beam buzzed faintly, as though the wiring strained to stay alive inside the blackout. The rest of the gym lay drowned in shadow: bleachers stacked to the ceiling, banners sagging from their ropes, metal equipment carts pushed into corners that fell away from the light.

Maya kept one arm locked around Lila, guiding her toward the center of the open space. The air felt thick, too heavy for a room this size, pressing softly against her eardrums with every breath she took. Lila's breaths came short and fast, each one trembling across Maya's sleeve.

A faint echo rippled through the rafters. Not a voice, not a footstep—more like a shift in weight somewhere above the lights, the kind of sound that traveled through beams before dropping into the room. The nearest floodlight flickered once, its cone shivering across the floor until it steadied again.

Maya scanned the gym quickly. Two portable floodlights stood abandoned near the far wall, their metal tripods knocked askew but their lenses still glowing, fed by emergency outlets along the base boards. They weren't aimed at anything useful—one blasted directly into a row of crumpled bleachers, the other into a wall of wrestling mats.

She pulled Lila with her, feet skidding slightly across the polished surface. Lila clutched at her arm with both hands, her pulse thundering against Maya's ribs.

The room carried strange acoustics—each sound arrived a fraction later than expected. Every step they took landed soft, muted, like the floor absorbed too much of the impact. Something shifted in the far shadows, a subtle drag of air as if a corner of the gym deepened without changing shape.

The high lights flickered again—three quick pulses in uneven rhythm. The portable floodlights responded with a faint crackle of their own, brightness wavering just enough to pull Maya's attention upward.

A thin draft slipped through the gym, brushing across their legs with the faint bite of a temperature drop. Maya felt Lila tense violently beside her.

"It's here," Lila whispered, voice strained around panic. "Inside."

Maya didn't answer. She dragged the closest portable floodlight by its handle, rotating its beam toward the center court, widening the spread. The heavy tripod scraped across the floor in a grating arc as she repositioned it.

The rafters creaked overhead—slow, deliberate, as if something shifted to keep pace with her movement.

She pulled Lila tighter against her side and angled the second floodlight toward the bleachers, forcing the beams to overlap and cut through more of the shadowed space.

The air inside the gym thickened again, a slow pressure settling beneath Maya's sternum.

The floodlights steadied for a breath, humming in uneven harmony overhead. Their glow washed across the center court in wide, unbroken sheets, leaving only the far edges of the gym hidden behind heavy stacks of equipment.

Maya pulled Lila toward the joined cones of light. The overlapping beams carved a narrow island across the floor—bright enough to see, but offering no sense of safety. The air against her arms felt charged, as if the humidity had thickened into something weighted.

A low vibration rolled through the rafters.

Dust drifted down in lazy spirals. The metal supports overhead gave a strained groan, followed by a sudden shift in pressure—an abrupt squeeze inside Maya's ears, as if the altitude had changed by inches in a heartbeat. Lila gasped beside her, knees buckling for half a second before she found her footing again.

Another tremor crossed the gym floor, more focused this time. It rippled through the hardwood beneath their feet, traveling in a slow wave that passed directly under the floodlights. The cones of brightness shivered, their edges warping as though pushed inward by an unseen force.

Maya angled the first portable floodlight again, dragging its tripod a few inches to tighten the overlap. The lens buzzed sharply, then steadied, its beam catching dust in a long, suspended shimmer.

A shape flickered behind the bleachers—too quick to resolve, a blur of dark mass squeezing through narrow space. The metal rows rattled in response, a chain reaction of soft impacts clicking down the stack. Something moved across the rafters next—another rapid shift, heavy enough to dislodge a small cascade of grit.

Lila pressed her forehead into Maya's shoulder, her breath stuttering hard. "It's circling."

Maya pressed her free hand to Lila's back, steadying her, though her own pulse hammered in her throat. She guided them deeper into the overlap of the lights, forcing her eyes to stay locked on the shifting corners of the room.

The second portable light flickered. Its beam wavered, dimmed, then surged back with a sharp flare that washed the bleachers in cold brilliance. For a split second, the rafters above them seemed to bend—straight lines warping just enough to trigger a pulse of nausea low in Maya's gut.

The vibration returned, stronger, rolling straight down the beam of the high floodlight. It resonated down the metal frame, then through the floor, then through Maya's bones.

Lila's voice fractured. "It's choosing where to strike."

The rafters groaned overhead.

The next impact came from the left—hard, sudden, driving a deep shockwave through the bleachers. Metal screamed as entire rows folded inward, collapsing in uneven layers that sent a plume of dust rolling across the floor.

Maya jerked Lila back. The floodlights bucked on their mounts, beams slicing wildly across the gym. Shadows stretched in long bands that slithered over the collapsed bleachers, creeping up the far wall before thinning again under the shifting light.

A heavy exhale drifted through the space.

Wet. Ragged. Close enough that the sound vibrated along Maya's ribs.

Lila gagged, bending forward with both hands pressed to her sternum. Her pulse thrashed beneath her skin, her breathing sharp and uneven. Maya pulled her upright, forcing her into the densest overlap of the remaining floodlights.

The light carved out a thin barrier, nothing solid—just enough illumination to slow whatever moved outside its reach. Something large swept along the far wall, quick enough to blur at the edges, its motion bending the glow as though the air thickened around it.

One of the ceiling floodlights blew with a sharp pop.

Half the gym sank into darkness.

A shape surged through the shadows—massive, angular, a torso twisting at an angle that made Maya's breath catch. Broad shoulders grazed the rafters. A limb slammed into the floor beside the collapsed bleachers, carving a deep gouge through the hardwood that sent splinters flying across the court.

The portable floodlights wavered again. Their beams jittered across the creature's outline in fractured glimpses—an arched spine, joints bending in directions no human limb could track, movement too fast to resolve before the silhouette vanished back into a thicker seam of dark.

Lila cried out, doubling over as a wave of pressure squeezed the space. Her vision blurred; her knees pitched inward. Maya scooped an arm under her shoulders, hauling her upright while adjusting the nearest floodlight with her free hand, angling it to cut off the creature's path.

The beam collided with a rushing blur.

A stuttering shudder rippled across the mass—its movement lagged, limbs twitching as if forced through denser air. For the briefest slice of a second, the creature's posture faltered—the twist of its torso catching in the light, its elbow locked mid-motion before snapping back into a faster, violent rhythm.

It lunged sideways, slamming into an equipment cart. Metal shrieked as the cart skidded across the floor, scattering cones, mats, and twisted bars in a clattering mess.

The sound ricocheted through the gym, echo catching up to itself with a delayed, warping pitch.

Maya shoved Lila backward toward the center court, her hands shaking from the raw power behind each displacement of air.

The creature surged again.

A violent tremor rolled across the gym floor, pushing a burst of cold air past Maya's legs. The portable floodlights rattled against their tripods, their beams quivering in thin, trembling arcs. Lila clung to Maya's arm with both hands, her breath hitching in tight, shallow bursts that cut off at the top of each inhale.

Something swept across the upper rafters again—fast enough to bend the emergency floodlights in a shimmering distortion, their beams warping as though dragged through shifting pressure. Dust rained down in thin sheets. A cable snapped overhead with a sharp crack, whipping against the metal supports before falling limp into the shadows.

Another impact followed—heavy, deliberate—driving a shockwave through the bleachers. Rows of metal seating buckled forward, folding under the pressure. The collapse sent a cloud of splinters and dust drifting across the court in swirling currents.

Maya angled the nearest floodlight with one hand while steadying Lila with the other. The beam flared across the gym floor, slicing through the haze. The light caught a flicker—broad mass shifting behind the dust, ribbed shadows rippling across an immense silhouette that strained against the brightness before slipping out of its reach.

A low, guttural exhale pushed through the space.

Lila doubled over, clutching her abdomen as her breathing fractured. "It's close," she choked, voice thin and shaking. "Right at the edge."

Maya dragged her backward, deeper into the overlap of the lights. The hardwood stung her palms where debris caught her skin. Every vibration from the creature's movements pressed into her bones—deep, rhythmic pulses that synced with each breath it expelled.

One of the ceiling floodlights flickered hard, then dimmed to half strength. The new darkness opened a wider path across the rafters. The air tightened in response, pressure squeezing inward from both sides of the gym.

A blur shot across the court—too fast for detail, only a distortion sliding through the leftover dust. The portable floodlight nearest the bleachers skidded several inches, metal scraping sharply as though struck from behind.

The remaining ceiling floodlight threw a harsh beam toward the center. The creature swept through the edge of it—a partial glimpse that carved itself into Maya's vision: a massive upper frame, shoulders angling with sickening precision, elbows bending sharper than anatomy allowed. The light tore at the silhouette, slowing it, forcing its movement into staggered frames before it dropped out of the beam again.

Lila sobbed, clutching at Maya's sleeve. "It's breaking through."

The floor trembled.

The creature lunged.

Maya seized Lila around the waist and ran—dragging her toward the far end of the gym, toward the last cluster of floodlights still burning on the opposite wall. The concrete beneath the hardwood vibrated in rolling pulses, chasing their footsteps.

The overhead lights flickered a final time

The last cluster of floodlights hummed unevenly against the far wall, their beams forming a fractured shield across the gym floor. Maya pulled Lila into the overlapping glow, her own breath sharp in her ears. The air pressed inward from every direction—thick, weighted, vibrating with each shift somewhere beyond the light.

The creature moved again.

Pressure rippled along the rafters in a rolling pulse. Dust cascaded from the beams, drifting like ash across the half-lit space. The portable floodlight nearest the bleachers tilted on its tripod, its legs scraping against the tile as though nudged by a massive weight just outside the beam.

The wooden floor groaned, boards flexing under sudden, concentrated force. A deep indentation formed across center court, stretching in a bowed line toward the floodlights. Maya tightened her grip around Lila, bracing her stance.

A violent gust swept across the gym, carrying a shock of cold that stung her throat. The floodlights flickered under the strain, cones of brightness pulsing in and out of focus. Lila's knees buckled again; Maya dragged her upright, holding her close enough to feel each tremor running through her frame.

Something rushed along the far wall—fast, dense, hard enough to shove a thick wave of air across the court. Mats toppled from their stacks, slamming into the floor in heavy smacks. The chained bas-

ketball hoops rattled overhead, metal rings clicking against their sup
ports.

A sudden impact cracked through the gym.

Bleachers folded inward in a cascading collapse—first one row, then the next, metal screaming under the pressure. The shockwave traveled across the floor, nearly knocking Maya off balance. She pulled Lila back as a scattering of broken boards skidded into the floodlight's glow.

Lila's voice quivered against her shoulder. "It's aligning with us."

The rafters trembled.

The remaining floodlights buzzed harder, their glow shrinking as strain built in their bulbs. Shadows along the walls began to stretch, pulled toward the gym's center by the force of the creature's circling mass.

Maya repositioned the closest portable floodlight, dragging its tripod several inches to widen the barrier. The beam cut through drifting dust, forming a sharp line of brightness across the floor. The light trembled—momentarily revealing a warped silhouette slipping along the boundary, its scale immense, movement jagged from forced deceleration.

A heavy exhale rolled past them, low and uneven. The air thickened, squeezing Maya's lungs.

Lila tightened her hold. Her pulse hammered against Maya's forearm. Her eyes flicked toward the windows high above the bleachers—tiny rectangles framing a horizon still deep in night, but thinning at the edges.

The pressure in the gym surged.

Wood cracked behind them.

Something dropped from the rafters.

The floodlights shuddered under the impact, beams widening in a frantic stutter as Maya dragged Lila toward the faintest shift of color gathering in the upper windows—a thin wash that hinted at a coming change in the sky.

Behind them, the gym floor heaved under immense weight.

Maya ran.

Chapter 35 — Withdrawal

Maya didn't look back.

The gym thundered behind her—another impact shaking dust from the rafters as she dragged Lila along the wall, shoes slipping on splintered boards. The floodlights stuttered overhead, their beams stretching and collapsing across the bleachers in jagged bursts that made the space pitch and reel.

Something landed again. The floor trembled under their feet.

Lila stumbled. Maya hauled her upright, breath tearing in and out of her chest. Ahead, the narrow doorway to the east corridor glowed faintly with the weakest rim of color leaking through the high windows—a smear of early dawn, thin but growing.

"Move," Maya breathed, forcing her legs to keep pace with the rising tremor in the building.

A long, uneven drag sounded behind them—heavy, deliberate, following their path along the bleachers. One of the metal supports groaned, bowing inward as weight pressed down from above. The sound of shifting mass rippled through the space, a deep vibration that crawled up Maya's spine.

The floodlights flickered again. One died with a sharp crack.

A slanted shadow bulged across the floor, stretching toward them in irregular pulses.

Maya shoved Lila through the doorway first. The moment her shoulder hit the frame, another impact slammed into the gym floor—strong enough that ceiling tiles broke loose and shattered across the boards where they had just been.

Maya leaned her weight into the door, pulling it shut behind them as the corridor lights buzzed to life in faint, stuttering lines. The walls shook once more under the force of something striking the opposite side.

She tightened her grip on Lila's arm.

"Keep going," she whispered, pushing forward as the hallway trembled under another heavy shift of weight behind the gym wall.

They ran.

The hallway lights flickered in uneven strips as Maya pulled Lila deeper into the east wing. The floor trembled again—lighter this time, but steady enough that dust sifted from the ceiling in a thin, drifting veil.

Behind them, something shifted its weight at the gym threshold. The metal frame creaked under the strain. A low, dragging sound followed—mass sliding, limbs adjusting, the scrape of something large trying to force itself forward.

Maya didn't turn. She felt the movement through the soles of her shoes as the pressure rolled along the corridor floor, traveling in uneven pulses. Lila gasped, one hand pressed to her chest, her steps breaking into short, frantic bursts.

A shape pushed into view at the far end of the hall, distorted by the failing lights—broad at the top, tapering in irregular angles that jittered with each stutter of fluorescent glow. It leaned, paused, then advanced again in a dragging lurch as if each step required a recalibration of mass.

Maya yanked Lila toward the fractured line of dawn filtering through a row of shattered windows ahead. The pale color deepened by degrees as the sky shifted, spilling across the tiles in long slanted bands.

The creature's advance slowed. Its silhouette stretched thin at the edges, flickering with the corridor lights. A hard, uneven exhale traveled down the hall—wet in places, shallow in others, its cadence unsteady.

Lila clung to Maya's sleeve. "It's coming," she whispered, voice trembling.

"I know," Maya said, forcing her legs to keep her moving. Her breath burned in her throat. Her pulse thudded in her ears. She could feel the weight closing in behind them, but something in its movement had changed—still dangerous, still massive, but no longer building speed.

Another ragged exhale echoed down the hall.

The creature dragged itself one step farther, then faltered as another thin wash of dawn slid across the floor.

Maya tightened her grip on Lila's hand.

"Run," she said, pulling her forward just as the lights surged once, then dimmed, leaving the corridor trembling behind them.

They reached the east corridor's wider stretch, where a row of high windows spilled a faint wash of early color across the floor. The light wasn't strong, but it carried weight—thin, steady, and growing.

Maya slowed just enough to pull Lila behind a toppled display case. Her chest heaved. Her hands shook. She kept her eyes locked on the far end of the hall.

The creature emerged at the corner.

Its outline wavered in the failing lights—broad shoulders tapering into limbs that shifted unevenly, as if parts of its mass fought to stay anchored. It pressed one limb to the floor, dragging its body forward in a heavy sweep. Another inhale rolled down the hall, deep at first, then breaking midway through, the sound catching against its own bulk.

The first angle of dawn touched its form.

A distortion rippled across it. One limb contracted sharply, pulling upward as if relieved of weight. The torso thinned along one side, portions of it slipping out of view before stuttering back into shape. The drag of its movement slowed, its body adjusting again and again, each shift less coordinated than the last.

Lila's fingers dug into Maya's sleeve. Her breath hitched, not in panic but in recognition—something inside her reacting before thought could catch up.

The creature tried another step.

Its mass rolled sideways instead, sliding along the wall as though pulled by the corridor's darker recesses. Its posture sagged. The next inhale rattled through the space, shallow and disjointed, like a body losing the rhythm that kept it moving.

Maya felt the change settle around them. The gym chase had been relentless, every movement sharp and decisive. Now the creature's effort sagged under early daylight—a strain that showed in the angles of its limbs, the inconsistent drag of its weight, the way its outline frayed at the edges.

The light strengthened by another fraction. Dust in the air caught the new brightness, swirling in faint motes.

The creature recoiled from it.

Not with fear—Maya saw no hesitation, no backward retreat—but with the involuntary response of something whose body no longer matched its environment. Muscles—or whatever structure guided its movement—tightened and collapsed inward, as if its frame compressed under external pressure.

Lila whispered, "It's changing."

Maya didn't answer. She kept her eyes locked on the creature as it swayed, its silhouette thinning further, its reach shortening with each unsteady shift.

The first true stroke of dawn crept across the tiles.

The creature jerked back a full step, its mass folding toward the darker intersection behind it. Sections of its body slipped out of the corridor's light entirely, dissolving into broken angles as it pulled it-self from the growing brightness.

Maya set her hand on Lila's back.

"Stay with me," she murmured, guiding her toward the next stretch of windows as the creature dragged itself into retreat, piece by piece.

Maya guided Lila along the wall, keeping close to the growing bands of dawn that streaked across the corridor. Each new sliver of light stiffened the creature's movement behind them. The scrape of its weight grew uneven—long pauses between drags, as if its frame struggled to coordinate where to place itself next.

They reached the threshold leading back into the gym.

The room was wrecked: splintered bleachers, collapsed rafters, scattered floodlights sputtering in erratic pulses. Patches of frost clung to indentations in the floor where impacts had landed hours—or minutes—before. Their breath stirred the dust hanging in the air, illuminated by the thin, rising light pressing through the up-per windows.

A shift of mass pulled every sound toward the far side of the gym.

The creature dragged itself into view.

It moved slower than before—far slower—its limbs folding and unfolding with irregular timing. One arm-like structure buckled as it reached toward the darker recess beneath the toppled bleachers. Its torso bent inward, narrowing with each attempt to pull itself forward. Portions of its outline rippled, losing shape for a moment before re-forming in distorted angles.

The first full ray of dawn touched the surface of its back.

The creature's structure tightened instantly. Its mass drew inward, compressing as if pulled by an unseen pressure. Maya heard a low, strained sound—air forced through a body adjusting against the envi-ronment, not reacting to pain but reacting to change.

It tried to shift farther into the darkness.

The attempt faltered. Its bulk collapsed a few inches toward the floor before it caught itself against metal beams twisted from earlier collisions. Its limbs contracted again, thinner now, their reach short-ened by the strain of holding form in the growing light.

Maya kept Lila close, stepping carefully across broken boards and frost-slick patches. She recognized the pattern—the slowing, the fold-ing, the retreat—not because she had seen it before, but because every movement told the same story:

the creature wasn't stopping.

It was winding down.

The bleachers offered the deepest shadow left in the ruined gym. The creature angled toward it, pulling its mass through the remaining pockets where the dawn couldn't reach yet. Its outline jittered once, twice, then slipped through the gap beneath the collapsed seating.

A final, dragged inhale traveled across the wreckage.

Then the shape thinned, stretched, and folded into the dark until nothing remained except a distorted smear of shadow that faded as the light strengthened.

Maya didn't wait for silence to settle.

She tightened her hold on Lila and stepped toward the nearest exit, the sound of their footsteps mixing with the soft creak of metal cool-ing in the dawn.

Maya pushed the warped side doors open with her shoulder. The hinges groaned, stiff from the cold that had settled into the metal overnight. Dawn spread across the cracked pavement outside in a pale, fragile wash—light that felt too thin for a world that had been torn apart only hours before.

The air hit her first.

Not warm—not yet—but free of the crushing pressure that had filled every corner of the gym. Her lungs finally expanded without resis-tance. Lila sagged against her side with the same shuddering release, her breaths coming fast and uneven.

They stepped onto the school's front steps.

The town below lay in scattered fragments of the night that had passed. Traffic lights blinked through empty intersections, their col-ors repeating with no rhythm. A cruiser sat diagonally across the main road, doors open, lights still rotating in a slow, unfocused arc. Somewhere far off, a siren wailed once and died out. No voices carried. No engines ran. Just the stillness left behind when something larger has already taken what it came for.

Lila caught Maya's sleeve again. "Do you think it's gone?"

Maya didn't answer—not because she doubted, but because the word *gone* didn't fit anything she'd witnessed. The gym behind them was proof enough. Frost clung to the concrete around the doorway. A strip of shadow beneath the bleachers still held a faint, unnatural depth, like a bruise that would take time to fade.

The creature hadn't been defeated.
It had finished.

Maya guided Lila down the final step. The gravel crunched under their shoes, too loud in the morning quiet. She kept her eyes scanning every alley, every doorway, every lingering pocket where darkness still clung to corners untouched by dawn. Her muscles refused to loosen, even as the sunlight stretched farther across the street.

"We're heading to the road," she said quietly. "We stay in the open. We keep moving."

Lila nodded, wiping her face with the back of her hand, her eyes locked on the empty street ahead as if the night might still be hiding in it.

Together, they began walking across the fractured asphalt—
each step deliberate, each breath unsteady—
the town's silence closing around them as the first full light of day crept over the roofs.

Chapter 35.5 — 2019, Suburban Illinois

The basement glowed in shifting colors from the television—blue, then red, then a quick flicker of white as the game menu cycled. Posters covered the concrete walls. A laundry basket sat half-folded near the stairs. The boy sat cross-legged on the carpet, controller in hand, headset lying unused beside him.

A faint draft curled under the basement door.

He glanced toward it. The house usually held a steady hum—furnace, dryer, vents moving warm air through old ducts—but the sound thinned around him. First the tumble of the dryer quieted, then the furnace fan slowed, the air settling in a soft hush across the room.

The ceiling bulb blinked once.

Then again, shorter this time.

He paused the game.

The sudden stillness pressed against his ears, a silence deep enough to feel inside his jaw. The draft brushed his ankles again, cooler now, though the room's temperature hadn't dropped enough to see his breath. The chill just lingered across his skin, a thin thread weaving along the carpet fibers before fading.

He set the controller down and reached for his phone.

The quiet unsettled him—no background whir, no distant engine thrum from the street above. The house felt wrapped in a layer of dense air, heavier than before, as if the pressure outside had shifted while the basement lagged behind.

He unlocked his phone and opened the home security app. Four camera thumbnails loaded across the screen. The driveway. The kitchen. The living room. The basement.

Before he tapped anything, the ceiling bulb blinked a third time—quick, sharp—throwing a brief stutter of light across the posters near the far wall.

He frowned at the bulb.

Then at the basement door.

Then back at the screen.

His thumb hovered above the camera feed.

The feeds loaded with a slight delay, each thumbnail flickering before stabilizing. He tapped the living room camera first.

The image sputtered—horizontal bands sliding across the screen—then dissolved into grey static.

He tried the kitchen next.

That feed blinked twice, froze on a skewed frame of the empty counter, then washed out in digital noise.

The driveway camera collapsed a moment later.

A smear of light, a sudden dip of brightness—gone.

He exhaled, confused, tapping the screen again. Only one window still responded: the basement feed. He hesitated before pressing it.

The view expanded across his phone.

A familiar frame filled the screen—the back of his chair, the glow of the TV, the outline of his own shoulders. Everything looked normal at first. Still. Quiet.

He shifted the phone in his hand.

The reflection on-screen didn't match.

His seated shape remained motionless, shoulders squared toward the TV. No tilt of the head. No shift of posture. No recognition of the device he held inches from his face.

His pulse thudded once against his ribs.

He lifted his free hand slowly, testing the image. His real hand rose toward his forehead; the reflection stayed anchored in place, frozen in the exact pose from seconds earlier.

The ceiling bulb blinked again.

A faint echo rolled through the basement—soft, delayed, as if the room absorbed too much of the sound before returning it.

He stared at the screen.

Behind the still outline of himself, a second shape hovered at the edge of the captured frame.

Tall.

Bent.

Shoulders angled deep, as though leaning too far forward to balance.

The shape flickered in small, uneven increments—tiny jumps across the pixel grid, as though the camera struggled to keep up with its movement.

He lowered the phone an inch.

His breath tightened.

The basement behind him remained empty in the low glow of the TV.

He raised the phone again.

The shape in the feed had shifted closer.

The feed stuttered—frames sliding out of order as if the phone struggled to decide which moment belonged next.

The outline behind his seated reflection advanced in uneven increments, each jump separated by a fractional smear of shadow across the pixels.

He swallowed hard and twisted in his chair.

Nothing moved in the basement.

Just the soft hum of the paused game, the faint shake of the rattling ductwork as the furnace tried and failed to restart.

He turned the phone back toward the screen.

The shape now loomed almost directly behind the frozen version of himself—shoulders pitched forward, limbs angled in ways the compression couldn't fully render. The distortion spread around it, darkening the corners of the frame until the edges bled into black.

A pulse thrummed through the room.

The TV flickered.

The overhead bulb dimmed to a low red glow, as if the filament strained under sudden pressure.

His breath hitched in his throat.

He tapped the screen again, desperate for a different angle—garage, front door, anything. Every feed remained dead.

The basement view jittered.

The distorted dark pushed closer to the reflection of his neck.

He jolted to his feet.

The air shifted—dense, thick, as though the room inhaled and held it. His ears popped from the sudden pressure change. The cold rolling across the floor brushed his ankles, moving in a slow, directional sweep.

He glanced toward the stairs.

Still empty.

Still quiet.

He lifted the phone again with a shaking hand.

The distorted shape in the feed had reached the chair—his chair. Shadow warped around the frozen outline of his own shoulders, bending inward with mechanical hunger.

The next frame crashed into static.

For a split second, the pixels realigned—dark limbs stretching forward, the entire feed pulled into a tight, collapsing smear.

The basement behind him remained silent.

Then the temperature punched downward again, hard enough to sting the back of his throat.

The static thickened across the phone screen—bands of gray stacking over one another until the image looked crushed under its own compression.

The sound from the TV dropped into a low mechanical groan before cutting out completely.

The basement lights died.

Not a pop.

Not a flicker.

Just gone—like the room had been unplugged from the rest of the house.

The cold rolled across the concrete in a single, steady push, rising past his knees. His lungs tightened with the sudden density of the air, each breath squeezing thin and shallow. Dust along the baseboards vibrated, lifted, and drifted toward the center of the room as though drawn by pressure instead of wind.

He staggered backward, shoulder hitting the wall.

His phone vibrated once—an alert the system shouldn't have been able to send with the network down.

BASEMENT FEED RESTORED.

The screen flashed.

The camera showed his gaming chair—empty.

The distortion pooled behind it, pulling the shadows long and vertical, stretching them upward like something preparing to move through them. The entire frame bent inward around that central dark, pixels dragged toward a single point.

His throat tightened.

Another surge rolled through the basement—thick, airless, heavy enough to force him a half-step forward without meaning to move. His breath left him in a weak gasp. The cold pressed deeper into his chest.

The feed jumped.

In the new frame, something tall occupied the warped dark behind the chair—rendered only by the camera's inability to process its shape. Shoulders sloped into angles the compression couldn't smooth. The head dipped toward the lens. The shadow around it folded as if drawn into a narrowing funnel.

The next frame collapsed.

Light smeared.

Dark bands twisted across the screen.

The entire basement feed folded into a single narrow strip of motion.

The phone slipped from his fingers.

The cold seized the room with one final surge.

His breath broke into a thin, strangled gasp.

And the basement went still.

The TV cast its shifting blues and reds across the carpet, colors bending whenever the frame on the frozen security feed warped. The boy's headset lay crooked on the floor, one earcup still faintly humming as the console menu droned its idle tone. A controller rolled in a slow arc until it tapped the leg of the coffee table and stopped.

The air held an edge that hadn't been there minutes earlier—dense, unmoving, as if the room were still adjusting to something that had passed through. Dust motes drifted at odd angles. The furnace clicked twice, trying to restart, but the attempt died mid-cycle, leaving the house in a thick, oppressive quiet.

On the couch, the boy's phone screen remained open to the basement camera.

The final frame hadn't refreshed.

The walls behind him looked stretched, the angles pulled inward. A smear of dark tone bled across one corner of the image, the kind that came from compression artifacts—too uniform to be natural shadow, too sharp to be a glitch. The faint outline of a limb had caught mid-motion before the feed froze, joints bent in a way the human eye resisted parsing.

The timestamp continued in the corner, counting silently upward.

Upstairs, a refrigerator relay clicked on. Lights along the staircase flickered once, twice, then steadied. The house resumed its usual sounds—electrical thrum, settling wood, the normal rhythm of an occupied home.

Only the basement remained wrong.

Faint frost traced the edge of the couch, a thin film that hadn't been there before. The condensation on the walls glimmered in irregular patches, as though a cold front had pressed inward and vanished. A single wet footprint—shallow, heel dragged—marked the carpet near the far stair.

The boy's chair sat empty.

No sign of struggle.

No scattered belongings.

No door opening or closing.

Just absence.

And the frozen frame on the phone, showing the same room, the same angle—

except for the blurred shape leaning closer behind where he had been sitting.

The battery icon pulsed once before the screen dimmed. The house held its breath.

Somewhere deep in the structure, a soft vibration passed through the vents—brief, rhythmic, almost like the echo of something retreating into a space no room should contain.

The basement lights flickered again.

Then steadied.

The house returned to normal.

The room did not.

Chapter 36 — The Official Lie

The sun was barely a presence—thin, pale, still fighting its way through the low gray sky—but it was enough to push back the weight that had clung to Maya's skin all night. Not erase it. Just loosen it.

She and Lila moved down the broken street in silence, their footsteps soft against the uneven asphalt. The quiet was wrong. Too still. Too hollow. A town waiting for someone else to speak first.

A block ahead, faint sirens began to rise—not frantic, not coordinated, but scattered, drifting in from multiple directions. Something had finally started moving again. Emergency crews. Responders. People waking into a world that didn't match what they remembered when they went to bed.

Lila stayed close at her side, eyes flicking from doorway to doorway as if expecting something to peel out of the remaining shadows. Her breaths were shallow, uneven, but she kept pace.

They rounded the corner toward Briarwood Court.

Maya stopped.

Her rig sat exactly where she'd left it hours earlier—driver door still shut, windshield scattered with a thin, uneven frost that dissolved as the sunlight touched it. The hood wasn't rimed in thick white anymore. No cold vapor leaked from beneath it. The air around it felt... normal.

Lila exhaled shakily. "Does it—does it work now?"

Maya didn't answer. She moved toward the vehicle, keys already in her hand, her pulse loud in her ears. The engine had refused to respond the night before—dead under her palms, as if something had held it still.

She slid into the driver's seat. The interior smelled of stale coffee and the faint medicinal scent from the trauma kit tucked behind her.

Her hand hovered over the ignition.

Not from fear of the Maw.

From the world they would have to walk back into.

She turned the key.

The engine sputtered once. Coughed. Then caught.

Alive.

Lila sagged against the passenger door. "Okay... okay."

Maya kept her eyes on the windshield. Emergency sirens grew louder now—multiple units converging somewhere east. The direction of Main Street. The police station wasn't far from there.

They were going to have to drive straight toward it. Straight into whatever explanation the town would build for the night.

She put the rig in gear.

"Seatbelt," she murmured.

Lila clicked hers into place with trembling fingers.

Maya eased them forward, the rig rolling cautiously over fractured pavement. As they pulled into the main road, smoke drifted from somewhere deeper downtown. A firetruck blocked one intersection. Police tape fluttered limply from another. People stood on their porches, wrapped in blankets, faces pale with disbelief.

Everywhere Maya looked, she saw the same expression—

They don't know what happened.

They don't want to know what happened.

The rig continued toward the heart of town, sirens growing clearer with each turn.

By the time Maya turned onto Main, the street had become a hive of fragmented response—clusters of officers, firefighters, EMTs, and stunned townspeople scattered across the blocks, all trying to impose order on a night that had shredded every rule they knew.

The rig rolled past a fire engine parked sideways across the road. Its lights spun silently, as if even the siren couldn't decide whether to break the quiet. Frost glittered on patches of asphalt where the sun hadn't reached yet—thin, uneven shapes that made no sense with the rising temperature.

Lila stared at them through the window, knuckles white around the seatbelt strap. "Those weren't here earlier."

"No," Maya said softly. "They weren't."

Bodies were being moved. Not many. Not whole. Black bags lay on stretchers, some sealed, some hastily wrapped. She saw an officer avert his gaze as another zipped a bag that shouldn't have needed two people to lift.

At the curb outside the courthouse, a huddle of detectives argued over an evidence kit. One gestured in frustration toward a camera that replayed nothing but warping static no matter how many times he hit the side of it.

Maya slowed.

A line of county officials stood outside the sheriff's temporary command post—grim, exhausted, exchanging clipped phrases she couldn't hear. One scribbled something onto a clipboard, then scratched it out hard enough to tear the page.

As Maya pulled to the edge of the scene, an officer signaled for her to stop. She lowered the window.

"You two alright?" he asked, voice thin from lack of sleep.

Maya nodded. "We sheltered in place and waited for daylight."

The lie came out smooth. Not practiced—just necessary.

The officer exhaled, relieved. "Good. Good. We've got EMTs staging behind the station. Sheriff'll be giving a statement soon. They're… trying to piece it together."

There was a tremor in his last words. Something like disbelief wearing a uniform.

Behind him, two paramedics rolled a stretcher toward an ambulance. Maya caught a glimpse of the body bag on top—angled oddly, as if something inside had folded in ways bodies shouldn't.

Lila pressed a hand to her mouth.

Maya touched her arm lightly. "Look at me," she whispered.

Lila did. Her eyes were glassy, but focused.

"We're leaving after the announcement," Maya said quietly enough the officer wouldn't hear. "We don't stay in this."

Lila swallowed hard. She nodded.

Voices rose near the precinct steps—equipment being moved, a microphone being tested. People drifted toward the makeshift podium, seeking answers they couldn't possibly accept.

Maya eased the rig into park.

"Come on," she said. "We listen. We hear what they decide happened."

Lila hesitated, then climbed out.

They stepped together into the brittle dawn, joining the crowd forming around the sheriff—

and the lie already taking shape in the air.

The sheriff stepped up to the podium—uniform pressed, jaw set, eyes sunken from a night no explanation could anchor. Pale morning light washed across the crowd, uneven and sickly, as though the town itself was trying not to look too closely at what had been left behind.

Microphones crackled. A deputy adjusted a cable. Someone cleared their throat.

Then the sheriff spoke.

"Last night," he began, "our community experienced a series of tragic, chaotic events resulting in multiple fatalities, widespread injuries, and significant property damage."

Maya felt Lila stiffen beside her.

"We believe," the sheriff continued, choosing each word like it might explode, "that a combination of power failures, structural accidents, and mass panic contributed to the... circumstances you've all witnessed this morning."

A murmur spread across the crowd—some relieved, some incredulous, some simply too exhausted to question anything.

Maya kept her face unmoved.

Behind the sheriff, a whiteboard was angled just enough for her to glimpse crude diagrams: intersecting arrows, red X's marking locations, and beside them—photos printed in haste, each heavily redacted. She recognized the patterns beneath the censor bars. Frost arcs. Distortions around wounds. Ribcages forced outward.

Someone behind her whispered, "Panic did *that*? Jesus..."

The sheriff pressed on.

"Reports circulating online include altered videos and manipulated images. These are being investigated. We urge everyone to refrain from sharing unverified content. Panic only breeds more panic."

Lila's fingers curled into Maya's coat.

Maya leaned closer. "Almost done," she murmured.

But she wasn't sure whom she was reassuring.

Near the ambulance row, a coroner's assistant struggled to lift a stretcher. A body bag slid slightly, the shape inside stiff, twisted—wrong. He caught it and glanced toward the stage, jaw tight, as if waiting for someone to admit the truth that would never be spoken.

The sheriff took a breath.

"We will issue a full report once our investigation concludes. For now, we encourage families to gather, support one another, and allow emergency personnel to continue their work."

He stepped back.

Questions erupted immediately, a wall of them—What caused the collapse on Seventh? Why were there no alarms? Why did the cameras fail? Why were some victims frozen? Why did some show pressure trauma with no point of origin?

Each question cracked the surface of the lie.

But officials blocked follow-up responses, redirecting, insisting on calm, urging patience, offering reassurances that dissolved even as they were spoken.

Lila looked up at Maya, voice barely audible. "They know they're lying."

"They have to," Maya said quietly. "It's the only story anyone can survive."

The sheriff gave a final nod to the crowd before stepping away from the microphones. Deputies started guiding people back, dispersing clusters of anger, confusion, disbelief.

Maya exhaled slowly.

The official lie had settled—thin, brittle, already fracturing at the edges.

But it was enough for the town to cling to.

Enough for Maya and Lila to slip away.

Maya guided Lila back through the thinning crowd, the morning light cutting through the wreckage and the exhaustion that clung to everyone still standing. Their rig sat exactly where she had left it beside the sheriff's temporary command post—closed up, untouched, streaked faintly with the grime of the night.

Two detectives argued over an evidence bag near the courthouse steps. A paramedic leaned against an ambulance with hollow eyes, staring at a stretcher he clearly didn't want to unzip. Reporters clustered around the podium where the sheriff tried to make the town's nightmare sound orderly, containable, explainable.

Maya kept Lila moving.

They reached the rig. Maya opened the driver's door, and Lila climbed in without a word, curling into the seat as if trying to take up less space in a world that suddenly felt too exposed.

Maya slid in beside her and shut the door. The sounds of the courthouse—the reporters, the generators, the brittle scrape of early cleanup—muffled instantly.

She turned the key.

The engine came to life on the first attempt, clean and steady.

Lila stared straight ahead, her hands clasped tightly, knuckles pale. She didn't look toward the corners of the windshield, didn't risk following the angle of any shadow.

Maya rested her grip on the wheel for one slow breath, steadying herself.

Outside, the sheriff ended his statement. Reporters raised their hands. Cameras clicked. Someone started rolling up yellow tape that cordoned off an intersection where no intact bodies had been found.

It was all theater now—
a performance for a town desperate not to understand the truth.

Maya shifted the rig into drive.

As they eased forward, no officer stepped out to stop them. No one called after them. People only watched—blank, relieved, terrified to question the quiet escape of those who had seen too much.

Lila whispered, barely audible, "Are we really leaving?"

Maya nodded once, eyes fixed on the road opening ahead.
"We are."

The rig rolled past the command post, past the courthouse lawn, past the curated lie being fed to the daylight.

And then the last piece of the town fell away behind them, swallowed by the brightening morning.

They didn't look back.

They drove in silence.

The town thinned behind them—storefronts still dark, traffic lights blinking without rhythm, intersections marked by cones and tape. A fire engine idled near a collapsed awning. Two officers stood beside a patrol car whose doors were open, staring at a cracked sidewalk like it still carried an answer.

Lila drew her knees up in the seat, arms wrapped tight around them. She hadn't spoken since they pulled away. Maya didn't push. The world outside said everything for them—too quiet, too hollow, too recently occupied by something that had finished what it came to do.

They crossed the city limits.

The highway opened.

Wind pressed against the rig, steady and warm, carrying none of the cold that had stalked every mile of the night. Maya felt her shoulders drop by degrees, muscles loosening in ways she hadn't realized were clenched. The morning sun crept higher, washing the road in a harmless pale gold.

For a moment, it looked like escape was possible.

Miles later, Maya turned into a roadside motel—one of the few still operating after the blackout. A single clerk stood at the reception desk, exhausted but functioning, handing over a key without question. She didn't ask where they came from. She didn't ask why they looked shaken. Dawn always delivered people like this.

Inside the small room, Maya locked the door and checked each window. Lila sat on the edge of the bed, hands loose in her lap, eyes fixed on the carpet. She breathed carefully—slow, measured, as though the air still carried memory.

Maya crouched in front of her.

"We're safe for now," she said softly.

Lila nodded, but didn't answer.

Hours passed before either of them slept. When they finally drifted, it was from exhaustion, not peace.

Hundreds of miles away, in another town waking under another harmless sunrise, a young girl stirred from a nightmare. She pushed herself upright and blinked at the soft glow of her nightlight.

"Mom?" she whispered.

Footsteps approached down the hall. The bedroom door opened. Her mother stepped in, brushing hair from her eyes.

"What is it, sweetheart?"

The girl lifted a trembling finger toward the far corner of the room.

A coat rack stood there. A pile of toys. Wallpaper patterned with fading stars.

The mother glanced over her shoulder.

"Nothing there," she said gently, sitting beside her. "Just shadows."

The girl's breath hitched.

The corner's darkness shifted—subtle, almost imperceptible—but enough that the faint spill of the nightlight bent around the edge of something unseen.

The mother didn't notice.

But the child did.

She tightened her grip on her mother's sleeve.

"Mama… it's watching."

The room fell quiet.

Morning waited beyond the curtains.

The cycle had ended.

Hunger always returned.

The End

NIGHT MAW FILE —
RESTRICTED

UNITED STATES OFFICE OF SPECIAL PATHOLOGICAL EVENTS

CLASSIFIED REPORT – LEVEL 5 CLEARANCE REQUIRED

SUBJECT: Unexplained Lethality Cluster – Case Series #47-B
LOCATION: ██████████████ County, USA
DATE: Post-incident compilation
INVESTIGATOR: ████████████
STATUS: CLOSED / SUPPRESSED (Pending Cycle Completion)

EXECUTIVE SUMMARY (REDACTED)

Between ██/██/20██ and ██/██/20██, a total of 10 confirmed death... inconsistent with any known human, animal, or mechanical agent.

Public explanation: Mass panic and misidentified human homicide.

Actual classification: Predatory entity, unidentified biological origin.

All physical evidence collected must remain under seal.

Further civilian awareness deemed "catastrophically dangerous."

FORENSIC NOTES (EXTRACT)

Core temperature anomalies: up to 28°F below ambient.

Ribcage deformations: outward bending consistent with internal pulling force.

Laryngeal collapse: puncture marks along interior cartilage; impossible without specialized tools.

Spinal fluid absence: complete drainage in two subjects; no puncture wound.

Shadow distortion: documented in five incident photographs despite no environmental cause.

Video evidence: corrupted by extreme data warping; analysts not... artifacts consistent with Case Series #32-D, #11-F, and #04-A.

Full autopsies filed under Restricted Archive: Vault Θ-9.

HISTORICAL PATTERN RECOGNITION (REDACTED)

Analysis confirms this event is part of a wider temporal cycle occurring approximately every 14–31 years across multiple regions.

Previous clusters:

1347 — Iberia

1682 — Eastern Seaboard

1793 — New England Interior

1911 — Pacific Northwest Corridor

1952 — Central Rockies Region

2019 — Northern Illinois

(See Appendix B, REDACTED)

Each cluster ends following 10 total casualties (combined confirmed deaths and unaccounted disappearances). Current incident reached 10 with the death of Det. R. Graves.

Subsequent activity halted within 30 minutes of dawn, correlating with known withdrawal patterns.

BEHAVIORAL SUMMARY (REDACTED)

Entity demonstrates:

• Selective predation based on awareness state

• Attraction to fear-response biochemistry
• Ability to disrupt electronic surveillance
• Locomotion inconsistent with human biomechanics
• Occupancy of shadowed spatial pockets not measurable by standard light refraction

Attempts to neutralize, track, or contain the entity have resulted in multiple losses (see casualties in Case Series #11-F and #32-D).

INTERNAL TAXONOMIC ADDENDUM (RESTRICTED)

Internal classification term: **NETHERKIN — TYPE VII**
Regional folkloric designation: "Night Maw" (local usage; non-taxonomic).

Cross-case comparison (47-B, 32-D, 11-F, 04-A, and historical clusters listed above) confirms:

• Identical cold-zone formation during active intake phases
• Recurrent shadow-lag and reversible shadow displacement in proximity to deaths
• Consistent internal trauma signatures (vacuum-type organ collapse; non-instrumental)
• Multi-event predatory cycle terminating after ~10 total casualties per emergence
• Zero confirmed successful containment or termination across all recorded incidents

Note: "Night Maw" refers to symptomatic manifestations perceived by civilian populations (darkness, pressure, environmental cold, unexplained presence). Internally, threat is indexed under Netherkin Type VII predatory bioform classification.

Further taxonomic details remain restricted to higher clearance tiers (see NETHERKIN MASTER INDEX, REDACTED).

RECOMMENDATIONS

Do NOT release full autopsy or forensic findings to local authorities.
Do NOT pursue follow-up investigation unless new cluster initiates.

Prepare regional alert protocols for next emergence cycle.

Suppress all leaked footage via federal DMCA emergency override.

Public safety rationale:

"Any increase in awareness has historically preceded accelerated predation."

FINAL NOTE (HANDWRITTEN, SOURCE UNKNOWN)

(Recovered from the margin of an internal printout. Handwriting does not match any cleared personnel.)

"You treat this as a case.

It is not a case.

It is a cycle."

"It sleeps only when it has eaten its fill.

And it has never forgotten a single face that looked into the dark."

"It will wake again."

The End

"The Maw is not a monster in the dark.
It is the reason the dark learned to hunger."

Thank You For Reading

Your time means everything.

If this story resonated with you, please consider leaving a brief review on Amazon.

Even a single sentence helps new readers discover my work.

Explore More Books by Gerald Locke

For a complete list of published works—including horror, epic fantasy, cosmic fantasy, modern hidden-magic, and stand-alones—visit:

GeraldLocke.com

You'll find:

- full book catalog
- reading guides
- future releases
- world lore
- author updates

Connect With the Author

For book trailers, updates, and behind-the-scenes content:

TikTok: **@geraldlockeauthor**
Facebook: **Gerald Locke – Author**
Website: **GeraldLocke.com**

Thank You for Supporting Independent Fiction
Your curiosity keeps these worlds alive.
I hope we cross paths again in the next story.

www.ingramcontent.com/pod-product-compliance
Lightning Source LLC
Chambersburg PA
CBHW020653010826
48969CB00013B/1069